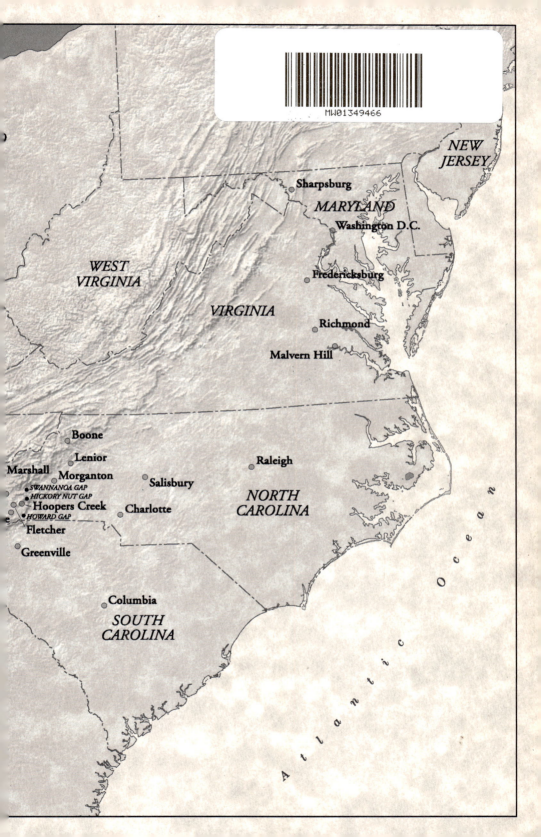

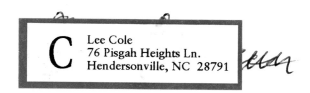

The Secret of War

A DRAMATIC HISTORY OF CIVIL WAR CRIME IN
WESTERN NORTH CAROLINA

The Secret of War
A DRAMATIC HISTORY OF CIVIL WAR CRIME IN WESTERN NORTH CAROLINA

Terrell T. Garren

Assisted by
Trena Parker

THE REPRINT COMPANY, PUBLISHERS
SPARTANBURG, SOUTH CAROLINA
2005

Copyright © 2004 Terrell T. Garren
All rights reserved

An original publication, 2004
The Reprint Company, Publishers
Spartanburg, South Carolina 29304
Second printing, 2005

ISBN 0-87152-545-3
Library of Congress Control Number: 2004105996
Manufactured in the United States of America

Endpaper map by Mark Stroud
Durango, Colorado

The paper used in this publication meets the minimum requirements of
American National Standard for Information Science—Permanence of Paper
For Printed Library Materials, ANSI Z39.48-1984.

DEDICATION

WILLIAM JACKSON PALMER
This work is dedicated to Brevet Brigadier General William Jackson Palmer of the Fifteenth Pennsylvania Cavalry, United States Army. He was a man who conducted the ugly business of war with honor and integrity. He is the quintessential example of the American citizen-soldier.
(PHOTOGRAPH COURTESY THE U.S. ARMY MILITARY HISTORY INSTITUTE)

Preface

This work is an historical account of the life and times of my great-grandparents, Joseph Youngblood and Delia Russell Youngblood. It is presented as an historical novel using the real names of historical figures in most cases.

In situations depicting specific war crimes the names of the individuals used are totally fictional. These fictional characters have no relationship to anyone living or dead.

Every effort has been made to present the story in historical context. Many of the battles and events depicted are reflected in documented history. In such cases, every effort has been made to present accurately the history of the period.

Acknowledgments

There are so many to whom I owe gratitude that I fear I shall miss someone but I want to thank those identifiable. A special appreciation goes to my wife, Maria, and my daughter, Solari, for putting up with a decade and a half of supporting my obsession. I would also like to thank Trena Parker, who was my loyal assistant and the feminine advocate for the work; Dr. D. Newton Smith, who provided the professional guidance for formulating the work; and Phyllis C. Corley for her logistical support.

I must thank my cousin, Nonnie Dellinger, who is also a great-grandchild of Delia Russell Youngblood. Her moral support and advocacy for revealing this painful part of family history was crucial for me. Thanks to Vickie Rowe-Currence, MSW, for helping me understand obsessive-compulsive disorder (OCD) and posttraumatic stress disorder (PTSD); Dr. Rob Merrill, DDS, for explaining the makeup of the human jaw and the implications of breaking it; D.A. Ledford, who helped me understand old time medical remedies; Bill Youngblood, for showing me the location of the Civil War hideout; and Nathan Youngblood, who told me direct accounts of his grandfather's experience as a Confederate deserter. Special attention is directed to the late Elspeth McClure Clarke, whose childhood memories are reflected in the work. Her stories of Union soldiers at Sherrill's Inn represent a priceless piece of oral history.

My sincere appreciation goes out to Leah Davis Witherow and Dr. L.W. Halling and all the staff at the Colorado Pioneer History Museum in

Colorado Springs; the Indiana Historical Society; the Tennessee State Archives; the North Carolina Department of Archives and History; Dr. Richard Sommers and the staff at the National Military History Institute in Carlyle, Pennsylvania; the South Caroliniana Library; Marcelle White with the Dalton Georgia Historical Society; the entire National Park Service for their assistance on my many visits to historic battlefields; and the staff of Hunter Library, Western Carolina University.

I express my warmest gratitude to the entire staff of Pack Memorial Library in Asheville, North Carolina. I worked there sporadically without ever identifying myself. The staff always helped whenever possible and conducted themselves efficiently and professionally.

My deepest appreciation goes to Dr. George A. Jones of the Henderson County Genealogical and Historical Society. He has inspired me more than any other one person with his firm direction and emphasis on "get it right." I also want to thank Evelyn Jones, Bert Sitton, and all the others at the society who helped me through the years.

I must also recognize Ed and Sharon Bonnville for their assistance and Mark Stroud for outstanding cartography.

I thank Susan Snowden for the outstanding editing job. The second printing of *The Secret of War* is much improved thanks to her skill and attention.

The Secret of War

A DRAMATIC HISTORY OF CIVIL WAR CRIME IN WESTERN NORTH CAROLINA

Chapter 1

―― JANUARY 13, 1928 ――

Hendersonville, North Carolina Her work had become extremely difficult. She had lost so much weight and could hardly eat. The condition was terminal and she knew it, yet she forced herself to move. Under no circumstances would she yield to disease or anything else that might diminish her resolve. Her work must be done.

She reached to the right and grasped the bedpost, hoisting up to a sitting position on the side of the bed. Even this simple movement left her with a quickened breath. Once upright she stilled herself and listened carefully, as she always did. It was 2:00 A.M. and there was no traffic to be heard, even at the normally busy intersection of Third Avenue and Grove Street. It was a dark, foreboding winter night with frost collecting on the windows and a bitter cold riding the wind from the north.

Delia Russell Youngblood was now eighty-one years old. She lived with her daughter, Tekoa "Cora" Youngblood Cunningham, at 301 Third Avenue East in Hendersonville. They occupied a simple bungalow with a small dirt basement. She had moved to Cora's house five years earlier. Leaving Hoopers Creek had been very difficult, but she had slowly gotten used to her new home. Even the move to town had not stopped her work.

The youngest of Cora's children, Madge Cunningham Steedman, had married the year before and her husband, Preston Cunningham, had passed away years earlier. The presence of Cora and her family had often hindered Delia's ability to do her work, for it had to be accomplished surreptitiously. Still, she managed to carry on.

Despite the overall condition of her cancer-ridden body Delia's hearing was excellent. She sat on the side of the bed contemplating mistakes of the past. Things might have been different. She thought of Hoopers Creek and the beautiful mountains that surrounded the pristine little valley. She had lived in the same house for more than sixty years. She had done her work well at home.

Delia sat enveloped in darkness and listened as she had done all her adult life. She had become adept at identifying the slightest sounds: the pipes, the heat, even the popping sounds made by the expansion and contraction of the glass as it warmed and cooled. Darkness had always been her friend and protector.

"Only fools cast light on themselves," she thought. There could be no relaxation; one could not be too careful. Ever wary, her mind evaluated the sounds of the January night. Despite the silence she listened for over an hour before moving again. She was always on the alert for the dreaded sound of horses, but there were no such noises carried by the wind on this moonless ebony night.

In the course of uprighting herself she had disturbed her emaciated little body. Delia spit out a dab of reddish-brown blood, which was oozing from the suppurating wound inside her left cheek. The once broken jaw was now ravaged by a rapidly growing tumor. She captured her spittle in the small towel she kept at her bedside but was forced to swallow some of the discharge.

Delia reached under the pillow and clasped the fruit jar in her right hand and pulled it from its hiding place. This simple act of passing the small fruit jar from hand to hand sent a jolt of pain up her arm. The cancer was in her bones now, and her suffering was beyond normal human endurance. Delia's aged fingers held the tiny treasure as she steeled herself to the pain. Motionless for another hour, she sat keenly alert for any sounds that might pierce the night.

CHAPTER ONE

Satisfied that all precautions had been taken, she mustered all of her strength and stood beside the bed. As if inspired by the simple accomplishment of standing, she seemed to experience a slight renewal of energy. With considerable effort, Delia hobbled to the door. Now breathing rapidly, she made her way to the basement entrance. Again her ears perked and she listened. Delia stood only a few minutes for fear she would fall. She knew she must hurry before her energy faltered.

Her eyesight was nearly gone, but it made no difference. She was accustomed to the lightlessness of the dirt basement. She had always done her work in the dark; she preferred it that way. Descending the steep stairs was slow and agonizing, but her pace was not hampered as a result of the darkness. It was the weakness of her body that slowed her.

She walked directly to the predetermined spot, placing her treasure on the floor. She picked up the spade as if in full light of day. She turned and walked across the small concrete pad to the dirt floor that made up the majority of the basement. Her mind had previously recorded the exact point where she would dig. The soil had been prepared during the preceding week. In total darkness Delia placed the spade at the edge of the loosened soil. As always, she paused and listened. There was no sound save the wind.

Delia began to dig. By now she was gasping for breath. Her lungs could carry only a modicum of what her delicate body needed. The strain had forced her heart to a quickened pulse. The physical discomfort caused her to tremble, but she continued to dig. The joints of her hands ached, and each movement was more difficult than the last.

The tiny scoops were placed beside the hole as she dug. Working very slowly she finished the hole. Her normally expressionless face featured a modest smile that no one could see. Satisfied, she returned to the concrete pad and replaced the spade in the exact spot where she had retrieved it. Unimpeded by the total darkness, she picked up the fruit jar and returned to the hole, carefully placing the tiny treasure in the bottom. Slowly she swept the loosened soil into the small opening, covering the jar. She worked the dirt into the hole and packed it into place. She stood erect and pressed the loosened earth farther down into the hole using her foot. With tiny circular motions she dragged her feet over the spot to disperse any excess soil.

Her work completed, she stood in silence, once again listening and waiting. There was still no sound outside her world. Satisfied that the exercise had been completed in stealth, she started up the stairs. Grasping the handrail, she forced herself up one painful step at a time. Delia's knees quivered, her lungs strained, and her ancient heart pounded. At last she reached the top of the stairs where she stopped to catch her breath. For a moment panic struck her mind. Her breathing had become so labored that she could not hear. The struggle and the pain were of no consequence to her, but she must hear. By the force of sheer determination she shuffled through the hallway and into the bedroom. She reached the bed and sat on the edge. Reluctantly she allowed herself the luxury of relaxation as she slowly lowered herself into the bed. Within minutes she was asleep.

Delia Russell Youngblood had buried three dimes, five nickels, and seventeen pennies on this winter night. In the five years she had lived on Third Avenue she had buried 193 fruit jars, tins, or other metal containers of various description. There were more than two thousand burial sites at the old home place of Joseph and Delia Youngblood on Hoopers Creek. She knew where they were buried and what was in them. As she lay in her bed that night she was content, sensing that this burial would be her last.

Delia was entirely unaffected by any presence now. She lay silently and prayed. Delia had always been a religious woman. The prayers offered comfort for the pain. It was not the physical pain that tormented her. It was the emotional pain that twisted her smile and stifled her enjoyment of life. Within the prison of her mind she fought the memories each and every day of her life. Only her children and her husband, Joseph, offered brief respites of joy in the midst of each painful day. Her wonderful and loving Joseph; she knew she'd be joining him soon. He had married her even though he knew. She smiled warmly as she remembered her lasting affection for him.

CHAPTER ONE

Into the night her condition worsened, and on the morning of January 15 she began to cough up more blood as her time grew near. The constant strain on her heart was too great and the weak, irregular beating finally yielded and slowed to a stop. A cold darkness slowly extinguished the only remaining light that was her mind. As the light faded, the woman that had never known peace in all of her adult life was now at rest.

Chapter 2

— JANUARY 16, 1928 —

RITES FOR MRS. YOUNGBLOOD TUESDAY
Rev. A. I. Justice to Conduct
Services at Patty's Chapel
Hendersonville News

FLETCHER, NORTH CAROLINA: The many friends and relatives of Mrs. Delia Youngblood, age 81, were greatly saddened and shocked to learn of her death, which occurred yesterday morning at the home of her daughter, Mrs. Cora Cunningham, Third Avenue and Grove Street, after a short illness.

The deceased came to Hendersonville a few years ago to make her home. Mrs. Youngblood lived the greater part of her life on Hoopers Creek where her husband, Joseph Youngblood, until his death 21 years ago, was a prominent and prosperous farmer of that section. After Mr. Youngblood's death Mrs. Youngblood managed the farm for a number of years.

Mrs. Youngblood was for many years a faithful and consecrated member of Patty's Chapel Methodist

CHAPTER TWO

Church, where she held her membership until her death. The deceased was of a very friendly and kind disposition and had a large circle of friends in this county.

The Rev. A. I. Justice will conduct the funeral services at Patty's Chapel tomorrow at 3 o'clock.

Mrs. Youngblood is survived by six children: Mrs. Cora Cunningham, Mrs. Lonie Roach, and Miss Dovie Youngblood, all of this city; Mrs. H. H. Wolfe of Fletcher; Revis Youngblood of Biltmore; and Russell Youngblood of Fletcher.

Hoopers Creek, North Carolina Many of the mourners had arrived in automobiles with a few of the older folks still traveling by wagon or on horseback. The severe weather of the previous week had moderated to some degree, but it was still very cold and damp in the valley. The yard at Patty's Chapel was crowded and active. On this occasion the assembly moved slowly and quietly.

Just before the service an old clapboard wagon arrived, driven by a young black man with an elderly white-haired gentleman seated beside him. The wagon pulled into the churchyard as the old man scanned the grounds. He sat motionless beside the driver. The young assistant climbed down from the wagon and walked swiftly around the muddy churchyard to help his passenger down. Others who were close turned and stared.

Almost everyone recognized the elderly gentleman as Pinkney Youngblood, the last surviving member of the original Youngblood family that had settled on Hoopers Creek almost a century before.

Mr. Pink, as he was often called, waddled toward the church, aided by his loyal employee. He carefully made his way across the muddy ground, taking short steps and grimacing a bit as he walked. His gout, worsened by the weather, made walking much more difficult.

Those still outside parted to make way for his passing. Most of the old Hoopers Creek families were gathered there on this damp January day: Wards, Garrens, Whitakers, Paces, Russells, Barnwells, Lannings, and many more. Gazing into the eyes around him, Mr. Pink offered no expression or greeting of any kind. He reached the top step and turned, looking back across the churchyard toward the cemetery.

When he was a young boy there had been only a few graves in that cemetery. There had been plenty of room for the many tables that the womenfolk would set up for food and drink at church socials. There was always room in the yard for a game of ball, and the grass usually revealed just where the games had been played that season. There wasn't so much room there now. Pinkney scanned the tombstones and thought of those who had been with him during those happy times. He also thought of the long gray lines of men, imagining them shrouded in the flame and smoke of the past. A morose consciousness rippled through him as he realized that he must return to the present if he were to make it through this sad day. Still expressionless, he looked out beyond the corner of the church where his eyes caught the image of a very elderly black man dressed in a dark ruffled coat and large floppy hat. For the first time his expression changed. Smiling ever so slightly, he looked over to his companion and instructed, "Help me back down these steps."

Again he advanced with his wobbly steps toward the back of the crowd where the old black man stood alone.

"Is that you, George?"

"Yez, sir. It sho' is," the obscure visitor responded.

Pinkney Youngblood took the man's hand in his. Turning back to his servant, he motioned in the direction of his old friend and spoke softly.

"This here is George Mills, Otis. Do you know him?"

The two black men exchanged courteous handshakes while Youngblood and George Mills stared knowingly at each other.

"Good to see you, George."

CHAPTER TWO

George looked back at him with the same warm but now toothless grin he had carried all his life.

"Good to see ya too, sir. Mighty good to see ya."

Mr. Pink looked back at the church and turned toward George.

"I guess we best git on with business."

Pinkney Youngblood slowly turned and feebly made his way back across the muddy ground to the steps of Patty's Chapel. Again he made the painful climb upward to the pine-encased doorway. The boards to the old steps creaked as he climbed.

Otis opened the door for him, and the two entered the church. Most every head in the room turned to peer at the tardy mourners. Pinkney walked toward the front of the small sanctuary, passing the pine pews, and found his way toward the white stage that held the open casket. He looked down into the casket and lifted Delia's tiny hand. Briefly he scanned her motionless body and shook his head. He took long and special notice of her face, remembering the bright eyes and beautiful laugh. Sadly he also took notice of the ugly depression that dominated the left side of her face, still apparent after all the years. Pinkney Youngblood then took his seat on the end of the pew with the other members of the Youngblood and Russell families.

Reverend Justice began the service by calling upon the congregation to stand and sing "Amazing Grace." Standing but not singing, Pinkney again drifted back to years of long ago and to the other occasion at which he had heard this song. As the service ended, Pinkney chuckled. He'd hardly heard a word. But he was not ashamed, nor did he mean any disrespect. He had just held a service of his own, deep within the confines of his mind.

The old Youngblood home place on Hoopers Creek was not large. Many friends and family members had been coming and going all day to pay their respects to the children of Joseph and Delia Russell

Youngblood. As was customary in the community, the women brought food and drink of every description. There was lots of eating and chatting as the afternoon wore on.

Pinkney Youngblood did not want to be there, but he had forced himself to come out of a sense of obligation. It was not to the living that he felt obligated, and he certainly did not care about making impressions. His only sense of obligation was to those who'd gone on.

Pinkney was the youngest of five Youngblood sons, and the recently departed Delia Russell Youngblood was his sister-in-law. She had married his brother Joseph many years before during the difficult period of Reconstruction, but she had been his friend even before that. He had known her nearly all of his life, and Delia was the last relative who had lived through those tumultuous times with him.

It was late in the evening now and Pinkney sat in the corner and watched and listened. There was a new generation of Youngbloods now, some of them young adults, many of them children. All six of Delia's children were living and in attendance. Many of the nephews and nieces were there, as well as Delia's grandchildren. There was no one left of his generation, and as he listened to the younger ones, an anger and resentment began to rise up inside him. It was only a smoldering anger at first, but as he began to evaluate some of their conversations, he became increasingly agitated.

Pinkney looked to the other side of the room and saw Russell Youngblood staring silently as if his mind were also roaming to another time. Pinkney knew that young Russell, who carried his mother's maiden name, had secondhand knowledge of Delia's difficult life. He had not seen or witnessed the horrors of her early years, but he had vicariously experienced the emotional strain almost every day of his life. He had helplessly witnessed his mother's agony, and Pinkney felt sorry for him.

Pink had once been a big man with a really big heart. But the years had taken their toll, and while he was still a tall man, his blue bloodshot

CHAPTER TWO

eyes often matched the hardness of his heart. His heavy jowls and bald head made him look much older. Like all of the Youngbloods he was usually a man of few words.

Throughout the day Pinkney had heard little of the banter going on around him. Nothing the minister said nor the greetings from the mourners meant much to him. His ears had accepted only a few select phrases of his choosing. But now his ears perked as he listened once again to the descendants of Delia Youngblood.

"Damn fools," he whispered to himself.

He could not help but hear the things that were being said, and he overheard one of the grandchildren questioning Cora Youngblood Cunningham.

"Why *did* she crawl around in the basement at night?" the teenager asked her mother.

"Sshh, child. Don't say nothin' about that," Cora responded.

One of the other grandchildren overheard the question and snickered slightly.

"Yea, what was that all about?"

Cora looked nervous and tried desperately to change the subject. She knew of Delia's secret, but it was not to be spoken of and she certainly was not going to have that discussion in this setting.

"Yea, she sure was strange. She buried stuff all over that basement."

This time several others joined in light chuckling.

The old man sat in the corner as both his wrinkled forehead and rutted nose reddened with the flow of blood. His face turned a scarlet red, and he slowly separated his leathery hands and balled them into fists at his side. Unable to ignore the chatter, he rose to his feet and shouted at the top of his lungs.

"You goddamn ignorant fools!"

The roar of the old man's voice sent a shock wave across the room, and everyone in the house stilled in silence. Cora started to say something, but before she could speak Pinkney glared at her, his smoky blue eyes flaring. With his hands shaking, he pointed straight at her.

"Don't you say a goddamn word," he roared.

The mourners stood at the entrances to the living room and the dining room as Pinkney glared at them all. He raised his hand again and pointed around the room as he began to rant.

"You damn fools. You sit here drinkin' your punch, eatin' your fine food, and ridin' around in your highfalutin motor carriages like you don't have a care in the world," he said as his body trembled with anger.

"You make fun of a poor old lady who suffered more than any of you can ever imagine. None of you know how really hard life can be and how hard it was for her. You have no idea how lucky you are that you've never seen a single day like the days that she lived. There ain't a one of you snivelin' shits that could survive what she did."

He paused briefly, taking a moment to look around the room at Delia's children.

"Yea, you think you know a little bit of it, but thinkin' and knowin' is way different. You just know enough to be silly and squirmy about it."

He turned his head toward the eldest of Delia's children and then continued.

"You're scared of the whole truth."

Bob Youngblood, Pinkney's nephew, was there with his young-adult children. He could see where Pinkney was headed and thought it best that the ghosts of the past remained buried with those who lived it. He did not want his mother's secret told now, not in this setting, especially with young children in attendance.

"Uncle Pink, don't do this."

Pinkney glared back at him and almost shouted.

"Can't you see they need to know this? They need to know what is really important when the sweets are stripped away. They need to know of the unending sufferin' and cruelty brought on by war. They need to

CHAPTER TWO

know that war changes not just those individuals who live through it, but generations beyond. Our lives have roots. Roots in the sufferin' of that fine lady we buried today. Yea, Bob, I think it's time they know."

Delia's children were now quite alarmed. Again there was an effort to stop him, this time from one of the younger in-laws. The entreaty made Pinkney even more furious. With his face contorted and his body hunkered down in threatening posture, Pinkney shouted them all down.

"'You shut your damn mouth, too. I may be an old man, but I'll come over there and knock your goddamn teeth out if you say another word."

All resistance was gone. The family stood staring and captive, not sure of what to expect.

Pinkney turned to Russell's wife, who now shared the Youngblood home place with her husband.

"Leave if you want to. If you stay, you're not leaving until I finish what I've got to say."

He then took slow steps and walked to the center of the house where the dining area joined the living room. From this position everyone could hear and see him. Pinkney paused, allowing time for those leaving to clear the room. He pretended not to notice as Russell Youngblood picked up his coat and started for the door. Pinkney waited until it got quiet again, and then he began.

"So, you wanna know why your grandmother was so strange and peculiar, do you?" he said, looking over at a few of the offending grandchildren.

"Well, I'm gonna tell you of a time that was like no other. In the beginning it was a time when things were simple and mostly beautiful. We all worked hard, but we enjoyed our work and we enjoyed each other. The air was clean and beautiful. The horses and the cattle grazed on lush green grass. There was a time when the sun shone on Hoopers Creek valley as if it were a place blessed from heaven and God himself.

Then that peaceful time of our lives was destroyed. Torn to pieces and ripped to shreds almost overnight. The world turned mad like a rabid dog. Smoke and flames seemed to burn and kill everything. Men's guts and brains were scattered across the fields like rotting cow patties. The rivers and streams flowed red with blood. Death, starvation, and destruction knocked at every door, sparing almost no family of the horrors that marched to the deadly drumbeat of war.

"There was five of us boys and I was the only one who came through it unhurt, saved only by my youth. You see, men are supposed to bear the burdens of war. Fighting is men's business. At least that's what we thought. But war also eats and swallows women and children as if they are grapes on the vine. No one is safe. I remember thinking that those who died were the lucky ones. I remember feeling so sad for the bodies and souls that were mutilated but still lived. There were tens of thousands who were tortured and consumed. One of those was Delia. You wanna know her secret? So be it."

Chapter 3

―― MARCH 1861 ――

Hoopers Creek, North Carolina Robert Russell stood on the porch of his beautiful new home, his eyes scanning the mountains around him. He had made substantial sacrifices to purchase the house and a thousand acres of land from the Merrimon family. He grimaced at the thought. One thousand dollars in gold and ten slaves was a tremendous price, and although there was always some lingering doubt, he felt confident when he looked out over the valley and contemplated all that was his. The house was a large, distinctive structure dominating the surrounding landscape. It was L-shaped with ten rooms, including a formal parlor. The rooms boasted sixteen-foot-high ceilings, which kept the house cool in the heated days of summer. On one end there was a large kitchen, and there were three stone chimneys, which gave the house a towering appearance. Originally constructed by the Branch Merrimon family some years earlier, it was still considered new by mid-nineteenth-century standards. The staircase was ornately fashioned, and many of the rooms were wallpapered with the finest material of the day. There was a generous display of windows on all sides and on both ends of the house.

In addition to the house there was an enormous barn and stabling for several horses. The stone springhouse was a reliable source of water through even the driest periods. There was also a chicken coop and smokehouse for storing dried and salted meats. The Merrimon family had drawn off a sizable plot for the growing of vegetables and herbs for household use.

Thanks to the generosity of his father-in-law, John Livingston, Robert and Susannah Russell occupied one of the finest properties in all of western North Carolina. But Russell was now short of cash and had only two slaves left. Zeke and Nanny Mills were getting old, but he knew there was a lot of good work left in them.

He could no longer count on Susannah to work her normal share. His wife suffered from some unidentified illness that generated pain in her joints and often rendered her immobile. She was small and frail but still managed to command a pleasant smile most of the time. She spent most days in her room but would hobble down when the weather was warm. Susannah always wore a plain black dress over layers of petticoats. Her bonnet was kept tight around her head, revealing very little of her face.

Robert Russell's many children were counted on to do a lot of the basic chores. The three girls, only teenagers, were responsible for much of the housework. The youngest, Delia, was very good with horses, yet she was only fourteen. Sarah and Mary were excellent gardeners, and they helped with many household and farm chores. Of the boys, James, the eldest, was now married and lived in his own house. He still worked for his father. Joe Lee and John, the youngest, were at home along with their sisters.

Delia was a pretty girl. She had coal-black hair with sparkling blue eyes. That combination gave her an exotic look. She was slightly less than five feet tall and weighed just under ninety pounds. She had milky-white skin and beautiful high cheekbones. Delia's face was accented with a pert little nose and a shapely mouth highlighted by a beautiful set of teeth. Her petite body was healthy and strong. Her tiny hands were graceful and dignified.

Sarah and Mary were larger. Both had dark hair but not as dark as Delia's. Sarah also had blue eyes, but Mary's were brown. The two of them were jovial and outgoing while Delia was quiet and reserved.

CHAPTER THREE

James was now a mature man with dark, curly hair. He had broad shoulders and big hands like his father. He had brown eyes, and his otherwise good looks were somewhat diminished by acne scars.

The other two boys were more like the Livingstons, small but solidly built. They both had light brown hair and brown eyes.

Joe Lee was now eighteen, and Robert depended on him as his personal assistant. The Russells were farmers and they raised corn and other grain to supply the drovers traveling through western North Carolina. As Robert Russell looked out over the farm he thought to himself, "This will be a good year. I will soon have even more land and more slaves."

He stepped off the porch and limped toward the barn. The soreness in his leg would always be with him. Many years ago a horse had fallen on his leg, breaking it severely. It never healed quite the way it should have, and he cursed the doctor who set the break, mumbling audibly, "Damn fool!" as he hobbled around the corner of the house. He immediately saw his three teenage daughters laughing and giggling as they walked from the well.

"Hello, Papa," they all said in near unison.

"Papa, something's wrong with Ole Star," Mary said.

"What you talking about, child?" her father replied, seemingly annoyed at the interruption.

Delia answered, "Papa, her nose is hot and she don't act right. I think she's sick or something."

"You girls take that water on up to the house and I'll go have a look."

Robert Russell hobbled down to the barn. He opened the door and walked into the stall where Ole Star was stabled. The barn smelled of manure and hay, but there was a relaxing quality about being there. Russell had only owned the home a few months, but he loved everything about it. Even the odor of the barn appealed to him as he made his way around the stall. He patted Ole Star on the forehead and felt her nose. He was immediately concerned. Something wasn't right, but he didn't have any idea what could be done. Joe Lee entered the barn and approached the stall.

As he looked at Ole Star he said, "Look, Papa, she's frothing a little bit."

"Yea, I see that, boy. She ain't right."

Ole Star was a good mare, fourteen years old and still capable of good work if she stayed healthy. Remembering how he had stretched financially to buy the Merrimon place, he didn't want to think of losing a horse now. He turned to Joe Lee and said, "I can't afford to buy a horse now, boy. You see if you can get her to drink some and we'll watch her through the night."

Robert left his son to tend to Ole Star while he slowly and painfully made his way back up to the house. He struggled up the back steps and into the kitchen where Nanny Mills and the girls busily prepared the evening meal.

Nanny Mills was a big woman. Her black face and brilliant dark-brown eyes sparkled as she worked at the iron cookstove. She not only took care of the house and everything in it but she also supervised and raised the girls as if they were her own. Susannah Russell was a Livingston, a family of privilege and wealth. Although Mrs. Russell still tried to help at times, Nanny Mills carried the burden of household chores with the aid of the Russell daughters. Nanny was as excited about the new house as anyone in the Russell family. She loved her work and the girls so much that she seemed to forget that she was a slave and that the children were not her own. "Miss Susannah" was generally nice to her and treated her with courtesy and civility. Master Robert, however, had a bad streak, and if things did not go to suit him he was mean to her and her husband, Zeke Mills. When things were at their worst Master Robert would threaten to sell them off separate, leaving Nanny crying and groveling at his feet. Even when he beat them, as he did occasionally, it didn't hurt her as much as the thought of losing her husband. Zeke was a good and wise man. His ability to negotiate their difficult lives demonstrated his keen intellect and sound judgment. She loved Zeke and he loved her. Now in her late fifties, she could never bear him children, but he did not seem to mind. The slave couple had originally belonged to John Livingston, but when Susannah married

CHAPTER THREE

Robert Russell, she and Zeke were given to the newlyweds as a wedding present.

Nanny and Susannah had grown up together on the Livingston farm, and the move to the newlyweds' home suited them as well as possible. The young couple started out in a small house outside the Livingston home, with the two slaves living in a one-room shack nearby. Now the Russells had their own house, and a fine house it was. The slave quarters were small but decent, and Nanny and Zeke were as content as slaves could hope to be. They made it a point to stay out of "Massa Bob's" way and do what he said as quickly and efficiently as possible.

As she prepared the evening meal with the Russell girls milling around her, Nanny Mills thought of her years on Hoopers Creek. She considered herself blessed. For a slave who could bear no children she had fared well.

Sarah chased Delia around the kitchen, smacking her on the backside with a wooden spoon.

"Quit dat, child," Nanny Mills said. "Ya girls actin' like it be playtime and it ain't. We gots work to do."

The trio of girls continued to laugh and chatter as they sat down at the large kitchen table. "Massa Bob gonna whop us all if we don't git his suppa ready," Nanny Mills scolded the three girls. Delia was stringing beans and Sarah and Mary were shucking corn. The girls told stories and speculated on their oldest brother, James, and his new bride. Mary whispered something to her sisters about what a young married couple would do in their home. Her whisper was at a level that prevented Nanny Mills from hearing all of it. Nanny Mills turned from the cooking pot and shook the large ladle at the girls.

"Ya girls ain't got no business talkin' 'bout nothin' like dat."

Her indignation was apparent. Recognizing that their bawdy topic had been exposed, all three girls burst out laughing, not threatened by the fact that Nanny Mills knew the theme of the conversation. Nanny Mills turned back to her pot and Delia whispered to Sarah, "Do they really?"

"Yes, they do."

Her sister responded and the girls giggled again. Robert Russell reentered the room, and his presence quelled the festive atmosphere. The girls turned back to their chores and Nanny Mills picked up the pace of stirring the pot.

"Where's Zeke?" Robert Russell gruffly addressed Nanny Mills.

"He be down workin' de field, Massa Robert," Nanny responded with her usual deference.

"Delia, you go down and fetch Zeke, take him up to have a look at Ole Star. I'm worried about her and maybe Zeke can do something."

"Papa, Ole Star ain't gonna die is she?" Delia asked.

"Of course not, girl, we are gonna see that she gets well."

Delia bounded out the back door and scampered across the open yard, down toward the fields where James and Zeke were working. Delia was used to moving with a heavy dress and layers of petticoats surrounding her body. With only her hands and face exposed the sun did little to change the color of her skin. All the Russell girls wore bonnets to protect their skin and contain their hair. Delia looked out over the valley as she trotted across the field. Life was so wonderful, she thought. Everything around her was beautiful. Spring was in the air and new growth was beginning. The land was verdant, and life was shrouded in intriguing new mysteries. Her mind drifted to thoughts about her brother's young wife and the things that Sarah had said about the couple. She blushed at her own thoughts even though she was alone. Then she smiled to herself as she went. Life promised so many exciting and interesting things. She felt she couldn't wait to experience and understand all of it. Just then she spotted Zeke as he worked on the fence below the field.

"Zeke, Zeke, Papa says for you to get up to the barn and tend to Ole Star. She's sick or something and we're worried about her."

Zeke dropped the fence section he was working with and pulled the handkerchief from his pocket, wiping his sweaty brow. Zeke was a tall, lean man with chocolate skin and large white teeth with decay emerging between the gaps. He had long arms with big hands. There was a fatherly

CHAPTER THREE

air about the man that had a comforting effect on all who knew him. He was a wise man but was careful not to reveal that around Master Robert. Master Robert did not like "niggers" who were too smart.

Zeke smiled at Delia as he delighted in her youthful energy.

"What's wrong, child?"

"I don't know," Delia said, "but Star is hot and frothing at the mouth."

"Dat ain't good. We bes' have a look."

Delia trotted along behind him as they made their way toward the barn. They entered through the large doors and continued to the stall where Ole Star was housed. Delia could see the look of concern on Zeke's face as he first looked at the horse. Delia watched him as he held the mare's head and then walked from one side of her to the other, looking into her eyes. He looked over at the little girl and said, "I don't like de look of dis. Dis ole horse be mighty sickly. We bes' cool her down some. Ya go fetch some rags while I git a bucket of water."

Delia was only fourteen, but she had been around horses all her life. She was worried about Ole Star and anxious to do what she could to help. Delia went into the house and told Nanny Mills that Zeke wanted rags. Nanny looked at Delia and asked, "How's dat horse doing, child?"

"I don't know, but Zeke looks worried."

"Lordy child, don't y'all let nothin' happen to dat horse or Massa Bob git mighty mean." Nanny scrambled around in the cupboard and pulled out two old linen rags and handed them to Delia. "Now you git on down there and help Zeke git dat horse well."

Delia ran down to the barn and entered the stall where Zeke stood with the bucket of water. Zeke shook his head and said, "She ain't drinkin." He soaked the rags in water and wiped them over the horse's head and neck while Delia rung them out for him in the cold water.

"Ya bes' go on now, child, ain't nothin' more ya can do down here. I'll stay a spell with Ole Star."

Delia went back to the house and continued helping her sisters and Nanny Mills prepare supper. She could smell the cornbread baking and the beans and corn boiling over the fire. Nanny turned to the girls, "Now ya girls go git cleaned up, supper'll be ready 'fore too long."

The Russell girls chattered and laughed as they got ready for supper. Sarah and Mary continued their frivolous but rather mature speculation on their brother and his new wife. To Delia it was all very fascinating and entertaining. Such discussions were new to her. Initially it was embarrassing and somewhat uncomfortable. Her mother would be outraged if she knew they talked of such things. Nanny Mills wouldn't tell and they knew it.

At supper that night the whole family assembled. John and Joe Lee sat side by side near their mother. Mrs. Russell had to be helped to her seat. James and his new bride, Minerva, sat side by side near the end of the table with Robert Russell. The three girls were scattered among them. Delia sat across from her sisters. The girls looked at each other and blushed with guilt. Watching the two made Delia wonder if it were true. Might Minerva be carrying a baby now? She shivered guiltily at such thoughts as though someone might be reading her mind. She was quickly brought to reality when James asked her father if there was going to be a war.

"I don't know if there is or not, but I know one thing. We'll whip those Yankees. One southern boy can whip ten Yankees any day. They're all a bunch of silly citified boys that can't ride nor shoot. If they don't leave our niggers and us alone then we will teach 'em a thing or two."

Young James Russell responded, "Every man I know in both Buncombe and Henderson counties can ride and shoot a rabbit at three hundred yards. I can't imagine missing somethin' as big as a Yankee. I reckon if there is a war, I'll be going." Young Joe Lee excitedly raised his head. "I'll be going too. I'm eighteen now and I can shoot as good as any man on Hoopers Creek."

"Y'all hush now," Robert said. "If there is a war, you'll be going soon enough. I 'spect it'll last three or four months, six months at the most. A heap of them Yankees will die before it's over."

CHAPTER THREE

Delia looked at the men around the table, and suddenly she was jolted by the real possibility of a war. She didn't have the nerve to probe but was nevertheless very curious. Her older sister repeated James' question.

"Is there really going to be a war, Papa?"

"Looks like there might be, child," Robert Russell responded grimly.

Delia was again shaken. Would her brothers really go off to war? Who'd run the farm? Where would the war be? Would it be nearby? she wondered. Will people really die in the war? Delia had been taught to read and write, and she had some education in literature and religion. She knew about the Revolutionary War, but very little. Her father often talked about the Declaration of Independence and the Constitution. She did not know or understand what those documents were about, and according to her father the Yankees didn't understand either. She wondered about the Yankees and what they were like. She imagined them as uncivilized, beastly men with little or no respect for freedom or for God. Such men could never win a war against God-fearing men like those she knew in the South. At least her father and her brothers assured her so.

Delia woke up early. Her sleep was a restless one as the discussion of the previous day had troubled her. She climbed out of the bed, being careful not to awaken her sister who slept alongside her. She put on the flannel robe that covered her nightgown and felt for her shoes in the dim morning light. She made her way through the yard to the outhouse. Closing the rickety door she seated herself. She thought of Ole Star and her trepidation returned. Delia made her way from the outhouse to the barn carefully in the early morning light. The cool air felt refreshing on her face as she walked. She went in the barn and stepped over to Ole Star's stall. Looking in the stall she was immediately shocked. Ole Star was down. Despite her youth she recognized the seriousness of the situation. She knew what it meant to see a horse down. Delia had seen it before and the horses usually died. Instinctively she turned and ran for the house, bursting through the back door and calling out loudly.

"Papa, Papa! Ole Star is down. She's down in her stall," she shouted, bounding up the steps. Her father was dressed and coming out of his room when he growled at Delia.

"Hush, child, I heard ya. You go out to the shack and fetch Zeke."

Joe Lee was now standing in the hallway in his nightshirt.

"Papa, I'll be there in a minute. Let me get my clothes on," Joe Lee shouted, not wanting to be left out. Bob Russell clutched the banister as he hobbled down the stairs. By the time Delia reached the slave shack Zeke was already on his way to the big house.

As usual, Nanny Mills had been up for two hours and was cooking in the kitchen. When Zeke and Delia reached the stall Robert Russell and Joe Lee were already there. The pain associated with Russell's arthritic, crippled leg nagged him as he tried to think it through. Feeling the strains of his financial burdens, Russell was at the edge of his tolerance.

He screamed at Zeke.

"What have you done to my horse, nigger? If my horse dies, I'm gonna tie you to the fence and thrash you 'til you bleed to death."

Zeke, sensing the gravity of the situation, tried to calm his master.

"I ain't done nothin', Massa Bob. I ain't done nothin'. I swear I ain't. I just tried to take care of Ole Star and get her heat down."

Still in a rage, Russell turned to the horse, unsure of what to do next. This was not the time to lose a horse, and his potential misfortune worried him. It was young Joe Lee who calmed the situation.

"Papa, why don't you get the Youngbloods up here? You know how good they are at taking care of lame and sick animals. They might be able to help Ole Star."

"I ain't goin' beggin' to no damn German Kraut for nothin'. Old man Reuben can't hardly speak English, much less doctor a damn horse," he yelled.

The German families on Hoopers Creek lived somewhat separate from the rest of the community. There were no educated or certified veterinarians in the area, but the Germans seemed to have a way with taking care of livestock and other animals. The elders in these families

CHAPTER THREE

still spoke German at home. Between the Scotch-Irish and English families, the Germans had been looked upon with disfavor in the early days. Still they were a friendly clan, generally willing to help their neighbors. The younger generations were now intermarrying.

Joe Lee calmed his father with logic.

"Papa, what do we care if they speak English or not, if they can save our horse? A horse don't speak German or English."

Bob Russell looked at Ole Star and pondered the question.

"All right, boy. You run on up Hoopers Creek and see if you can find Reuben Youngblood and tell him I want him to have a look at this horse."

Even though he was reluctant, Bob Russell was in no position to be particular. He considered calling on the Krauts for help a desperate measure, but one that had to be taken.

Delia Russell and her sisters could see the two figures coming up the road from a distance. One they recognized as their brother, but the man riding behind him on the horse was taller than their brother. He stared at the girls as the horse carried them into the yard. The taller rider quickly dismounted and approached the porch with a wide grin on his face.

The stranger looked to be about six feet tall with fair skin and light wavy hair. He had large, bright hazel eyes and a bushy mustache. His clothes were modest, but he was clean and tidy. He seemed to walk with confidence, and there was a disarming, kindly quality about the man.

"Howdy, ladies," he said, taking off his hat and slightly bowing to the three girls. They all giggled shyly, for they weren't sure how to respond to a young man addressing them directly.

Young Joseph Youngblood bounced onto the porch, not one to miss this kind of opportunity. Several pretty girls gathered in one place was more luck than he had counted on this early spring morning. Sarah finally worked up the nerve to speak.

"Papa's in the barn with Ole Star." Those were the only words she could muster. She was otherwise speechless; Mary and Delia could only stare. Joe Lee rescued them by calling on this brazen young man to follow him to the barn. Joseph continued to stare at the three girls with a conspicuous grin on his face. Each of the girls looked down or glanced to the side. They looked up only briefly to encounter the grin on the face of Joseph Youngblood. It was beyond Delia's comprehension to speak, but she could not resist looking up to catch a glimpse of the stranger on her porch. Only this time, he was staring directly back at her. Her eyes met his and she found herself locked to his gaze. She could feel her face flush with embarrassment yet she sensed an unfamiliar attraction. She felt the urge to turn away yet she couldn't. A warm, dizzy feeling passed over her as she stared at him. Briefly the scurrilous talk of the previous day flashed through her mind. Joseph Youngblood started for the steps, following Joe Lee, but his eyes stayed fixed on Delia. By the time he reached the stairs his head was turned all the way around looking back at her. The wide grin was now even wider. This young man was enjoying himself. After all, he thought he was coming to look at a sick horse and now he was looking into the piercing blue eyes of the prettiest girl he'd ever seen.

At that moment he reached the edge of the steps, his eyes still fixed on the young girl. She was now in a state of near hypnosis, not moving or talking; she only stared. Joseph started to turn, but it was too late. He missed the top step and fell headlong sprawling into the yard, muddying his clothes and face. The two older girls burst into laughter and Joe Lee came over to help him up. But Delia was frightened. She still could not move, but she was worried that he was hurt. She had the urge to rush to his aid but didn't dare move. Youngblood got up and chuckled at his own embarrassment as he looked at the two older girls, who were now laughing hysterically. Not knowing what else to say, he looked at Joe Lee and said, "I reckon I better go have a look at that horse, before I come up lame myself." At that the girls laughed even louder and Delia giggled a little, realizing with relief that he was uninjured. As the two young men started toward the barn, Joseph turned again, staring back at her.

Delia's sisters teased her. "I do believe that boy was staring at you."

"He was not!" Delia lashed back.

"Yes, he was, I believe he's sweet on you."

CHAPTER THREE

"Ain't so!" Delia shot back.

"He was staring at you, Delia."

This time she didn't respond. She just stared off toward the barn.

I know he was, she thought.

But when she spoke she said, "Oh don't be silly, Mary. He wasn't staring at me. He's probably sweet on one of you two."

The attempt to reverse the accusatory atmosphere failed. Mary and Sarah rolled their eyes as if to discredit Delia and the three girls separated.

Delia went up to her room and closed the door where no one could see her. She dropped to her knees and began a silent prayer. "Dear God, let it be me. Let him look at me. Let him think of me like I'm thinking of him." She rose to her feet and felt herself trembling with a nervous energy. Delia tried to overcome her anxiety. She longed to go to the barn to help with the horse but was afraid of what she might do or what she might say. Would her father see her trembling and know what she was feeling? Would this Youngblood boy know she was nervous? She pulled back the window dressing and peeked toward the barn, hoping to catch another glimpse of him.

It seemed as though he had stared straight into her, that he had looked into her heart. But then she thought he looked so pleasant, he had smiled. Maybe she saw into his heart also. She decided it didn't matter. Her motivation was of sufficient strength. Her only choice was to follow her heart, Delia smiled as she thought. She worked up her courage and started for the barn. Frightened as she was she couldn't stop. Her father might be irritated with her but still she marched on as if pulled by some unseen force. As she opened the barn door the voices of the men could be heard echoing faintly from the back of the barn.

Closer to the stall her father's gruff voice could be heard, "Where's your daddy, boy? This is man's work, not fit for no damn boy."

Joseph Youngblood calmly addressed the older man.

"My father is not at home, sir, and your son told me you needed help. My father is good with livestock, but he ain't no better at horses than I am. Do you want me to help you or not?" Joseph said firmly.

Robert Russell pondered the question and begrudgingly responded, "Well, at least you're one Kraut that speaks good English. At least I'll understand what you're sayin'."

Joseph looked at him but refrained from further comment.

By this time Delia had reached the stall. Her father, Joe Lee, Zeke, and the tall young stranger were gathered around the downed horse. Joseph Youngblood was now all business. He squatted beside the horse's head and began to speak gently to the horse.

"What's wrong with you, girl? You feeling pretty bad, aren't you?" He patted her head and lifted it slightly and opened the horse's mouth. He examined her gums and teeth and felt her nose. He turned to Bob Russell with a worried look on his face.

"I don't know if I can help her or not," he said with a genuine air of concern.

The young man looked around the barn as if sizing up the situation. He looked at Joe Lee and the old slave and said, "Can you two help me?"

"Sure we'll help."

"This is gonna take a while," Joseph said seriously.

Robert Russell turned to them saying, "There's nothing more I can do here. I'll leave you with it." He turned on his stiffened leg and started out of the barn.

"Come along, Delia."

She wanted to stay and help, but mostly she wanted to remain in the presence of the handsome young man who was doctoring her horse.

"Let me stay, Daddy."

"No, you go on," her brother said. "You'll just get in the way."

Joseph was still busy examining the horse and at this point seemed indifferent to her presence.

"Come on, girl," Robert Russell said, leading Delia from the barn.

Joseph turned to the old slave and Joe Lee and told them they were going to need some rope and two stout blankets as well as some strong backs.

"We got to get this horse up or she'll be dead by tomorrow morning."

CHAPTER THREE

The two men went about their business of retrieving the rope and blankets. Joseph talked to the horse as he planned what he was going to do. He opened the worn leather bag that he carried with him and pulled out smaller pouches that were full of dried herbs and bags of dried leaves of a weed known as Mountain Planting, common in Appalachia. He rolled out a broad piece of linen about a foot and a half square. He had Joe Lee and Zeke build a small fire just outside the door of the barn.

"I need some kind of cooking pot," he told Joe Lee. Zeke went to Nanny Mills and returned with an old black pot that she used for dying cloth.

"Dis here work for you, Massa Youngblood?" he asked tentatively.

"Yes, that will do fine," Joseph said as he continued to work.

By now he had the little fire glowing, and he filled the black pot with herbs and Planting. He added water and brought the mixture to a boil. Horse urine was poured into the mixture to add acid, which helped to break down the leaves and roots to a soupy gel. He continued to stir and cook the strange ingredients, bringing the thick mixture to a slow boil. Soon the air was filled with a noxious, pungent odor. More herbs and Planting were added, and the three men took turns working the pot with a wooden stick.

Joe Lee waved his arm and quipped, "I hope you ain't gonna make her drink that. She'll die for sure. It's about to kill me just smellin' it. Whew. Aw, damn," he almost gagged as he turned his head away. He had inhaled the strong fumes, causing his nose to run profusely.

"No, it ain't for drinking," Joseph said calmly.

"I'm making a poultice."

The day wore into the evening and Delia and her sisters again joined the family at the dinner table, but Joe Lee wasn't there. Joe Lee arrived in the middle of the meal and asked that food be sent down to the barn for Zeke and the Youngblood boy.

Delia bounded to her feet.

"I'll take it. I'll take it. Please let me take it." It was obvious to everyone that her voice was filled with an urgency that was unlike her. She was a little unnerved when she realized that her emotions had been exposed.

"What's wrong with you, Delia?" her mother asked.

"Nothing, Momma," she replied sheepishly.

"I just want to take them some food and I want to see Ole Star."

Her two sisters weren't fooled. They looked at each other and grinned.

"She's sweet on that Kraut boy," Sarah said, laughing.

"I am not," Delia responded indignantly. Her two sisters laughed uproariously.

"You're too young to think such things," her mother said.

"Nanny, you fix up some food and take it down to the men. I think they'll be pretty hungry."

"Yes, ma'am," Nanny Mills said respectfully. Delia's hopes were dashed, missing this great opportunity. Everything was happening down at the barn and she couldn't be part of it. When supper was over the girls helped clean up the kitchen while Nanny prepared a basket of biscuits, ham, and apples to take to the men. Mrs. Russell retired to her room when Nanny finished the food basket. Mary and Sarah were off to the parlor.

The white folks had been discussing the day's events as if the black woman wasn't there. Nanny Mills hadn't said a word, but she didn't miss a thing. She knew those girls like her own and better than their own mother. She also had a special sensitivity to issues of the heart, something her master lacked. Hers was nearly torn out when Master Bob threatened to sell off either her or Zeke, splitting the couple.

As Delia started to leave the kitchen, Nanny bent to pick up the basket. "Ooo, ow," she screeched and put her hand on her back. Delia turned in alarm to see what had happened.

"My ol' bad back gone a hurtin' me again. I reckon Miss Delia gonna have to go down to dat ol' barn after all. Ya git dat stuff there and carry it down fer me, ya hear?"

A sly smile crossed the dark black face, and she saw the joy in Delia's eyes.

"I be right behind ya now. You min' yourself."

Delia was at first concerned about Nanny's injury, but she quickly

CHAPTER THREE

deciphered Nanny's true intentions. Nanny knew how bad she wanted to go down to that barn and she was making it happen.

"Don't you hurt your back none, Nanny; you know you gotta lot of hard work to do."

Her two sisters were leaving by now, and Delia was picking up the basket.

"I'll carry it for you, Nanny."

As they walked to the barn Nanny turned to Delia.

"Is you really sweet on dis boy, child?"

"No, I ain't, Nanny. I just wanna see Ole Star."

Delia looked up at the kind black face and into her big dark eyes. Those eyes saw right through her. The slave woman chuckled, "Now ya be careful child, ya mamma ain't gonna take kindly to ya courtin' no man at your age."

Delia smiled back at her. The old woman looked ahead as she walked. She laughed slyly and then said softly, "Um hum. You isn't sweet on that boy and I ain't black neither."

Delia could not believe her eyes. She marveled at the warm fire in the pit just outside the back door near Ole Star's stall. There were ropes running from the rafters in the barn under the horse's body and tied to the blankets that were holding her up. Joseph Youngblood was boiling something and putting the pot under Star's nose, making her breathe the vapor. The barn was filled with a strong foreign odor so intense that it muted the normal smell of manure that usually dominated the barn. Layers of linen cloth were tied under the horse's neck and upper chest area. The linens were layered thick with the herbal poultice that Youngblood had concocted. All the while he continued patting the horse's head and talking to her softly. To those in observance there seemed to be an immediate affection between the gentle young man and the sickly horse. Still more blankets were draped over the horse's back, and Star was standing up with the help of the apparatus Youngblood had rigged for her. Joe Lee and Zeke chatted aimlessly, while keeping the fire going.

Mucus ran profusely from Ole Star's nose as she tossed her head from side to side. The men were sweating, and the air was filled with a fog-like mist of smoke and steam from the cooked poultice.

"If the horse has a fever why are you keeping her so warm?" Joe Lee asked.

"'Cause that's how she got the fever," Joseph answered. "She got cold."

"She won't get well 'less we keep her warm," Nanny Mills blurted out as if she were now the designated person in charge.

"Now ya men hol' on here a while. Ya gotta stop'n eat somethin', else ya be sicker'n dat ole horse. I ain't taken kere of no sick men tomorrow."

"Suits me, ma'am. I'm mighty hungry right now," Joseph said, looking away from the horse for the first time in a while.

"I don't know if I can eat or not with that damn smell in here," Joe Lee said, holding his nose. Youngblood looked at the old black woman and smiled. She grinned back at him.

"You bes' fix dis ole horse boy; ifen ya don't Massa Bob gonna make it bad on all us."

"I'll do my best, ma'am," Joseph said smiling. Nanny Mills looked back at him, thinking to herself, "He called me ma'am." That had happened before because some white folks forgot who she was. They soon changed their tone after they realized their mistake. The black woman looked into Youngblood's eyes and immediately understood that he hadn't made a mistake. Overcoming the distraction, she turned to her husband with a look of obvious affection.

"Ya bes' eat somethin' too, old man. I ain't havin' ya propped up like dat ole horse." Everybody laughed and began to pass around Nanny's fixings.

Joseph chewed into the biscuit as his head turned to the figure in the shadows. As Delia stepped forward his face formed into an awkward grin. He stopped chewing, swallowed the last bit of biscuit, and stood from his crouch. He stared motionless, and she stared back. The others in the barn observed the couple as they gawked at each other. Joseph had

CHAPTER THREE

forgotten the horse, and Delia had definitely forgotten the food.

There was an uncomfortable silence when Nanny Mills chuckled; "I reckon dis boy ain't got nothin' on his mind 'cept fixin' dat horse." She turned to Zeke and rolled her eyes.

"Don't ya let nothing happen to dat basket and I'll see ya at home tonight. I'm gonna take this girl back home while she can still walk. Sumpum down here catchin'." The others burst out laughing while Delia and Joseph smiled.

"Come on, child. Let's go home and leave these men to do their work."

Delia ignored the teasing from her two sisters. As she climbed into bed she pondered the day's events. The banter didn't bother her because her mind was elsewhere. It was obvious that he was interested in her, and at the moment that was all that mattered. She thought about what her father might think and that did worry her. Delia's sleep was again restless and uncomfortable. She was awakened periodically during the night as her mind tormented her with thoughts of the future. She arose early the next morning while her two sisters were still asleep. Downstairs she found Nanny Mills in the kitchen already preparing for the day's meals.

"Ya bes' mind yourself, girl. Ya be swimmin' in a deep pond," she said in a motherly tone.

"Oh, Nanny, I ain't courting."

"I know ya ain't, but ya would be if ya could. And when your daddy finds that out, things ain't gonna be so good, so you bes' be careful."

Delia wanted to go to the barn, but she was afraid to go on her own. She knew that Joseph Youngblood was still there, and she thought her brother Joe Lee would also be there.

Nanny Mills turned to her and handed her the basket.

"Ya go on down there 'n take this food to the menfolk, but don't ya get in no trouble now, else Massa Bob be mad at everybody."

Welcoming the opportunity, Delia took the basket and started for the barn. It was another crisp spring morning, but she was not bothered by the cold. When she entered the barn she could still smell the pungent odor generated by Youngblood's poultice. Approaching the stall, she saw Joe Lee sleeping in the hay across from Ole Star's stall. She could hear Joseph softly talking to the horse and coaxing her along. Stepping softly, she tried to hear what he was saying but couldn't make out the words. As she moved closer, Joseph detected her presence and rose to his feet.

"Please come in, Miss Delia," he said politely. "And good morning to you."

Suddenly Delia was shaking and lost her ability to speak. She demurely nodded back in response. Joseph smiled at her and then turned back to Ole Star.

"You know, I think her fever is broke. I didn't really do nothin' except get her on her feet, but this old horse got better on her own."

Finally, Delia found her voice.

"Oh, that's wonderful," she said. "Papa will be so pleased."

Joseph turned back to her, "I hope to come calling on you, Miss Delia. I'm gonna tell your daddy so."

Delia blushed at his words and was dumbfounded again. She was pleased and excited, but then reality sunk in and she worried about what her father might say. She managed to utter, "But . . . uh . . . thank you."

She handed him the basket. "There's apple butter and biscuits that Nanny Mills fixed. It's for you."

She looked into his eyes, and when he took the basket he clasped her hand around the handle. The sensation of his touch was unlike anything she'd ever experienced. She pulled her hand away, leaving him with the basket. He smiled at her broadly, realizing that he had embarrassed her.

Her face was now fully flushed and she quickly stammered, "I best be going now." She rushed out of the stall and toward the barn door. Joseph laughed and shouted after her, "I'll be calling on you, Miss Delia."

He began whistling as she exited the barn. Delia rushed back into the house and through the kitchen in a flurry. She bounded up the stairs and into the room where her two sisters were busily gossiping. She lay down on the bed, closed her eyes, took one hand in the other, and mentally replayed every second of her encounter with the tall young healer.

CHAPTER THREE

Later that afternoon Delia and her two sisters sat on the porch with their little brother John. Joe Lee came up from the barn, laughing and talking amiably to the girls as he approached the porch.

"Why that old horse is a sight better. I don't know what Youngblood did down there all night, but it worked."

A few minutes later Joseph Youngblood came walking from the barn with Master Bob at his side. Delia overheard her father saying, "Thank you for doctoring my horse, and you tell your daddy we'll see him at the meeting. If you want to court my daughter you best be at the meeting with all the other young men. My daughter ain't courting nobody, especially some Kraut, unless he proves himself a good man."

Joseph Youngblood glanced over at Delia, then turned back to Bob Russell.

"Yes sir, Master Bob. I'll be at any meeting you think a good man ought to be at. Thank you, sir." Joseph Youngblood took one last glance at Delia and started walking for home.

Chapter 4

——MARCH 15, 1861——

Joe Lee Russell steered the buckboard into the yard with his older brother James at his side. Bob Russell sat on the porch as his two sons approached him.

"Did you find any decent help down in Fletcher?"

James spoke up immediately. "Yes, Papa, there's a pretty good crew available. It's some East Tennessee boys working out of Mitchell County. They did some work on the plank road and the sheriff says they do satisfactory work."

Bob Russell tilted his head, contemplating his son's response.

"Well, this ain't road building, this is fence building."

"I talked to him, Papa, and he said they was likely to be good at building fences."

"How many men have they got?"

"At least four: a man named Matthias Dees, his two sons, and another boy I believe to be a cousin."

"How much money do they want?"

"He says they'll work a full day for six bits a day."

"Six bits a day!" Bob Russell scowled in anger. "I wish I hadn't had to give that damned Merrimon all my field hands."

Joe Lee listened to the conversation and then interjected his own view of the matter.

CHAPTER FOUR

"Papa, those Dees boys are the nastiest looking men I ever saw. They smell like a chicken coop, and I don't reckon any of 'em ever got within a day's ride of a bath."

His older brother looked at Joe Lee with some contempt as if challenged by the younger man. "Joe Lee, we ain't inviting 'em to a party. We're getting them up here to work."

"That's right, boy. I don't care how nasty they are if they can do good work. They better do a lot of work for six bits a day. You go on back down to Fletcher tomorrow morning and tell them they can start work Monday."

Monday morning was dreary and overcast, but no rain was falling. Matthias Dees and his two sons, Carl and Rupert, made their way up Jackson Road with their cousin to the new Russell home place. Matthias Dees was thirty-nine years old, but he looked much older. He was a scrawny man with long, pointed fingers and a face accented by a sharp chin and a constricted upper jaw. His naturally dark brown hair appeared even darker because its greasy condition caused it to collect soil. He had small, deep-set eyes and terribly rotted teeth, discolored from years of chewing tobacco. His two sons were very different in appearance. The older one, now nineteen, was short and stocky with a full, heavy beard. But he also appeared dirty and unkempt. The younger boy was not as stocky but had similar facial features, and all three members of the Dees family had dark brown beady eyes. A fourth man who accompanied them was equally unkempt, but he was a tiny fellow, maybe less than five feet tall and very small in weight and stature. He had very little facial hair but what there was had grown to several inches long and hung in stringy little collections.

The mountain coves of the backcountry in western North Carolina were sometimes populated by an unsavory people. In the early days of the nation's history criminals often found refuge in these remote areas. Matthias Dees and his sons were descendants of a man who'd raped and murdered a child. Their criminal ancestor had escaped the hangman's noose in Baltimore, Maryland, fleeing from that state to the highlands of southern Appalachia. There he was lost to civilization and authority.

The Dees men and others like them usually confined themselves to the highland coves. Sometimes they traveled to towns and cities nearby looking for work. They preferred to make a living the easy way, but if they had to they would work for short periods. On this occasion the Dees family was engaged in honest work while they searched for dishonest opportunity.

The four men walked up to the Russell house and Joe Lee met them on the porch. "You men hold here and I'll get Papa."

Matthias Dees immediately spoke up.

"Yes, sir, brother, God bless you. We'll wait right here as long as the Lord's willin'."

Bob Russell came onto the porch and struggled with his bad leg down the steps to greet the four men.

"They say you men can do good work," Bob Russell said skeptically after looking at the unsightly crew.

"Yes, sir, Brother Russell. We're good workers. We work for the Lord and the Lord willin' we'll give ya a good day's work for honest pay. God bless ya, brother."

Bob Russell looked at Matthias Dees and raised an eyebrow. He had dealt with many Bible-toting, preaching kind of men in his day. You never knew which ones were really on the Lord's side and which ones were on the other side. To hear them talk, they all said the same things.

"Well, I got a thousand acres of land and near half of it needs fencing and I don't have a lot of time."

"Yes, sir, Brother Russell. Ain't no better workers that God done put on this here earth. Me'n my boys here, we done good work over in Mills River and the Lord rewarded us for it. Now the Lord sends us to you and we gonna serve you like the Lord guides us. Praise be, yes sir, brother."

None of the other three men said a word. They stood behind Matthias Dees while he negotiated their fate.

CHAPTER FOUR

Russell turned to his son and said, "Take these men down to the lower field and get them started down there. James and Zeke will bring some locust stakes and the tools down behind you. Y'all go on now."

The four men started to turn and leave when Matthias Dees turned back to Bob Russell. "One more thang, Brother Russell. Me 'n my boys, we ain't got nothin' to eat brung with us. I know'd the Lord will provide. God bless you, but would you be willin' to give a po' man a little blessing of ya bread each day?"

Bob Russell shrugged and responded, "Yea, yea, I'll give y'all something to eat. Just get down there and get this work done."

———— MARCH 30, 1861 ————

The group of young men huddled around the campfire. There were four Youngbloods: William, the oldest; Joseph, now twenty-three; J. N., nineteen, and Hiram, eighteen. The youngest of the Youngblood clan was left out, being only nine years old. Pinkney was considered too young to hunt with the older boys. The rest of the group was made up of three Garren boys, Will, David, and Elisha. The two families shared a common bond. They came from German families, and there were many relationships between the Garrens and the Youngbloods. Reuben Youngblood's wife was a Garren. So the young men were not only friends but also cousins. They laughed and played around the campfire as Hiram and J. N. roasted the rabbits they had killed earlier that Saturday. They teased each other about who was the best shot. The truth be known none of the group was likely to miss any sizable target. But this evening's teasing was not about marksmanship. It was about courtship.

"One more day with that pretty gal in your eyes and you won't be able to hit anything, Joseph," Will Garren chuckled.

"Hell, he won't even be able to pull the trigger," Joseph's older brother said laughingly. The members of the group took turns teasing him as Joseph stared into the fire.

"I tell you she's the prettiest girl I ever saw."

"From what I hear, you hardly saw her," Will Garren said. All the men laughed. They passed around the little brown jug of Garren's Tonic, each of them sipping it when their turn came.

When the jug reached J. N.'s hands he lifted and tilted the jug, taking in as much of the smooth corn brew as he could gulp. He wiped his mouth on his sleeve and smiled at his companions.

"Well, I reckon we'll all be going to dinner at Patty's Chapel tomorrow so you can see that pretty girlfriend of yours," J. N. Youngblood said.

"I've heard so much about her, I'm gonna go just to see her myself," David Garren responded. Joseph glanced at David and there was a flash of jealousy in his expression. The other men noticed it and they all laughed.

"Reckon Joseph's gonna whop you for looking at his girl?"

The mood quickly turned to a more serious matter when Will Garren, who was older than the rest of the men, warned them about what was to come.

"You know boys, they say there's gonna be a war. I reckon old Daniel Blake, Bob Russell, and all those rich old men ain't gonna fight no war. Who do you 'spect they thinks gonna do the fightin'?"

The group got quiet for a moment while they contemplated what Will had said. With fire in his eyes, young Elisha Garren looked at the older man and said, "By God, I'll fight. I'll fight any Yankee to the death that tries to come down here."

"Seven states have already left the Union and nobody knows what's gonna happen next. There's an election soon. If a war starts I reckon North Carolina will be next."

Joseph Youngblood looked at Will Garren, calculating where he would be in all of this. "I don't want to go to no war. I wanna get married and have a whole lot of children."

A smile broke out on his face and the other men laughed as if they knew what he was thinking.

"Don't get your buggy ahead of the horse, Joseph. I wouldn't be having no children just yet."

CHAPTER FOUR

Will Garren calmed the group down again and said, "This dinner we're all going to at Patty's Chapel tomorrow ain't about church. It's about leaving the Union and fighting the war."

Bill Youngblood was a quiet man with a dry sense of humor.

"I reckon we all have our reasons for going. Will's going to fight a war. Joseph's going to have children."

At that comment they all roared with laughter. Continuing, he said, "But I'm going to eat. I guarantee you the ladies will have the best fixin's you ever saw."

The men nodded in agreement as they pulled the roasted rabbits from the fire and ate their supper.

---MARCH 31, 1861---

The traffic on Jackson Road was unusually heavy on this Sunday afternoon. Politics was not something that ordinarily attracted attention on Hoopers Creek. But the politics of the spring of 1861 was different. It was now on most every man's mind day and night.

As the buggies made their way up the rutty dirt road to Patty's Chapel it was difficult to steer them in the midst of the foot traffic. Reverend Patty stood on the church porch greeting the men as they came in. The slaves in the yard tended to the horses as the men herded in and around the church. The crowd was so large that Reverend Patty directed that all the windows be propped open so men could gather outside to hear. The ladies were out on the lawn setting up tables to feed the men after the meeting. It was a pretty day though somewhat cool as it could often be in early spring in the North Carolina mountains.

The Russell girls were there with their mother and Nanny Mills. A chair was carried for Susannah Russell in the back of the wagon. Mrs. Russell sat out on the grounds the entire time covered with two blankets.

Robert Russell was an important man and the family knew it. Even though the women were not allowed to participate in the meeting, they all recognized that important events were occurring. Delia, however, had other matters on her mind. She strained her eyes and looked toward the church as she spread a tablecloth. Delia had hoped to catch a glimpse of him, maybe even speak to him. She considered what to say even though it was unlikely that they would talk. Delia had never seen so many people gathered in one place. She could see through the church window that Patty's Chapel was packed to its limit. Reverend Patty stood at the altar and addressed the men in dramatic fashion. He was a secessionist and believed that there was no other alternative. Delia did not know what a secessionist was but thought it must be a good thing because her papa was also one. She could hear them speaking but could not make out the words. Delia felt a sense of pride when she saw her father step up behind the church podium. Inside the church the crowd was hushed as Robert Russell began to speak.

"God gave you men freedom, but he didn't give it to you for nothing. Sometimes a man has to stand up for what he believes in. That time has come for us. And if we are going to be free men we are going to have to stand up for it. I believe a war is coming and we're going to have to fight to protect our land, our homes, and our freedom. The founding fathers of our country gave us the right to independence and freedom. It says so in the Declaration of Independence, and the Yankees signed it just like we did. This Lincoln is a tyrant who wants nothing but power for himself and his cronies. If he has his way, we'll all be slaves."

The men in the room applauded his words and other speakers took to the podium to speculate on what was next. Speakers informed them that seven states had left the Union and North Carolina was now locked between the seceded states in the South and the states to the north, determined not to let them go. Still other men pleaded for restraint and order. There was still a majority that did not want secession.

With all of the talk of freedom at Patty's Chapel that day, not a word was uttered about the quiet black men who tended to the horses, buggies, and carriages in the churchyard. When the group came out of the church there was a cluster gathered around the Youngbloods and the Garrens. Robert Russell saw them and wondered to himself if the

Germans could be counted on to join them if it came to a fight. He hobbled over to the group. An elder named Absalom Garren was at the center.

Robert Russell had always treated the Germans in his community with mild contempt. It was a difficult thing for him to ask for their help. He stepped forward, holding himself up with his cane clasped in his left hand. He extended his right hand to Absalom Garren.

"Mr. Garren, sir, I trust we can count on you and your boys in a time of need," he said, shaking the patriarch's hand.

"I reckon this is our land too," he said. "If fightin' is to be done, we'll do what we gotta do."

Robert Russell seemed relieved and expressed his gratitude. "My boys will fight side by side with yours."

The elder German-American bowed his head and nodded slowly. He cut his eyes upward, looking at Russell as if he doubted his confidence. The lingering effects of war in Europe were still present in the minds of many immigrant families. Garren considered his knowledge of wars past when he replied to Russell.

"I pray to God that they don't die side by side."

As the two patriarchs spoke Joseph Youngblood glanced over them in the direction of the tables in the yard. The silence was broken when William Youngblood said above the crowd, "Let's don't do any fighting yet. Now's the time for eat'n." They all laughed mildly, and one could sense relief among the men as the serious tone of the moment was diminished. They scattered and began walking toward the tables, and the ladies directed them in line to get a plate and start eating. There was chicken and rabbit and canned tomatoes and beans from last season. As they went through the line Joseph had difficulty loading his plate because his eyes were scanning the area, visually seeking what he had hoped to encounter that day. Finally he saw her with her back to him. She had not seen him as she was busy at work.

Sarah saw Joseph first, and she tapped Delia on the shoulder.

"Look, little sis, he's looking at you."

Mary and Delia looked up at the same time. When Delia's eyes met his, Joseph broke into his broad grin and nodded in her direction. She felt overwhelmed at this attention. For a girl her age to attract this man ahead of her sisters was a source of pride that overwhelmed her. They stared at each other briefly until J. N. Youngblood goosed his older brother along.

"Either you move on or get out of line else we all starve to death."

David Garren, who was in front of him, turned around and looked at the others. "Boy, he's a sick lovebird."

They all laughed as Joseph continued to glance toward Delia as he made his way through the line. She felt it necessary to turn away and look busy even though she was no longer sure what she was supposed to be doing. Joseph watched her as he continued to fill his plate. He worked his way around the tables in a discreet and tactful way. When he knew she was in earshot, he spoke to her quietly.

"Hello, Miss Delia," he said, smiling broadly as she turned in response. She blushed and smiled back at him. Her bright eyes darted from side to side as if she were engaged in a criminal act fearing that she might be observed. She wanted to say something to him, but she could not summon the words. Her embarrassment caused her to bow her head and stare at the ground. He spoke her name again.

"Miss Delia," and she looked back into his eyes.

"I'm gonna come calling on you."

He smiled that huge broad grin and chomped a big bite of cornbread, never losing eye contact with her. Joseph nodded with a slight bow and walked away. Delia had still not uttered a sound.

—— SUNDAY, APRIL 7, 1861 ——

Joseph Youngblood sucked in his breath and stepped into the front yard. He laughed internally and felt slightly embarrassed. He shook his head from side to side and chided himself.

"You damn fool, why are you so scared? Her daddy ain't gonna kill you. After all, you saved his horse."

CHAPTER FOUR

Then he thought, "Well, he might yet." Joseph had shined his boots and put on clean pants and the only good shirt he owned. He climbed the stairs onto the porch and knocked on the door. The door opened, and Joseph found himself staring into the eyes of the pleasant black nanny he had met earlier at the Russell farm.

"Good afternoon, ma'am," he said sheepishly.

Nanny Mills chuckled, "Ain't ya a sight, boy? Come on in. I reckon ya come a courtin' Miss Delia." She looked him up and down and laughed again as she turned. Joseph felt foolish as he thought of his own appearance. He concluded that he must look like a buffoon or something. Nanny Mills said, "You best wait here. I'll be right back with Madame Russell."

Joseph stood in the hallway getting more self-conscious by the moment as he waited for Nanny Mills to return with Delia and her mother.

The three women walked into the room. It was a warm spring afternoon, but Mrs. Russell still draped herself in a large quilt. She smiled at Joseph and suggested that they sit on the porch. Delia trailed along behind her mother, looking beautiful but very nervous. She was dressed in a full dark-blue dress with layers of petticoats underneath, all of which hung to the floor and covered her tiny feet. The long-sleeved dress had wide buttoned cuffs that came down her arms to the tops of her wrists. As did all the women of that day on Hoopers Creek, she wore a tied bonnet around her hair, which was knotted in a bun at the back of her head. Her dark hair barely peeked out of the sides of her bonnet. She had a youthful glow about her that impressed Joseph each time he saw her.

Delia had hardly looked up as they walked out on the porch. Mrs. Russell and Delia sat on a bench seat made for two. Mrs. Russell gestured toward a straight-back chair against the window, and Joseph took his seat after the ladies were in place. Nanny Mills stood in attendance and glanced over at Joseph. Smiling, she shook her head again slightly. Joseph was disconcerted by her gesture. She seemed to suggest that he wasn't going to do so well.

"Can I get y'all somethin'?" Nanny Mills said to Mrs. Russell.

"No, Nanny," Mrs. Russell replied.

"Would you like something to drink, Joseph?"

"No, ah, no, ah, I mean, no thank you ma'am." Joseph couldn't believe his nervousness. He had courted women much older than this young girl and it hadn't bothered him, but for some reason this experience was very unnerving. Mrs. Russell stared at him as if waiting on him to say something, but no one said anything and the silence became strained.

"How's your farm doing?" Mrs. Russell asked.

"Oh, uh, okay, well fine right now. We've been doing lots of plowing and we're about done. Paw says if the weather is good, we'll plant soon."

"Good, that's good," Mrs. Russell nodded back at him. The silence continued and Mrs. Russell just stared at him. Delia still hadn't looked up. She seemed to be staring at the floor. Joseph thought he had never been so uncomfortable in all of his life. Think of something to say, he told himself. But he couldn't think of anything. Finally, he muttered, "Uh, how's your farm?"

Mrs. Russell looked at him, calmly nodded, and said, "Right good, Joseph."

Delia remained bowed. She hadn't said a word nor made eye contact with Joseph. Joseph wanted to speak to Delia but was afraid to. Finally, something came to him.

"How's Ole Star doing?" he said with relief as if he had come up with a great discovery. The question brought a smile to Mrs. Russell's face, and Delia's eyes lifted from the floor and sparkled as she looked at Joseph. Slowly a big grin came across her face, but it was Mrs. Russell who responded.

"Ole Star is doing just fine. You made quite an impression on Master Russell. How'd you learn to take care of animals?"

"Oh, I just took to it as a boy. My daddy had an old sick dog, and I nursed that dog day and night 'til one day he just up and got better. Later I learned from Dr. Fletcher how to set bones. Can't hardly set a horse bone though, but a dog you can. Depending on how bad the break is."

Joseph relaxed a little as he found himself in comfortable territory.

CHAPTER FOUR

"You know I can sew up a bad cut or a wound on 'bout any animal. I just take an old razor, clean out the wound, get a needle and thread, and sew 'em up like a tear in a shirt."

The two women grimaced at the mention of open wounds, and Joseph worried that he had gone too far. He tried to think of other things to say but nothing came to him. Delia still said nothing. It seemed that a great deal of time went by without anyone saying anything. The three sat staring at the scenery and occasionally glancing at each other with Delia mostly staring at the floor. She thought to herself, "I wished I could talk to him. There's so much I want to say, but I just can't do it with my mama watching over me."

On occasion she raised her head slightly and looked at him. She smiled as she wondered to herself why he was so attractive to her. Then she realized that the mere fact that he was attracted to her made him appealing.

Mrs. Russell called out to Nanny Mills and asked that she bring a pitcher of water. Nanny Mills came back with the tray and poured each of the three a glass of water. Joseph was relieved to have it. His discomfort had caused his mouth to dry, and he gratefully gulped the water. As if in afterthought he stopped quickly and said, "Oh, thank you very much, ma'am," looking at Mrs. Russell.

"You're welcome, Joseph," she said, picking up her own glass.

Joseph, Delia, and Mrs. Russell continued to sit in silence, but all seemed to be a little more at ease. Delia's brother James came around from the side of the house. He was a jovial young man who seemed to like Joseph. They had known each other for a while, and James shook hands with him.

"It's good to see you, Joseph."

"Good to see you, too, James," Joseph responded, smiling.

James looked over at his sister.

"So you come courting my little sister, have you?"

Joseph was worried and wasn't sure if the comment was friendly or hostile.

"Yea, uh, I reckon so." James laughed and looked back at Joseph.

"We sure do appreciate you taking care of that horse."

"Oh, I didn't do much. I just got her up and got her warm. She pretty much got well on her own."

"Folks around here say you have a way with doctoring animals, and I believe you got a gift for healin'. Thanks for your help."

He patted Joseph on the shoulder, smiled at his sister, and walked into the house. Joseph sat back down, and again unpleasant silence dominated the atmosphere as the two adults stared at each other and Delia stared at the floor. Joseph shifted nervously in his seat as the afternoon wore on. He was determined not to leave early, but he got little response from anything he thought to say. It occurred to him that matters could be worse; he could be sitting with her father.

Then Joseph spoke directly to Delia. He was afraid this would offend Mrs. Russell, but he decided to do it anyway.

"Miss Delia, I want to thank you for bringing me that bite to eat while we was caring for Ole Star."

Delia looked up at him, and their eyes met. She smiled broadly and responded, "Thank you, Joseph, for saving our horse."

They stared at each other with eyes fixed. Mrs. Russell shifted her gaze back and forth between the two. Joseph thought to himself that the visit was worth the effort. The walk down Hoopers Creek, the hike up Jackson Road, and this strained afternoon sitting on the porch brought him that much closer to Delia. He was smitten by this young girl, and she was clearly responding to him. Finally, as the sun began to lower in the sky, Mrs. Russell broke the silence.

"It's gettin' on kinda late now, Joseph. Delia you best be helping with supper."

Joseph quickly rose to his feet, somewhat relieved.

"Yes, ma'am, I better be gettin' on now. Thank you for your hospitality."

He turned to walk away and leave, but he looked back at Delia one more time. "Good evening, Miss Delia."

"Good night, Joseph."

CHAPTER FOUR

He started on the long walk back up Hoopers Creek Road to the Youngblood farm.

The next morning Delia dressed and bounded down the stairs and into the kitchen.

"Good morning, Nanny."

"Good mornin' to ya too child. Ooh Lordy, what's got you so bubbly?" she asked.

"Nothing."

"I believe ya been courtin'," Nanny Mills said, now laughing out loud. "Ya best go down to the well and git some water."

Delia grabbed the large bucket and went out the back door and down the stairs, almost skipping through the grass toward the family's well. She hooked the bucket onto the rope and watched down in the depths of the well as she lowered the bucket. Her mind was full of daydreams as she thought of Joseph, and she imagined their wedding with flowers and music and her sisters and all the other girls looking at her with envy and adulation. She thought of Joseph all dressed up walking beside her. In her daydream she was so confident and mature, but in reality these images frightened her. Delia cranked the bucket back up from the well and watched it as it got closer to the top.

As she reached for the bucket and unhooked it, she heard something and felt a presence behind her. Delia turned around and was startled. There were four men close to her, almost trapping her against the wall of the well. The older man was a grungy, dirty-looking creature with rotten teeth and a foul odor about him. The three younger men with him were equally soiled and unkempt in appearance. The older man grinned at her, almost leering as he leaned close to her face.

"Well, well, ain't you a mite purdy thang, missy."

"Mmhum, sweet smelling too," said the younger man on his left.

Delia was frightened and uncomfortable at how they crowded around her. She wanted to get away or to run, but she had nowhere to go.

"Ah, now missy. You're such a purdy thang. Won't you give a poor man a drink of dat thar water?" he said, smiling and winking at her.

She thrust a bucket out in his direction as if to say, take it, but no words escaped her lips. One of the other younger men now crowded her from the side, and she felt his body make slight contact with hers. He seemed to snicker in her ear, and as she turned toward him she smelled his foul breath. Suddenly a loud, booming voice overrode the words of the men around her.

"Ain't nobody gettin' a drink 'round here less'n they gits back to where they belongs," Zeke Mills bellowed at the four men. Matthias Dees turned in surprise and apparent contempt toward the black slave.

"Ya ain't got no business tellin' me nothin', nigger," Dees said with obvious animosity in his voice.

"Ya bes' git away from dat child and you bes' git away now," Zeke Mills said, shifting the pitchfork from his left hand to his right.

The four men had been posturing in an aggressive manner until they saw the old slave shift his grip on the pitchfork. Matthias Dees quickly assessed the situation and realized Zeke Mills was not a man to be pushed around, slave or not.

"Hol' ya horses, old nigger. We jus be wantin' a drink o' water," he said with an unctuous smile on his face. He stepped aside and made a grand bowing gesture. "Ya go right ahead, Miss Lady," he said sarcastically.

Zeke Mills stared at the four men and shifted to his right as Delia passed, putting himself between Delia and the men.

He motioned to his left, "Now ya men bes' git on back down there 'n finish Massa Russell's fence. And don't be causin' no trouble."

Saving face, Matthias Dees chuckled and laughed, "Sho, sho, that's where we's a goin' anyway. God bless ya, old nigger."

Zeke Mills watched as the four men walked away toward the pasture where the fence building was in progress. He had never been given the opportunity to learn to read and write. He never thought of himself as a smart man and always believed Massa Russell to be a wise man, but as he watched Matthias Dees and his boys making their way down the hill, he thought to himself, he'd do all the work himself before he would hire men like that.

Chapter 5

—— APRIL 13, 1861 ——

Fletcher, North Carolina James Russell worked the buggy whip hard against Ole Star's flank, lashing her with an urgency that was unlike him. The buggy bounded to and fro as his eyes searched ahead, looking for the sweeping turn up Howard Gap Road. Two men passed on horseback riding with a similar urgency, for they carried the same news. The riders continued up Howard Gap Road.

As James made the turn his mind raced with many thoughts and images of the news he carried. A soaking rain had fallen through the previous day and night. The road was muddy and soft in places so as the buggy bounced and sloshed up the road, mud and water splashed Ole Star and the wagon. James Russell had Ole Star in a full trot, but he slowed her down as he approached the bridge across Cane Creek. Time moved slowly to him as he crossed the bridge and made another left turn up Jackson Road. He thought ahead to the climb he must make up the steep incline back to the Russell farm. The distance between Fletcher and the Russell house was just two and one-half miles, but on this Saturday evening, it was the longest journey in James's young life. As he passed the Lanning farm, he saw John Lanning plowing near the road. James could not resist stopping briefly and shouting out the news.

John Lanning looked stunned at first but then shook his head and ran toward his house. James whipped Ole Star back into full speed as he continued to climb Jackson Road. Near the top he passed a wagon loaded heavily with firewood. It was Fred Pitillo and his son. James pulled around them and shouted out the news. Fred looked as if he'd been lashed by lightning. He just stared back in open-mouthed astonishment. As James sped away he looked back long enough to see Pitillo whipping his old mule in a frenzied attempt to hurry him home.

Finally James topped the hill, and Ole Star started down the last leg of the journey to the Russell farm. James continued to whip her almost irrationally. She pulled the wagon on as it splashed through the wet ruts and gullies of Jackson Road. The cool air and the cold splashes now aided the overheated horse as she moved toward the final leg of the journey. He could see the farmhouse in the distance as he continued down the hill. He pulled into the yard and drove the buggy toward the house, reining in Ole Star at the porch.

James leaped straight to the ground, screaming as he jumped, "Papa! Papa!"

He dashed up the steps into the house and shouted with all his energy.

"Papa! Papa! Where is Papa?"

The old man sat in the parlor working on his ledger as he heard his son's cries. He rose to his feet and shouted back.

"I'm in here, boy."

James dashed into the parlor and nearly ran into his father who was now standing in the doorway.

"Calm yourself, boy," the old man said firmly.

"It's started, Papa! The war, it's started! They fired on Fort Sumter!"

The two looked at each other with eyes wide open.

"What's Fort Sumter? Where is it? I never heard of it! Who fired at it?"

Robert Russell frantically tried to sort out the meaning of it all.

"I was in Fletcher late this evening and riders came in from Columbia, South Carolina. There were telegraphs from Charleston to Columbia. The South Carolina militia fired on a fort in Charleston harbor; they said it was Fort Sumter, that the Yankees wouldn't give it back to South Carolina."

CHAPTER FIVE

He paused to catch his breath, "It's true, Papa, they had the telegraphs with them. At 7:30 on Friday night the Yankee commander surrendered the fort to South Carolina. The war has started, Papa. It's started!"

Robert Russell turned and slowly sank back down into his chair. Although he had anticipated this day, even looked forward to it, there was something about it that disturbed and worried him. From his chair he looked back at his oldest son and nodded.

"Yes, son. I reckon it has. This means war."

Delia had never witnessed such excitement in her fourteen years. Everyone in the family appeared to be besieged with anxiety and tension. Fort Sumter was a place she had never heard mentioned before, but it had been bombed. Although she was not allowed to participate in the discussions, Delia listened to every word with great interest. Nanny Mills had told her that "such talk be for the men folk" and that she shouldn't be listening. But the discussions completely absorbed her. It seemed that the Fort Sumter incident was all that her father and her brothers could talk about. She could not comprehend everything, but she knew for certain that this commotion was upsetting her mother a great deal.

In yet another foreboding development, Delia's father told her that she would be going with him to an important meeting at The Meadows, the Blake home in Fletcher. Bob Russell's disability required that he be assisted at all times. While he could steer the buggy, he required help up and down as well as assistance with his bags. Because her brothers were busy with their own preparations, Delia was chosen to accompany her father. She had no idea who would be at this meeting or what would be done. Whatever had been planned for the meeting, it was all changed now.

Her father reined the buggy to a halt in front of the door of The Meadows and then impatiently scowled at Delia.

"Get my step down, girl."

For an instant Delia did not hear him, for the yard was full of other buggies and horses and men talking and whispering to each other. As she raced to place the step that aided her father in exiting the buggy, she noted the black man who came and tended to the horse. She looked into the eyes of the slave who took the harness of her father's horse. His weighty expression was telling yet puzzling. It was apparent that this strange black man seemed to know and understand, more so than she, the magnitude of the moment.

Delia briefly studied the imposing structure that dominated the little hill across the road and down a short distance from Calvary Episcopal Church. The large, square, two-story structure was constructed in a simplified form of Italianate style of coursed granite rubble and featured three chimneys piercing a low hipped roof.

"Get my bag, girl," Bob Russell snapped as he hobbled on his cane toward the front steps of the Blake house. As he approached the door a white-haired black man offered his assistance.

"Let me help you, Massa Bob."

Bob Russell rudely brushed him aside and approached the figure standing in the middle of the foyer. He switched his cane to his left hand as he extended his right. Daniel Blake shook his hand and never once glanced at Delia.

"Welcome, sir. We are indeed honored by your presence. This is a most important day."

"Thank you. I am here as your obedient servant, sir."

Getting to the point, Russell asked, "Are the others here?"

"Yes, most of them. We will assemble in the parlor," Blake said.

Suddenly the gregarious Mimi Blake appeared in the hallway. She greeted Bob Russell, and unlike the men, she immediately took notice of Delia holding her father's bags.

"Hello, Miss Russell. So nice of you to come and help your father."

Delia was relieved that her presence was being acknowledged. She managed to nod in recognition at the same moment her father switched his cane back to his right hand and snatched his bag from her. He

CHAPTER FIVE

walked away, marching in his chopping triple step toward the door of the parlor, apparently having totally forgotten that his daughter had accompanied him.

Much to Delia's relief Mrs. Blake took her hand and said, "Come with me, dear. You can help." Mrs. Blake took her to the kitchen where three black women were working furiously to prepare tea and cakes for the men. Two neighbor women sat together by the window whispering with worried expressions etched in their faces.

The Meadows boasted a large parlor with a huge ornate fireplace trimmed out in solid white oak. The rectangular room was more than fifty feet long with sixteen-foot-high ceilings, yet there was not enough room for those in attendance. Bob Russell quickly grabbed a seat and began making mental notes of the leaders who had traveled from other neighboring counties. In attendance were politicians, judges, lawyers, and clergymen. The room was buzzing with chatter and the air was filled with tobacco smoke as the men traded rumors, opinions, and stories related to the Fort Sumter attack.

A hush fell over the room as two well-dressed men entered. The former U.S. Senator Thomas Clingman and Congressman Zebulon Baird Vance made their way around the room. As the whispers passed throughout the parlor, the identity of these two were known to most and quickly revealed to all. A somber mood settled in the room as Daniel Blake stepped to the center.

"Gentlemen, as you know, we face a great moment in the history of our state and our country. We have gathered here today to discuss our plans for organizing our people and our men for the struggle that is before us. I have asked the experienced and respected attorney A. S. Merrimon to assist us in conducting this meeting."

The tall, dark-haired, and stately figure of Merrimon slowly rose to his feet.

"Gentlemen, as most of you know, I have been a pro-Union man. But the conduct of the U.S. government and President Lincoln's call for troops is a violation of our rights and the Constitution on which this nation was formed. It is disturbing enough that President Lincoln would call for troops to invade our neighbors to the south, but it is even more appalling that he would force North Carolina to provide the men and arms to carry out his illegal invasion."

A roar and a cheer erupted in the room. There were cries of "Yea!" and "Here, Here!"

Merrimon raised his hand to settle the men and turned to the two gentlemen who had recently served in Washington as their senator and their congressman.

"Senator Clingman, Congressman Vance, have you anything to add?"

Zeb Vance rose and carefully surveyed the room.

"As most of you know, I have been a loyal and true Union man throughout my life and my career." A seriousness of purpose defined his face as he bowed his head slightly.

"The circumstances of this time and the gravity of the moment dictate that I must stand with my people and my state, and I am now a secessionist through and through." The room exploded in thunderous applause. The exhilaration of the moment was such that some dropped their teacups in a rush to clap. Vance raised his hand and cocked his head as if to scold the men for their emotional outburst.

"Listen to me, gentlemen. There is nothing in this to celebrate, but every reason to dedicate ourselves to the task before us. It is indeed a time for planning and for prayer. We must make every effort to conduct ourselves carefully and responsibly in the coming days. And with that in mind, I call upon Senator Clingman to address you concerning the legal implications of this situation."

Senator Clingman stood and slowly scanned the room as if he were assessing his audience and organizing his words accordingly. The group waited patiently, using the time to shift their stance or sip their tea.

In a tone that was notably sadder than the others, he began.

"Gentlemen, as Congressman Vance pointed out, we are men who believe in and respect the law. That is why the actions of the U.S.

government are so deplorable. Seven of our neighboring states have seceded from the Union. Governor Ellis will very soon call an emergency session to consider the question of secession for North Carolina. The bombing of Fort Sumter and the president's call for troops to invade the South most probably means that North Carolina will join her neighbors in secession. That's why Congressman Vance and I felt that we had no other choice but to resign our seats in Congress and return home. Meetings like this are going on in many other southern states, and I suspect that Arkansas, Tennessee, Virginia, Maryland, and Kentucky will all join us. I have given this matter serious thought and have asked God for his divine guidance, but I see no alternative for us. The only answer is an independent South."

Again the men resounded in agreement. Congressman Vance raised his hand again, quieting the group. He then addressed Senator Clingman directly.

"Tom, please take a moment and explain the legal situation, as you and I have had an opportunity to consider such matters and some have not."

"Gentlemen, it is fairly simple. The U.S. government and President Lincoln are calling us traitors, when the legal facts clearly demonstrate that it is they, not we, who are traitors. Let me not express it in my words, but in the words and wisdom of our founding fathers."

Clingman then stooped and reached into a worn leather bag, removing a rolled parchment. He unrolled the document and held it up for all to see. "Gentlemen, allow me to share with you the last two paragraphs of the Declaration of Independence."

> We, therefore, the Representatives of the United States of America, in General Congress, Assembled, appealing to the Supreme Judge of the world for the rectitude of our intentions, do, in the Name, and by Authority of the good People of these Colonies, solemnly publish and declare, That these United Colonies are, and of Right ought to be, Free and Independent States; that they are Absolved from all

Allegiance to the British Crown, and that all political connection between them and the State of Great Britain, is and ought to be totally dissolved; and that as Free and Independent States, they have full Power to levy War, conclude Peace, contract Alliances, establish Commerce, and to do all other Acts and Things which Independent States may of right do.

And for the support of this Declaration, with a firm reliance on the protection of divine Providence, we mutually pledge to each other our Lives, our Fortunes and our sacred Honor.

Clingman read the eloquent writings of the founders with such emotion and flair and with particular emphasis on the words "independent states" that the room burst forth in a frenzied emotion rarely shown by mountain men. Indeed, to Clingman's surprise, the unmistakable glisten of tears was present throughout the room. As he took his seat, he pondered. There is no doubt that these citizens are but a generation removed from the Revolutionary War and the founding of the nation. Its visceral effect still lingers in this community and its leaders need no further persuasion.

When order was returned, the learned Mr. Merrimon posed a question.

"As a legal matter, Senator Clingman, is there any provision of the U.S. Constitution that would supersede this portion of the Declaration of Independence?" Clingman turned to Vance and offered him the opportunity to respond to the question. Both men knew that A. S. Merrimon already knew the answer. He had asked the question for the benefit of the others in the room. Vance rose to his feet.

"I have studied the words of the founding fathers regarding this question. It is abundantly clear to me that the right to sovereignty of the states was reserved and included in the thoughts and minds of every member of the Continental Congress. No state: not New York, not Massachusetts, not North Carolina, nor any other state would have ratified that Constitution if they had any indication that they were giving

CHAPTER FIVE

up their right to leave the Union should it become necessary and in the best interest of their people. The idea that the states would have given up irrevocably their right to be separate is not only radical but also a new concept created by President Lincoln. I refer you to the Constitution itself. While there are many references granting specific powers to the federal government, some of them superseding state authority on various matters, there is no mention of any state surrendering their right to sovereignty. The Constitution specifically states that all powers not granted to the federal government are reserved for the states."

Vance then produced a copy of the Constitution and read the Tenth Amendment to the Bill of Rights:

> The powers not delegated to the United States by the Constitution, nor prohibited by it to the States, are reserved to the States respectively, or to the people. . . .

"It is clear to me that because there is no prohibition anywhere in the Constitution that would prohibit a state, acting on the will of its citizens, from leaving the Union, then it is perfectly legal. It is therefore clearly and indisputably a state's right. Mr. Lincoln's claim otherwise appears to be an outright act of aggression born of tyranny."

Bob Russell spoke from his chair. In an urgent voice he shouted, "It's plain as mud on your face that the people of the northern states are the real traitors. Why, I don't believe the Yankees will last more than a few weeks in this war. When they suddenly realize that their people are dying for a treasonous cause, they'll turn their backs on the president and his cronies. I believe they will throw Mr. Lincoln and all of those scoundrels out of office."

Many of the men nodded and shouted in agreement. Congressman Vance lifted his hand again and rose to his feet.

"Bob, I wish that were true. Let me ask a question of all of you. How many of you have a copy of the Declaration or the Constitution in your home?"

Only two hands went up, that of Merrimon and Clingman. The group quickly recognized the absence of hands.

THE SECRET OF WAR

Vance continued. "I hope this demonstrates my point, gentlemen. You are the leaders of our community, and none of you, except these two learned jurists, have such a copy. Just how many farm boys in Illinois or factory workers in New York do you think have copies of the Declaration of Independence and the Constitution?

"We are clearly right in our interpretation of these historical documents, but I believe it unrealistic to think that the president and his associates are going to tell the people of the northern states the truth about the crimes in which they are engaged.

"I am afraid, gentlemen, that instead of telling them the truth about the founding of the Union and our clear legal right to sovereignty, they are going to use the institution of slavery as a means to make demons of us all. They have little contact with us and don't understand us. I own some slaves myself, and I know how important they are to some of you. To the people of the North slavery is evil. They will, most assuredly, use it against us."

It was clear that Vance's remarks had a disconcerting effect on the men in the room. But no one seemed to have any inclination toward modifying his position. Mr. Merrimon again addressed the group.

"Gentlemen, then we are all agreed?" There were nods and murmurs of acknowledgment throughout the room. Drawing on his sense of legal conduct Merrimon then stated, "Is there a dissenting voice among us?" He paused and looked around the room. The men searched each other's faces for signs of dissent.

A tall, dark-haired man rose at the back of the parlor.

"I reckon it don't matter none," he said with sad resolution apparent in his voice. It was Joseph Hamilton. He was almost fifty, his dark hair graying around the ends and completely gray at the sideburns. Most of his ragged beard was gray. He was there with his three brothers. They'd ridden across the county to attend the meeting.

"I've know'd you men dang near all of my life. Up until a few weeks ago you was all God fearin', law abidin' men. Now all of ya went and gone plum mad. It's like sick cattle, all of ya damn fools herdin' off in

CHAPTER FIVE

the same direction without nary an idy as to where ya goin'."

Hamilton looked around the room and his emotions overtook him as he continued his tirade. He shook his head and his lips quivered.

"I ain't got no book learnin' like these fancy lawyers here, and I ain't read them fancy papers neither, but I reckon you gonna read 'em like ya wanna and them Yankees are gonna read 'em like they wanna and y'all are gonna kill each other to see who gits to say they's right." He continued, now almost wailing. Some of the men murmured in disagreement; others shook their heads negatively as he went on.

"I done been a Union man all my borned days, and I ain't quittin' now."

Hamilton then turned to Zeb Vance and said, "I've knowd you since you was a boy, Zeb, and I'm glad you said what you did about slavery. But you ain't said enough, don't matter what no Yankee says. Don't matter what none of you'ns says. Slavin' is a sin against God the Almighty, and it be a curse on us all. It's an evil that's gonna smite you and your children and their children. You go fight this damn fool war if ya have ta, but you bes' leave me and mine out of it. We ain't havin' no part of this here madness."

Hamilton glared at the men around the room as they booed and shouted him down. He looked at his brothers and motioned toward the exit. They worked their way toward the door and made their way out. There were more boos and shouts when two of the Jones boys fell in behind and left with them.

As the men made their exits Merrimon raised his hand again to settle the group. "Gentlemen! Gentlemen! Quiet please. Do we have any further comment?" Zeb Vance stood once more.

"Yes, there is one more thing I'd like to point out," he said thoughtfully, looking around the room slowly and deliberately. Then with his head bowed he started to speak. "Those fancy papers Joseph Hamilton was talking about may not mean much to him, but they mean a lot to me and they should mean a lot to all free men. With that in mind I will quote from memory a passage from the Declaration of Independence that inspires me to be at this meeting, to stand with you, and to die with you if it comes to it. The passage is the fourth paragraph:

> That whenever any form of Government becomes destructive of these ends, it is the right of the people to alter or abolish it, and to institute new Government, laying its foundations on such principles and organizing its power in such form, as to them shall seem most likely to effect their Safety and Happiness. Prudence, indeed, will dictate that Governments long established should not be changed for light or transient causes; and accordingly all experience hath shown, that mankind are more disposed to suffer, while evils are sufferable, than to right themselves by abolishing the forms to which they are accustomed. But when a long train of abuses and usurpations, pursuing invariably the same Object evinces a design to reduce them under absolute Despotism, it is their right, it is their duty, to throw off such Government, and to provide new Guards for their future security.

Vance calmly seated himself as the room exploded in a roar that turned heads all the way to the far end of the Blake yard. Vance's rendition of the Declaration spurred emotions to a frenzy. All thoughts or considerations of Joseph Hamilton's words were now lost.

Merrimon shook his fist in the air, overtaken by the excitement of the moment, and shouted, "Then secession it shall be!"

Again the men shouted and cheered.

Clingman stood again, "As most of you know, this probably means war. It could last six months, even a year. All of you will have to support this effort fully with your resources and your sons.

"My friends, we have reached a firm decision and may God guide us and protect us. Reverend Patty, will you lead us in prayer?" Caught up in the moment, Patty didn't react immediately as he was unable to muster a prayer. Eventually his traditional religious training saved him.

CHAPTER FIVE

"Gentlemen," he bellowed in his thick Irish accent, "Please bow your heads and join me in reciting the Twenty-third Psalm."

The kitchen was a flutter of activity. Delia stood by the entrance, feeling as if she were the only stranger in the house. Sensing this, Mimi Blake took a bucket and approached Delia.

"Would you be so kind as to carry in some water from the springhouse?"

"Yes, ma'am, I'll be happy to if you will guide me in the proper direction," Delia replied properly.

Mrs. Blake handed the bucket to Delia and directed her to the springhouse, which sat adjacent to the main house. Grateful for something to do, Delia thanked Mrs. Blake and began a slow gait across the yard. The Blake yard was full of men, slaves, and horses. There were several small groups standing in the side yard chatting and sporadically laughing in a low volume. Near a large apple tree Delia observed what she thought to be several of the Blake children. Two boys and a girl were feverishly involved in a game, and the older boy seemed to be winning. She wondered if Mrs. Blake would approve of her joining the children, at least to watch. Then suddenly Delia was jolted by what she thought was a familiar voice.

"Delia."

She turned tentatively and immediately recognized with excitement that the voice was Joseph's. He had come to The Meadows with his father.

"Why, good afternoon, Joseph," she stammered demurely.

Joseph looked at her as if puzzled, "I am quite surprised to see you here, Miss Delia. Did you come with your father?"

"Yes," she replied. "It seems that my brothers either had work to do or another meeting to go to. I ended up escorting my father this afternoon. He needs help, you know."

"I see. Well, I am quite pleased that the Russell family is so busy," he said with a sly smile.

Silence followed as Delia deciphered the meaning of Joseph's statement. Realizing the intended nature of his comment, she smiled but was unsure as to what her response should be. Joseph spotted the bucket she was carrying and offered to assist her. The two meandered toward the springhouse, and Joseph reached over to take the water bucket from her. Not feeling at all comfortable with entering the springhouse with him, Delia remained just outside the door while Joseph filled the bucket.

He exited and declared, "Now you must allow me to carry this to the house for you."

Delia meekly responded, "Maybe just to the door, Joseph."

He nodded in understanding, and the two ascended the slope toward the back door of the Blake house. Neither made an attempt to talk, but they shared occasional glances. As they reached the house, Delia stopped and reached for the bucket.

"I can take it from here," she quipped. Joseph passed her the water bucket and stared intently at her hand as she reached to take it from him.

"I'm looking forward to coming to call on you again, Miss Delia," he said. For the first time, he saw Delia relax as she allowed her beautiful smile to emerge. Totally enamored by every feature, Joseph walked away pleased.

As the meeting broke up the men spilled into the yard. Robert Russell searched the landscape until he caught sight of Delia coming toward him. As she placed his stool for him and he climbed into the buggy he turned to her and said, "I know this was hard for you, to come to this meeting when you'd rather stay home, but even the womenfolk are going to have to help out in this war."

Delia said nothing to reveal how much she had enjoyed herself or to enlighten him about her experience on the grounds.

"I'm glad to help, Papa."

Chapter 6

—— JULY 12, 1861 ——

Hoopers Creek Thomas Clingman was now a former U.S. senator. He had been a politician and community leader all of his adult life. His decision to raise a regiment for the Confederate army was one that came to him naturally. Although he had no formal military training, serving in the army was a responsibility that most southern men considered mandatory.

He and his party of nine had been making rounds in Henderson County for several days. There were numerous farm families on Cane Creek and Hoopers Creek with many healthy sons. He had hoped to gain both the support and the enlistments of these families. As he rode into the yard of the Youngblood farm with Daniel Blake and the others traveling with him, he was very optimistic that all would go well. The level of enthusiasm for supporting the cause had overwhelmed him. Lincoln's call for troops to invade the South had motivated almost everyone, even some of the strongest Union supporters, to join the Confederacy. The anticipated invasion of the South whipped the population into a frenzy, quickly spreading war fever to every hamlet and town.

As the party approached the house, Reuben Youngblood walked out onto the porch, his five sons following him. Clingman and his entourage seemed out of place in this rural setting. Reuben Youngblood walked down the steps and greeted Clingman and Blake as they dismounted. These men shook hands while the others remained in their saddles. The two older Youngblood sons, William and Joseph, descended the steps and joined their father and the two dismounted visitors.

"Mr. Youngblood, I am here to . . ."

The elder Youngblood held up his hand to stop him in the middle of his speech.

"I know why you're here; everybody knows why you're here. You want my sons for the army."

Youngblood made it clear that he didn't need to be briefed on anything. He turned partially, gesturing to his two older sons. "These are my two oldest boys. They can go with you and your army," he said in his German accent.

"Good, very good. Thank you, sir," Clingman replied gracefully.

Before he could comment further, Youngblood continued. "My youngest is only a child, and my other two sons must be here to farm. I must have their help."

"It is good to have your support," Clingman said, gesturing to Mr. Blake, the man standing beside him.

"Mr. Blake and others in the community have agreed to pay the bounty for the men joining the army."

Bill Youngblood then spoke up.

"Senator Clingman, sir. It is our understanding that the enlistment will be for one year and no more than that."

"That's right," Clingman responded. "You don't have to worry; you'll probably be home in less than six months. Probably in time to work on your farm by the first of next year."

On the porch young J. N. and Hiram Youngblood restrained themselves. Both young men were consumed by anger and disappointment. They had desperately wanted to go with their older brothers. It was only the adamant resistance from their father that had prevented them from doing so. Even nine-year-old Pinkney would have gone, had he been allowed to.

Daniel Blake shook hands with the two young men and happily welcomed them to state service.

CHAPTER SIX

"Mrs. Blake and I are most pleased to invite you to a barbeque to be held for all the young men joining the army. There will be food, drink, and much celebration in your honor. Please give us the pleasure of your attendance on the fifteenth day of July at Calvary Episcopal Church in Fletcher," Blake said.

Clingman then asked with concern, "What about the Garrens? Will they be with us?" Reuben Youngblood turned to his sons as if to indicate he knew that they could answer that question better than he could. As if on cue, Bill Youngblood replied, "Yes, they are with us and they will be at the meeting at Calvary Church."

Nodding his head with pleasure, Clingman added, "All of them?"

"Yes, I think all of them . . . who are of age," Bill Youngblood replied.

"Good. Then there will be no need to ride all the way up Bearwallow Mountain." The two younger men nodded in affirmation.

Joseph Youngblood had said nothing until the meeting was nearly over. "I wanna know about just one man," Joseph said, indicating that he thought it was important.

"Who might that be?" Clingman asked.

"Solomon Cunningham. He is older but he is still the best shot on Hoopers Creek, and the men of the valley admire him," he said with an anxious plea in his voice, as if to make sure Clingman understood the importance of this one man.

"I don't know. We went by his home place and talked to him about it, but he wouldn't say. You know he has his own family—a lot of children—and he's thirty-seven years old. I guess we can't expect him to join us if he doesn't want to."

Clingman seemed to be conceding that Cunningham would not be with them, but Youngblood pressed him further.

"If you don't get anybody else off of Hoopers Creek you need to get him. He is an honorable man and highly respected by everyone."

"We'll do our best," Blake answered. Clingman and Blake remounted their horses. There were more families to call on and more recruiting to be done before sunset.

THE SECRET OF WAR

——JULY 15, 1861——

William and Joseph Youngblood hugged their mother on the front porch as they bade her farewell. As they turned to say good-bye to their father, the old man could not look them in the eyes. When he finally raised his head, he had managed to clear the tears that had escaped his eyes. He hugged them both and turned without saying a word. The three younger brothers were down off the porch, excitedly encouraging their older brothers. A cluster of other young men waited in the yard. All the Garren boys had walked down from Bearwallow Mountain to Hoopers Creek, and the Garrens and the Youngbloods started on the walk to Fletcher. There were other families already on the road. Some on horseback, some in wagons, but mostly on foot. All the young men who were going with the army carried a blanket roll as well as their personal belongings.

Having endured the difficulty of saying good-bye, the group of German Americans-turned-Confederate soldiers were now busily engaged in chatter about their future. Immediately the teasing and joking was under way. Joseph paid little attention as he looked northeast, inspected the outline of Bearwallow Mountain in the distance, and thought of Delia.

Joseph was amazed at the size of the crowd. Since the whole issue of states' rights, secession, and the bombing of Fort Sumter had started, the crowds at every occasion seemed to grow larger and larger. But this crowd was beyond anything they had ever seen. Everyone on Cane Creek and Hoopers Creek seemed to be there. There were scores of young men, many of their parents, and a multitude of children. The atmosphere was both festive and celebratory. As the Youngbloods and Garrens waded into the crowd Bill Youngblood turned to the others, "Man, I bet there's a lot of good eatin' here tonight."

"Well, you better eat good now. 'Cause I reckon we won't eat too good, once we're in the army," David Garren quipped.

Elisha Garren, beaming with excitement, said, "I bet all the girls are here."

CHAPTER SIX

"Do any of y'all see Delia?" Joseph said.

"Oh no, not that again," Will Garren bellowed.

"Are y'all gonna have a family tonight?" he added. The others laughed hysterically, but Joseph continued to search the crowd. He was paying no attention to the teasing from his friends.

As they approached the wooden canopy that had been built for the church, Daniel Blake, who had another young man with him, greeted them.

"Hello. Hello. Welcome. Welcome," Blake announced with his usual officious tone. As he shook hands with the new recruits he gestured to the young man to his left.

"This is my son Fredrick. He is going to be your captain," Blake said confidently.

No introduction was necessary as young Blake was known to all. Bill Youngblood and Will Garren glanced at each other as they looked back at the baby-faced Blake. Fredrick Blake was only twenty-three and had no practical experience at anything that the other men were aware of. To the farm boys he was just a little rich kid who had lived a soft life. The little cadre remained silent until they secured their place in line.

"Who elected him captain?" Joseph said to his older brother.

"I don't know," Bill replied.

"I don't know either," said Will Garren, who overheard them talking.

"I guess they think that we're goin' to a picnic."

Elisha Garren, the youngest of the group, intruded into the conversation, saying, "He don't look any older than my baby sister."

"Yea, but his daddy is paying the bill," Will Garren shrugged.

After waiting in line for a few more minutes they reached the table where the enlistment rolls were being completed. Joseph was first to step forward. An unfamiliar man sat at the desk and said calmly, "State your full name, age, and home county."

"Joseph Youngblood, twenty-three, Henderson County."

"Sign right here," the man said. Joseph took the pen and signed his name to the document, and the man gave him a ten-dollar note.

"Next," he said as Joseph moved to the side. He could faintly hear his brother signing up behind him as he looked around for the only person who mattered. The crowd was so thick that it took him awhile to work his way to where the women were working at the tables.

Joseph had never seen so much food, and he chuckled to himself, as he knew that this would make his brother very happy. The tables were filled with roast beef, ham, fried chicken, and baked bread. Fresh vegetables were in season, so the green beans and tomatoes were also plentiful. Joseph surmised that his brother would eat enough to last for the first half of their enlistment. At the back of the covered area there was a clear dirt patch with local musicians playing the fiddle and picking the banjo.

A large group of men had gathered out by the wagons, and Joseph knew that the whiskey was flowing. Then he saw her. Delia carried a basket from the wagon, placed it on the table, and returned to get another. He moved toward her, amused because he knew that she had not seen him. He took this opportunity to watch her for several minutes as she repeated her trip to and from the wagon. Her mother and sisters helped while Nanny Mills spread the food on the table. The excitement seemed to consume everyone. The girls and the women showered the young men with attention and adulation.

Joseph felt proud to be among them and to be serving his state and defending his home. Like those around him, Joseph found himself caught up in the fever that dominated the community. In truth, he'd decided to join the army because he knew that Bob Russell would never allow him to marry his daughter if he did not serve. He looked at Delia's face and thought, "Hell, I'd fight the whole Yankee army by myself for her."

A smile took over his face at the moment she looked up and spotted him. Caught up in the moment, Delia didn't think or care about what her parents might see. She dropped her basket and forced her way through the throng of people until she reached him.

Joseph took both her hands into his, and their eyes locked for a long moment. "Oh Joseph, I'm so proud of you. My father is so pleased that you are joining the army. It's wonderful."

CHAPTER SIX

"I'm only doing my duty," he said.

"You look so handsome," Delia whispered, her face beaming. Their enjoyment was interrupted by the loud booming voice of Nanny Mills.

"Miss Delia, ya git yoself back over here," she said, seemingly concerned that Delia might be drifting into a pattern of inappropriate behavior. Delia tore herself away from Joseph and returned to the table. As she walked away from him, he shouted at her.

"I will see you again later tonight."

She turned, looked back at him, and nodded frantically in the affirmative. Joseph walked back through the crowd, noting all of the people that he knew. There were Fletchers, Carlands, Lewises, Bishops, Brysons, Freemans, Hendersons, Fowlers, Whitakers, Wheelers, Summeys, Russells, Barnwells, Wards, Lannings, and Hammonds. It just seemed like everybody was either joining or cheering them on.

Joseph felt good. He knew that if there was going to be a fight he would like to have them all in it. There was a commotion at the far end of the large shed. He saw his older brother and the Garrens move in that direction. It was almost a cheer, and he couldn't determine why everyone was cheering. He worked his way around some women who blocked his view until he could see the table where the men were signing their enlistments. Then he understood the cheer, because standing at the table was Solomon Cunningham. That's everybody, he thought to himself. The highly respected Cunningham signed his papers and walked through the crowd with a group of young men around him. Joseph joined them and shook Solomon's hand at about the time several of them started talking. Sam Wheeler grabbed Solomon by the shoulder and said, "Sol, we want you to be captain." "Yea! Yea!" many nodded in agreement. Cunningham raised his hand, stopping them in their tracks. He sternly looked them all in the eyes.

"No," he said firmly. "It's already been decided. Young Blake is going to be our captain."

The other men grumbled, but Cunningham would hear none of it.

"It's settled. Now let's get down to the business that we have to do. You boys go on and have fun tonight 'cause I reckon there won't be much fun come tomorrow morning."

"We're glad you're here," Elisha Garren said, beaming. Cunningham looked back at him with a scowl on his face.

"I ain't here 'cause I wanna be, but a man's got to do his duty."

The mood had gotten too serious and Sol knew it, so he lightened the atmosphere. "Besides, I figured I better come look after you boys, so you don't get in any trouble."

They all laughed briefly as the group waded into the crowd.

It was now late in the evening. Every available man had enlisted that night. The festivities were at their peak. The corn liquor was flowing freely, and even some of the teetalers were drinking. The musicians were lively and the crowd was rowdy and jubilant.

Daniel Blake stepped in front of the musicians, and his son dragged a large wooden box to the front, which Blake then stood upon. Holding a tin pan and wooden spoon, he began banging on the pan until he had the crowd's attention. He began a long dissertation laced with accolades for all the men who were joining the army, as well as the leaders in the community. While he held the crowd's attention, Joseph worked his way out through the side of the canopy and stealthily circled all the way around behind the food tables. Everyone was watching the ceremony so intently that they did not notice him slipping in among the women. He came so close behind Delia that his body made contact with hers. She froze at first, and then she heard him whisper, "Meet me at the bell tower," he said quietly.

Just as stealthily as he had arrived, Joseph slipped away from the crowd and into the darkness. It was some distance through the cemetery to the church bell tower. He could hear the speeches in the background as he picked out a spot and waited. For a minute he was deathly afraid that she might not come. If she didn't come to him he thought he'd be unable to leave. He could not march off to war the following morning without seeing her. He paced and fidgeted as he waited. The short wait seemed like an eternity, but then he saw her silhouetted against the light of the lanterns in the background. She saw him and immediately lost all inhibitions. She threw her arms around him, and he hugged her tightly. Delia pulled back only to look at him. Her eyes had not yet adjusted to the darkness, and she was totally unprepared for his kiss.

Joseph kissed her deeply, and to her surprise she was disappointed when he finally pulled away. Delia was drawn to this man in both mind and body in a way that she had never experienced. She briefly thought of her parents and quickly looked back to see if anyone had followed her. On so many occasions she had been speechless when she had been with Joseph, but after seeing that no one had followed she turned back to him and words came easily.

"Oh, Joseph, I think of you day and night. I have thought of nothing else."

She started to say more, but he kissed her again.

"I think of you day and night, all the time, too," Joseph responded.

"Oh, Joseph, I love you. I love you more than life itself."

"I love you too, Delia, and I'm going to marry you. I'm going to go fight this war for your daddy, and I know he will let you marry me when I return."

Suddenly she was stricken by fear. The realization that he was leaving tomorrow morning hit her hard.

"Oh, Joseph, I can't bear you leaving. I can't stand the thought that you might be hurt," she said with tears coming into her eyes.

"It's only a few months at the most, and lots of folks think it will just be weeks," he said, trying to calm her. "I will come back to you, I promise. I swear on my life and I swear to God. I will come back to you."

Their eyes now adjusted to the limited light, and they could make out each other's features. Joseph looked over Delia's shoulder to see if anyone was near. They could hear the ceremony as the speakers continued their rousing under the canopy. Confident that there would be no interruptions, he turned back to Delia, reached his arms around her, and kissed her passionately again. He took her hand and led her around the bell tower. Slightly stumbling, she followed him unquestioningly.

"Come with me," he said as he pulled her behind the bell tower.

"Here, take this," he told her, placing a large gold coin in her hand.

"What is it, Joseph?" she asked curiously.

"My great-grandfather fought in the Seven Years War in Germany against France and Russia. He served a great Prussian leader called Frederick the Great. After the war my great-grandfather was rewarded with solid gold coins. There were only five coins, and they were passed down through my family. My father carried them to America with him, and he gave one each to his sons. I want you to put this one in safekeeping for us. It's worth a lot of money, and we'll use it to start our new lives together when I come home. Promise me you'll keep it for us. Put it somewhere safe."

"Oh, yes, yes, Joseph. I'll keep it until you come home to me. I shall cherish it with all my heart," she said, looking at the beautifully minted coin with the strange German crest on one side and the bust of Frederick the Great on the other. She looked at him and pressed the coin to her breast.

"It's so beautiful," she repeated.

Joseph fell to his knees, looked up at her, and recited the words that he had planned for weeks. He bowed his head, cleared his throat, and then looked up at her again.

>My dearest Delia,
>It is to thee that I commit my heart.
>It is to thee that I commit my life, my spirit, and my soul.
>It is to thee that I will return to take as my wife.

Delia looked down at him with tears flowing from her eyes. Dropping to her knees to join him, she took his hands in hers and said, "And I commit to thee, Joseph. I will be your wife and I commit my soul and my life to you forever."

The couple embraced, their knees now embedded in the dirt. Not

CHAPTER SIX

wanting to separate, they continued to hold each other, as the music and the murmur of the crowd signaled the end of the program. Reluctantly the two turned their faces toward the light that outlined the bell tower. Anxiously Delia told him, "I must go back now, Joseph."

"I know," he said.

They rose to their feet and hand in hand walked back toward the sound and light. Delia tightly clutched the precious gold coin in her other hand as she tried to imagine the details of their future. She knew that in his absence the coin would serve as a tangible symbol of their union, a symbol that she would hold and protect until his return.

―― AUGUST 1861 ――

Camp Patton, Asheville, North Carolina Joseph had never been so miserable in his life. Camp Patton was now crowded with hundreds of men. His company was crammed into a small area next to Balous Edney's company, another group of Henderson County men. The food was unfamiliar and the tents were of such poor quality that the men joked that they could stay drier in the rain. They marched daily, this way and that, for no particular purpose or reason. Young Fredrick Blake seemed to whine constantly about the slightest discomfort. Solomon Cunningham stayed to himself mostly. He did speak up when the younger men griped or complained. He would tell them to be quiet and go along with it.

As the days went by and the marching continued the men became increasingly disgruntled with their situation. The men joked that all the marching must be part of a grand plan to stomp the Yankees to death.

The Cane Creek Rifles and the Hoopers Creek boys huddled together for the most part. Earlier they had agreed to call themselves the Cane Creek Rifles, and formal elections were held for officers. The men wanted Sol Cunningham, but he still refused to serve so they elected Fredrick Blake, mostly because Cunningham told them to. Blake spent little or no time with the men as he had a very nice, elaborate tent, larger than the others. He had silver goblets for drinking and real plates to eat on. One of his daddy's slaves attended him at all times and kept several changes of clothes washed for him. Most of the men only had one extra shirt and an extra pair of socks.

The Garren boys joked that Blake was a dandy, ready for the Easter parade in New York. Wisely, they complained only to themselves and continued to carry out the boring drills. Bill Youngblood commented to the others, "We might as well surrender to the Yankees if this is all we are gonna do. I'm damn tired of marching."

"Oh, no, we'll whip 'em this way," said Elisha Garren.

"Them that marches best wins the war."

The Hoopers Creek boys now teased Will Garren constantly, for he had been elected corporal. They would do what he said during the day but at night called him "Napoleon" or "general" and constantly asked him where his horse was.

"And why don't you have one of them big, fancy swords with pearls on it? And maybe you'll get ya a silver goblet like that Blake boy."

Will Garren stared back at them with a mixture of embarrassment and contempt as they crowed with laughter.

"I didn't ask to do this. You damned fools elected me. As soon as we get to a battle, I'm giving you boys over to the Yanks. We got a better chance of winning with you fellers on their side."

The days turned to weeks, and on August 11 Captain Blake gave the order for the men to form up. He stood before them and addressed them with great pomp and arrogance.

"Men, we have been assigned as part of the 25th Regiment of the North Carolina Infantry. We are Company H, and our colonel will be Thomas Clingman. He will be addressing us tomorrow morning to give us our orders."

As he completed his remarks and released the men, someone whispered to the others in the back row, "He tries to act like a general, but he looks like a girl." Those men within hearing distance burst forth in laughter.

Sensing that a demeaning comment had been made, Blake angrily rushed into the company, "Just what are you men laughing about?" All the men looked at each other, back and forth, as if no one knew what he was talking about.

"Was that you, Youngblood?" Blake asked Joseph.

"No, Freddy. I didn't say anything."

Blake's face turned red.

"Don't call me Freddy anymore," he screamed.

"It's Captain. Do you understand?"

"Yes, Captain. Sorry, Freddy, I mean Captain," Youngblood slipped again as the other men snickered.

"I'm sorry, Captain," Joseph said, trying to recover. "It's just that I've known you since you were a boy."

Blake, now furious, looked at the other men who were attempting to keep a straight face.

"It's Captain now. And don't any of y'all forget it."

He stomped back to his private tent, allowing the men to break apart on their own.

The following morning the men were formed up again, and this time all the companies were arranged in order and marched together. There were eleven companies from Henderson, Jackson, Haywood, Cherokee, Transylvania, Clay, Macon, and Buncombe counties.

Some of the men expected improved conditions now that they had been made part of a regiment. Such expectations were unfounded. Colonel Clingman, their commander, was adamant that they maintain the strict vigil of drill. Their lieutenant colonel, Saint Clare Dearing, was a career military officer who had resigned his commission in the U.S. Army. Dearing and a young major, Henry M. Rutledge, directed the training. Although he was a boyish-looking young man, only twenty-two years of age, Rutledge boasted a military education and training.

Day after day, the men marched and drilled. They had no uniforms, and the only weapons they had were ones that a few of the men had brought with them. The majority carried sticks or boards as substitute rifles. Sunday was a blessed relief for the men, and although some of them had not been that religious prior to the war, the escape from the drudgery of their daily activity inspired many of the men to find a new interest in their religious betterment.

There was much enthusiasm and uplifting of spirit generated by the news from Virginia. By now the men had heard much talk of the grand battle and the great victory the Confederates had achieved at Manassas, Virginia, in July. Many of the men took great relish in hearing and repeating the stories about the Yankee retreat and the civilian audience skeedaddling back to Washington. There was lots of worry that the Yankees might quit this war before they had had a chance to get into it. Also boosting their spirits was the fact that North Carolina had been involved in the victory.

Morale was high on September 17 when Colonel Clingman gave the order to the captains to form up their companies. He then advised the regiment that they would depart at sunrise for Morganton, where transportation by train had been arranged. A great cheer arose from the regiment.

David and Elisha Garren rushed over to Joseph and Bill Youngblood.

"We're going on a train," David said excitedly.

"We've never seen one," Elisha added.

"We've never seen one either," Bill told them. Elisha then stated that maybe all they were going through was worth it for the train ride to Raleigh. Joseph Youngblood looked at him contemptuously.

"I've always wanted to ride a train, but it ain't worth marching my feet off for it."

"Yea, and I reckon it's gonna take you someplace you'd rather not be, before this war is over."

—— SEPTEMBER 18TH, 1861 ——

The officers and the men rose early and began rolling their blankets and putting down their tents. The regiment's wagons were in place to carry the bulky supplies. The sun had yet to rise over Beaucatcher

CHAPTER SIX

Mountain, but already Camp Patton was stirring with activity. The men fried bacon and drank coffee, many waxing sentimental as they prepared to leave their mountain home. There was also great excitement about what was to come. Many comments had to do with the common belief that anything would be better than more days of marching back and forth to nowhere.

As the sun peaked over the ridge Captain Blake called the men into formation. The order to march was given, and the regiment marched toward Asheville. Soon they approached the center of town, crossing the square and passing the Eagle Hotel, proceeding down South Main Street to the Swannanoa River. The men were surprised and amused to find that the entire town seemed to be out that morning. Hundreds of people ran beside them and followed along the road in various groups and clusters. There were young boys on horseback, women and children in wagons, and town leaders cheering them on their way.

The stirring notes of drum and fife and the waving of flags added to the thrilling and patriotic atmosphere. A group of citizens gathered near the Eagle Hotel and sang "Dixie" as the men marched by. This was not the first group of young men to enjoy such a send-off. Zebulon Vance and his Rough and Ready Guard had preceded them, but each time another group departed the fanfare and the emotions were the same. It was a curious mix of exhilaration, pride, and sadness. Although the atmosphere was celebratory, both those in the marching columns and the citizens on the street knew that many of these men might not return.

The march turned east at the Swannanoa River. The formal atmosphere and military structure that had carried them through the streets of Asheville now moderated to some degree, but the men kept a steady pace. They looked back and forth at each other with some amusement at the surprising number of citizens still following or marching along beside them. As the sun set in the western sky the men soon found themselves marching out along the old Cherokee trails headed toward the landmark known as Swannanoa Gap. By the time they began the climb passing through the gap, the heat of the day was upon them and the reality of their struggle began to affect even the most dedicated participant.

Joseph Youngblood was past all concept of celebration in his mind. He tried not to look at the citizens who gathered at every convenient point to urge them on. His thoughts were only of Delia and sadness was his only emotion. He was so frightened that he might not see her again. Glancing occasionally at the groups of people gathered here and there, his love-stricken mind played tricks on him. For a brief instant he would think that he saw her in the crowd. He displaced such ideas knowing that she couldn't possibly have come from Henderson County to participate in the march. He steeled himself to only one idea. I will return. I shall return, he swore to himself as he marched along the dusty road.

As the sun began to set behind them the exhausted men were called to a halt in a grassy valley along the river. They settled into camp, grouped by companies. The sun cast a strange and beautiful orange light on the Black Mountains to the north. The men ate what they could and were very thankful to the many citizens who brought them cakes, coffee, and vegetables.

Joseph wondered if it would always be this way. At sunrise the men marched on and camped the following night at Old Fort, only to rise again the following day. Finally, on the afternoon of the fourth day, the spent and sweating men arrived at Icard Station in Morganton, where the nearest railhead was located. They camped again around the railhead to wait on a train. There was great interest on the part of the citizens of Burke County. Many of the county's men had left on earlier train rides as new regiments were being organized. The camp that night was peaceful and the rest extended due to their somewhat early arrival. The following morning the mountain men of the western counties awakened with a frightening start. Many of the men thought that they were under attack. Hardly anyone in the group had ever heard the roaring of a steam engine. Soon the hissing and whistling iron monster pulled into the station. The men rushed to the tracks and cheered with whoops and hollers at the amazing sight before them. The soldiers compared this

CHAPTER SIX

new spectacle to forest fires and monsters and thunderstorms. While the journey had been difficult indeed, these mountain men couldn't help but appreciate this part of their arduous adventure.

Joseph and the other men from the mountains were totally unprepared for the strange environment they encountered when the train pulled into the station in Raleigh, North Carolina.

"Hell, they ain't a hill, not even a bump nowhere," Bill Youngblood said as the men climbed off the train.

"It's hotter'n hell twice over too," Will Garren added.

Joseph didn't say anything, as he was concentrating on what had to be done, what was going to be required to get him through this.

Captain Blake called the Cane Creek Rifles into ranks. The company formed up with the others, and soon they were marching through Raleigh as the 25th North Carolina Infantry Regiment. In the next few days they were issued new uniforms and brand new 1842 British-made Enfield rifles. The weapons were prized for their quality and accuracy. The guns weighed nearly nine pounds. Each man was given ammunition and percussion caps for the weapons. Joseph looked at his new weapon with interest and appreciation. There was nothing in the process to indicate what these rifles would mean to them in the continuing drama of war.

The uniforms were typical gray sack coats reaching halfway down the thigh. The coats had loose collars that could be worn turned down or standing up. On the shoulders there were strips of black cloth, which indicated that they were North Carolina infantry. The trousers were of matching gray cloth with black stripes running down the seams. They were also issued leather double cross belts.

The men looked at each other and made fun of the new look. But down deep they were all proud, for the uniforms seemed to unify the men as a single military unit. They'd mostly thought of themselves as boys from Cane Creek and Hoopers Creek playing soldier. Equipped with their new uniforms and their new rifles, they were real soldiers.

Joseph looked at his brother and chuckled.

"Ain't you a fine lookin' thing?"

"I can't be no prettier than you are," Bill responded.

Joseph looked down at himself. The pants were a little short and the waist was too big, but all in all he felt pretty good.

Solomon Cunningham approached as the men continued to admire themselves.

"I don't know why you boys are so worked up over the uniforms. Have you taken a good look at these rifles?" he said in a serious tone.

"These are the finest guns I've ever seen. They're British I think."

The men began to examine the new Enfields with appreciation.

"Whew! I can pop me some Yankees with this thing," Will Garren said confidently.

"You ain't kiddin' me, they're beautiful," Elisha Garren said.

The newly outfitted men marched back to camp. Their boredom and apathy had been replaced with excitement and confidence. They were there to defend their homes and their families, and at that point they were proud to be part of the southern cause.

Chapter 7

―― MARCH 16, 1862 ――

Hoopers Creek Delia joined her mother and Nanny Mills in the parlor early that morning. Mrs. Russell handed her the knitting basket, and soon all three women were knitting at an industrious pace. The three were knitting socks to send to the men in the army. Letters to home from the soldiers often included requests for various household items. Socks were always listed as a priority. Women on the home front worked constantly on making and collecting items to send to their loved ones in the army.

Delia looked at her mother with growing concern. No one in the family spoke of it, but Mrs. Russell's condition seemed to be slowly deteriorating. Her weight was on the decline, and the color of her skin took on an unhealthy sallow look. She could no longer walk and had to be helped from room to room in the house.

Delia worked diligently at her knitting, but her major task this day would be escorting her father to Asheville. She was looking forward to this small adventure as it made life interesting. Delia had nearly finished the sock she was working on when she heard the familiar thumping of her father's approach. He took two steps, planted his cane, and then took two more.

"Good morning, Papa," Delia said.

"We best be going," Bob Russell told Delia.

Delia stood and passed her knitting basket to her mother as she made her way to the front of the house, collecting her father's leather satchel and her own small basket of belongings. Delia found Zeke waiting with Ole Star already hitched to the buggy. He held the harness as Bob Russell climbed onto the step that Zeke had placed for him. Delia followed behind, and soon both were in the buggy and ready to depart.

"Zeke, you keep those boys working on the fence. I'll be back early tomorrow evening," he told the slave.

"Yes sir, Massa Bob. I keep 'em workin' from sunrise to sundown. Yes sir, Massa Bob, we be workin'."

Delia was now capable of steering the buggy, so she took the reins and nudged Ole Star, pausing to wait for Matthias Dees and his crew to cross with a load of fence rails.

Dees turned toward the wagon, took off his hat, and bowed theatrically.

"Good morning, Mr. Russell. God bless you this fine morning. Good morning to you too, Missy," he said, smiling at Delia.

He stood upright, replaced his hat, and turned, walking away from the wagon. Delia had ignored him, staring straight toward the road, as he engaged in his overly embellished greeting. She was not fooled by his theatrical performance even if her father was. She did not trust this man or his unsightly crew.

Delia led Ole Star and the buggy with reasonable skill as they plodded down the soft muddy road toward Fletcher. The town center was bustling with activity. Two large freight wagons were parked in front of Johnston's store and many smaller wagons were parked around it.

Ole Star rambled past Johnston's store and stopped at the post office. Delia climbed down from the buggy, and her father waited while she went inside to retrieve the family mail. Claude Ward was the local postmaster and a relative of the Russell family. His mother was a Livingston, and he was especially fond of his nieces, Delia and her sisters. He greeted her warmly and smiled.

"My, my. Have I got good news for you! A big passel of mail came in yesterday, and there were several things for the Russell family."

CHAPTER SEVEN

He reached behind the counter and retrieved a bundle of envelopes that he handed to Delia. She was beside herself with anticipation as she looked through the stack. She knew immediately that the letter on top was from Joseph and as she thumbed through the others she discovered yet another.

"Thank you, Uncle Claude. I was hoping there would be mail today."

He waved her on.

"Sure thing, Miss Delia. Glad to help."

Delia pranced out of the door and down the steps, climbing back into the buggy.

Her father impatiently snapped, "Give me that mail, girl. I'm expecting an important letter from Raleigh."

He looked through the parcels quickly, noticing a letter from his son James, who was also in the 25th North Carolina Infantry. He tucked the others in his jacket pocket while he opened the official-looking brown envelope from Raleigh. Delia knew better than to ask about the contents of the envelope. Her father had become quite influential with the new government and could have gone to the legislature and possibly even the Confederate Congress, but Bob Russell had elected to remain at home. His bad leg was the secondary reason for his staying at home, as he calculated that the required travel would be difficult. However, his primary reason for staying home was strictly mercenary. Bob Russell figured there was money to be made off of this war, and he was going to figure out how to do it.

Delia steered Ole Star down the Asheville Road as they passed numerous walkers and plenty of other four-wheeled horse traffic. There were two oxen-pulled freight wagons headed south, and her father concluded that they were probably headed toward Hendersonville and Mills River. The wagon traffic would eventually assemble in Asheville and then make the difficult journey across Swannanoa Gap to the railhead at Icard Station in Morganton.

Delia demonstrated her confidence and skill as Ole Star plodded on toward Asheville. By late morning the Russells had arrived in

Shufordsville, a small hamlet between Asheville and Fletcher. Delia guided the buggy and Ole Star into the yard of the Baldwin store. R. L. Baldwin, like most of the people in the area, was well known to the Russell family. R. L. walked out onto the dock in front of the store and waved as the wagon came to a halt.

"Howdy, Bob. How y'all doin' today?"

"Just fine, R. L. Just fine. Did you get my ax for me?"

"Yes, came in two days ago. I've been holding it for you."

The two men continued to chat as Delia held Ole Star in check. R. L. Baldwin went back into the store and came out a few minutes later with a brand new double-bladed ax. Knowing Russell's physical limitations, Baldwin carried the ax down the steps and placed it on the back of the buggy and then returned to Bob Russell's side of the wagon. The two men made small talk while Bob Russell reached into his money belt and collected the coins necessary to pay for the ax.

"How's business, R. L?"

"Business is good, only I can't get enough supplies. They only sent me about two-thirds of the salt I ordered last week."

"Oh, I wouldn't worry about that. They'll catch up with you next week I'm sure."

Recognizing that Russell carried some influence with the new government, Baldwin requested, "Bob, do what you can to see that they keep me supplied, will ya?"

"I'll do it. Don't you worry," Russell reassured the storekeeper. He waved good-bye and the storekeeper returned his wave.

It was a good distance from Shufordsville to Asheville, but Ole Star kept up a steady pace. Many of the people they passed along the way were familiar to them; some were not. But all greeted each other cheerfully. There seemed to be a heightened spirit of camaraderie in the community since the Blake barbeque.

Late in the day the wagon began the climb up South Main Street into Asheville. Delia did not get to the busy city very often, but she had an idea that these trips were going to become a regular occurrence. She

CHAPTER SEVEN

noted with interest that there were soldiers milling about Asheville in new Confederate uniforms. When Joseph and the others had departed they didn't have uniforms, and she couldn't help but wonder what Joseph would look like in his. She was certain that he would be the most handsome man in his company, maybe even his whole regiment.

They pulled into the livery area in front of the Eagle Hotel where two slaves greeted them immediately and took Ole Star's harness. The hotel proprietor stepped onto the porch and greeted them also.

"Welcome, Mr. Russell," he shouted from his perch.

Delia felt a vicarious sense of importance as the hotel staff hurried to help them. She grabbed her father's satchel and her own bag. They were led into the hotel where many men were standing and conversing. Recognizing her father, several of the gentlemen came over to greet him. Delia stood patiently and silently behind her father as he exchanged greetings.

A slave woman took Delia's bag and led her to the back of the hotel as another slave took Bob Russell's bag and helped him to his room. Delia was led to a smaller room next to the kitchen. She and two other single women would occupy the room. One of the women was from Warm Springs and had accompanied her brother. She greeted Delia warmly, and the two of them chatted amicably.

"I'm here with my older brother. He's come for a meeting tomorrow," she said, holding Delia's hand.

The young girl looked at Delia and asked, "How long will you be staying?"

"Only until tomorrow," Delia answered. "My father is here for the meeting too."

"What is your name?" Delia asked her.

"Martha, Martha Anderson."

The young woman was tiny. She had small hands and stood only to Delia's eyes. Light blond hair peeked from around her bonnet, outlining her attractive facial features. She had brilliant eyes that were almost golden. Delia marveled at her innocent beauty.

"My name is Delia Russell. My brothers are in the army, except for my little brother. He's only nine."

"My two other brothers are in the army also," Martha Anderson responded.

The two of them made the best of their day while Bob Russell continued with the business at hand. After getting situated in his room he returned to the parlor where a group of men gathered informally. They were discussing the recent news from Fort Donelson and Fort Henry. It was not good. The reports that they had received revealed that the Confederate commander had surrendered both of the forts without much of a fight. Many of the men were smoking, either cigars or pipes. Consequently, a strong tobacco odor and a pale plum color dominated the atmosphere in the hotel parlor.

"The damn fool should have fought it out with them. He could have gotten reinforcements. At least he should've put up a fight," Bob Russell scowled.

The local favorite, corn whiskey, was now circulating in small glasses. The always-plentiful mountain brew loosened tongues and magnified courage, and as the evening wore on the swearing and boasting intensified. Delia and Martha Anderson spent the evening in their tiny room comparing details about their lives. They had both brought food with them, and they chatted endlessly as they ate. Exhausted after the day's travel and activities, the two women finally took to their beds. But Delia did not sleep at first. She huddled in her bed and clutched the two precious envelopes that had come from Joseph.

> My Dearest Delia,
>
> So much has happened since I last wrote you. We are now marching toward New Bern for the city is under attack by a Yankee general named Burnside. Many of the men are glad to be leaving Granville and Hilton Head as this part of South Carolina seems to be commanded by a creature called a "bed bug." Most of

us would rather fight Yankees than bed bugs as we suspect their bite can't be any worse.

We know we'll soon be going into battle. The men called a meeting and we voted young Freddy Blake out. Solomon Cunningham is now our captain and we're all glad for it. I don't think a single man was for Freddy. Poor Freddy up and quit, got up his fancy tent and his slave and skeedaddled for home. A lot of the men are complaining, wanting to know why an officer can quit and we can't.

I hope the fightin' don't get too bad but I guess I'll get by somehow. I think of you constantly and I am sustained by your image. It is for you that I carry on and pray for the day that we are together again.

All my love,
Joseph

It was well past midnight and through many cigars and too much corn whiskey that the men finally concluded their discussions and went to their rooms to retire for the evening. As Bob Russell dozed off to sleep, he was proud of himself. He had made a good showing. His pledge was larger than most and a great deal larger than many others. Pleased with the outcome of the evening and groggy from the corn whiskey he had consumed, he fell immediately to sleep.

Matthias Dees and his boys moved methodically by way of the light provided by a partial moon. They crept silently from their camp through the pasture toward the Russell home. Dees talked quietly to the men as they moved toward the house.

"Okay boys, dat gull of an old man done gone off to town, 'n his sons have done joined dat crazy army. There ain't nobody up thar except the old lady, the little boy, and them two old niggers to worry about. Now 'em purdy little girls ain't a worry."

The others snickered at the comment.

"Rupert, I want ya to watch dat old nigger's shack. He's the only one we have to watch."

The Dees gang continued on until they reached the smokehouse. Rupert posted himself on the side of the little building, serving as a lookout. They worked silently and adroitly for several minutes. Soon all of the hinges were off. Even in the difficult light it was a task easily accomplished by these experienced thieves. Once inside they looked about for the most valuable items.

"Now boys, take 'em two hams," he said authoritatively.

"Oooh doggies!" Dees howled.

"Looky here. Damned if they ain't got a whole sack of salt. Ya git dat, boy."

The men grabbed all they could carry, placed the items outside the smokehouse, and calmly replaced the door and all the hinges. The group of men collected their ill-begotten gains and headed off toward the pasture.

Their work on the Russell farm was to be finished the next day, and they would collect their pay. Matthias Dees knew what to expect when missing items were discovered. It took some extra time, but Matthias made the group walk quite a distance and string their stash up in a tree along their departure route, deep in the woods. Then they returned to their camp at the farm and retired for the remainder of the evening. As he lay down on his blanket roll Matthias Dees laughed out loud.

"Well, 'em damn fools must've prayed for us tonight, cause God sure been good to us. He give us their ham."

They all laughed.

"What I really's hankerin' fer now to save my soul is one of 'em purdy little girls up thar," he sneered.

The laughter got even louder.

Bob Russell was up early the next morning. His head hurt and he was a bit stiff from having slept on his moneybag. He opened the door and growled at the slave who was in attendance in the hallway.

CHAPTER SEVEN

"Fetch my daughter Delia for me. She's in the kitchen quarters."

"Yes sir, yes sir," the small black man replied as he dashed down the hallway out of sight.

Delia and Martha had slept later than they meant to. Delia dressed and rushed to her father's room and helped him gather his things. They went to the parlor together where the room was packed with various clusters of men and even a few soldiers. Delia and her new friend huddled in the corner mostly unnoticed. Delia greatly appreciated having a new friend to experience all the excitement with. Martha Anderson's golden eyes beamed as she and Delia took it all in.

The meeting began with several speeches and then ended with several reports of the war.

Bob Russell's most important business was to be done at the bank. He left Delia at the hotel and walked to the bank with a group of other men.

Delia and Martha decided to take their breakfast in the yard. Delia had fried apples, and her friend had fresh cornbread. The two shared with each other. After talking the kitchen help into loaning them a pitcher for water, they went about making a picnic for themselves.

Later that morning Delia's father returned, and the livery slaves soon had Ole Star and the buggy ready to go. Delia hugged her new friend good-bye and climbed onto the wagon where her father was already seated. Her eyes caught sight of his bulging leather satchel, but she said nothing. They headed south toward the Swannanoa River and then to Henderson County in the distance. Soon they crossed the river and continued their journey. As her father turned to her she noticed something different in his tone. He was serious but surprisingly respectful.

"Delia, you're gonna have to do some quick growing up. Unfortunately, this war is going to make you face certain responsibilities before your time. I'm gonna have to trust you with some important family matters. You know how your mama is, being sickly and all. She just don't concentrate too well anymore. So anyway, I need to tell you what I have in my satchel. It's money, lots of money. I took silver and gold to the bank today and exchanged it for money. When we get home

I am gonna show you where I hide all of our money. If anything bad happens you need to know where it is, and you need to take care of it until your brothers get home, or until your little brother John gets old enough to help you."

Delia couldn't believe her ears. Her father was going to trust her with the family money. "My, my!" she thought to herself. "This is really something." She was astonished yet confident. She knew she could handle this new responsibility. She was smart and responsible. Her father had made a good choice, and she would show him so.

"Don't worry, Papa. I can do it. I will take care of everything for you."

"I know. I know you will. That's why I'm telling you this. Just never trust anybody, Delia. Never trust anybody. Remember that. You are never to tell anyone about this and never discuss it with anyone, except me, until James comes home from the war."

The rest of the trip was quiet and uneventful. Delia thought of her role and was so proud. She thought about Joseph and how pleased he would be that she was capable of handling such responsibility. She thought, "I will make a good wife for Joseph. A very good wife."

Delia swung the buggy to the left, turning down the road past Calvary Episcopal Church. As she drove by she glanced at the bell tower and reminisced about her last night with Joseph. She would never forget the promise that he had made to her that night. It warmed her heart and gave her comfort as she repeated his words in her mind. Reciting them made her feel somehow connected to Joseph.

She knew that the shortcut by Calvary Church would have them home sooner. It was considerably shorter than going to Fletcher and then up. They arrived mid-afternoon, and Delia drove the buggy through the yard and Ole Star brought them to a stop in front of the house. Zeke had seen them from a distance and was already on his way from the pasture. Susannah Russell sat out on the porch covered with a quilt. She greeted her husband and her daughter as they climbed the steps.

"Oh, I'm so glad you are back. How was your trip?"

CHAPTER SEVEN

"Fine. Fine. It went real well." Bob Russell clutched his satchel tightly under his arm as he made the cumbersome climb up the step. Delia helped him as best she could, but he would not let her carry the satchel. Zeke approached and spoke to his master.

"I be stabling up de horse for ya, Massa Russell," he said, taking the horse harness.

"How is the fence work going? Is it finished yet?"

"De work goin' real good. Yes sir, Massa Russell, we be most finished. Mr. Dees say he needs his pay today. He be going back home this evening."

"Yes, I know. Send them on up here when y'all are done."

Turning toward the door, Russell went into the house and seated himself in the parlor. Mrs. Russell returned to the kitchen, and he called Delia into the parlor.

"Close the door, Delia."

Delia closed the door and Bob Russell walked over to the window and looked out as if to verify that no one was peeking. He went to the desk, opened up the leather satchel, and placed several large bundles of the new Confederate currency on the table. Delia had never seen the new money before, and she thought it looked odd compared to the money she was familiar with.

"There's a lot of money here, Delia, and I'm gonna show you where I hide it. I changed some of my silver and gold into money, but I still have a reserve of gold and silver coins in case we need it."

Bob Russell took Delia to the corner of the room where the fireplace met the wooden planks. He then removed two pieces of the paneling that slid up and out from their positions, with their ends positioned behind the fireplace rock. Next, he slid another large, roughhewn board out from behind the two pieces of wooden paneling. He then slid out a large, flat, wooden box with metal bands hidden in a compartment in the wall of the house. The box was secured with an old padlock. Her father pulled a key from his pocket and unlocked the box.

Delia was fascinated. Inside the box were numerous little leather pouches and some U.S. greenbacks.

"Hand me the money, Delia."

Delia picked up the money and handed it to her father as he stacked it neatly into the box. By the time the task was completed, the box was nearly full. He closed it up, put the lock back on it, and slid it back into its hiding place. He then replaced the large, roughhewn board covering the compartment. Sliding the two pieces of paneling back into place he stepped back, looked at his work, turned to Delia, and smiled.

"What do you think of that, child?"

Delia was awed.

"You can't see a thing, Papa. It looks just like all the other boards," she said, continuing to study the mysterious wall.

He then walked around to the other side of the fireplace and motioned for her to follow. Down near the bottom he removed a loose stone, placing the key in the empty socket. Then he put the stone back in its place.

"Now listen to me, Delia. If the house should ever catch fire you must get this box out of here. This is a well-built house, and we're not likely to have a fire, if we're careful. But you never know. Lightning could strike or something."

Russell paused and then instructed his daughter. "Now you go on and help your mama, I'll see you at supper."

Bob Russell collected the remaining currency that he had left out and put it into his pocket. He went out to the front porch and looked out over his property to inspect the fence work. He seated himself and waited for the work crew who he knew would soon be finished with their project.

It was late afternoon when Zeke came walking back to the house with Dees at his side. The two men approached the porch, and Dees immediately began his annoying blessings.

"God bless you, Brother Russell. Lord bless your soul. I hope you're having a mighty fine day today," Dees said effusively.

CHAPTER SEVEN

"Yes, I am having a fine day today. I just got back from Asheville and our boys are doing real well. I wonder when you and your sons are gonna join the army," Russell asked, applying some pressure to the slovenly character.

"Oh, I don't know, Brother Russell. Soon as the Lord calls us, I guess. Yep, soon as the Lord calls us."

Russell took the money from his pouch and handed Dees the pay for him and his crew. Dees had not seen the new currency, and he looked at it puzzled.

"What's this?" he asked.

"It's the new money. It's the money you'll be seeing from now on in the South. It's Confederate dollars."

Dees cocked his head, looked down at the strange notes in his hand, and eyed them like a robin looking for a worm. He didn't know if he was entirely comfortable taking this different looking new money.

"Are you sure this money is good money, Brother Russell?"

"Yes sir," Russell replied confidently. "It's as good as gold. In fact, I exchanged gold for it."

Dees folded the money, put it into his pocket, issued some more blessings to Russell and his family, and bade his farewell.

As the sun crept up behind Bearwallow Mountain the dim morning light began to illuminate Hoopers Creek valley. Nanny Mills was already busy in the kitchen when she instructed Zeke to go to the smokehouse and collect the ham needed for the family breakfast. Zeke retrieved the key and started down the pathway to the smokehouse. The heavy fortress-like log structure was reasonably close to the house. Zeke unlocked the large padlock on the heavy door and drew a match to light the lantern kept inside. As soon as he struck the match he realized something was amiss. At first he hoped that his eyes were deceiving him, that perhaps the sack of salt had been placed elsewhere in the smokehouse. But as the lantern shed light on the grim situation Zeke began to panic. He knew his master's temper, and he had been entrusted with the key. He dropped to a seat, using the ledge at the side of the smokehouse, put his hands over his face, and covered his eyes. He slid his hands down, exposing his eyes to the light as he continued to evaluate the situation. He noticed that the hams were also gone. Now desperate for some sort of explanation, he went outside the smokehouse and examined the lock, the large chain, and the hasp. There was no damage.

Zeke collected himself, and as he walked back to the main house he shook his head back and forth in utter disbelief. He looked at the key in his hand as his befuddlement continued. There was no evidence that anyone had entered the smokehouse. No animals could have gotten inside, and besides an animal wouldn't take salt. He opened the kitchen door and went inside, his heart filled with fear and confusion. He wanted to run but knew he couldn't. It would be useless. He looked into his wife's eyes, and she could see that something terrible had happened.

"What is it, Zeke?" she asked fearfully.

"Somebody's done been in de smokehouse," he said, shaking his head.

"Who? How could they?" Nanny asked frantically.

"I don't know Nanny, but dey done went 'n stole Massa Robert's ham and salt," Zeke said, bowing his head sadly.

"Oh Lawdy, oh Lawdy, Massa Robert gonna be in a fit," Nanny Mills exclaimed.

"What's we gonna do, Nanny? What's we gonna do? Massa Robert gonna kill me."

Nanny Mills stepped back, dropped to a chair, buried her face in her hands, and began to cry. She looked up and tearfully told Zeke.

"You gotta find 'em hams. You gotta find 'em. Oh, and de salt. Oh Lawdy, we gots to have dat salt." The two of them continued to try to sort out the disastrous development while their minds were overwhelmed with confusion and fear.

Susannah Russell came into the kitchen with Sarah helping her. She was feeling somewhat better and cheerfully greeted them. She looked into the faces of the two slaves and realized that something was seriously out of order. Nanny was crying and Zeke had the look of death on his face. His lips quivered as he told her what had happened. She was stunned but thought that possibly there was another explanation. She had not seen her husband go to the smokehouse the previous day, but maybe she had simply missed it. But then her logic told her that that would not make any sense. Where else could her husband have possibly put such items? Susannah continued her evaluation as she turned and left the room, and within a minute or so the triple thump of Robert Russell's footsteps could be heard moving rapidly toward the kitchen. He burst through the room, shouting at Zeke as he headed straight toward the back door.

"You git your black ass down there to that smokehouse, nigger. You better find that damn ham and if that salt's gone, you won't eat again 'til Christmas, if ever."

Zeke meekly fell in behind his master as he hobbled down the back steps and waddled toward the smokehouse. Many thoughts rushed through Robert Russell's mind as he pondered what possibly could have happened. Did someone break in? There were already known deserters in the mountains. Could there be a group of them nearby? Could they be responsible? That thought occurred to him, but maybe the old nigger simply had lost his mind. Zeke had left the lantern lit when he returned to the house, and he watched as his master panned the interior of the smokehouse. His head bowed and his lips quivered as he awaited his fate. Robert Russell came out of the smokehouse with his eyes aflame. Zeke bowed his head and began to shake his head side to side, mumbling sadly.

"I swear Massa Russell, I swear I ain't done nothin'," he began his pleading.

Robert Russell closed the door and carefully examined the lock, the chain, and the hasp. He released the chain and stepped back, and his eyes scanned the entire door area. It was clear to him that there was no sign of forced entry.

His rage overwhelmed him as he swirled and turned toward Zeke. Zeke resumed his pleadings and looked into his master's eyes. He could see his master's face now turning to a crimson hue. He dropped to his knees and began to beg, bowing his head.

"Please, Massa, please, I swear I ain't done nothin'."

Bob Russell screamed so loud that Nanny could hear it in the kitchen.

"I trusted you with the key, you crazy old nigger! I trusted you with that damn key!"

Zeke continued to beg, his mumblings now senseless sobs. Bob Russell wielded his cane and swung wildly, crashing it onto Zeke's back with all his force. He switched his cane to his right hand and continued to lash him severely across the back. His anger was so overwhelming that, for the moment, he intended to kill him.

Russell redirected his blows and aimed for the gray turf that covered the old slave's head. He struck him across the back of the skull, cutting him deeply, and blood began to flow. This had no effect on Bob Russell, and he continued to beat him. Zeke instinctively covered his head with his hands and cried out for mercy as the ferocity of the assault increased. Many of the blows were wild and misdirected, glancing off of his hands, head, and neck. Bob Russell wielded the cane overhand, and it came down solidly on the back of Zeke's left hand, the sound indicating a certain fracture. Russell's screaming and Zeke's wailing had not gone overlooked in the house. Nanny was now completely frantic as she raced out the kitchen door. Tripping on her dress, she crashed into the ground, skinning her hands and face. She screamed and cried as she approached them in the midst of the terrible beating Zeke was receiving. He had now drawn himself into a fetal position as Bob Russell continued to strike him, again and again. Nanny began wailing her pleadings well before she reached the two men. The exertion of Bob Russell's terrible deed was by now becoming exhausting, but the beating continued as Nanny reached them.

"Please, Massa, please, ya gonna kill him!" She begged him, now overwhelmed with tears and emotion. She fell over Zeke, covering his body with hers. The sweating and gasping master continued furiously and wildly swinging his cane. He beat Nanny as he had beaten her husband. He struck her in the head several times, but her bonnet with the bundle of hair underneath cushioned the blows. Bob Russell stepped backward and nearly fell. This provided a brief respite for the crying, begging slave woman to look up at him and again plead for mercy.

Delia was still in her nightgown, rushing toward them. She had almost reached them, she too crying and screaming. Sadly, she was a second late as Bob Russell sent one last blow of the cane crashing down on Nanny Mills's face, striking her across the bridge of the nose at a slight angle. The blow broke her nose, and the blood spurted immediately. Nanny's eyes drooped as she fell stunned across her husband's body. Bob Russell raised the cane again as his daughter reached him, screaming, "Please, Papa. No, No."

"You bring back that damn salt and those hams or I'm going to hang your black ass," he shouted in his rage. Delia clutched him tightly as she sobbed into his breast.

"Please stop it, Papa. Please stop it."

The exhausted master was panting as his temper abated to some degree. The two slaves lay in a crumpled heap balled together as their master pushed his daughter to the side and walked away, mumbling his curses as he went. He stopped, turned again, and looked back.

"Find it, or I'll hang your ass."

Delia knelt beside Zeke and Nanny, trying her best to comfort the two victims of Bob Russell's wrath. Nanny was only semiconscious as she turned and looked at Delia, her face smeared with blood from her severely broken nose. Her eyes rolled back and Delia gasped, recognizing the seriousness of her injury.

"Oh God, Nanny, you're hurt bad," she said through her tears. "Let me help you."

Nanny did not respond to Delia's words; she only continued to mumble her husband's name, "Zeke, oh Zeke."

Her sisters rushed to Delia's side. Delia looked into her sisters' eyes with a fear she had never known before.

"They're hurt. I think Papa hurt them real bad."

Zeke was sitting upright as he held his wife in his arms, rocking her back and forth. The two of them held each other while blood spilled from their wounds.

Delia could see her little brother and her mother cowering at the door, staring as if transfixed. Delia now experienced her own rage as she screamed at her sister.

"Mary, get some rags, get some water. Quick, hurry!"

Her two sisters soon arrived with water and clean rags as Delia and her sisters helped the two injured slaves back into the house.

Bob Russell sat at the dining table and calmly ate his biscuits as the women nursed the two slaves in an attempt to stop the bleeding. The normal tranquil atmosphere on Hoopers Creek would not be the same this day, nor ever again.

Chapter 8

―― JUNE 29, 1862 ――

My Dearest Delia,

We have been on the march for days now and we know not what our fate might be. All the men are anxious for what the morrow brings. There has been fighting all around us for days, but for the mercy of God we have seen little of it. The roads and fields are filled with many wounded and dying men. I want to stop and help some of them but I am ordered to keep moving.

There is much talk in camp as to where we will be tomorrow. Captain Cunningham has been called with the other captains to meet with Colonel Rutledge. I fear that sunrise may bring our regiment into deadly contact with the enemy. I can hear young Elisha Garren sobbing as I write. He has received some ominous premonition; he suspects from God that he will be taken tomorrow. His brother comforts him but it seems of little good.

My love for you and thoughts of home weigh heavily on my heart as the image of you burns deeply into my soul. Please know my dearest Delia that if I should go into battle and God takes me my last thoughts shall be of you. Please give my love to Mama and Papa, as I know they worry a great deal about Bill and me. Give my love to my baby brothers as I thank God they are not here in harm's way. If it be God's will that this letter should be my last, know that my soul shall carry your image as I go to face my maker.

With deepest love and affection, I am

>Sincerely yours,
>Joseph

——JUNE 30, 1862——

Glendale, Virginia Captain Solomon Cunningham called his men to formation and waited as Colonel Rutledge ordered the regiment to march. The regiment was part of Confederate General Robert Ransom's brigade that included the 24th, 25th, 35th, 48th, and 49th North Carolina, as well as Zeb Vance's 26th North Carolina Regiment. The brigade muster rolls included the names of more than seven thousand North Carolina men. General Ransom issued the order to march to his colonels. Obediently, they rode back to their regiments and passed the order on to the captains.

Captain Solomon Cunningham called his men to the march. The men of Company H fell into the ranks and began to march down the Virginia peninsula toward the southeast. Along the way they could hear the sounds of battle, rattling and popping in the distance. They were marching toward the unfamiliar town of Glendale, a town that had been the scene of a serious fight only hours before. The sights and sounds of the march gave the men an ominous indication of what was to come. For days time and luck had protected them. But there was no more time and their luck was exhausted.

At nightfall they camped in a beautiful little pasture just northwest of the town. The soldiers had little in the way of rations, but they ate what they could find and tried to rest. The men in gray learned that their brigade

CHAPTER EIGHT

had been attached to Confederate General Huger's division. No one seemed to know whether or not this development might be favorable.

―― JULY 1, 1862 ――

At 4:00 A.M. General Ransom sent for his colonels. The officers assembled around the campfire, and General Ransom gave them their orders for the day.

"Gentlemen," he said in a most serious tone. "General Lee wishes to pursue the enemy with all due speed. We are to assemble the men and begin our march behind General Jackson down the Willis Church Road."

He spoke of General Jackson with reverence in his voice. Jackson had already won fame at Bull Run and in the Shenandoah Valley. The Confederate commander, General Robert E. Lee, had been in charge only a few days. Almost every soldier on both sides already knew who he was. His skill and aggressive style were succeeding in driving the enemy back toward the James River and away from Richmond. The men were in the highest spirits, fully motivated and ready to face the ultimate challenge.

"General Hill has been provided with a guide, Reverend Allen, who is familiar with the ground around the enemy's position. It is a formidable position. When we arrive on the field we will await orders from General Huger as to our exact position."

General Ransom paused.

"Gentlemen, we must drive the enemy from that hill at all hazard. May God go with you."

It took more than an hour to assemble the brigade and begin the march. Willis Church Road was crowded with men and horses. General Jackson's men were halted in front, preventing their advance. There were many wounded as well as cowardly skulkers milling about, which further added to the delay.

At about 1:30 P.M. Joseph heard the sound of an opening artillery barrage to the south of their position. In what seemed like seconds a thunderous roar erupted from the southeast.

"Those are Yankee guns," Will Garren said.

Joseph recognized a bit of fear in his friend's words. The roar continued with the sound of crackling musketry mixing in soon after. Finally the march continued as the men in gray made their way down the road. They moved toward the home of a Mr. C. W. Smith as Joseph heard cheers coming from the ranks in front of him. He glanced at Bill as they wondered what the cheer was all about. Soon the companies in his regiment began to approach the house, and the cheering grew louder. Word passed back through the ranks that their new commander and Stonewall Jackson were up ahead. Eventually, the house and the porch came into view. Standing on the porch were generals Lee and Jackson. Joseph and the other men soon joined in the wild and emotional cheering.

The soldiers became caught up in the moment as Jackson mounted his horse, Little Sorrel, and rode away. General Lee waved in acknowledgment, then went back into the house.

Most of the men had never seen Lee or Jackson, and for them the sighting was an inspiration. The adrenaline flow was almost palpable as pulses quickened and hearts pounded. The noise from the battle grew louder as they were again halted. By now it was 2:30 in the afternoon, and the brigade was still more than a mile away. The brigade was ordered to the right and through a large patch of woods. When they emerged from the woods Joseph was amazed at what lay before him. They had exited behind what was left of Confederate General Magruder's artillery. Many cannons lay broken and smoldering. Many bodies lay bloodied and scattered about, some with their gray uniforms torn from their bodies.

Still the brigade did not move. Through the smoke and the roar in the field beyond them it was evident that a great battle was in progress. The 25th North Carolina Regiment and the 26th North Carolina Regiment, commanded by Zeb Vance, were to take a position on the far right of the Confederate line. Joseph could see General Ransom and the commanders clustered in front of the brigade. A lone officer came riding frantically at full gallop from the direction of the battle. Joseph could see him approaching General Ransom and the other officers, but he could not hear their conversation.

"General Ransom, sir. General Magruder requests your assistance with all due speed, sir. He urgently requests that you advance immediately," the rider shouted.

Colonel Rutledge looked from the officer to General Ransom.

"Sir, should we not move immediately?"

General Ransom looked frustrated and confused.

"But I cannot move. I have no orders from General Huger."

General Ransom grimaced and darted his eyes from side to side. He looked back at the messenger and sternly replied, "Tell General Magruder that I am assigned to General Huger and that I cannot move without orders from him."

The visibly exhausted messenger looked back at General Ransom in utter astonishment. Before he could protest General Ransom shouted, "Go! Go now and report to your commander!"

The officer responded curtly.

"Yes, sir."

He turned his horse back toward the sound of battle and rode away.

Colonel Rutledge and the other regimental commanders were somewhat vexed as to what they should do or say. General Ransom called for a messenger.

"Find General Huger and tell him that General Magruder has requested my assistance and urges me to advance. I await orders from General Huger. Ride with all urgency and find him. Now ride!"

The messenger rode away in full gallop, and the other officers looked toward the battle. From their vantage point they could see thousands of Confederates advancing on Malvern Hill while receiving a murderous fire. Another half-hour went by before the messenger from General Magruder returned. This time he was breathing harder and also bleeding from the face.

"General Ransom, sir. General Magruder begs you to please come to his assistance. He is at the enemy's mercy and must have your help."

Colonel William Clarke, commander of the 24th North Carolina, sheepishly approached General Ransom.

"Sir, should we not move to their aid?"

Frustrated and angry, Ransom shouted his reply, "I still have no orders from General Huger."

Colonel Paul Faison, commander of the 56th North Carolina, pleaded, "But sir, we do not know where General Huger is. I urge you, sir. We must move now."

Robert Ransom was a professional soldier and West Point graduate. To move without orders from his commander conflicted with his professional military training. No doubt though that the sun was setting in the west, and if he were to join in the battle the decision must be made without further delay.

"Gentlemen, form up your regiments and prepare to move on my signal. We will march all the way to the right. We will come in around to the right of General Mahone and try to flank the enemy."

The six colonels rode back to their regiments and called their men to formation. Joseph Youngblood saw Colonel Vance ride by the 25th North Carolina, as he spurred his horse. The horse reared as Vance gave the order for the 26th North Carolina to form. The men of the 25th were already coming to their feet as Colonel Rutledge rode up and began barking his command. The captains in turn followed, and Captain Cunningham called the men of Company H into formation.

The 7,000 men that made up Ransom's brigade began to move to the south. As they proceeded shells began to burst overhead once they were within range of the Union artillery. Men began to falter as their officers urged them on. There were 163 soldiers in Company H now marching in attack formation, 6 rows of approximately 26 men per row. Joseph and his brother found themselves on the back row.

General Ransom rode up and down the line and began to turn his brigade toward the enemy that was clustered menacingly on the hill beyond. The thousands of blue uniforms swirling together in the distance created an ominous image like dark clouds forming before the

CHAPTER EIGHT

storm. Descending a small hill the Confederates in gray entered a long, winding ravine. Soon they came within range of distant musketry. Men began to fall and screams pierced the air. The mass of men ascended the ravine with Captain Cunningham running in front of the men of Company H. He shouted the double-quick order with all the strength he could muster.

All the men began to yell as they ran forward. By this time the Union guns of Buchanan and Griffin's brigades began to turn and lower their muzzles toward the charging men in the ravine. The Union gunners switched to grapeshot and canister, loading and ramming as fast as they could. The exploding shells began to tear gaps through the ranks as the Confederates came into the hellish fire. Their advance was only slowed as they stopped to fire their muskets. The Confederate volleys began to rain in on the Union positions in response to the vicious artillery barrage.

Several cannon blasts struck Company H across the front of their formation. Solomon Cunningham was hit first, and a canister blast tore through the line in front of Joseph, hitting all three of the Garren boys right in front of him. Wounded and bleeding, Cunningham managed to rise to his feet. The injured captain half-ran and half-staggered up and down the line, urging his men down. Joseph could not hear him at first, but as he ran closer to their position he heard him shout, "Take your position and fire, men." Captain Cunningham was hit again and fell crashing to the ground. Joseph fired his musket into the cluster of cannons on top of the hill just west of Crew House. He could see blue uniforms moving into position in front of the cannons as he rushed a few feet forward to where Elisha Garren lay bleeding from the throat and abdomen. His immediate reaction was to roll him over and try to help him. He reached around and grabbed the mortally wounded man and frantically pulled his friend toward him. Joseph's hurried grip had landed at a tear in the soldier's abdomen. He tugged hard, trying to bring the man to safety. The effort caused the tear to open fully as Joseph accidentally pulled Elisha's bowels from his lower body cavity. The gruesome contents spilled onto Joseph's hands. He gasped in horror as he felt the heat and moisture from his neighbor's intestine. Elisha's head drooped and his eyes fell fixed. As Joseph stared into his lifeless face, yet another ball struck Elisha in the back. The stench from the young man's torn body sickened Joseph as he tried in vain to help him. Realizing that Elisha was dead, Joseph rolled him forward against another man he did not recognize. He crawled in behind them and ducked behind the mound created by his two dead comrades.

Will and David Garren lay a few feet away to either side of Elisha, both severely wounded and bleeding. Joseph recovered his musket just in time, for he looked through the smoke toward the hill and was engulfed by fear. Through the fire and blaze of cannon and dense smoke he could see the forming Union soldiers beginning to advance. The air was thick with the smell of burning cordite and the sounds of ferocious gunfire. Mixed with the sounds of battle were the faint, pitiful cries of the wounded.

"Fire, men! Fire!" he heard someone yell.

Instinctively, Joseph quickly loaded and laid the barrel of his Enfield rifle across the body of Elisha Garren, sighted into the enemy, and fired. He knew that he had hit someone, as there was no way to miss. Strangely, he felt nothing at the thought of killing another man, barely noting it as the instinct to survive took control. He rolled over onto his back, continuing to cover himself with the bodies of his comrades and scanning the area behind him as he rammed and loaded his musket. The ravine, both sides of the hill, as well as the area to the rear were covered with hundreds of dying and wounded men. Many soldiers were busy at the same task as he, loading and firing, loading and firing. Joseph could see that many of these courageous men still fighting were wounded.

Joseph cocked his musket, rolled over again, and fired another round into the advancing bluecoats, once again certain that he had made another hit. The blue mass was much closer now, and panic began to grip him. He again rammed the cartridge load into his Enfield, ramming the bullet in behind it and placing the percussion cap on the nipple in just seconds. He rolled back over and cocked the musket at the same time. He fired again, and this time he actually saw the face of the man he killed.

CHAPTER EIGHT

He couldn't run. Certainly he would be shot from behind if he stood. There was no choice but to stay and fight.

As he loaded and turned to fire for the sixth time, he pulled down at the exact moment that he looked into the face of a young boy. His surreal image popped out of the smoke only a few feet in front of him. Joseph's shot struck the boy through the heart just as he was about to fire at Joseph. The youngster fell forward, carried from the momentum of his run, as blood spewed from the gaping wound in his body. The young soldier in blue toppled directly onto Joseph as his body began to convulse. Reflexively he vomited the contents of his stomach. Joseph froze briefly as the ghastly scene unfolded. He screamed in horror as he frantically threw the boy's convulsing body off.

As his instinct for survival took hold, Joseph's mind raced with confusion. He studied his immediate surroundings and tried to determine his best course. Joseph could readily see that there were many more Union soldiers approaching. Even though he was terrified and hindered by the slick dampness of blood and human excrement he fumbled for his weapon and reloaded again.

As he reloaded and turned toward the sea of advancing blue uniforms it now seemed a certainty that Joseph was to meet his maker this day. He knew he could not possibly shoot them all. A strange feeling of relief and then tranquility came over him as he watched the mass of blue advancing. He was going to die and there was nothing he could do about it. Something about that knowledge seemed to calm him. Joseph readied himself again and prepared to fire.

At that moment he heard a terrific cheer and a thunderous volley from the right. Hundreds of musket balls tore into the ranks of the blue uniforms coming down the hill. Almost all of the soldiers in the Union front were either killed instantly or severely wounded. Men in blue fell by the score. The advancing Union line began to falter as the men of the 26th North Carolina moved forward and poured a second volley into their ranks. Colonel Vance himself ran forward among the men.

Joseph looked at him and shouted out loud, "Zeb! Get down!"

His shouts were in vain, for surely only God could hear his words. Vance did not alter his path as the myriad bullets and canisters burst around him. "God is with you, Zeb," Joseph said aloud.

"Dear God, save us all," Joseph mumbled as he watched the scene unfold. He took one last look at Vance, then turned to fire again.

Vance ordered his men down to cover and fire, signaling to them with his outstretched arm. Some of them began to mix in and fill in the gaps where the dead men of the 25th lay among the wounded and the few unhurt. The advancing blue line continued to falter as the men of Ransom's brigade kept up a constant though intermittent fire. By now the smoke was so thick that it was hard to see anything. Joseph simply fired in the direction of where he knew the enemy to be. The smell, the smoke, and the din of battle created an eerie, almost supernatural atmosphere. Joseph loaded and fired although he could no longer see the rounds hitting the enemy before him. His eyes burned from sweat and smoke, but he continued to load and fire into the direction of the enemy.

As the smoke cleared slightly Joseph could see that the Union soldiers had fallen back to their position behind their guns. He silently prayed a prayer of thanksgiving, for God had surely spared him from certain death.

Finally the sun began to settle in the west and the firing began to dissipate. Targets were much harder to identify, and the men slowly began to absorb the awful scene that surrounded them. Joseph continued to stare toward the white house and the hill for fear that the Union army might advance again. He also began to take in the ghastly sights before him. He heard a moan and then a cry for water from a voice that he recognized as Will Garren's. Gently crawling from behind the riddled bodies that had protected him, he reached Will, who was bleeding from the upper left arm and the left side of his chest. Will pleaded for water as he looked into his friend's eyes.

"Please help me, Joseph. I'm hurt bad."

Joseph's eyes tired.

"I know you're hurt, I know, but I'm gonna get you outta here."

CHAPTER EIGHT

The scene that surrounded the pair was completely horrid and frightening. So many of the men were screaming, bleeding, and writhing in pain that the field took on a singular, insect-like crawling effect.

Joseph held Will Garren and pulled him to a safer position. He dragged his friend through a maze of maimed soldiers and discarded equipment. As he held the older bleeding man he began to sob. Suddenly he was overcome with a strange sense of guilt. He had been spared and so many of his friends had not.

Joseph tried to collect himself and concentrate on his duties as nurse for Company H. He pulled a bandana from his pocket and tied it around Will Garren's bleeding upper arm. He whispered to him, "Will, this is gonna hurt. I'm gonna have to drag you outta here." Will Garren only nodded. They heard the whistle of a bullet as the random shot flew over their heads. Joseph Youngblood, still prostrate, began dragging his hometown friend toward the rear of the lines.

As they slowly scooted toward the rear Joseph continued to view the disaster on the field. The cries of the wounded would haunt him for the rest of his life.

But in the darkened confusion of that morbid night one cry was familiar.

"Joseph! Joseph!"

He had now moved Will Garren a few hundred yards from the Malvern Hill battlefield when he heard his brother's voice.

"Bill! Hey, Bill! I'm over here!"

He could barely detect the outline of his brother and another man as they approached through the darkness. David Garren held onto Bill Youngblood, who was helping him along. Garren had a bullet hole clean through the left leg.

"David needs help," Bill said to his brother frantically.

"Will is hurt bad too, I'm afraid. Help me get them to the rear and we'll get a surgeon."

When they were safely behind the battle lines Joseph laid the two men side by side and shouted at his brother to get a surgeon. He tended to the men's wounds as best he could while he waited for help. Finally, his brother returned with a face etched in despair.

"There ain't no help, Joseph. There's thousands of wounded men out on that field. We're on our own."

Joseph looked around to assess the situation. David Garren, still conscious despite the wound through his leg, calmly said, "Hell, I'd rather have you than some damn fool surgeon who'd surely cut my leg off. I've seen you fix horses, cows, and even dogs. Ain't much difference." Then he laid his head back calmly as he placed all his faith in his old friend.

"Bill, can you find me a big bucket or a pan in one of these camps? I've gotta have water."

James Miller from Company I approached carrying Joyce Marion, who had been hit twice.

"Won't somebody help me? Joyce is hurt bad," he pleaded.

"Lay him here," Joseph said calmly. "We need a fire. Build a fire as fast as you can."

He began giving other directions as if he were an officer. Joseph tried to stop the bleeding of the various wounds and dressed them with the few rags he had. He then took off his cross belt and laid it aside. He opened the leather pouch and placed it between two of the wounded men.

Soon his brother returned with a large metal pot.

"I stole it, but I'm sure the Lord won't mind this time," he said with pride at having obtained the precious item. Soon Joseph and the other men had a fire going and the pot of water boiling rapidly. Joseph dropped in the bundle of herbs he had brought from home. Thankful that he had carried them along, he stirred the boiling concoction and wondered whether or not the healing power came from the herbs or the boiling heat.

"As long as it works," he said almost prayerfully.

Joseph moved over to Will Garren. He'd been somewhat encouraged because even though Will's breathing was labored he did not hear any gurgling and he was not coughing up blood. He rinsed his hands in the

CHAPTER EIGHT

boiling water, then opened Will's shirt and felt for the wound. Fortunately he found the bullet lodged between two ribs, and as far as he could tell the body cavity had not been penetrated. The next step was to dowse the knife in water and probe for the bullet.

"It popped out just like a cork in a jug," he said to Will, smiling. Soon he had cleaned and sewn both of Will's wounds.

Joseph worked through the night and into the next morning. His hands were burned and red from the boiling water. More and more wounded men had been brought to him. Sidney Williams and the other Williams boys from Buncombe County brought their brother to him. Sadly the poor fellow bled to death while Joseph worked on him. It was well into the next morning before the ghastly work came to an end. With no training and little help he had treated many. Those who could not find a surgeon often fared the best, if fate placed them in the hands of the nurse from Company H.

Amazingly David and Will Garren seemed to be recovering. The first cousins were overcome with gratitude for the care Joseph had provided. In the desperate quest for survival there had been little time to think of others, but in the solitude of that July evening, David questioned Joseph.

"Do you know where Elisha is, Joseph?" he asked, fearing the answer. Nearing the point of total physical and emotional exhaustion, Joseph nodded his head affirmatively. Tears rolled down his cheeks as he looked at his friend.

"I was with him on the field, David. He's dead."

David looked over at his cousin with tears welling up in his eyes.

"I promised my sister that I'd take care of 'em. What will I tell her?"

CONFEDERATE STATES OF AMERICA
ARMY OF NORTHERN VIRGINIA

CASUALTY LIST
25th North Carolina Infantry Regiment
Battle Of Malvern Hill, Virginia
July 1, 1862

Buncombe County	*Rank*	*Status*
Almon, Henry G.	Private	Wounded
Anders, David H.	Private	Wounded
Arial, Harvy O.	Private	Wounded
Banks, Henry H.	Private	Killed
Barnett, Columbus V.	Corporal	Killed
Boyd, Daniel A.	Private	Killed
Brooks, David W.	Private	Wounded
Bryant, Columbus D.	Private	Wounded
Cannon, Watson R.	Sergeant	Killed
Carson, Newton F.	Private	Wounded
Cartner, Daniel W.	Private	Wounded
Clements, Joseph R.	Private	Killed
Courtney, John H.	Private	Wounded
Dotson, Josiah H.	Private	Wounded
Drake, Elias A.	Private	Wounded
Edmonds, Samuel R.F.	Private	Wounded
Gudger, Jessie Giles	Private	Wounded
Garland, George W.	Private	Killed
Gillespie, James L.	Private	Killed
Holder, Hamilton	Private	Wounded
Hyatt, Samuel P.	Private	Wounded
Ingle, Albert L.	Private	Killed
Joyce, William M.	Private	Wounded
Justice, William W.	Private	Wounded

Knight, Thames M.	Private	Killed
Merrill, Henry C.	Private	Killed
Morgan, Perminter P.	Private	Wounded
Pearson, William I.	Private	Wounded
Penland, Alexander M.	Private	Killed
Pinner, Solomon B.	Private	Killed
Ramsey, Anderson W.	Private	Wounded
Riddle, Marvil M.	Private	Wounded
Whitaker, George W.	Private	Wounded
Whittemore, James B.	Private	Wounded
Williams, Lewis D.	Private	Killed

Henderson County	*Rank*	*Status*
Allen, David J.	Private	Killed
Allison, Isaac	Private	Wounded
Anders, George W.	Private	Killed
Barnwell, John A.	Private	Wounded
Cunningham, Solomon	Captain	Wounded
Enloe, Thomas J.	Private	Wounded
Featherston, Calvin R.	Private	Wounded
Head, Anderson C.	Corporal	Wounded
Garren, David	Private	Wounded
Garren, Elisha	Private	Killed
Garren, Williamson	Corporal	Wounded
Holder, Lyttleton I.	Private	Killed
Ingram, Joel	Corporal	Wounded
Ingram, Robert	Private	Killed
Johnson, Creed F.	Private	Captured
Kuykendall, John Allen	Private	Wounded
Laughter, Hampton	Private	Wounded
Lister, Thomas R.	Private	Wounded
Love, Mathew Nixon	Captain	Wounded
McKillop, Jacob	Private	Killed

Nix, Francis	Private	Wounded
Owenby, Francis M.	Private	Killed
Payne, Cary J.	Private	Wounded
Ruth, Braxton R.	Private	Wounded
Rutledge, Henry Middleton	Colonel	Wounded
Taylor, Jesse W.	Private	Killed
Taylor, Wilbourne	Private	Killed
Vermillian, James M.	Private	Killed
Wheeling, Samuel	Private	Wounded
Cherokee County	*Rank*	*Status*
Aldridge, James E.	Private	Wounded
Johnson, Benjamin C.	Private	Wounded
Jordan, James H.	Private	Wounded
Martin, William J.	Private	Wounded
Parker, William J.	Private	Wounded
Sharp, William W.	Private	Killed
Clay County	*Rank*	*Status*
Smith, George W.	Private	Killed
York, Jeffery S.	Private	Killed
Haywood County	*Rank*	*Status*
Anderson, Jasper N.	Private	Wounded
Anderson, Josiah M.	Private	Killed
Chambers, George W.	Private	Wounded
Buchanan, Julius L.	Private	Killed
Fie, John C.	Private	Wounded
Fry, Neely D.	Private	Wounded
Green, Jeremiah	Private	Wounded
Griffith, William D.	Corporal	Wounded
Inman, William P.	Private	Wounded
McCracken, Joseph M.L.	Private	Wounded

Reese, Isaac	Private	Killed
Smathers, William Burton	Sergeant	Wounded

Jackson County	*Rank*	*Status*
Allen, Joseph, J.	Private	Wounded
Allen, William	Sergeant	Wounded
Bryson, Samuel H.	Private	Wounded
Cogdill, Joseph W.	Private	Wounded
Collins, Joseph A.	Private	Wounded
Cowan, David L.	Private	Wounded
Cowan, James W.	Private	Wounded
Crawford, Andrew J.	Private	Killed
Frizzle, James H.	Private	Wounded
Hemphill, Robert S.	Private	Wounded
Hooper, Daniel H.	Sergeant	Wounded
Keever, David M.	Private	Wounded
Long, Peter G.	Private	Killed
Moody, Joseph H.	Private	Wounded
Moss, John J.	Private	Killed
Norton, William V.	Private	Killed
Parker, Henry H.	Private	Killed
Parker, Samuel J.	Private	Wounded
Parris, Alfred W.	Private	Wounded
Queen, John B.	Private	Killed
Watson, Benson N.	Private	Wounded

Macon County	*Rank*	*Status*
Atkins, Alfred A.	Private	Killed
Blackman, Jacob	Private	Wounded
Bane, George W.	Private	Wounded
Byrd, Robert	Sergeant	Wounded
Kelly, George W.	Private	Wounded
Lilley, Thomas	Private	Wounded

Lockaby, William C.	Private	Killed
Long, Henry C.	Sergeant	Killed
Netherland, George M.	Lieutenant	Wounded
Peeler, Jacob F.	Corporal	Wounded
Sellers, Felix H.	Private	Wounded

Transylvania County	*Rank*	*Status*
Cagle, Leonard C.	Private	Wounded
Case, Elisha G.	Private	Killed
England, David H.	Private	Wounded
Fowler, William H.	Private	Wounded
Hogsed, Walter L.	Private	Killed
Magaha, Thomas J.	Corporal	Killed
Raines, Christopher C.	Private	Wounded
Ray, William C.	Private	Wounded
Scersey, David W.	Private	Wounded
Scruggs, Richard M.	Private	Wounded
Thompson, James W.	Sergeant	Killed
Wilson, John C.	Private	Wounded
Wilson, Robert	Private	Wounded

Chapter 9

—— JULY 1862 ——

Fletcher, North Carolina Normally the Fletcher post office was a lazy, quiet gathering place with a few gentlemen assembled to chat on the front walk or a lone farmer checking in occasionally. Today the post office was the center of activity. Word had spread rapidly throughout the community, and at least two hundred or so of Fletcher's citizens had traveled for miles for an anxious visit. The casualty lists from Virginia had arrived and had been posted.

Delia was weak and jittery as she began to climb the stairs. She observed poor Mrs. Allen sitting on the dock screaming and wailing at the loss of her son David. She soon overheard the story of how David was killed at a place in Virginia called Malvern Hill. She also overheard Reverend Patty lament, "There are so many. So many."

Apparently one of the Barnwell boys had been shot in both thighs, and many more men had been killed or wounded. Delia worked her way through the cluster of people, squeezing in between the pressing crowd to read the list. The men of Henderson County were posted in alphabetical order, and Delia immediately dropped her eyes to the end of the list, searching for any names that began with the letter Y.

An overwhelming sense of relief came over her as she realized that Joseph's name did not appear. With her heart still pounding and her mind strained with trepidation she searched for her brother James. To her great relief, his name was nowhere to be found either. She stepped back, allowing others to approach, and immediately offered a prayer, thanking God for protecting Joseph and James. Still keenly cognizant of the pain in the faces and eyes that surrounded her, she decided that the people of this valley would never forget Malvern Hill.

Delia returned to the buggy and joyfully gave her father the good news. In a rare display of emotion, Bob Russell bowed his head in demonstrative relief. Delia unhitched the buggy, and the two of them continued the journey along Asheville Road. They turned down by Calvary Episcopal Church and traveled the short distance to The Meadows, the home of Daniel and Mimi Blake. The Blake home was a solidly built mansion. Delia always marveled at the huge square structure. It had many rooms, all of which were ornately decorated, and she loved the high ceilings and large windows trimmed in polished oak. It was one of the finest homes to be found in the upper Carolinas.

Still somewhat shaken from the emotional trip to the post office, Delia found that steadying her father was also quite a challenge. She stared in appreciation of the stately Blake home as they approached the front door.

Mimi Blake cheerfully offered her greetings and invited them into the house.

"Come in. Please sit," Daniel Blake said, gesturing to Robert Russell. Russell settled himself in the rust-colored armchair and motioned for Delia to bring his leather case. She dutifully handed him the case as he took his seat. Mimi Blake then escorted her to the other side of the parlor, and the two of them perched on small chairs by the piano.

Delia was pleased that she was being permitted to remain in the room. Mimi inquired about the health of Delia's mother as well as that of her siblings, and they engaged in small talk until the men began their discussion. Mimi Blake quickly changed her focus, and it was apparent to Delia that she was not the only one intent on listening to the men's conversation.

"Thank God your boy is okay, Bob."

CHAPTER NINE

"That battle at Malvern Hill must have really been terrible," he added.

"Yeah, but at least we whooped 'em. Our boys ran those Yankees clean out of Virginia," Bob Russell said almost defiantly. Blake wasn't sure if he was trying to convey confidence to his friend or to himself.

"You know, Daniel, we are going to need more money and more men. Even though the Congress passed that Conscription Act, we're still gonna need every single body we can get," Bob Russell said.

"I know," Blake replied.

Then he looked at Russell inquisitively and said, "Don't you think maybe the Yankees will sue for peace now?"

"I don't know, but I sure hope so," Bob Russell responded.

"This war has already lasted longer than anyone had foreseen. Many good boys have died on both sides."

"I don't know if conscription is going to be fully accepted by our people though. A lot of folks are really riled up about it."

"I know, but it had to be done. There wasn't any other choice. Too many men are choosing not to volunteer. And that brings me to ask you about Freddy. Is he gonna go back?"

"Now Bob, you know officers can resign. He doesn't have to go back," Blake responded, somewhat offended.

"Yes, but you'd think he might want to. He is a healthy young man and most of the others have gone," Russell said with disappointment.

"Well, Fredrick is staying here. There's a lot he can do to help by staying with me," Blake said. "We're going to be raising money and supplies for the troops, and we are helping others organize regiments."

Blake continued his defense.

"I was in Asheville just last week. A Colonel Lawrence Allen formed a new regiment in Madison County, and it was designated as the 64th North Carolina Regiment. There's also a company of men from Polk County set to go over and join them, and then the 64th will be over 900 strong. Company B was raised here in Henderson, and they will also join up with the 64th," Blake said.

"Yes, I know. The whole Jackson family joined that regiment. J. L.

Ward is a captain," Bob Russell added.

"With all of our Henderson County men and B. T. Morris's Company out of Polk County, it should make a fine regiment," Blake said. "By the way, Bob. There were three men from Mitchell County who signed up here in Henderson County with Company B. You might know them. I think they did some work for you. They've done a lot of work around here."

"Who would that be?" Bob Russell inquired.

"A man named Matthias Dees and his two sons," Blake said.

"Hmm, I don't know much good about those fellows. I guess their work would pass. But they are a questionable bunch," Russell said.

"Yea, but I believe that they're just poor, Bob. That Dees appears to be a deeply religious man, a reverend I think."

"Well, I'm not so sure about that," Bob Russell replied suspiciously.

Delia bristled when she overheard the discussion about the Dees men. She had to restrain herself from speaking her mind. It was obvious to her that the Dees men were responsible for the disappearance of the hams and the salt from their smokehouse. She knew Zeke didn't do it, and there were no other suspects. Besides, the Dees gang had left just that morning. She wondered why her father could not see it. As she assessed her father's remarks since that terrible day, she had calculated that he probably did know. He was just too ashamed to admit that the crew he hired had stolen from him and, even worse, that he had so wrongly punished Zeke and Nanny.

"Have you heard any more about the value of our currency?" Blake asked Russell.

"No, I have not, but I'm really concerned. It already takes twice as many Confederate dollars to buy anything as it ought to."

"Yes, and as much as you and I have invested in Confederate money things could get disastrous if the valuations keep dropping."

After the men resolved to keep in close touch, Delia and her father said good-bye to the Blakes and thanked them for their hospitality. They returned to the buggy and climbed aboard. As the slave handed Delia

CHAPTER NINE

the reins she looked over at the grand stone structure and wondered why the Blakes' son was too good to fight with the rest of the men. She also wondered about the new Confederate government that her father seemed to be so proud of. Why would such a government pass a law that would allow a healthy twenty-four–year-old like Freddy Blake to sit at home in wealthy comfort while Joseph, her brother, and the others risked their lives defending them? She had been able to gather that if enlisted men elected not to serve they could be arrested as deserters and sometimes even shot. But it seemed obvious that the wealthy were often given rank, and then they could just choose to resign and come home. She not only didn't understand this but she also didn't like it. It wasn't fair at all. If Joseph had been wealthy, maybe he would have been an officer and maybe he would now be on his way home.

> My Dearest Delia,
>
> I can't begin to tell you of the suffering I have seen. The horrors of Malvern Hill never leave my mind and I shall be haunted to my last breath with these awful visions. As you probably know thousands were wounded and killed. Both Captain Cunningham and Colonel Rutledge were wounded. There is talk among the men that maybe the Yankees won't come back. May God make it so.
>
> I know you have heard about the Conscription Act. While I am desperately forlorn about the prospect of having to remain, I take heart in the fact that I have been granted a furlough. So not all the news is bad, my dear. I will be able to come home soon! Only a few at a time will be furloughed and they're letting the wounded go first. That's if they are well enough to travel. Alas, so many are not. Judging from the roster, I should be coming home in the middle of September. Some of the

men think that this war will be over soon. Others think it will be over by Christmas. So you see, one way or the other, our time apart will be short-lived. Soon I will be able to hold you and to plan our life and our marriage. I hope your mother, father, and sisters are all well. My brother Bill and James Russell are here with me and God thus far has protected us. As I close my eyes to sleep each night I remember your grace and beauty and it comforts me. Remember us all in prayer.

With love,
Joseph

Matthias Dees sat on the stump whittling a hickory stick, watching the other men out of the corner of his eye. He leaned over and whispered to his son Rupert, who was sitting on the ground beside him.

"Reckon all these regiments are paying a $15 bounty?"

"I ain't got nary an idy," Rupert answered with his hat drooping over his eyes.

"Seems a heap o' money to be layin' on a man jes' for signin' up," Rupert added.   Dees laughed loudly.

"Hell, yea, it's a heap for signin', but it ain't near enough for fightin'. I ain't gettin' my arse shot off for no $15 note. I reckon if a feller was a thinkin' right, he might just slip around here, there, and yonder 'n go to signin' a bushel of times. Don't ya think, boys?" he questioned in a sly and calculating tone. Their devious conversation was interrupted as one of the officers walked by.

"God bless you, brother. I'm praying for you," Dees chirped at the officer. The man nodded and continued walking.

"Rupert, the way I figger it the longer a man hangs 'round here with these damn fools, fightin' a rich man's war, the more likely he is to git a musket ball up his arse. Me and you knows these here mountains as good as any. All we got to do is wait 'til it gets good 'n dark and then we'll skeedaddle. With all 'em men off fightin', leaves a lot of fishin' to be done," Dees continued devilishly.

Rupert shrugged, looked back at his father, and contorted his face into a sly grin.

"Yep, and ya know with all 'em boys off fightin' it sure leaves a bunch of purdy gals that ain't got no man." They grinned at each other.

The newly formed 64th North Carolina Infantry Regiment was camped along the French Broad River, just south of Marshall. It was warm, and due to summer weather the foliage was thick and green. The rhododendron and laurel so common to Madison County were dense and twisted all along the steep slopes above the river. It was well after midnight when the summer shower began to pelt down on the leaves of the forest and the tents in the field. For Matthias Dees and his two boys, this perfect summer shower and the early morning darkness provided convenient and easy cover for their departure. The three of them slipped quietly through the camp and out among the trees. Soon they had picked up the trail that wound up the steep slope east of the river. In a short period of time they were out of sight and beyond detection. The Dees boys returned to their element.

The Russells were used to visitors these days. It seemed to Delia that someone was always coming and going. Today's visitors were old friends. W. W. Hutchison was a prominent man of modest wealth. He had a large family, and his son John was considered a genuine hero, his battlefield exploits now well known to every family with a connection to the 25th North Carolina Infantry.

Those who knew W. W. Hutchison simply called him "Hutch." He had another son who was accompanying him on the visit to the Russell farm that day. His name was Daniel Washington Hutchison, but most everyone called him "Wash." Delia had always liked Wash, but most of all she respected this strange figure of a man. He was in his early twenties, strong and healthy. But Wash Hutchison had not joined the others in the army because he had no feet. Tragically, Wash had gotten lost in the snow as a toddler. Forced to wander through the night, he'd been found near dead the next morning. His life was saved, but his frozen feet had to be amputated. But unlike others with such disabilities, this young man had overcome many obstacles and was an amazingly wise and capable human being. He moved ably about on his knees, which were covered by homemade leather knee shoes that tied around his legs. He had developed great upper arm and chest strength. Surprisingly he had become a logger and a woodworker, buying a small patch of land on Souther Road and building a modest cabin for himself. Delia had seen Wash at work. When trees were cut, other men would run clear. But Wash simply watched carefully, then maneuvered swiftly around the trunk to ensure that he was clear of the falling tree. He had figured out how to do many things in spite of his peculiar disability.

Hutch and his son Wash entered the yard while Delia walked out to greet them. She was used to Wash's disability but was still impressed with how easily he was able to maneuver.

"Come on in. Papa's in the study," she said pleasantly.

"Thank ye, ma'am," Hutch responded as they followed her into the house.

Robert Russell sat in his study deep in thought. He worried daily about finances and was continually devising solutions that would restore his financial stability.

"Howdy, Hutch, how ya doing?" he asked reflexively.

"Doing good, Bob. Doing pretty good. You know my boy, Wash?"

"Yea, howdy Wash," Russell responded.

"What can I do for y'all today?" he asked.

Both men took a seat while Wash popped up into a chair like a bird jumping from limb to limb.

"Bob, I wanna talk to you about building a hideout," Hutch told him in a serious tone.

"A hideout? What exactly do you mean? A hideout for what?" Russell asked him.

"In case the war reaches here," Hutch replied calmly.

"The war coming here?" Russell asked in apparent disbelief.

"Yes, I think we should get ready, just as a precaution. I've got family to protect, my wife and daughters. I'm real worried about it," Hutch said, hanging his head.

"We've got to protect the women," Hutch added.

"Hutch, I don't think you have to worry about the war coming here. Our boys whipped 'em pretty good at Fredericksburg, and lots of folks think the Yankees have had about enough. Besides, they couldn't get here. We're hundreds of miles away, and they'd have to come through our mountain passes. Our men would cut them to pieces if they tried it," Russell said, trying to convince himself as well as the Hutchisons.

Delia listened anxiously. Her father had always told her that the war would never reach western North Carolina because the mountains protected them, but she wondered. He had been wrong about the money. Maybe he was wrong about this too.

"Maybe so," Hutch responded, "but I don't see why it'd hurt anything to be ready just in case."

"What ya got in mind, Hutch?" Russell asked him.

"My boy Wash here has a good plan. Tell him, son."

The strange young man with no feet suddenly broke his silence, spurting out his defensive ideas. Obviously he'd given the whole concept lots of thought.

"Mr. Russell, if you go up the road past my new cabin, it's only a half mile or so uphill to the top of a little knoll. From the top of that knoll you can see most every corner of the valley. We'd be able to spot anybody coming or going, without them knowing we're there. That little hill has a curl in it, kind'a like the end of a pig's tail. It's natural ground, just hankering to be a dugout. I can dig back in there, put logs against the back wall and the sidewalls, then put a lean-to roof over it, and you'd never be able to see it from Hoopers Creek valley."

The strange young man reported all this in serious military style.

"That sounds like a mighty big project to me. Where you gonna get the manpower to build such a thing around here?" Russell asked with skepticism.

Wash Hutchison was taken aback and clearly offended.

"Why, I can do it, sir!" he said defiantly. "I need some tools and supplies, but I can do it mostly by myself. I'll only need another man when I hoist some big logs into place. That Youngblood kid Pinkney, he's willing to help some, and I was hoping I could count on your man, Zeke. He could help me with the heavy part."

"If you could help us with supplies and let Zeke help with the heavy stuff we could have us a right comfortable and safe place to hide out if we needed it," Hutch added.

"I don't know," Russell responded.

Delia could not sit in silence any longer.

"Papa, why not? The supplies can't cost that much, and I know Wash can do it with just a little help."

"I don't know. I don't have enough help around here as it is. All my boys are gone and Zeke can barely get everything done," Russell said.

"Papa, I'll help some so Zeke won't get behind here. I'll see to it. Besides, Ma's not well and you've got a bad leg. It's not like we can get around as quickly as others might be able to. We might need a safe place to go, and this would give us a surefire answer should something happen," Delia said thoughtfully.

Robert Russell paused for a minute to think about this plan. He didn't want to admit that he feared invasion or that he couldn't endure such a small financial burden.

"All right, y'all go ahead and build your little hideout. It's a waste of time and money, but if it makes y'all feel better, then go ahead."

"But I ain't buying no nails though; you're gonna have to do it with notched logs," he told the group in a pious tone. The footless man responded quickly.

CHAPTER NINE

"No problem, Mr. Russell. I built my cabin with no nails. I can do it." Wash looked over at Delia, taken by her charm and warmed by her support. Delia looked back at Wash Hutchison fondly. What a man, she thought. If Wash had feet like anybody else, he'd be at the very front of the battle lines in Virginia.

"Good, then it's decided," Delia said in a way that was designed to commit her father to support the project. "Mr. Hutchison, when you need Zeke please let me know a day or two ahead of time and I'll arrange to get him up there."

Delia's father gave her a strange and challenging look but said nothing.

Chapter 10

―― SEPTEMBER 1862 ――

Leesburg, Virginia Joseph could hear men stirring outside his meager tent. What is it this time? he wondered. Solomon Cunningham was back, having recovered from his wounds. He pulled back the flap on Joseph's tent as he shouted, "Fall in formation, boys. The colonel is coming over to say something."

Joseph roused himself and soon joined the other soldiers in the large clearing in front of their camp.

It was a brisk morning and none of the men were very pleased to be called out at such an early hour. At first Joseph feared they might be under attack or something, but the lieutenant had assured him that the formation was for an announcement only. Knowing this, Joseph was able to relax a bit. He didn't care what the announcement was. His furlough was only two days away, and that was the only thing on his mind. He had been quite lonely since his father had sent a paid substitute for his brother Bill. Will and David Garren were still home on wounded leave, and Elisha was dead. While there were plenty of men around, the absence of his brother and his best friends had been difficult. His thoughts drifted, as they often did, to Delia.

"I can put up with two more days of marching and drilling, because I'll soon see my sweetheart," he stated dreamily as he walked with the others.

Colonel Rutledge stood before the regiment and shouted as loud as he could.

CHAPTER TEN

"Gentleman, General Lee has reorganized the army. I am most pleased to report that our brigade will now be part of Longstreet's corps, Walker's division. You have served honorably and bravely through great adversity. It now falls upon us to do our duty once more. General Lee has announced that we shall be taking this war to the enemy. You are to prepare your belongings for the march. We will break camp and begin the march into Maryland at daybreak tomorrow."

Rutledge scanned the faces of his men, half-expecting to hear a cheer. He had hoped that they would at least be happy about joining Longstreet's corps. What he saw were only stunned expressions and what he heard was silence. After an uncomfortable moment he prepared to dismiss the men, but then he hesitated and stopped.

"Oh yes, one more thing: all furloughs are canceled," he said calmly. The colonel dismissed the regiment, then walked away, leaving the men standing stiffened by shock and disappointment.

Slowly and quietly at first, the men began to groan and grumble.

"What in the hell?" one man finally said loudly. Others were visibly puzzled and shook their heads in disbelief.

"I thought we got in this war because they was invadin' us."

"Now we go off and invade them?" said another.

"If I was them Yanks that'd make me mighty mean. Give me a hankerin' to fight even harder."

"Hell, they'll also be closer to their supplies."

"Makes no sense."

"That's why we got in this thing; they was threatening our homes. It just ain't right!"

Joseph rushed to pull Captain Cunningham aside.

"Sol, please God; I've got to have my furlough! All the other men got one, I gotta have it!" he said, pleading passionately.

"Joseph, you know I can't do anything about it," Cunningham replied sadly.

"Sol, I ain't goin'. I've done all they asked me. I've marched from here to hell and back, I've worked and I've killed. They got to give me that furlough!" he said with tears now gathering in his eyes.

"Now Joseph, calm down and for God's sake don't go thinking up nothin' stupid. Ain't you heard there's a war on? If you run off and get caught, you'll be shot," Cunningham warned with genuine concern in his voice.

"What the hell is the difference? They're gonna keep on 'til we're all killed anyway," he muttered as he walked away.

Cunningham followed and put his arm around Joseph.

"I know you love that gal back home, but you gotta hang on. The best way to get back to her for good is to go on and let's get this done. Listen, if we take this war up to them for a while maybe they'll back off and leave us alone. How would you feel if you ran off, got yourself caught, and then the war ended right after this Maryland campaign? Don't risk it, Joseph. Hang on now. We need you. I promise you'll be the first man furloughed when the colonel says we can have 'em again."

The wise and compassionate Captain Cunningham backed away, leaving Joseph to his tears.

All through the night Joseph wrestled with his deep disappointment. No matter how he tried to calm himself, the anguish and sadness enveloped him. The massacre at Malvern Hill had shaken his entire belief system. Joseph couldn't help but wonder if the Cause really justified this massive destruction of human life. On the other hand, he had witnessed such bravery and inspiration of spirit. Surely God was present in those selfless, heroic acts. Adding to his internal struggle was the idea of invading someone else's home. He got up repeatedly during the night and often contemplated running as he quietly shuffled about the cold camp. He knew that the sentries had been doubled. The officers were smart enough to expect that some might try to desert, rather than face another hard march and possibly another deadly fight. Joseph thought about Sol Cunningham and what he had said. He knew that if there was one man in the whole army who'd keep his word, it was Sol. The sky had begun to turn a beautiful pink by the time Joseph was able to reach his decision and regain control of his emotions. He would march one more time and then go home with or without permission. Pushing himself to that quiet place inside, he prayed, "God, just help me make it through this last march. I swear I'll never kill again. Please, Lord, just get me through this last fight and get me home."

——— SEPTEMBER 17, 1862 ———

Sharpsburg, Maryland It was three o'clock in the morning when Ransom's brigade moved to the far right of the Confederate line away from Antietam Creek. The men were exhausted from the march and the expectant grip of the excruciating wait. A great many of the men tossed and turned in their bedrolls, while many had passed out in exhaustion hours earlier. When the sun finally peeked over the rolling hills of Maryland, the 25th North Carolina Regiment and Ransom's brigade found themselves in a safe, inactive position. At about 9:00 A.M. Captain Cunningham came with the formation order.

Joseph and the others were alert and ready despite their exhausted physical state. Soon they were marching through Sharpsburg as the citizens of the town peered at them curiously. Someone in the ranks suggested that they were marching around to the far left of the Confederate lines. The sounds of battle could be heard in the distance and seemed to grow louder with each step. The march began to remind Joseph of that day at Malvern Hill. He quickly pushed the memory aside and tried to concentrate on one thought: "Get this done and get my furlough." He began to repeat his earlier prayer, "Please God, get me through this. Let me go home." He then steeled himself for what was to come.

The march continued until the regiment moved around Dunker Church and into a patch of woods. They took position to the left of Confederate General Barksdale's men. During their march through the woods they met men of Hood's and Early's units leaving. Immediately behind them was Union General John Sedgwick's men marching forward in force. They proceeded confidently, having just celebrated the success of routing the men in gray and being totally unaware that the Confederates had been reinforced. As the men in blue marched toward the woods and the Confederate position, Ransom's brigade formed and prepared for the Union advance. The clatter of shouldering muskets rattled through the Confederate ranks.

Joseph took his position and waited. The minutes seemed like hours as he prayed silently for relief. Soon the order to fire was given, and a murderous volley poured into the oncoming Union soldiers. Joseph reloaded and fired another round. Smoke and flame filled the air. The smell of burning cordite once again tortured the nostrils of the soldiers in the ranks. Both fear and adrenaline now energized Joseph and the others. They loaded and fired as fast as they could. The Union lines faltered, and the men in blue began to fall back. Relief fell over him as Joseph heard the order to cease-fire. The roar of battle dimmed all around them as they held the line and waited.

The men of the 25th paused anxiously as they watched the officers preparing for the advance.

"Oh, God, no!" the man next to Joseph exclaimed.

"They'll march us right into their guns," he said, shaking his head. But before the order to charge could be given the Union men had reorganized. Their blue ranks were reformed, and they were advancing again. This time they were allowed even closer before the order to fire was given. The Confederates again opened up on Union General Sedgwick's men with a volley that sounded like crackling thunder. The flame and the smoke roared out of the musket barrels as hundreds of balls could be seen tearing into the blue uniforms. The return fire was scattered and ineffective.

"Why don't they stop?" Joseph shouted as he rammed his musket. He could see scores of them falling to the ground and could hear the screams of agony through the boom and clatter of gunfire. The Confederates kept firing and the men in blue kept advancing. It was developing into a terrible slaughter. Finally the blue line faltered and the Union soldiers fell back.

"Thank God. Please don't come back."

But much to Joseph's astonishment the Union soldiers tried to advance for a third time, finally retiring after more losses.

CHAPTER TEN

These mountain boys were now veterans, and any illusions about the enemy had long since dissipated. They now looked across the field at men they respected. These men, like themselves, were courageously fighting and bravely dying for their country. It sickened Joseph as he looked over the rolling ground at the dead and dying men in blue. He knew they'd come again if they had to.

Joseph desperately hoped that the battle would end. Unfortunately, he soon learned that the Union army had a better idea than advancing at them head-on. Artillery batteries had been moved into position on the opposite hill. The Union gunners could be seen working in the distance, and soon shells were whistling into the nearby woods. The distance was great and the gunner's aim less than perfect, but still the effect was frightening. The men wanted to move, but General Ransom held them. Shells burst about them throughout the afternoon, but the Union infantry made no further attempt to advance. As the day wore on the men began to hope that maybe they'd be spared. The artillery continued intermittently as the sun settled behind the rolling Maryland hills.

The 25th North Carolina Infantry Regiment had fared well. There were only a few dead and a scattering of wounded. Today had been a good day for the 25th, but not for others. That night Lieutenant Henry Garren, an old friend and neighbor and a cousin to Joseph's good friends, came into camp. He was in the 35th, another of Ransom's regiments, and was accompanied by a nice-looking young black man named George Mills, a servant to Lieutenant Garren's captain, Watt Bryson. He'd been allowed to travel with the regiment. Slaves weren't allowed to join the Confederate army at that time, although George had tried.

"Joseph, can you help us?" Henry asked, his voice tempered with sadness.

"Why, what is it?" Joseph asked.

"Watt was killed today, and his body is still out there somewhere."

Upon hearing the words the poor black man with Henry burst into tears.

"George here was raised up with Watt. They was like brothers."

The young black man continued sobbing uncontrollably as Lieutenant Garren went on.

"You see, George here promised Watt's daddy that he'd bring Watt home. We want to go out there and find him. I know about where he is. We got some others to help, and I thought maybe you'd want to help too," Henry said sadly.

Joseph was overcome with grief; the Bryson family were friends and the news of Watt's death hit him hard. He choked back his own emotions as he wondered how long this could go on. Joseph figured he'd gotten through the day fairly well. Now this.

"Sure, I'll help, but let's don't get anybody else shot."

The small cadre of Henderson County men snaked their way out onto the dark and bloody field. Lieutenant Garren led them, and soon they found the body. Captain Watt Bryson had been shot through the chest, and it appeared to Joseph that he had probably died instantly.

Poor George Mills was devastated as they carried the body back to their lines. He lay on the ground holding his dead master in his arms, rocking and chanting incoherently. The scene was so morose that many of the men watching were also driven to tears.

"I gots ta take Massa Watt home," the poor black man managed to blurt through his mournful state. "I gotta take him home!" He screamed, half-crying as he said it.

Lieutenant Henry Garren returned after a brief departure.

"Men, the colonel says he can go. George is gonna need money to get the body home. Everybody, give me all you can spare," he said knowing all would be willing to provide what they could. The men collected their money, and Joseph gave all he had left. He approached the poor fellow and patted him on the shoulder.

"I'm so sorry, George. I know some of your folks back home. I believe you're kin to Zeke Mills and his wife that lives on the Russell farm, aren't you?" Joseph asked in an attempt to comfort the man. George looked up at Joseph and nodded his head in acknowledgment.

CHAPTER TEN

"Yeah, Zeke be my uncle. Does ya know 'im?

"Yes, I know him. Delia Russell is my fiancée. I'm going to marry her soon as I get home."

Lieutenant Garren interrupted them.

"George, you and some of the men bring Watt with me and we'll get him on a wagon. We'll get you back to Virginia and you can take him home."

Joseph turned back to George Mills.

"If you see Delia when you get home, will you tell her I miss her, tell her I'm thinking of her, and I'm gonna come home?"

George was regaining control and managed a wobbly smile.

"Yez, sir, Mr. Youngblood. I tells her fo' ya."

Joseph patted George Mills on the back, shook hands with Garren, then returned to his regiment deeply saddened by the experience. He knew that the Brysons would never get over the loss of their son.

Through the night the 25th remained in the same position. After a long and tense night with the painful cries of the wounded filling the air, the sun rose over the battlefield the morning of the 18th. The Confederate left remained stationary while rumors circulated among the men, many speculating and passing on disturbing information about the Confederate right and a big fight over a bridge that spanned Antietam Creek. Joseph considered that maybe God had intervened somehow and answered his prayer. They had been moved from the Confederate right all the way around Dunker Church to the West Wood on the Confederate left. He hadn't appreciated the long forced march at the time, but now he suspected that it might have saved his life. He only wished God had done the same for Watt Bryson.

All through the day the men waited. From experience they knew that the brave men in blue might surprise them at any time or, worse yet, their own officers might order them to march toward the Union-occupied hill. The order never came and neither did the men in blue. Both sides simply held their positions and waited.

The soldiers in line were always watching the officers behind them for some signal or indication of what was to come. Joseph saw the riders and then he saw Captain Cunningham approaching.

"Joseph, come with me," he said firmly.

Joseph fell in behind him and followed him to the rear. There was an unfamiliar officer waiting with Colonel Rutledge.

"Is this the man?" the stranger asked, looking straight at Joseph.

"Yes, that's him," Cunningham replied curtly.

Joseph was stricken with fear. What could possibly be behind this? Why did it involve him? He had told no one about his plans to leave. He was sure that he hadn't told a living soul.

"We have many wounded," the stranger said sadly.

"I understand that you have a surgeon's skills?"

"Sir, I'm not a surgeon, I'm just a nurse," Joseph said humbly.

"He's better than most any surgeon in the army," Captain Cunningham blurted out confidently.

"He saved more men at Malvern Hill than most surgeons there. And he did it without cutting off a single leg or arm."

The stranger looked at him with apparent disbelief.

Uncertain as to where this was leading, Joseph continued his humility.

"I don't know how to amputate, sir."

"Guess it don't matter if he's the best or the worst. He's needed real bad one way or the other. Come with me, soldier."

Joseph looked at Colonel Rutledge and Captain Cunningham seeking approval.

"Go on now, go with him. They need you," Colonel Rutledge said with approbation.

Joseph joined several other men who were gathered nearby. The small group walked at a fast pace behind the officer. One of the men said that he thought they were headed toward the town of Sharpsburg.

"Yes, I think that's where we're headed. My regiment marched through here yesterday. Looks like we're going back in that direction," Joseph added as he pointed.

The officer leading them didn't turn around. He maintained his

CHAPTER TEN

swift and resolute gait. He seemed to be in a hurry to get these men into town.

Soon they approached the outskirts of the bustling small village. Joseph could not believe his eyes. There were people moving in every conceivable direction. Wagons and horses were coming and going. Men were carrying other men. Wounded were being unloaded at every house and building. The moans and cries of the injured created a macabre, morbid atmosphere in the streets. The citizens of the town had opened their homes to the wounded, and the women fluttered and scurried about, taking charge of much of the activity.

The young Virginian who'd come in the little procession with Joseph was taken aback.

"My God, there's hundreds of them! What are we to do?" he said, running his hand from his forehead down the length of his face.

Joseph looked back at the young man.

"Were you at Malvern Hill?" Joseph asked calmly.

"No, this is my first," the young man said with a sickened expression.

"Well, if I had to guess, I'd say all the wounded ain't here yet," Joseph told him. The young man looked back at him as if in shock.

Joseph approached a bloodied man with a splotchy red apron that had once been white. He was standing over a soldier on the side of the street and appeared to be a surgeon.

"Sir, what do you want us to do?" Joseph asked.

The visibly exhausted man turned to him and in exasperation told him, "Just pick out someone and go to work. There's plenty to do."

Joseph looked away from the surgeon and turned back to the young Virginian.

"What's your name?" he asked calmly.

"Jacob, it's Jacob," the young man answered.

"Well, Jacob, looks like we've got another Malvern Hill here. We're on our own. Many of these men won't get any help lessen it comes from us. Come with me," he said, taking charge.

"We might be able to save some of them."

Before Joseph could proceed an officer with an escort approached him. He was a major and seemed to be in authority.

"Come with me, soldier. I have a wounded man you must treat."

Joseph and Jacob followed the officer into a small house on the main street. Inside, two Confederate soldiers stood guard outside a bedroom. The guards snapped to attention as the major approached. The major ignored them and led Joseph into the room.

The officer turned to Joseph and gruffly ordered him, "Treat this man immediately; he must be taken back to Virginia as soon as possible."

Joseph looked at the young man in astonishment. He wore civilian clothes but was neat-looking and seemed out of place. He calculated that the man was about his age.

Before Joseph could speak the major continued. "This man is a spy. As soon as you can get him ready, I'll be back for him."

The major marched out of the room, leaving Joseph and Jacob to treat the mysterious stranger.

Joseph approached the small bed where the man was stretched out. He could see that his right arm was wrapped. Joseph looked at the poor man and could see that he'd lost a lot of blood. His face was ashen and he suffered from a cold sweat.

"Let me have a look at that arm, mister."

"I'm not a mister. I'm Captain William Palmer of the 15th Pennsylvania Cavalry," the young man said defiantly.

"Don't make no difference to me, Captain. I'm just trying to heal ya." Joseph spoke to the young man in a kind and considerate tone. He felt sorry for him. It was apparent that the man was very young, and he probably had a sweetheart and a family back home like Joseph did. Joseph looked at his youthful features and wondered how such a man ended up in such a predicament. He was small with dark hair and a clean-shaven face. He had dark eyes surrounded by smooth, handsome features. He conducted himself with dignity despite the pain and his serious physical condition.

CHAPTER TEN

"Tell me, Captain Palmer, how'd you end up here?" Joseph asked as he worked on the man's arm.

"I might ask you the same thing."

Joseph laughed and nodded in agreement. "Yea, I reckon so. I wish I knew."

"I suppose I got here the same way you did," Palmer answered.

Joseph contemplated his response while he continued to clean the wound.

"I reckon I thought I was doin' the right thing by my folks, seeing how y'all come down and started this war," Joseph said in a low, monotone voice.

"We didn't start this war, you people did. Bombing Fort Sumter and defending slavery."

Joseph stopped briefly and looked into Palmer's eyes and responded firmly. "I ain't fightin' for slavery. I don't give a damn for slavin', never have."

Joseph finished cleaning the wound and began sewing up the gash. "How come that major is calling you a spy?"

"They caught me out of uniform, that's all," Palmer replied.

"That's all?" Joseph repeated in a challenging tone.

"Don't they shoot people who are spies?"

"God's will be done," Palmer answered without any sign of fear.

"Have you got family back home?" Joseph asked.

"Yes, my mother suffers considerable due to me being in the army. We're Quakers, and my family is opposed to violence."

"I reckon my family is against it too," Joseph responded.

The two talked on as Joseph continued his treatment. The more they talked the more they found they had in common.

When the major returned Joseph had completed treating the wound. He spoke up firmly when the Confederate officer approached.

"This man is not a spy, sir. He is a captain in the 15th Pennsylvania Cavalry."

"The man is out of uniform. That makes him a spy," the major responded.

"Hell, if that's so then half the Confederate soldiers are spies. Most of the men in my brigade don't have uniforms anymore. Many of us don't have shoes. Does that make us spies?"

The officer looked at Joseph, asking in a threatening tone. "What is your rank? Are you a surgeon?"

Fear gripped Joseph as he realized he'd crossed a dangerous line. His new friend from Pennsylvania saved him.

Before he could respond Palmer interrupted them.

"Are we going to stay here all night or are you going to take me to a superior officer?"

The question irritated the Confederate major, but it also distracted him from his interrogation of Joseph Youngblood.

"Don't worry about where you're goin', Yank. You'll soon be shot!" he said hatefully.

"Guards, take this man."

Joseph and Palmer exchanged glances as the guards in gray took the young captain away. Once Palmer and his guards were gone Joseph and Jacob returned to the street to see where their services might be needed.

Joseph stopped a passing lady and explained his status and asked for her help.

"Do you have a pot or something we can boil water in?" he asked.

"Yes, doctor, I do," she replied. Joseph started to correct her and explain that he wasn't a full-fledged doctor but decided against it. It didn't matter anyway.

She was a pleasant-looking lady of small stature. Her head was bare with her gray-speckled hair tied in a small bun at the back of her head. They followed her through a winding path in the midst of the Confederate wounded and street traffic. The lady led them to her large and stately home which was close by. Joseph then directed several men on the street to bring in four or five of the wounded. Young Jacob was quite shaky at first, but he was able to maintain his composure and willingly jumped in. He stayed with Joseph all through the night and with guidance was soon sewing up wounds on his own.

CHAPTER TEN

By morning the pair had saved many men, and Joseph couldn't help but be proud of the long night's work and their accomplishments. The lady of the house now slept in a chair nearby, and the men they'd been working on were now resting as best they could. Two were permanently at rest.

The young Confederate healer and his friend were not even aware that a new day had dawned. Their clothes were completely stained with the blood and discharge. Exhausted they stepped out onto the street. It was early morning on the nineteenth. Their relief from concentration and lack of sleep left them drowsy. The sun blinded Joseph as he briefly took in the surroundings.

"Halt!" he heard someone shout.

"Halt or I'll shoot!" the man shouted again. Joseph's eyes adjusted and he found himself staring at the muzzle of a Springfield musket held by a man in a blue uniform with sergeant stripes. Several more men in blue ran up and pointed their guns at him and Jacob. Joseph looked over at his new friend and saw terror in his eyes.

"Put your hands over your heads. You two crackers are now prisoners of the United States Army."

Chapter 11

—— CHRISTMAS 1862 ——

Hoopers Creek Life on Hoopers Creek was not as Delia remembered it in her childhood. She was certain that those days would never return. The hardships were mounting, and they were running out of food. But most worrisome for the Russell household was the faltering economy. The huge investment her father had made in Confederate currency was proving to be a disaster. The many uncertainties had pushed her father into periods of depression, anger, and even rage. Robert Russell could not accept the fact that he had miscalculated to such a great extent. He continued to fantasize that Confederate currency would make a miraculous recovery and still held out hope that his wealth would be restored.

Her father's behavior began to worry Delia more than the difficulties that they were experiencing. His instability was often frightening. On a day-to-day basis she had had to take on more of the family responsibilities. Her mother's health and spirit continued to deteriorate and her sisters were little help. John was ten and tried to help, but his thoughts were often consumed with the welfare of his big brothers. It was hard to get a youngster to take any initiative. She and Nanny and Zeke carried the burden of maintaining the household. Without them Delia was sure that the Russell family could not function.

It was the night before Christmas when Delia walked into the study to check on her father.

CHAPTER ELEVEN

"Hello, Papa. How are you feeling?" she asked.

Her father did not answer, and Delia saw the glass on the table beside him and the jug of whiskey on the floor.

"Never did I think that I'd be worried about money at this stage of my life," he said sullenly.

"It's going to get better though. Our boys are holding up well and Zeb Vance is going to make a great governor," he said, lighting up substantially.

"Yea, I think it's gonna get a lot better with Zeb in the governor's office. Zeb will do something to help turn around our Confederate money," he said.

Quickly his emotions dipped once more, and he looked at Delia and said, "You can't hardly buy anything now with Confederate money. You need a basketful just to buy a loaf of bread."

"I know, Papa, but it will get better. This war is gonna end soon and everything will work out. You'll see."

"Close the door, Delia, and get the moneybox down. I want to have a look."

Delia went to the fireplace and removed the two pieces of paneling and the rough sawed lumber that covered the hiding place. She slid the large box out of the hole and brought it to the table, placing it in front of her father for the tenth time this month. She retrieved the key and unlocked the box. Bob Russell opened it and began to examine the contents, removing the stacks of Confederate money and placing them on the table beside the box. He removed the leather pouches and opened them one by one, counting the few gold and silver coins that were still inside.

Delia reached for the lone velvet pouch that was hers. While her father counted his money, she walked to the other side of the room and beside the candlelight opened the soft velvet pouch and dropped the large, German gold coin into her hand. It's beautiful, she thought. Delia brought it up to cover her heart, and tears came to her eyes as she thought of Joseph and his awful predicament. She had heard horrible stories about the prisons up north. Delia worried about the cold and dampness. Many men from the South did not fare well in the brutal winter climate. If only she could go find him. It had been so very long since they had seen each other. She was worried that he would be changed, that maybe he wouldn't love her anymore, or worst of all that he might die at the hands of his captors. Delia placed the coin back in the velvet pouch and returned it to the box.

Her father had finished counting his money. The two of them refilled the box and locked it, and Delia carried it back to the hiding place. She fitted the rough sawed lumber into place and slotted the two pieces of paneling. She turned to her father, saying, "Please, Papa, it's late. Shouldn't we go to bed now?"

"You go on, child. I'm not sleepy," he said sadly.

"But tomorrow is Christmas, Papa. You should rest."

Delia gave up on her father and walked down the hall to her room. With a lighted candle at her bedside she started the letter that she'd been composing all day.

> My Beloved Joseph,
>
> I pray that this letter finds you well and that God will protect you. I don't know if you will ever receive this but I did so want to write you. There are so many things to tell.
>
> Most of the young men have gone now. They are going to form a new regiment here after the first of the year. Since your brother Bill came home your other two brothers will have to go. I have heard that J. N. and Hiram are going to join the new regiment. That will leave only Bill and young Pinkney to help your mother and father take care of the farm. I also have terrible news. You may not have heard that Solomon Cunningham was killed at a place called Fredericksburg just a couple of weeks ago. His poor widow Saphrona is

devastated. She is left with the children to raise by herself. My brother James is now a sergeant and seems to be doing well, but I fear for him.

Things here are very difficult, as Confederate money seems to be losing its value. Some people think that life will be better with Zeb Vance as governor.

If you get this letter know that I love you and think of you every day. I pray for your safe return that we may be joined together as we planned. I have committed to memory the vow you made to me behind the bell tower that night at the church. Those words sustain me and help me through each day. I pray that this war will be brought to an end and you will be returned to me safely.

              With deepest affection and all my love,
              Merry Christmas,
              Delia

---JANUARY 1863---

Asheville, North Carolina Delia guided Ole Star up through the muddy lane that was South Main Street as they approached the Eagle Hotel. She didn't know what this meeting was about, but a rider had come to Fletcher the previous day asking her father to attend. Climbing the stairs and entering the large hotel parlor, they could see that a crowd had already gathered. Once again A. S. Merrimon seemed to be conducting the meeting. Delia was ushered to the back of the room where other women gathered informally.

Merrimon started the meeting by making an announcement.

"Gentlemen, for those of you who do not already know, I must make you aware of a dastardly act that occurred in Madison County on January 8. A group of deserters and conscription evaders made a raid on Marshall. They broke into the warehouse at Marshall and stole the county supplies of salt, flour, and general merchandise. In addition these heartless criminals broke into the home of Colonel Lawrence Allen, where they beat and molested his wife and children. Two of Colonel Allen's children were in bed terribly ill with scarlet fever. These demons dragged the two sick children out of bed and took their blankets. Sadly, I report to you that Colonel Allen's six-year-old son and four-year-old daughter died shortly thereafter."

There was a great outcry from the crowd. An air of vengeance permeated the room as all of the men present swore to do everything possible to bring the rogues to justice.

Merrimon raised his hand quieting the crowd.

"Governor Vance has requested military aid from General Heth in Knoxville. General Heth has dispatched Colonel Allen and the 64th Infantry Regiment to Madison County for the purpose of apprehending these perpetrators. Now it is requested by Governor Vance that we do everything possible to maintain law and order in our communities. Anyone having information regarding these Tories is to provide it to Colonel Allen or to me. The individuals involved will be arrested and taken to Knoxville for a military trial."

Delia and the other women gasped in horror at the back of the room.

"How could these people be so inhuman? Did they not even care about innocent children?" Martha Anderson said to Delia.

"Where will this all end?" Martha shook her head and her eyes teared as she told Delia that one of her brothers was killed at Fredericksburg.

"I'm so very sorry. It's so awful," Delia responded empathetically. "Oh, Martha, my beloved Joseph has been taken prisoner, and I fret daily for his health and safety."

The meeting in the parlor went on for some time, and there was considerable celebration over the great victory at Fredericksburg. Yet many of the men questioned why the Yankees weren't quitting.

Delia got up and dressed herself as usual. She had a lot on her mind these days that either kept her awake at night or caused her to rise early. This day in particular one subject had been troubling her, and she

CHAPTER ELEVEN

decided that today was a good day to address it. Delia was up early, and her sisters, brother, and parents were still fast asleep. She crept down the stairs being careful not to wake anyone. She went into the kitchen, finding Nanny Mills at her usual station. Delia walked up beside her while Nanny stirred a pot and placed her hand on her shoulder.

"Nanny, may I have a word with you?"

Detecting the seriousness of the young woman's tone, Nanny turned to her and said, "What be on your mind dis mornin', child?"

"Nanny, do you know about President Lincoln's proclamation?" she asked curiously.

"Lawdy child, what you aks me 'bout sumpon like dat fo?"

"I just want to know, Nanny. Do you know about it?"

"Now, you bes' go on child and don't be talkin' 'bout none of dat," Nanny said, blandly staring at the pot and avoiding Delia's eyes.

"I really want to know, Nanny. I really want to know the truth," she said seriously.

Nanny Mills was silent for several seconds, continuing to stir the pot on the stove. She slid the pot off to the side, wiped her hands on her apron, and looked Delia directly in the eye.

"Miss Delia, I raised ya up like a bean sprout. I been wit ya through yo' whole life. Lawdy child, I held ya when ya first seen de light o' day. Come sit wit me."

Nanny led Delia to the kitchen table and sat down beside her.

"Ya see child, black folks always knows a lot more den white folks thinks they does. We don't got no book learnin' and we ain't got nobody to teach us the written word. But we do know what's goin' on. We just aks like we don't, so white folks leaves us alone. Yes, I knows about Mr. Lincoln's proc-a-ma-shun and Zeke knows too. We know he sez we free and we be free to go. But Miss Delia, where we gonna go? What we gonna do? We ain't got nothin'. We don't have no book learnin'. They ain't neither one of us can read 'n write. We can't even sign our own name."

Tears came to the old slave's eyes briefly. Laughing slightly she said, "Besides, child, who gonna take care of ya? Dem other girls and little

John, who gonna care fo' them? Poor Miz Russell can't hardly git herself outta bed and Massa Bob can't hardly walk. I reckon if we's free we needs to be where folks needs us. We ain't got nowhere else to go, so we bes' stay here and take care of them that we been with all of our lives.

"Sides, we don't know who be the boss, Mr. Lincoln or Mr. Davis."

The two sat staring at each other, contemplating the seriousness of the moment.

Projecting resolve, Nanny rose to her feet.

Delia understood how the old slave woman felt. Delia got up from her chair, grabbed the old black lady, and hugged her, and Nanny hugged her in return. With tears in her eyes, Delia looked at her and said defiantly, "Nanny, if it was up to me you'd been free a long time ago." The old black lady chuckled, rolled her eyes, patted Delia on the shoulder, and said, "Lawdy, child, Lawdy, I knows dat. Now me and you bes' be gittin' on back to work. Ain't anythin' around here changed for us. Only thing we bes' do is get breakfast ready." The old black lady returned to the stove, humming a field hymn as she went.

Chapter 12

―― APRIL 5, 1863 ――

Hoopers Creek Matthias Dees and his son stood on the rock outcrop overlooking Terry's Gap and the valley below. It was still early spring and the leaves had only begun to form on the trees of the mountain forest. Dees had a commanding view of the area as he waited for Rupert's return. He couldn't help but think about how glad he was that war had come to the mountains. The war had turned out to be a most fortuitous opportunity for him and his boys.

"Endless opportunities for men like us," he chuckled.

In the distance he could see Rupert working his way up the trail. It was still a substantial distance so it was almost an hour before Rupert completed the climb to the top of the rocky crags where his father and brother waited.

"Well, what did you find out, boy?" Matthias asked his son.

"We're in luck, Paw," Rupert answered with a sly grin.

"I did just like you said. I told 'em I was a Confederate soldier headin' home on furlough and that I just needed a bite to eat 'n somethin' to drink. They give me water and cornbread 'n then I found out everythin' from 'em two niggers they got," he said proudly.

"They got a papa, but he's gone to Asheville and ain't expected home 'til tomorrow night. Thar ain't nobody there 'cepting 'em two niggers, and they live in a shack a fer piece from the house. Then there's 'em little kids, three of 'em, but they're little tiny thangs."

Matthias Dees punched his son in the shoulder and cocked his head, staring at his son with an evil expression.

"Tell me 'bout the gal, son. I wanna know 'bout the filly."

"Paw, she's a purdy thang, little tiny thang too. She ain't gonna give us no trouble."

Dees turned and looked away toward the valley below. He nodded his head affirmatively.

"Naw, she ain't gonna give us no trouble a'tall. We'll head down the mountain soon as we see the lanterns go out."

—— APRIL 7, 1863 ——

Delia did not know what all the fuss was about, but she could tell that it wasn't good news. A rider had stopped by the night before and talked to her father. Mr. Russell seemed to be expecting company this morning. He told Delia that he was going to be leaving for the day, but she would not be going with him. Her father had not been anywhere in months when Delia had not accompanied him. She was unhappy with her exclusion but concluded it must be some men's issue.

Delia watched through the bedroom window as the unfamiliar wagon approached the yard. There were three men on the wagon and two more on horseback. One man climbed down from the wagon and walked toward the house. Delia ran to the door to greet the man.

"Hello, miss. My name is Joseph Holbert, and I'm here to call on Mr. Robert Russell."

"Yes, I believe he is expecting you," Delia responded. She gestured to invite him in when she was interrupted by the triple clump of Robert Russell's approach.

"Good morning, Mr. Holbert," Russell announced officiously.

"Good day to you, Mr. Russell."

Mr. Holbert pulled out a piece of paper and handed it to Robert Russell saying, "This is your official appointment to the Board of Inquiry, and I trust it will be sufficient for you to proceed with this matter."

CHAPTER TWELVE

Brushing past Delia, Russell took the document, folded it clumsily, and stuffed it into his pocket.

"Yes, yes. That's fine. Now, let's get on with it. Let's go on up to the Barnwell house and see if we can figure out what happened."

"The rest of the men are ready. Let's go," Holbert responded.

Russell turned to Delia and told her, "I'll be home about dark."

The ride from Jackson Road to Terry's Gap was a short one. When the six men arrived at the home of Dave and Saphrona Barnwell, Russell could see a number of people gathered around and two men who appeared to be guarding the house. Two older women were over at the slave shack entertaining what appeared to be two small children. Nathan Drake greeted the men as they arrived. Holbert introduced the other men to Drake, who was also part of the Board of Inquiry. The other members of the board were already there, and the assembly was now complete. As the last members gathered in the front room, Mr. Holbert said, "Gentlemen, if you would please gather 'round. The court has appointed you to act as members of this Board of Inquiry with the charge of investigating the murder of Saphronia Barnwell. Mr. Drake here lives nearby and he is going to inform you of what we know so far and then we will go inside." Nathan Drake stepped forward inside the small circle of men.

"The two Barnwell slaves were in their shack, and apparently they didn't hear a thing. The two children are very small, and apparently they did not wake up either. Dave Barnwell was spending the night in Asheville, and he was seen there by several people." Drake paused long enough to be interrupted by Sam Fletcher, another board member.

"I know that's so, Nathan. I saw him in Asheville myself," Fletcher said.

Drake nodded and then continued with his appraisal.

"Sometime during the night somebody came into the house and murdered Saphronia," he said, bowing his head.

"I've been in there and seen it. It's quite unpleasant, gentlemen."

Robert Russell gruffly interrupted the men.

"Gentlemen, if you don't mind. I think we've had enough of this talking. I want to go have a look for myself."

Drake obligingly led the way. When the group got inside Drake pointed to a small lean-to covered room on the south side of the house that he indicated was the children's sleeping area. On the other side of the main room was a second room with a hinged door and latch on it. He led the group of men into the second room. The disturbing view of a bed completely draped with a large quilt immediately struck all those present. The form that was underneath the quilt was obviously a human body.

Robert Russell's eyes immediately shifted to the bedpost. He detected that a leather strap had been crudely tied around the top two bedposts leading from there to a point where it disappeared under the quilt. The men assembled in a semicircle around the bed. Holbert instructed Drake to remove the quilt.

Drake stepped forward and pulled the quilt completely off of the bed. The men gasped at the sight before them. The formerly beautiful young body of Saphronia Barnwell lay in the center of the bed. The lifeless woman had a horse harness pulled over her head and body, locking her arms at her side. Her naked form was covered in bruises. In some places there were bite marks that appeared to have been inflicted by a human. It took a moment for the men to recover from the initial shock.

Holbert calmly addressed the group. "Please note the blow at the top of her head near the scalp line."

Sam Fletcher was now completely on the other side of the bed. He leaned over, examined the wound, stood erect, and informed the others of his opinion. Pointing at the wound, he said, "That's what killed her."

Robert Russell was drawn by the expression on this woman's face and the look in her open eyes. He could see the fear etched in her expression and in her eyes. Suddenly shaken by the sight, he turned his face from the scene.

"For God's sake, in the name of decency. Please cover her! Have you no shame?" J. C. McDowell scolded Drake. Drake quickly covered her body with the quilt, and the inquiry continued.

CHAPTER TWELVE

Struggling to regain his composure, Russell looked around the room and began to talk in his official capacity.

"There doesn't appear to be any disturbance. It doesn't look like she fought," he said, somewhat puzzled.

"Yes, you are right, Bob. She didn't fight," Drake said, bowing his head sadly. His voice was laced with emotion as he choked on the words.

"I wonder why she didn't fight," asked McDowell.

"That's real easy to figure out," Drake responded.

"We already figured that one."

"What do you mean?" Fletcher asked, also puzzled by the lack of resistance.

"It's easy," Drake said.

"She had two little children asleep in that other room. Whoever did this told her that they would kill the children if she fought. She was protecting her children. I figure she cooperated completely. She had to or they'd a killed them little ones too, sure as sunrise."

"Yea, I reckon that's right," Holbert added. "Their mama made sure they slept through it and that's why they're alive."

"Well, if she didn't fight them, then why did they kill her?" Fletcher asked.

"We figured that out too. We figure she knew who they were. She may have known them or at least she could identify them," Drake replied.

"Yep, I bet so," Holbert added. "These mountains are full of unsavory characters. There's scores of them up in the high country now and more coming every day from Virginia, Tennessee, and God knows where else. If this war don't end soon, this kind of thing is just gonna get worse."

Fletcher, North Carolina Delia worked Ole Star gently as she guided the buggy into the large area in front of the post office. I can't wait until this is all over, she thought. Surely things couldn't get too much worse, and she was beginning to lose track of just how things had gotten to this point. All she knew for certain was that her beloved Joseph was in a Union prison camp and his two little brothers who Joseph had desperately wanted to keep at home had joined the 60th Regiment.

Delia tied Ole Star and climbed the stairs to the post office. She greeted Mr. Ward and handed him a letter. He slowly took it from her and looked away as he accepted it. Before he could say anything Delia asked cheerfully, "Do I have a letter today?" He didn't answer. She could tell from the look on his face that his answer was the same as it had been for months. He placed her letter in the basket and then reached forward and took her hand.

"Look, Miss Delia. You gotta understand. Joseph is in a Union prison camp now. You best go on living your life and you can think about Joseph again someday, if he ever comes home."

Delia perked up defiantly.

"What do you mean if, Mr. Ward? Joseph is coming home. He promised me he would and I know he will."

She fought back tears as she faced the older man.

"And he would write to me if he could. I know he would."

"Yes, yes, I'm sure he would," Ward said, conceding to her insistent demeanor. "But I can tell you, Miss Delia. He can't write you. Them Yankees don't let them write no more, and even if they did he probably can't get no paper to write on. They barely get enough to eat in those prisons, and they sure ain't gonna be handing out no paper."

Delia again spoke defiantly. "Mr. Ward. You will see to it that my letter gets mailed to him, won't you?"

Ward shrugged, shook his head, and looked back at her. "Yes, Miss Delia. I'll see to it. I'll see to it that your letter gets mailed."

Chapter 13

―― NOVEMBER 1863 ――

Asheville, North Carolina Robert Russell walked into the courthouse with Delia following behind him. It was an exciting day, and a large crowd had gathered for the purpose of seeing their local hero, Zebulon Baird Vance, now the governor of North Carolina. When the Russells reached the courtroom, no seats remained. Vance stood before the crowd and spoke briefly on issues relating to state government and the progress of the war. In a traditional town meeting style Vance engaged the local citizenry in an open discussion.

"Zeb, when are y'all gonna do something about all these Tories robbing and killing folks?" someone called out. Vance nodded his head, acknowledging the problem, and his expression indicated his own concern about the matter.

"Most of these Tories really aren't on one side or the other. They're just thieves taking advantage of the situation, and we're doing all we can to root them out."

"I say we shoot 'em when we find 'em," one man shouted. There was a "Here! Here!" and a general murmur of agreement with the man's statement. Vance raised his hand and shook his head negatively.

"Now hold on. We're gonna have none of that as long as I'm governor," he said firmly. The local prosecutor, A. S. Merrimon, gestured as he began a speech.

"If we find these Tories or anybody else breaking the law, then we'll arrest them and bring them to trial."

"No matter how bad things get we mustn't lose our sense of law and order. North Carolina is the only state left that has not eliminated the writ of habeas corpus. I'm proud of that and I want to keep it that way."

"What to hell is writ-a-corpus, or whatever you said?" one man asked.

"It's basically your rights, Sam. The right to due process and a fair trial."

"Yea, but we're dealing with men who just as soon spit on the law as not," another man shouted.

Vance responded to him, quickly saying, "Last winter two of Colonel Lawrence Allen's sick children were roughed up by some of the raiders. Two little children died as a result. Later some of our own men went into Shelton Laurel and rounded up a group of people and shot them without a trial, or a hearing, without anything. Now we find out that most of those shot were probably innocent. Killing innocent people is not going to bring law and order back into our lives."

There was a general, although reluctant, acceptance of the governor's argument. The focus of the meeting then turned to more immediate matters of concern. One older man stood and asked a simple question.

"When can we get more supplies, Zeb? I gotta hog past ready to slaughter, but I ain't got nothing to cure it with," he said sadly.

Vance grimaced. "I don't know, John. The blockade has kept us from bringing in much of anything and it's extremely difficult to get any more from Virginia."

Finally the group concluded that the governor would appoint a special commission to investigate and find a solution to the growing supply problem.

The meeting broke up, and Robert Russell went to the back of the courtroom to Merrimon's office where Vance, Merrimon, and others continued discussing important issues. Delia stood outside the door and listened as her father asked a nagging question.

"Zeb, is my Confederate money worth anything?" he asked. He got only silence at first, but then reluctantly Vance acknowledged his question.

CHAPTER THIRTEEN

"Not much, Bob. It's pretty near worthless now. I'm sorry," Vance said, trying to be honest. The strain was present on Russell's face as he shook his head and continued his questions.

"I don't know how much longer I can deal with this. My boys are gone. I invested heavily in Confederate script. I wasn't able to raise much of a crop. I don't know if I can hold on much longer."

"I know it's tough, Bob, but we're all in this together. They're just isn't anything we can do except keep fighting," Merrimon answered.

"I do hope things will get better soon."

"I hope so too, 'cause winter's coming and there's a lot of folks in Henderson County that I expect ain't got enough stored up for the winter."

Russell started to leave when he turned to Merrimon and asked, "I heard there's been another woman killed. Is that true?" Merrimon and Vance exchanged glances and then Merrimon looked back at Russell.

"Yes, I'm afraid so," he said sadly.

"I heard it was someone down in Madison County," Russell continued in a tone that indicated a question.

"Yes, it was," Merrimon replied.

"It was Martha Anderson, a real pretty girl with a full life ahead of her. It's a terrible thing."

"Was she murdered?" Russell asked.

"Well, I can't say for sure, but the sheriff thinks so. Her cabin burned up and the body was burned real bad. The sheriff says that he thinks her throat was cut first. Them that done it burned up the place so as to hide the crime."

Delia's heart sank as she listened to the men's discussion from the doorway. She spun around leaning against the wall to gain support for herself as she evaluated what she had heard. She closed her eyes as she thought of the beautiful Martha Anderson, her fair hair and her golden eyes lost forever. She had known her only briefly but felt close to her. Delia didn't have many friends, and losing Martha made her feel as lonely and hopeless as she had ever felt. With tears streaming down her face, she lowered her head and quickly returned to the wagon.

Delia turned the buggy onto Souther Road as her father pointed out Wash Hutchison's modest little cabin in the clearing to their right. Wash was on the porch anticipating their arrival. Ole Star tugged the buggy into the yard. Before the greetings were completed the footless man had bounced out of his chair, down the two log steps, and over to the wagon. Delia was about to climb down and help him by placing her father's step in a convenient position for him, but she had no time. Wash just approached the buggy, grabbed the back of the wagon frame from below, and flipped himself onto the back with what seemed like little effort.

"Good morning, folks," he said cheerfully as he positioned himself on his knees behind them.

"It's not far. Just head straight up the road," he said, pointing up the hill. They continued to climb for a ways before making a little turnoff to the left. Robert Russell looked around impatiently as he tried to see the strange man's handiwork.

"Stop here," Wash said, hopping down off the buggy and leading them through a little cluster of rhododendron. Delia helped her father down, handing him his cane; the pair followed Wash as he worked through the thicket on his knees. When they came back out into the open Delia was amazed at what she saw. They were standing on top of a knoll that provided a panoramic view of the Hoopers Creek valley. In back of the knoll Wash Hutchison had engineered an ingenious dugout lean-to structure that was approximately fifty feet long and sixteen feet wide where it was cut back into the bank. A lean-to roof covered the dugout just barely above ground level at the back of the structure. "This way," he motioned, as they stepped down a set of dugout steps into an opening in the earth. What greeted them there was most impressive. Wash had dug out the entire area by himself. He had placed most of the vertical boards against the earthen walls and positioned a large oak beam lengthwise over the structure. Lean-to slats ran perpendicular to the beam, creating a sound roof. Inside the structure itself were four equally sized partitions allowing for privacy when needed. After touring the

CHAPTER THIRTEEN

inside of the structure Wash led them back outside and marched them a short ways over the top of the knoll.

"Now look back," he said, obviously proud of himself. Nothing could be seen except an ordinary-looking hilltop flanked in the rear by woods and at the center some laurel and rhododendron. From anywhere in the valley the hill would give the appearance of being unoccupied. The only way to see it was to walk up on it in close proximity. Bob Russell supported himself on his cane as he studied the unique structure.

"What about water?" he asked.

Wash grinned.

"That's easy. There's a spring sixty paces away in the laurel thicket. We can get water in broad daylight and never be seen unless somebody comes all the way up here." The three of them returned to the buggy and climbed back on board.

"Over here," Wash said, as he directed them onto a trail that ran back in the woods to the northeast. Again they were astounded at what they found after traveling less than a hundred yards. Wash had constructed a small corral with high slat fences and a small gate. This structure could not be seen either until one got very close.

"Look at this," Wash said as he pointed to the back corner of the corral. "That's the hay you got for me, Mr. Russell. It should stay good and dry there." Wash had constructed another covered area with poplar bark shingles. The shed protected a sizable stack of hay for livestock.

Wash turned to Russell.

"Well, what do you think?" he asked, anxiously seeking approbation. Almost begrudgingly Russell responded, "It'll do. It'll do. Sure was a heap of work. It's a shame to let all that work go to waste. I just don't think we'll ever need it. I hope not, anyway," Russell said, indicating that he was unsure of himself.

"I think it's just wonderful, Wash," Delia said, smiling down at him. "It's beautiful and you did it all yourself."

Wash blushed and spoke with modesty.

"Naw, Zeke helped me some. Without him I couldn't have put up 'em big timbers."

"Well, still, it gives me comfort knowing we have a place to go if the war comes here. And what a safe and hospitable place it is!"

Wash looked up at her with great pride. He had become fond of Delia, as his work on the hideout had brought them into more frequent contact. Secretly his affection for her had progressed beyond mere friendship in his mind. He dared not show it for he knew that she was betrothed and he feared her rejection. Most of all he feared offending her.

Robert Russell calmly turned back toward the buggy and began walking away.

"Well, if nothing else, this would be a cool place to keep horses during hot weather." Looking back toward the hideout structure Russell shook his head negatively, then laughed, "I don't know what we'll do with that big hole in the ground." He walked away and climbed onto the buggy.

After supper that night Delia went into the kitchen to find Nanny Mills busy as usual. "Nanny, I'm worried about Papa. He seems to suffer so."

"I know, Miss Delia. He don't seem right 'bout half de time."

"He drinks that corn whiskey every night now; I don't think it's good for him," Delia said worriedly.

"Dat stuff sho nuff bad fo anybody. It be bad nuff it burn yo stomach, but it burns a man's mind. Dat be da baddest part."

"Nanny, everything is getting worse. We've hardly any money, and we'll have hardly any food before long. My brothers are gone. So is Joseph, and now Martha. What will we do when winter gets here?"

"Now don't you fret, child. The good Lord gonna provide. Ya jus has ta hang on. They be a better day comin'. If we has to we do without and if needs be we'll go up on de mountain and live in dat hideout thing 'til dis war be over. Someday it just gotta be a better day," Nanny said confidently.

"Nanny, I worry about Joseph every day and every night and I worry about my brothers too. I don't even know for sure if Joseph is still alive, but I pray he must be for I couldn't go on living without him."

CHAPTER THIRTEEN

"Naw, he gonna be all right. Dat Joseph he be a strong man, a smart man. He gonna survive dis war, and when he come home we gonna have a big wedding and Nanny gonna make ya de purdiest weddin' cake dat you ever did see." Delia smiled gratefully as she looked into the eyes of her trusted companion.

"Yes, Nanny. He will come home to me. I know he will."

Chapter 14

—— 1863 ——

Camp Morton, Indianapolis, Indiana Joseph Youngblood was up just as the sun was rising over the stockade wall. His tired eyes opened to another day of grim reality in a Union prison camp. He was shivering from the cold and closely huddled with the other men around the lone wood stove. The horse stable that surrounded the stove had served as home for Joseph and Jacob for months now. The two were among the strong that had survived the winter of 1862–1863. The Indiana winters always produced below-freezing temperatures and violent piercing wind from the north. Most of the prisoners had scant clothing and only one thin blanket. Making matters worse, the stable was missing planks along the outside walls. Even getting a spot on the inside of the stable was difficult given the overcrowded conditions at Camp Morton. Many inmates endured the temperatures outside of the walls, some having only a poorly dug hole to protect them from nature's frigid offerings. The prisoners lost many digits to frostbite and Camp Morton lost many lives to the Indiana winter. Joseph and Jacob were indeed lucky to be alive.

In the early days of 1862 Camp Morton had been a tolerable facility. It was located on converted fairgrounds and named after Indiana's governor, Oliver P. Morton. The property consisted of a 36-acre plot of knobby land in the northeast section of Indianapolis. A small stream ran through the middle of the camp, but it often ran low in the summer

CHAPTER FOURTEEN

months. There were four springs on the property which provided drinking water for the Confederate prisoners.

Richard Owen, the original commandant, had done his best to treat the prisoners well. In the spring of 1862 he was ordered back into military duty and replaced by David Rose, a former U.S. marshal. Reorganization and the confusion over exchanges left little time or money for those in charge to improve living conditions, and the prison environment began to deteriorate. The desperate need for clothing and shelter had turned many of the men into desperados. Personal belongings and even blankets had to be kept constantly on the person of each prisoner, else he lose them to a fellow inmate. Then, in a retaliatory measure, the Union secretary of war, Edwin Stanton, ordered rations cut for all Confederate prisoners held in Union prison camps.

The considerate Commandant Owen left for duty in June 1863, and while the prisoners were saddened, they soon had reason to hope. During the month of July famed Confederate General John Morgan brought his Kentucky cavalrymen north of the Ohio River for a bold raid behind enemy lines. The Confederate prisoners watched the flurry of activity around the camp with both interest and amusement. Rumors circulated among the prisoners that Morgan and his Confederate cavalry were on their way to Camp Morton to free them. The prisoners concluded that there was some truth to the rumor as a significant number of guards had been pulled away from the camp to help defend the city. Unfortunately for them, prospects for freedom faded when word circulated that Morgan had crossed into Ohio and was apparently not coming to Indianapolis. Finally, on July 23, all hopes were dashed as a new group of prisoners arrived at Camp Morton, among them more than a hundred of Morgan's men.

It was during this time that Jacob became seriously ill. Joseph had become his caretaker and provider. On this morning Jacob could not walk, so Joseph was intent on getting the prisoner who worked the serving line to pass him an extra piece of bread. Howard Turner had been one of General Morgan's Kentucky privates, and Joseph had befriended him upon his arrival. Finding Howard to be a kind and resourceful young man, Joseph quickly sought him out for help when he learned of Howard's chow-line duty. Howard had willingly participated in this mealtime routine. Joseph had asked that Jacob be hospitalized, but the guards scoffed and said that he was just lazy.

Joseph calmly strolled to the side of the yard and ate the half cup of mixed wheat flour and water and the small piece of bread that was his day's ration. The gruel that they were served was cold and mostly uncooked and the bread was hard and dry. Once strong and healthy, Joseph had become quite weak and emaciated. He lost a great deal of weight through the winter. He was fortunate compared to many of the men.

Joseph crept quietly back to the barracks where he unwrapped a small piece of bread, breaking off little pieces for his comrade to eat. Joseph held Jacob's head up to help him sip water as he attempted to swallow the dry bread. Even from the back of his head Joseph could feel the heat, and he knew that Jacob's fever was rising. He stayed with him until he managed to get Jacob to finish the modest meal.

Joseph looked at the dimly lit surroundings, then back at his friend and was overcome with despair. His stay had turned into weeks, then months, and there was now no sign of rescue, no chance of being exchanged, and no chance that the war would be coming to an end anytime soon. Joseph wondered constantly about home, his family, and Delia. He began to think that he might not see any of them again. At this point he didn't know how long he could survive in this awful camp.

Joseph looked down at his friend and became increasingly despondent. He knew that if something wasn't done Jacob would die. Moreover, he knew Jacob was slowly losing his will to live. He felt frustrated and had an urge to try to do more. Joseph recognized that Jacob needed strength, so he returned to the chow area and awaited an opportunity to get more food. There were many guards and success would not be easy.

Joseph put his hands in his pockets and loitered about as if passing the day. Turner saw him and surmised the purpose of his approach. The two men waited for an appropriate opportunity, and Joseph walked

CHAPTER FOURTEEN

over to Turner feigning small talk. As he turned to walk away Turner slipped him another piece of bread. Joseph thought that the exercise had been completed in stealth, but after he had taken only a few steps he heard a shout.

"Hey, you! Stop!"

Joseph heard the guard but pretended that he didn't. The guard ran forward with his rifle pointed at Joseph and shouted even louder.

"Hey, cracker. I told you to stop."

A Union sergeant who was standing nearby stepped forward.

"What's the problem, soldier?"

With his gun still pointing at Joseph the guard said, "That man stole some bread and that one there helped him," pointing at Turner.

The sergeant turned to look at Joseph and calmly ordered, "Put your hands in the air, Reb." Joseph put his hands in the air and the soldier searched his pocket, pulling out the modest portion of dried bread. The sergeant turned to Turner and ordered him forward.

"Guards, take these men to the front of the yard. They're going for a little ride."

Two armed guards marched Joseph and Howard along toward the front of the compound. One of the guards snickered. He appeared to be no more than a boy of seventeen or eighteen.

"Yea, boy, sho' enough. You Rebs will be goin' for a ride sho' enough. You're gonna ride Morton's Mule and that's a ride that you ain't ever gonna forget."

Turner glanced fearfully at Joseph and Joseph glanced back at him. The two men knew full well what it meant to ride Morton's Mule. Joseph tried in vain to explain his need for bread but knew not to go too far, lest the punishment be doubled or worse.

They were locked inside a pen outside the guards' barracks while they awaited their fate. Soon the sergeant returned with orders from the commandant. The two men were taken to the yard. Their hands were tied behind their backs, and they were forced to climb a ladder. Then they were made to straddle a large wooden beam. The beam was supported on either end by two other beams planted vertically in the ground like a giant sawhorse. Two more guards came along behind the others, and with leather straps they tied weights to the Confederate prisoners' feet.

At first the discomfort was marginal. Joseph looked across to the other sawhorse structure at his friend, Turner, who was seated in a position similar to his own. Turner looked at Joseph and tried to smile.

"This is the first time I been for a ride in a long time." Joseph smiled back.

"It is a nice day for a ride, isn't it?"

As the seconds crept by the joking ceased.

The leather in Joseph's boot soles was almost completely gone, but there was still a thin portion left around the ankles and feet. The weight of the rocks tied around his ankles was cutting off his blood circulation. As the strap became more and more painful, Joseph became fearful that this ride would result in permanent injury. How would he take care of Jacob? He worried that if he wasn't there, no one would help his friend.

The constant shifting of weight from one small point to another became unbearably painful. The insides of his thighs were chafed and sore and his crotch area throbbed with pain. Well into the evening both men slumped forward, and then backward, trying desperately to rest their weight on another part of their body. Finally the sun sank completely, and the dark offered Joseph the opportunity to relieve himself. At first the release felt wonderful, but it was quickly replaced with the severe sting of the acid passing over broken flesh. Joseph's feet were now fully numb, and he truly feared for his life.

Occasionally Joseph or Howard pleaded and groaned, but no one responded to their pleas. As the sun rose the next morning over the city of Indianapolis both men were in dire condition. Turner leaned to the left and slowly slid off of the beam and would have been seriously injured, but the rock tied around his foot and the leather strap caught and hung on the beam as he fell. He dangled in the air briefly until the strap broke, and he plopped to the ground with the now loose rock falling on him and bruising his ribs. A young guard in a blue uniform approached him, screaming and cursing.

CHAPTER FOURTEEN

"You get your ass back on that horse. Come here, soldier," he said to another guard.

"Give me a hand. Let's get him back up there."

Joseph was so weak that he couldn't tell for sure what was happening. Then he heard a loud voice overriding the others.

"That's enough, men. Take them down and take them back to their quarters. Cut their hands free," an officer firmly instructed the guards from a nearby perch.

Joseph heard the guards grumbling and chuckling simultaneously as they went about the job of releasing the two men from their torture. Two Union soldiers cut the rocks from Joseph's feet and pulled him off the beam, and he fell limp in their arms. After they cut the restraints from his wrist, Joseph slowly wrung his hands in an attempt to get the feeling back. However, the return of feeling was excruciatingly painful, and Joseph writhed on the ground desperately trying to find the strength to recover. Two guards hoisted him, one under each arm.

"Now march, Reb."

As the two men released him Joseph collapsed again in a heap. He raised his head weakly and looked over at Turner, who was in a similar state. Joseph reached down to his feet and worked them, rotating the ankles round and round, trying to gain some circulation. Eventually feeling began to return, and he could feel his toes. Tears came to his eyes; he was so relieved at the sensation. He remembered the Hutchison boy, Wash, whom he had grown up with. Much of the time he spent on the beam he considered the challenges that Wash had faced growing up without feet. The fear of facing a life like that had terrified him.

The Union guards laughed and cajoled as the two victims struggled to regain their step.

"You Rebs ain't worth much. Can't even stay in the saddle for a leisurely ride."

The other guards joined in the laughter. Joseph glanced back at the sawhorse structure and thanked God that their ordeal was over. The two men had struggled to their feet and were standing, albeit unsteadily. They helped each other as they staggered and stumbled back to the stable. As Joseph dragged himself back to the small patch of dirt and straw where he usually slept he saw Jacob still lying there. But as he got closer a sunken feeling began to develop in the pit of his stomach. There was no movement, nor any other indication of life. He had marched all the way from Sharpsburg, Maryland, ridden trains cross-country, and quartered with this man day and night for months. They had helped each other through the worst of times and had relied on each other for companionship, strength, and support.

Joseph dropped to his knees beside Jacob and took his hand in his own. It was cold and lifeless. In his weakness and sorrow he fell to the ground and lay beside his friend. He put his arms around Jacob's lifeless body as he sobbed silently. Joseph looked across the dirt floor of the stable and saw the others watching him. Glancing around the damp confines he could see nothing but filth, misery, and despair. One young man looked down at Joseph and said, "He's dead, ain't he?"

"He's deader than hell. We're all gonna die. This damn war is gonna kill us all."

—— AUGUST 15, 1863 ——

Howard Turner and Joseph Youngblood walked inconspicuously toward the spring at the east end of Camp Morton. Turner glanced about the compound to be sure that no one could hear them.

"We've got to get outta here. If we stay here through the winter, we'll die too," said Howard.

"You're crazy," Joseph responded while looking around anxiously. "You saw what happened to those men last month. They were all shot down, and even the ones that got outside were rounded up by the dogs."

"Yea, I saw that too. But they were stupid. They didn't do it right," Turner stated confidently.

CHAPTER FOURTEEN

"Forget it," Joseph said. "I ain't trying it. This war's gotta be over soon, and all I want to do is go home."

The two men were getting their drink of water when they heard a shout from the yard.

"New prisoners coming." The gates opened, and a large column of Confederate captives marched into the yard. They were flanked on either side by a single line of men in blue carrying muskets.

"Halt!" one of the guards shouted, and the men stopped in the middle of the yard. Prisoners came out of their barracks and from all around the camp to see the new arrivals. New prisoners were always a source of excitement. Having recently been on the outside, these men carried news from home and news of the war. Joseph and Turner quickly walked over to the new arrivals. When the guards dismissed them the other prisoners converged and intermingled with the new ones.

"Do you know my brother?"

"Do you know my father?"

"What was your unit?"

"Where are you from?"

"Do you have news from home?"

These questions and many more could be heard echoing through the ranks of the Confederate prisoners.

The chatter created a constant buzz with many soldiers making familiar connections. Howard Turner had found another man from northern Kentucky that knew his family. Joseph was with him while Turner was anxiously learning all there was to know about the conditions at home. In the course of that conversation Joseph overheard someone speak the words, "60th North Carolina."

His heart raced as he whirled to find the man who had said it. He started shouting loudly, "60th North Carolina? Where are you, 60th North Carolina?"

Joseph shouted as loud as he could.

A few feet away a man motioned from behind others, "Here, over here, 60th North Carolina."

Joseph worked his way through the crowd toward him.

The man looked at Joseph as if puzzled. Suddenly he screamed.

"Dan. It's you. Dan Taylor. Well, I'll be damned. It's you, ain't it, Dan?"

Taylor's face looked blank. He looked at the tall, gaunt, emaciated figure.

"Pardon me, but I don't believe I know you."

Joseph was now smiling broadly, exposing his rotten teeth as he approached the soldier and eagerly grabbed his hand.

"Sure, you know me. I'm Joseph Youngblood from Henderson County. Back on Hoopers Creek, you know."

Taylor's expression was aghast. Joseph's shrunken body was caked with filth, and his head and face were covered with grotesquely matted hair.

Meekly the man said, "Is that you, Joe? God, is that you?"

"Yes, yes, it's me. I know, Dan. I look like hell. I've been here almost a year now and let me tell you, it's been rough. Me and Turner there, we're good friends."

"Oh yea, that man Brown he's talking to, he was with us in Mississippi when the Yanks caught us. We were near Jackson, and I was trying to get back to the regiment when I ran into these Kentucky men. The next thing I know the Yankees had us all," Dan said.

"Is there anybody else with you from home?" Joseph asked.

"No, just me and these poor fellas from Kentucky and a couple from Tennessee."

"Come with us," Turner gestured, and the four of them walked to the converted stable that was their barracks.

"Come, let's see if we can find you a spot in this horse palace. The four men found a corner and, after bargaining for some spots near their own, sat down together and talked about home and the war.

"Tell us about Gettysburg," Turner asked. "We've heard some about it, but we don't really know that much."

"We don't know that much either. We've been stationed down in Mississippi and that battle was up in Pennsylvania. Heard tell nearly

CHAPTER FOURTEEN

forty thousand men were lost on both sides. But I reckon they whopped us if the truth be told," Brown said nodding his head.

"Is that right, Dan?" Joseph asked.

"Yea, I reckon so. It was a big battle and we lost. A lot of folks say that we lost our chance to win the war when we lost that one."

"You'd never know that down where we was," Brown added.

"We were still fighting right on."

"Tell me about my brothers J. N. and Hiram. Another prisoner told me they were in the 60th. Tell me how they are doing. Please tell me they are okay."

Taylor smiled and his expression brightened. "They're fine, Joseph, at least they was the last time I saw 'em, just fine. They were in the 60th with me, in the same company as me. J. N. is just as lively as ever, and that Hiram sings for the men around the campfire and he sings 'Lorena' so as to make your heart melt. I done miss those boys already."

Joseph leaned back and relaxed slightly. He thought that things could be worse and there was still a lot to be thankful for. J. N. and Hiram were doing fine and Bill was back home tending the farm, and it seemed like for the time being he was at least the only one in the tight spot, just rotting away waiting on the war to end. Then he thought of Delia and smiled again, assuming that she too was safe at home.

The other men were still talking when Joseph abruptly interrupted their conversation.

"Dan, have you been home? Have you had a furlough?"

"Yes, I've been home, but it weren't no furlough. Me and Hiram just skeedaddled for a few days, but we came back."

"Tell me, Dan. Did you see Delia? Is she okay?"

At first he wasn't sure whom Joseph was referring to. "Oh, you mean Delia Russell?"

"Yes, did you see her?"

"No, I didn't see her, but I saw her daddy down in Fletcher and he said they was all fine. He said that they didn't know if you were dead or alive. They heard that you were in a Yankee prison camp."

Taylor paused, laughed a little, and said, "I reckon now I can tell 'em that it's so."

"Yea, I reckon it's so, and I reckon we're stuck here 'til this is all over. Ain't nobody doing much exchanging."

Listening to the two men talk about home, Turner turned to Joseph with a measure of urgency on his face.

"You mean we'll be here when this war is over, if we live that long. Look at yourself, Joseph. You may not live 'til spring."

The long, miserable, hungry days turned into long, miserable, hungry weeks, and soon the sun was setting farther to the south. Fall settled over the grounds of Camp Morton, and the cool air from the north again threatened the men. That morning one of them had been caught "flanking." He went through the chow line on one end and moved around to the other side for a second helping of rations. The poor fellow was discovered and called out in front of the other soldiers for the purpose of being made an example of. The commandant stood before the men.

"Now you damn Rebs gonna go by our rules, and what we say you're gonna do. Now this fellow here decided to break the rules, and he needs to get his just rewards. He is going to spend his day on the chines and you fine gentlemen get to watch."

"Guards, put him up there."

Joseph and the other men watched as the poor fellow was marched forward and forced to stand on the edges of a large wooden flour barrel with the top knocked out of it. A large, heavy log was handed up to him. He was forced to hold the log while he balanced himself in the uncomfortable position. He had no shoes, and his bare feet were pressured from the edges of the barrel. The weak and malnourished man had been up there less than an hour when he began to falter. The commandant had gone back inside when the poor wretch dropped the log. The sergeant summoned the commandant who then returned to the scene. He looked at the poor man still standing on the barrel, leaning over and gasping with his hands on his knees, trying desperately to maintain his balance.

CHAPTER FOURTEEN

"Gentlemen," the commandant shouted.

"You know the rules. Guards, hoist that log back up there. If he drops it again, take him over against the stockade wall and shoot him."

A low murmur and a slight hiss circulated through the yard after the commandant gave his orders. He turned quickly, glared at the prisoners, and shouted at them.

"Would anyone like to take his place?" No one stepped forward, and the log was hoisted back to the fellow as the commandant calmly walked away. The man held on as long as he could, but finally he lost his balance and fell off the barrel. The prisoners looked at each other worriedly and hoped for some reprieve. The sergeant stepped forward shouting, "You heard the orders, men. Take him to the wall." The prisoners could hear the poor wretch begging for his life.

"Please, please. I have a wife 'n four little children. Please don't shoot me."

Again the sergeant shouted, "Take him to the wall."

Two guards looped an arm under each of the prisoner's arms and dragged him to the stockade wall.

As he was being dragged away the man shouted as if to someone in the crowd that he must have known. "Please tell Sarah and tell the babies I love them. Tell 'em they was my last thought."

He seemed to shout with newfound strength as he was pulled toward his end. Most of the men looked away as the poor prisoner was positioned against the wall. The sergeant told the guards to form a line twenty paces in front of the condemned man.

"Shoulder arms!" shouted the sergeant.

"Take your aim!" the sergeant shouted again.

"Fire," he commanded.

There was a singular boom as the six muskets seemed to fire simultaneously. A cluster of musket balls struck the man in the abdomen and chest. One ball miraculously struck the log behind him. Joseph stared in disgust as he watched the man fall into a crumpled heap at the base of the wall.

The men knew that no man in the army would likely miss a shot at only twenty paces. But they'd seen it before. One of the guards had missed, because he'd chosen to.

As this unfortunate drama played to its end, the men of the prison camp were finally dismissed. Relieved, the men returned in silence to the stables. Joseph broke the silence as they exited the yard. He looked at his friend Turner, saying calmly but with determination, "We need to talk tonight."

That night Joseph crawled over the ground and huddled close to his friend from Kentucky.

"All right, Howard. I think you are right. We won't survive another winter here. We'll die here for sure, one way or the other. You say you've got a plan. What is it?"

Turner looked about as to make every effort to keep the discussion clandestine.

"Well, it's like this, Joseph. You remember when those boys broke out back in July. What happened to them?" Turner asked, knowing the answer to his own question.

"They got caught. The dogs got 'em," Joseph said.

Turner's tone was more serious now, and he began to describe the nature of his ideas.

"You see, Joseph, the hard part is getting outside the walls. If you ever get outside, then you ought to be able to get away," he said smiling.

"Well then why does everybody either get shot or get caught by the dogs?" Joseph asked, frustrated.

Turner smiled again.

"Because the guards know where they're going."

Joseph was puzzled but intrigued by Turner's idea.

"What do you mean, the guards know where they're going?" Joseph asked.

"Every single man that has ever gotten out of here runs dead straight south, ain't that right?" Turner asked him.

CHAPTER FOURTEEN

"Of course they do, you damn fool, where else they gonna go? Take up residence in Washington?" he asked.

"Here's how we do it, Joseph. I have family in northern Kentucky. My pappy's brother lives in New Albany, Indiana. He's a southern sympathizer, a Copperhead. I know his place and I know how to get there. If we can get outside these walls, we're gonna do it different. We're gonna head straight north until we get clear of this damn place. Then we'll head west 'til we pick up a creek and we'll run in that creek for a while so no dogs can pick up our trail. Then we'll loop all the way around and make our way back south of Indianapolis 'til we pick up sight of the railroad tracks."

He paused waiting for a reaction but got none. Joseph only listened intently.

"Once we spot them tracks, Joseph, they'll lead us straight to home. Them tracks will be our map. All we got to do is follow the tracks toward Louisville. We'll stay in the woods but keep the tracks in view at a distance. Once we get all the way to the Ohio River we're safe, boy. We're safe. I'll find my uncle's place, and he'll take care of us. We can stay there a spell, get ourselves rested up, get good food to eat and a bath. It'll be like home, Joseph."

To Joseph it was a distant dream, seemingly unrealistic. He looked at the filth and squalor around him and knew that there was no other choice, no other option. If he stayed there he would surely die.

"Should we take Brown and Taylor with us?" Joseph asked.

"No, it's too risky. It's just gotta be the two of us," Turner replied.

Joseph nodded begrudgingly.

"All right," he said. "They're new here. Maybe they can last it out. But I still don't know how you think you're gonna get us outside these walls."

Turner looked at him and smiled, "The moon is almost gone, and on the night of the new moon, we'll go. Are you with me, Joseph?" he asked, reaching for his hand.

Joseph looked in his eyes, "Yes, I reckon I'm with you."

The designated night of departure was dark and cold. It was November, and the winter winds danced over central Indiana and Camp Morton. The two men lay huddled together among the others in the darkened stable. They waited until it was late and began to carry out their plan.

Saying loudly enough for others to hear, Turner grumbled, "Move over, damn it, I gotta take a leak."

"Damn you, Turner, I was asleep," Joseph responded according to the plan. Turner got up and started for the door as if to relieve himself. Joseph spoke as if trying to whisper but intentionally allowing others to hear.

"Wait a minute. Now, I gotta go too."

He climbed to his feet and followed Turner to the door. The outside walls were lined with lanterns and many guards overlooking the grounds. But the cold had driven some of them to sneak away from the yard where the wind was always strongest. Several were huddled together away from the wind. The two Confederate prisoners crawled slowly and quietly toward the north end of the compound where an opening had been left by the shivering guards.

Turner reminded Joseph to feel the ground in front of him. Even the snap of a twig or the movement of a rock would bring unwanted attention.

"Over here, Joseph."

Turner led the way to the north wall where the creek entered the compound. The Union guards had driven stakes into the ground and into the creek bottom to prevent escape by means of the channel. Turner directed Joseph to two of the stakes in the bank. While lying on their bellies the two began to rock each stake, slowly trying to raise it from its hole. The men worked feverishly, twisting and pulling until finally the two wooden stakes were freed. There was still inadequate room for escape, but the two men began to dig into the creek bank where it met the channel at the stockade wall. The pointed stakes made excellent digging tools as the men slowly continued to move aside the cold earth that separated them from freedom. They had worked for over an hour when Turner attempted to squeeze through. He climbed back out and whispered to Joseph, "A little more."

CHAPTER FOURTEEN

A thump was heard on the walkway overhead, and the two men froze in cold silence. Joseph could hear the pounding of his heart as the sentry walked directly above them. Soon he had passed, and they heard him in casual conversation with other guards at the corner of the stockade. They continued digging until Turner turned to Joseph and nodded, "I think that will do it."

He got down into the hole and squeezed himself through. Soon he was on the other side of the stockade wall. Joseph crawled out behind him, and after crawling about twenty more feet the two men stared into the night. Panic gripped Joseph as he looked into the darkness. What have I done? he thought. But there was only one thing to do now.

Turner turned to him, whispering again.

"Follow me."

Tiptoeing until they thought they were out of hearing distance, the men ran north, straight north, as they had planned for days. It made Joseph nervous, and he wondered about the wisdom of the decision. It seemed almost foolhardy, to be running in the direction of Union territory. They kept running, sometimes barely able to trot, until they saw the sun rising in the east. They stopped to drink from a creek and then hid themselves in a thicket, covering each other with leaves, branches, and pine needles so thick that only their faces were exposed. At last they rested and fell into a fitful sleep.

They awoke after sleeping only a few hours and were both still very tired.

"We have to stay here until it gets dark," Turner told him quietly.

Joseph's immediate concern was hunger. The two men had carried nothing with them, and Joseph knew that finding something to eat would be critical.

"How are we going to get food?" Joseph asked.

Turner smiled and said, "Don't worry about that. I'll see to it that you get plenty to eat."

Joseph could tell that there was some implication in Turner's tone.

"Wait here," Turner said.

Joseph watched from the little thicket as Turner peeled away his forest blanket and walked just a few feet away. He rolled over a large, dead log and began digging and sorting through the debris underneath. A few minutes later he came back to Joseph with a small handful of various grub worms and bugs.

"Shall we dine, sir?"

"We're not going to eat that, are we?" Joseph asked with a sickening expression.

"Well, sir, we might choose to select another dining hall, one with a spread more suitable to your tastes?" Turner said, continuing with the theatrics.

Giving himself up to the moment, Joseph smiled.

"Why no, fine sir. This will do just fine. Could I have a glass of port, please?"

"Sorry, my good fellow, we are out of port at the moment. Perhaps a handful of muddy water would suit your dry palate."

Joseph reached over and collected two of the ugly, crawling creatures from Turner's hand. He looked at them briefly, winced, and tossed them both into his mouth, swallowing them whole.

"Quite delightful, good sir. I find that it suits my palate better if I swallow them whole and very quickly, I might add."

The two men ate the remainder of the grubs and settled down for a rest while they awaited darkness. Throughout their stay in the little thicket, they were constantly alert for the sounds of men or dogs. Luckily, there were none.

"Well, Turner, it looks like the first part of your plan is a good one. If they were after us we would have heard the dogs by now."

Turner looked at him and said calmly, "The last thing those Yankees expect Rebs to do is head north. Now tonight we gotta get all the way around Indianapolis and then we can head south."

At nightfall the two men headed west. They came upon lights in the distance and knew that it was the city of Indianapolis. Turner was an excellent guide and seemed to know what he was doing. When the sun

CHAPTER FOURTEEN

rose the following morning they had reached the southern tip of the city. In the distance trains could be heard, which assured them that they were approaching the railroad tracks that ran from Indianapolis to Louisville.

"When we find those tracks we won't need a road map. They will lead us straight south," he told Joseph confidently. Night after night the men continued their southward journey, keeping the tracks a safe distance to the east. Both men were becoming weaker and weaker from the lack of suitable food and the constant dysentery they had brought with them. Joseph feared that he could not go on much longer. Each day they would use whatever cover they could find. One afternoon Turner said, "Wait here."

He crept from the pine patch they had settled in and soon returned with a gleeful expression on his face. He weakly slapped Joseph on the back in his excitement.

"It's there. It's there," he said, pointing south.

"What's there?" Joseph asked, anxious to understand what the excitement was about.

"It's the river, the Ohio River. We're almost there. Hallelujah!"

Both men were emotionally encouraged at having made it to the river. They started traveling along the bank, keeping the water within sight as they followed the course to the southwest. It was well into the night when they approached a small hilltop, and Joseph could see a large clearing and a little cabin in the moonlight. Turner turned to Joseph and grabbed him by both shoulders and shook him vigorously.

"That's it. That's it. That's my uncle's cabin. We've made it. Come on, let's get ourselves down there and get something to eat and then get a bath."

As they approached the little cabin it was clear to Joseph that its inhabitants were probably asleep. The cabin was dark, and there was no sign of activity other than a little smoke coming from the chimney.

"You best be careful, running up on your uncle's place in the middle of the night. You're gonna get us both shot. Shouldn't we wait 'til morning?"

"Yea, you may be right, and believe me, Uncle Toad would shoot you at the drop of a hat, but I'll be careful." Joseph waited a safe distance from the cabin as Howard continued his approach. Howard threw stones at the door and shouted, calling his uncle's name.

"Hey, Toad Turner, wake up! It's me, Howard, your nephew."

There was still no activity nor any light seen from the cabin. Then Joseph heard a voice coming from the darkened doorway that was now slightly ajar.

"Who's out there?" the man's voice echoed through the night.

"It's me, Howard Turner, your nephew. It's me, Uncle Toad." The introduction was followed by a long moment of silence. Then the voice called out through the darkness.

"What be your mother's name?" the stranger inquired.

Understanding that his uncle was attempting to verify his identity, Howard shouted triumphantly, "It's Juliana. It's Juliana. My mother's name is Juliana."

Within seconds a match was struck and a lantern lit. A tall, gray-haired man in a nightshirt stood in the doorway.

"I'll be damned, Howard. Where did you come from?"

Howard turned toward Joseph and motioned for him to come with him. The two sick and weakened men ran for the cabin as fast as their feeble frames could carry them.

Chapter 15

—— FEBRUARY 1864 ——

New Albany, Indiana Joseph had forgotten how good life could be. For the first time in years nobody was telling him what to do, what to say, or where to go. He had put on weight and gotten his strength back, and his diarrhea was completely gone. He was very happy to be staying in the Turner home. Toad and Alice were not only southern sympathizers but they were also good people with charitable hearts. Throughout that winter Joseph came to appreciate them and to love them like his own family. Thanks to the Turners' prosperity there was plenty of food and their large wooden cabin was warm and comfortable even in the Indiana snow.

Life was not always perfect, however. The presence of Joseph and Howard had to be kept secret. The nearest neighbor was a mile upriver, but still the possibility of visitors was a constant threat. There were often soldiers passing by, sometimes neighbors or local officials. When outsiders approached the cabin the two men were forced to hide in the loft. On one occasion the sheriff had seated himself in the front room while he talked to the Turners for over an hour. There were lots of southern sympathizers in southern Indiana and suspicions ran high, and the sheriff occasionally stopped by to inquire about things. Toad Turner was adroit at presenting himself as a loyal Union man. Listening from the loft, Joseph worried that something might go wrong. Finally the discussion came to a close and the sheriff departed, unaware of the two Confederate soldiers hiding only a few feet above him.

Early in the morning or late in the evening when it seemed to be safe Joseph would go stand by the river and look to the south. On the other side of the Ohio was Kentucky and beyond that, sparkling in the distance, was his beautiful mountain homeland. Joseph dreamed of the Blue Ridge Mountains and the rolling hills and valleys of home. He worried about his family, and of course he often thought of Delia. He had been unable to write or communicate with them for fear of exposure. Toad Turner feared that any attempt to mail a letter south would lead to trouble.

Joseph was troubled by unpleasant thoughts that drifted through his mind. He was particularly troubled by stories Howard had told him about some of Morgan's men.

"General Morgan is a tough man, a hard fighter he is. For the most part he treats his men all right. But some of them that rides with him did some terrible things," he had said.

"What might that be?" Joseph asked with nervous curiosity.

"When men go gallopin' off on their own they can do some mighty bad things. We got separated up in Ohio from the rest of the cavalry. We were tryin' to catch up." Howard paused and wrinkled his face in apparent disgust.

"We caught up all right. Some Confederate cavalrymen had come up on a house and raided it. There weren't any soldiers there, just old men, a few children, and a couple of women. We got there too late. They were all dead. Most of 'em were scattered in the yard, but we found the two women tied to the beds. We never did prove who did it. There wasn't time. We soon had to hightail it back to Kentucky."

Joseph was troubled by what he heard. He continued to worry about the security of his loved ones back home. He'd gone to war to protect them, but everything had gone wrong. The more he thought of home, the more he thought of leaving.

Toad Turner was a river pilot and had been so all his life. He regularly ran supplies up and down the Ohio River. Toad made good money running supplies of every description for the U.S. government. He was about to leave again on a run to St. Louis.

CHAPTER FIFTEEN

Joseph grinned at his friend Howard with deep appreciation. He thought of how he had saved him from certain death in prison. Joseph knew that if he had remained at the camp, he would have died. Of that there was no doubt. But still he was troubled. His mind and his heart were constantly pulling at him with thoughts and memories of home. After talking to Howard he decided that they should seek his uncle's help. As the family sat down for a hearty dinner of pork, potatoes, and corn, Howard began his entreaty on Joseph's behalf.

"Uncle Toad, Joseph has a hankerin' to go home. Do you reckon you can help him out any?"

Toad cocked his head and pulled at his whiskers.

"I don't know," he said thoughtfully.

"Be hard to get across that river. But I 'spect I could manage that well enough. The trouble is that even if I got him across that river, Kentucky is now Union territory and so is Tennessee. Be a long way to go on foot through hostile territory, and there will be thousands of Yankee soldiers."

Joseph hung his head looking dejected.

"Yea, I know. It don't seem possible. I guess a man ought to appreciate just stayin' where he is. But I want to go home so bad. I have no idea how my family's faring. I don't know how my fiancée is doing, and I just gotta go home."

Toad Turner chewed on a large piece of salt pork with apparent difficulty while he seemed to be contemplating the topic at hand.

"Well, if you stay here long enough, maybe this darn war will be over 'fore too long. Then again, I don't know. I thought it was going to be over in a few months. This war is liable to go on 'til there's nobody left. I just don't know."

He shook his head as he chewed another bite of his supper.

"I'm fixin' to take my boat to St. Louis tomorrow. But I'll think on it a spell. Maybe an idy 'ill come on me."

Joseph and Howard grew even closer as the weeks turned into months. They did as much work as they could for Alice Turner while being careful not to be seen. Alice enjoyed their company greatly, for she was often lonely. Her husband's trips up and down the river often left her at home alone for weeks. Life at the Turner cabin continued in uneventful tranquility.

Three weeks later Toad Turner returned from his river trip and was greeted cheerfully. Toad was cheerful too.

"Those damn Yankees may be fools, but they sure got a heap o' money. I've made more money running the river during this war than I ever did before."

Alice herded them all into the kitchen and seated them at the table while she laid out a feast. Two chickens had been killed, and jarred vegetables added variety to the meal.

"Howard, I reckon I got a plan to get Joseph home. It ain't a great plan, but it's the only half-decent one I can settle on."

He rubbed his chin as he began to explain his scenario.

"You know the army is paying good money for river pilots to go down south carrying cargo from up here. The Yankees control the whole river now; all the way from here to New Orleans they ain't nothin' but Yankees. They want river pilots to haul tobacco from Louisville to Vicksburg. It's a long way and it's a run I don't usually make. But it is good money, and I think that it would be the chance that Joseph is looking for."

"How so, Toad?" Howard asked him.

"Well, you see, it's like this. I could go over to Louisville and let them load me to the top with as much tobacco as I could haul. When I leave Louisville, instead of going all the way downriver, there's a place not too far down where I can pull in close to the bank, and we'll put Joseph on with the tobacco. You'll need to help me though, Howard, cause it will take some work. We'll need to move some of that tobacco out of the way and fix a place for him to hide. We'll need to work fast, so nobody sees us."

It was obvious to Joseph that Toad had given the plan serious thought. The idea of stealing away down the river frightened him, but Joseph felt he must try. He couldn't stand being away from home any longer. There was a lot of danger ahead and he accepted it. If they were

CHAPTER FIFTEEN

caught he would be sent back to prison. Or worse yet, maybe shot as a spy. Joseph was also concerned about the Turners. He worried greatly that he would get Toad in trouble. But the call from home often sounded in his mind. Like a siren in the distance, the southern highlands beckoned him almost constantly.

"It sounds like a good plan to me, Mr. Turner, if you're sure you're comfortable taking the risk. I'm mighty grateful for all you've done for me already."

"Yea, Joseph, it will be risky. We'll have to be extremely cautious. Even if we get to Vicksburg without any trouble, there's still a danger that you won't be able to make it to friendly territory. The Yankees are moving further and further south and I don't know where the Confederate lines begin or end," he finished worriedly.

"I'm willing to try 'cause I think you are a wise enough fella to help me carry it off."

"I'll pay you back someday. I swear I will. I'll pay you back somehow," Joseph said.

The rest of the meal was quiet as the reality of Toad's plan put a somber mood on the festivities. Alice was going to lose one of her boys, and her husband would be taking a great risk. Joseph faced all kinds of uncertainties, and he tried to sort them out in his mind. Even if he made it home, Joseph thought to himself, they probably would make him go back to his regiment, or what was left of it. He couldn't imagine it being the same, and he didn't have any way of knowing how many of his comrades were now dead. If he could just stay at home for a month or so to see his family and to hold Delia in his arms once again it would be enough. If he could stay home for a month or so, or even a week, Joseph decided that he would marry her. If only she would do it and her father allow it. He regretted not marrying her before he left. But he never dreamed that the war would last this long.

Toad Turner was a smart man. The Yanks would have a hard time catching him and Joseph knew it. With just a little bit of luck and the good Lord's help, he'd likely be home in a month or two.

Joseph and Howard waited in the bushes along the riverbank, carefully scanning upriver for traffic coming their way.

"He shoulda been here by now. I hope nothin' went wrong," Joseph said.

"Lord, boy, if you're gonna worry this much now, you're never gonna make it on that boat. If you think you're nervous waitin' on him to get here, what are ya gonna do when them Yankees get on that boat, inspecting the cargo?" Howard scolded.

Anxiety was overtaking Joseph as his many fears surfaced.

"Yankee soldiers are going to get on the boat?" he asked Howard.

"Sure, I reckon so. There's a war going on, in case you didn't know. Nobody trusts anybody, especially Yankees. They stop boats on the river right regular."

Their conversation was interrupted as the form of a small flatbed steamer heavily loaded appeared upriver. They watched at a distance as the boat chugged its way over toward the north bank and the skilled pilot guided it into position for landing. Howard ran down and waited while Toad threw him the lines. Joseph took another, and soon they had the boat tied off and stabilized.

"Now hurry, damn it," Toad shouted from the deck of his little steamer. He flopped a large plank out onto the bank, which made for an unsteady but usable gangway. Joseph and Howard quickly ran on board, and Toad barked off instructions.

"Over here, boys, over here!"

He motioned for them to take a position between two stacks of tobacco. He patted the top part of a tobacco pallet, which was more than head high.

"This one has to be taken all the way out. Set it over here for the time being." He then directed them to the only available space left on the deck. The two men worked quickly until the pallet of tobacco was completely removed.

Toad went to the engine compartment and returned with four short wooden planks.

CHAPTER FIFTEEN

"Here, boys, here."

He showed them the space that had been created by the removal of the tobacco pallet.

"Help me work these boards in here."

With considerable effort they had the boards in place running between two pallets of tobacco at about three feet off of the deck.

"In yonder, son. I'm sorry that it's such a small space," he said to Joseph.

"That'll be fine, Toad. It'll be all right," Joseph said, indicating he planned to meet the challenge.

"Now, boy, you are gonna be in there for days."

"Yes sir, I know," Joseph responded.

"See that hole in the deck?"

"Yes, sir," Joseph again responded.

"Well that hole is gonna be your outhouse. Don't use it except when we're moving and when we're sure nobody else is around. We're gonna pile tobacco up on top of you, on these boards, and we're gonna replace all this tobacco in front of you, so you're gonna be enclosed in this little tobacco room until I get you to Vicksburg. Now you remember, don't say nothin' to me. Don't forget that. Never, unless I talk to you first. I'll let you out some late at night if I can."

"Yes sir, Mr. Turner. Yes sir, I'll do whatever you say."

"Yea, I reckon you will, 'cause if you don't you may not live to see spring. Or if you do it might be back in that hellhole of a Yankee prison," Turner emphasized, making sure Joseph was sufficiently scared to ensure his silence.

Joseph climbed into the little compartment; then Howard handed him a bucket.

"Alice made this for you. It's got some good chow in it and a little bottle of water. Toad can refill it for you now and then. You got to go easy on the food though, 'cause you gotta make it last. Toad can't carry too much food with him cause it might raise suspicions."

"Yea, I'll get you some more water from time to time, but remember there's no more chow comin'," Toad Turner said as he began covering and enclosing the compartment with bundles of tobacco.

Soon his little compartment was complete. Joseph could see nothing except a few gaps of light here and there and the tobacco walls that surrounded him. He looked above his head in the cramped quarters and wondered if the wooden slats would be adequate to hold the tobacco piled on top of him. He could hear Howard and Toad talking and heard footsteps close to his compartment. There was a thump and then another on top of the tobacco piles. "Good-bye, my ole ridin' buddy, I'll see ya after the war," Joseph heard Howard shout to him, and he knew that departure was imminent.

Joseph shouted back.

"Farewell, Howard. Thanks for everything. I'll come back to see you when the war is over."

"You do that, Joseph, you come and see me." Then there was silence, and soon Joseph felt movement as the boat was untied and pushed out into the river.

Chapter 16

―― 1864 ――

Haywood County, North Carolina Matthias Dees and his two sons crept quietly through the woods, their eyes and ears constantly alert for signs of other life. The mountains had evolved into a violent, dangerous place.

The communities of western North Carolina had suffered greatly at the hands of desperados. The value of human life had plummeted even in the coves of Haywood County.

The normal order of life was often converted to chaos by the war. The conflict had brought all sorts of adversity to almost everyone. Threats existed at every turn.

As the Dees boys crept through the woods Rupert and his brother were on either side of their father. All three men carried loaded muskets. Matthias Dees also carried a Colt pistol in his belt. They came to a narrow point in the creek that was used as a crossing for foot traffic on the north side of Mount Sterling. The men looked about anxiously. They stopped on the creek bank, their eyes searching the foliage.

"Are you sure this is where we are supposed to meet them?" Dees asked while still scanning the ridge lines.

"Yep, I'm sure. Sure 'nough, he said they'd meet us up right chere."

"All right, ya boys keep a sharp eye while I git a sip of water and rest a spell. Now y'all holler quick if you see or hear somethin'."

Dees laid his musket across a log and knelt by the stream while he scooped himself a drink. He found a dry place on the bank of the stream where he seated himself and pulled his floppy hat over his eyes. He had rested only a few minutes when he heard a call from Rupert.

"Somebody's comin', Paw," Rupert whispered, breaking the silence.

Dees jumped up quickly but quietly and dashed behind the log, laying his musket across at the ready. Soon four men could be seen coming up the trail from the Tennessee side of the line. The Dees boys watched silently as they approached. Rupert whispered to his father, "I reckon that's 'em, Paw."

They waited a little longer until the men were close enough to see their faces. Dees called his two boys closer to him and whispered, "Now remember what I told you. If anything starts, fire one time and run, and we'll meet back at the road."

"Ain't nothin' gonna start. They ain't gonna ambush us," Rupert said confidently. Suddenly they heard a call as the four men stopped within voice range. They could clearly see the dark blue uniforms speckled by the foliage.

"Hey there, is anybody there?" a strange voice called out from the forest beyond. Dees paused briefly and then slowly rose to his feet.

"Yea, we're here. Is that you, Kirk?" Rupert called out.

"Yea, is that you, Dees?" the man called back to him.

"We're coming on up. Lower your muskets. I don't wanna be shot by mistake," the man in the blue uniform shouted after him.

Soon the seven men stood together on the bank of Cataloochee Creek.

"Paw, this here is the man I been tellin' ya 'bout. This here is Colonel Kirk of the U.S. Army," Rupert said, indicating he was impressed by Kirk's rank and title. Matthias Dees looked to his son with guarded contempt.

Kirk gestured toward the men with him. "This here is John and Bill Cooper from up in Yancey County and Joe Stewart from Mitchell County. Them boys is now privates in the U.S. Army."

Dees looked annoyed as if he were surprised by the introduction. He thought the men looked amusing. He saw them as a bunch of mountaineers like him who were just as dirty as he was, all wrapped up in fancy new uniforms. Their greasy hair hung down surrounding their bearded faces, creating a comical contrast with the new uniforms. The

CHAPTER SIXTEEN

three men Dees knew smiled at him, displaying their rotten discolored teeth, but Dees was not impressed.

"Oh yea, we've knowed 'em boys a long time," Dees said with inference.

"Now tell me Kirk, jus' what is it ya want with me and my boys?"

Kirk gestured to the three men wearing Union uniforms.

"Y'all know these men. I kin do for you the same thing that I've done for 'em."

"Now jus' what do ya figger ya gonna do for me?" Dees said contemptuously. Kirk pulled a pouch with tobacco and a cluster of fine papers from his pocket.

"Would ya men kere fer a smoke? We'll sit down and talk."

Dees and his sons stared at the tobacco anxiously as the tension eased. Such items were hard to come by, and tobacco was always a welcome gift or an appreciated bribe.

"I'm a colonel in the U.S. Army, and I've been authorized to form up a regiment made up of North Carolina and East Tennessee men. I want y'all to join up."

Dees puffed his cigarette, cocked his head slightly, and looked at Kirk. He squinted his dark eyes and looked about as if he were revealing a great mystery.

"I done been in one army and I ain't hankerin' on bein' in another," said Dees.

"I figgered on that," Kirk responded, "but there's a lot of opportunity in this for the likes of you. First off, I'm authorized to tell ya that the U.S. government will pay ya good money if ya fall in with the 3rd North Carolina Mounted Infantry with us."

Dees's eyes lit up and bulged slightly as he leaned forward. A sly smile wrinkled his mouth.

"Mounted? Did I hear ya say mounted? Are ya gonna give us a horse?"

"Yes," Kirk replied.

"How come you ain't got no horse now? Ya come walkin' up here same as I did." Dees questioned the colonel with cynicism in his voice.

"Well, we ain't got no horses yet. But we gonna git 'em in a few months."

John Cooper injected himself into the conversation.

"Matthias, you know me. I'll tell ya straight. Colonel Kirk, he's done right by us. Look at this here," he said, holding up his feet. The man wore a solid pair of quality leather shoes.

"Whew. Damn. Ain't dat purdy," Dees said.

"But I want me a horse. I'm done used to goin' barefoot such that I don't need no shoes. But I'm damn tired of walkin' these mountains."

All the men laughed.

"We're all tired of walkin', and the army's gonna git us horses in a few months. I'm gonna see to it," Kirk said.

Dees looked back at John Cooper and talked directly to him.

"Yea, I 'member ya. I wanna know who else done joined up with ya fellers I mighta knowed."

The three men with Kirk were all western North Carolina men. They called off names of various others who had joined. As the mountaineers recounted the various individuals now in Kirk's unit Dees nodded at some of the names. He commented intermittently that he knew this one or that one, that he knew him well, or the other not at all.

Dees turned back to Kirk.

"Tell me somethin', Mr. Colonel. How much the Union army payin' a man to sign up?"

The men in blue uniforms grinned broadly, and the Dees boys leaned forward, listening carefully.

"I am authorized to tell ya that the Union army will pay ya three hundred dollars to sign up."

"Whew. Hot-damn doggies! Praise be!" the Dees boys howled in astonishment.

"I tol' ya, Paw," Rupert shouted excitedly.

Dees motioned for his sons to be silent.

"Now that ain't Confederate money, is it? I done been paid with that worthless shit once and I ain't takin' no more of it."

Kirk and the others laughed hysterically. He shook his head negatively, "No. No. Hell no. We ain't takin' no Confederate money either."

"No sir. We're talkin' greenbacks, U.S. dollars guaranteed."

CHAPTER SIXTEEN

Dees found the offer incredibly intriguing. Three hundred dollars was a fortune in 1864, and it was hard for him to believe. Dees cocked his head and extended his neck.

He looked slyly at Kirk.

"Ya ain't got that money on ya person, now have ya?"

"No, no, you'll have to come to Greenville to git ya money," Kirk said.

"You mean if I come over to Greenville with you and make my mark, you just gonna hand me three hundred dollars?" Dees asked.

"No," Kirk responded. "Ya don't git it all at once. But if ya join up 'n make your mark, you'll git twenty-five dollars that day, a brand new uniform 'n boots like 'dis here."

Dees leaned back and scratched his head.

"Damn! I never'd thunk it. This war done created more opportunity than a gold rush."

"Now let me ask ya to ponder this, Mr. Colonel," Dees said, now comfortable with the man in the blue uniform. "Me and the boys gonna think this over. In the meantime, you gonna leave us alone?"

"Yea, you think a spell, and if you don't bother us, we won't bother you. But now don't you be joinin' up with no Confederates."

Dees looked back at his boys, and they all three burst into laughter.

"Mr. Colonel, sir. Hell'll freeze over 'fore me 'n my boys join up with 'em damn fools. I ain't sayin' that I'll join up with ya, but I won't bother ya and I won't join up with 'em neither."

"Don't figger on it too long. Many of the men hidin' out in these mountains are joinin' up with us," Kirk said.

Dees looked at him with concern registering on his face.

"Yea, I knowed that. I just wanna be sure that there's room for the likes of us."

The men shook hands and parted ways. Kirk gave them some tobacco and papers. The rough mountaineers–turned-Union soldiers turned around and headed back into Tennessee while the Dees boys headed back up to the top of Mount Sterling.

When they were completely clear of the Union soldiers Dees looked back and instructed his sons to "sit a spell" with him.

"Oh, lawdy. Praise be, money done gone to fallin' outta the damn trees." He wagged his head from side to side.

"I can't figger it. They're payin' a man three hundred dollars. That's a mighty heppin' o' greenbacks."

"Three hundred dollars would look like a bushel o' collard greens in August."

"Let's do it, Paw. Let's join up now. Let's git that money 'n 'em boots. Hell, if we don't like it we'll leave when it suits us, just like when we left 'em fool Rebels," Rupert said.

"Now ya listen here, boys. The Union is gonna win the war, and if a feller handles it right he might be in a powerful spot when this war is over. Them what stayed with the Union is gonna be bossing them ol' slaveowners 'fore it's over, you wait and see, and it don't matter none how long they stayed in jail before the war."

Dees was now engaged in deep concentration.

"But I ain't sure that this here Kirk fella is the one to sign up with. Remember what I told ya boys. If ya goes fishin' go fishin' where everybody else ain't fishin'. I reckon a feller'll catch a heap more fish if he ain't crossing lines with everybody else. Besides, he ain't givin' all the money at once," Dees said indicating to his sons that he'd thought of something they hadn't.

"Did ya hear 'em names Kirk called out? He called every thief, liar, crook, and scoundrel in the mountains. Them two Cooper boys with 'em is meaner 'n snakes. No sir, I reckon we'd be better off fishin' another pond. 'Sides, Kirk ain't got no horse. If a feller goes over to Tennessee he might git himself a few dollars more and a good horse."

Chapter 17

---MARCH 1, 1864---

Memphis, Tennessee Joseph had suffered substantially within the confines of his tobacco-enclosed cubicle. He had escaped it only briefly during the trip down the river. Turner had allowed him out for short periods in the middle of the night while they were traveling on the most isolated sections of the river. The weather had been kind for the most part, although it was still cold at times. The cold and the physical restrictions of his small space often kept him from sleeping. It was especially difficult on nights that he was not able to emerge from his tobacco hut to stretch before settling in.

Joseph was facing another challenge on this arduous trip. There was absolutely nothing to do but think. At Camp Morton he had at least had people to talk to. Encased inside his tobacco hut, there were only his thoughts to keep him company. Joseph could not keep from mentally replaying his war and prison experiences and was often overcome with sadness over the suffering and loss of so many. His sleep was interrupted with nightmares of the carnage recorded in his memory. He often conjured up images of the men he'd killed. He dreamed of the young boy he'd shot at Malvern Hill.

Occasionally other boats would pass, and his heart would pound louder than he thought possible. It was during these brief moments that he would question the wisdom of his decisions. Then memories of Camp Morton and the horrible conditions there would return. Joseph was certain that he would now be in the boneyard had he stayed. Joseph had at least enjoyed a few months of relative happiness that he wouldn't have otherwise. Perhaps he should've stayed with the Turners and waited out the war.

Thoughts of home and family often consumed him. Joseph worried that many of his friends had been killed or wounded since he had lost contact with the outside world. He so missed Delia and worried that she might have forgotten him or that she thought him dead or, worse yet, that she had married. These thoughts provided a source of resolve. Joseph knew that there was no guarantee he would make it, but he always reached the same conclusion. The risk was worth it. He was alive and would soon be home.

Looking through the cracks in the tobacco, Joseph could see light falling on the coming day, and he wondered about their progress and how far downriver they might be. Except for his discomfort and cramped confinement the last few days had passed uneventfully.

Suddenly he heard Turner's voice above him.

"Joseph, don't make a sound. A Union gunboat is coming on."

There was silence for a period, and then he could hear a voice calling across the water. He could not detect exactly what was being said, but he heard Turner shout back, "I have a load of tobacco for the U.S. Army."

The inquiring voice across the water came again.

Turner responded, "Yes, sir, I have papers."

Again came the voice and this time Turner paused and Joseph became concerned. Turner finally shouted back. "Yes, sir, I will make port. Yes, sir."

A few minutes later he heard Turner's voice again, this time low and directly above him.

"Dear God, Joseph. They're gonna board us. Don't make a sound. I pray you, don't make a sound."

Joseph immediately felt his heart pounding. His first thought was that he needed to station himself in a comfortable position. There was no way to know how long the visitors would remain on the boat. He

CHAPTER SEVENTEEN

knew that even the slightest move would be disastrous. He thought, I must be absolutely quiet or I'll go back to prison and who knows what Toad Turner might face.

The only sound he could hear was a little swishing of the water beneath him and the pounding of his accelerated heart. He could feel the slowing of the boat.

"Throw me your line." Joseph detected the voice of a different man.

Turner responded, "Aye, sir."

There was a bit more commotion, and he could feel the boat being pulled and then tied. The swish and thug sound of the rope was followed by footsteps. Then there were many footsteps. He could barely make out what was being said at the front of the boat, but he did hear a voice asking for papers.

He heard Turner's response, "Yes, sir. I have them here from the U.S. Army quartermaster, in Louisville, Kentucky. I am a loyal Union man taking tobacco to the army."

Again there was silence and then more footsteps shuffling about the boat. He heard the same voice again.

"Where are you from?" the voice asked.

Turner answered, "Indiana, sir."

"You wouldn't be carrying any contraband from Indiana, would you?" the voice said.

"Why, uh, no sir. No sir," Turner responded.

"We'll see. Okay, men. Search this boat."

There was more shuffling and footsteps. Then Joseph heard some very unfamiliar sounds. It was a noise like a swish, followed by a slight thump that accompanied the slow, steady steps. The sounds were repeated. Swish, thump. Swish, thump. Joseph began to seriously wonder about the origin of the sounds as they were coming closer and getting louder. Fear engulfed him as he thought of being discovered. The swish, thump sound was right beside him and then directly above him.

The reality of what generated the noise became immediately evident as a bayonet popped through the stacks of tobacco, piercing his right arm and tearing into the surface skin on his back. He was stricken with pain but forced himself to remain silent. The bayonet quickly withdrew. As Joseph grabbed his wounded arm, the swish, thumps continued down the length of the boat.

He heard the voice again.

"Hey, Indiana. My men could use a little tobacco."

"Sure," Turner responded. "Take a couple of bundles for yourself and your men. I reckon the army won't mind."

There was more shuffling about, followed by joking and laughter. He could hear Turner repeatedly expounding about his Unionism and profusely thanking the soldiers for doing their duty. Soon Joseph heard footsteps exiting the boat, and he could feel the boat being pushed off from the dock. It was quite a while before any other sounds were heard. Turner said nothing. Joseph figured that he was waiting until he had completely cleared the gunboats and the port.

Suddenly, he heard Turner's frantic voice above him.

"Oh God, Joseph. Are you all right? Are you hurt?" Turner said, anxiously waiting for a response.

"I'm hurt, but I don't think it's bad. I'll be all right if you can get me a bandage of some sort."

"We best wait for nightfall. You'll have to make do 'til then," Turner said apologetically.

It was after midnight when Turner uncovered Joseph's cubicle, allowing him to escape briefly.

"Where are you hurt, Joseph?"

"Here," he said, gesturing to the back of his right arm. The tip of the bayonet had gone through the back of his arm at a sharp downward angle, missing the bone in his arm with the tip, skipping off one of Joseph's ribs, and piercing the flesh on his back. Turner got some water and cleaned the cuts as best he could. As Turner cleaned the wounds Joseph stretched his legs and slowly breathed in the fresh night air. His need to move was about as great as his need for a bandage. As he took in the beauty of the starry sky, Joseph's heart was

CHAPTER SEVENTEEN

full of gratitude for the day. Certainly, he thought, this day could have turned out much differently.

"I have something to tie around your arm, but I don't have anything to put over that puncture on your back."

"That's okay," Joseph told him. "I felt it pretty good and I know it's only a skin wound. The blade bounced off my ribs. As long as I can keep it clean, it should heal fine."

"We'll be comin' in above Vicksburg day after tomorrow," Turner told him.

"I will hold back a little bit to be sure that we get there well after dark," Turner said.

"Joseph, you know you'll have to get off the boat in the river."

Joseph looked at him, realizing that the close scrape with the Yankees had truly frightened Toad Turner. He was pretty anxious to get rid of Joseph, and it was now quite obvious.

"Sure, Toad. I understand. It's best if I get off as soon as possible. You get me as close to the bank as you can and I'll go it on my own from there."

Two nights later as they began their approach to Vicksburg Turner freed Joseph from his cubicle.

"There's Union gunboats all over the river around Vicksburg. You'd best get off upstream."

Toad Turner was ready for this dangerous act of goodwill to end. Joseph could not be upset with his friend. The man had risked his life in addition to all that he had already done for him. Joseph was deeply saddened at the thought of not seeing the Turners again. Indeed, they had become very close.

Joseph looked at Toad, staring him in the eyes, and said, "I won't forget you."

He reached for Toad's hand and clutched it in his.

"Thank you so much for all you've done. I owe you my life."

Temporarily regaining his courage and his composure, Turner smiled back at him.

"Twern't nothin' to it. Proud to have done it for ya," he said while shaking Joseph's hand.

"Now move this boat over to the bank. Let me get off of here so you can sell that tobacco and take all that money back to Indiana. Please give my regards to Howard and Alice, and I'll see y'all someday after this war is over."

As the boat drifted toward the bank, Joseph packed up his blanket and consumed the remaining food. They were only a couple of miles above Vicksburg when Turner eased the boat into slower waters and Joseph slid down the side and into the river. His right arm was very sore but completely mobile as he paddled and kicked his way toward the bank. He came to an area that was too steep to climb, and he half-swam and half-bounced his way along the bank, feeling his way down the shoreline in the darkness. Soon he caught himself on a large tree that had fallen into the river. Joseph pulled himself up onto the trunk of the tree and rested.

He listened and looked for a few minutes to be sure that he was safe. Joseph was increasingly uncomfortable from the soaking cold that surrounded his body. Climbing along the trunk of the tree until he was above the bank, he stood up, took off his clothes, and wrung them out as best he could.

Soon the temperatures forced him to put his clothes back on, despite their dampness. His experiences with Howard Turner would serve him well. His life would now depend on these vital skills of survival and navigation. It was a clear night, so he was able to chart his route by the stars.

Joseph knew that Tennessee and a good portion of Mississippi were in Union hands. He had no idea how far south he would have to go to find Confederate lines. Again he thought of Delia and his spirits were rejuvenated as he took off walking. Checking the wounds to his arm and back and looking at the sky he quipped aloud, "Well, reckon you best be walking while it's still dark."

Joseph traveled as far as he could that night, and eventually his clothes dried out. He was still suffering from the cold when the sun

CHAPTER SEVENTEEN

came up and he made his camp. He covered himself as much as possible and then went to sleep.

Joseph woke up mid-morning to a warm, sunny day for which he was thankful. The relief from the cold soon turned to sweat from the heat. He knew he was somewhere in western Mississippi but was not sure exactly where. He walked inland all the way around Vicksburg and headed further south. Four nights later he came across an isolated cabin in the woods.

It was just before daylight when he approached the little structure. Joseph fretted about making himself known, but he was motivated by hunger. Finally he concluded that in this part of the country the inhabitants were most likely southern sympathizers. His biggest concern was getting their attention without being shot.

Smoke circled slowly from the stone chimney, and a lantern lit the inside of the little house. Joseph steeled himself for the approach, slowly getting within voice range of the door. He thought it best to lie on the ground as Howard had taught him and shout to announce his presence. Joseph called out, and soon a voice called back. He could hear some activity, but he wasn't sure what was happening. Eventually an old man's voice called back to him.

"Come forward 'n show yourself."

Joseph stood, raised his hands high in air, and walked forward. As he got closer to the cabin he could see the double barrels of a shotgun sticking out the door.

"Stop right there and state your purpose."

"I'm Joseph Youngblood, a Confederate soldier, and I'm starving to death. I need something to eat real bad."

"If you be a Confederate soldier what is ya regiment?" the voice demanded.

"I was with the 25th North Carolina, Ransom's Brigade."

Slowly the door opened, and the man stepped outside.

"I never heard of it, but it don't make no matter no how. Ya either is or you ain't, and we'll find out soon enough, I 'spect."

The old man lived with his wife, several children, and two young women whose husbands were in the Confederate army.

The two women dressed and cleaned his wounds, and then he was able to bathe himself and rest.

"Where am I?" he asked one of women.

"We're just a few miles northeast of Brookhaven, Mississippi. The Yankees come and go here now, but so do our boys. My husband is with Forrest's Cavalry, and they are in the area. If I can find him he could get you to Alabama and maybe you can get a train east."

The next morning one of the young women left and went into town. She was gone most of the day but returned near nightfall. She approached Joseph.

"Can you ride?"

"Yes, I can ride," he said, lacking confidence. "It's been a long time."

"Good. Be ready to leave in the morning," she said calmly.

"Yes, ma'am," Joseph responded.

Immediately after daylight they left from the back of the house and headed into the woods. Nothing was said as he followed the quiet figure through the forest. She was dressed in a long, full black dress and was surprisingly fast for a woman, Joseph thought. She hiked up her dress and took broad steps like a man. They moved rapidly most of the morning without rest. Joseph was tired but wasn't about to ask a woman to slow down.

Eventually they came to a small clearing. It was a pretty spot with large, old oak trees covered with lots of low-hanging Spanish moss clinging to the limbs.

The woman turned to Joseph.

"We'll wait here."

They sat on a log but very little was said. It was over an hour when Joseph heard what seemed to be horses in the distance. Soon there was no doubt; the sounds were horses, many horses. Within minutes the little clearing was filled with horses and Confederate soldiers. All the mounted men wore Confederate gray. One man moved in front of the group.

"I'm Lieutenant Wallace of the 8th Mississippi Cavalry. They tell me you can ride."

CHAPTER SEVENTEEN

Joseph beamed at the sight of friendly faces.

"Yes, sir, I can ride."

Lieutenant Wallace called out, and a youngster not much older than fifteen or sixteen rode up in front of the officer. He had an empty horse tied to his saddle.

"Climb on. We've got a ways to go 'fore nightfall, and there's lots of Yankees around here."

Joseph got on the horse and followed the young officer into line. They were maybe thirty strong when they rode off. Joseph was uncomfortable and awkward at first, but soon his riding skills came back to him. His new companions were expert horsemen, but he was able to keep up. The horse they gave him was calm and easygoing and for that he was thankful.

The Mississippi cavalrymen rode on eastward throughout the following day at a slow, steady pace. When they rode into camp that night they were met by more of Forrest's men. When the mounted caravan departed the next morning the cavalry was more than a hundred strong. Joseph couldn't help but be favorably impressed by the lively spirit of the men around him.

Five days later they rode into Tuscaloosa, Alabama. There the Confederates were met by cheering people who'd turned out to greet them. They went into camp that evening just outside the city. Joseph and his new companions were treated to good food by the townspeople. There was fresh meat and warm bread for them to eat. Joseph ate peaches for the first time in years. He was feeling much better every day and was thankful for his blessings.

Late that night as men gathered around the campfire Lieutenant Wallace walked over and sat down next to Joseph.

"You ain't the best rider I've ever seen, but you're gettin' better. We need good men, Joseph. This war is gonna go on for a while. Would you consider joining up with us?"

Joseph looked at Wallace and spoke to him in an earnest tone. "I ain't seen my family in over two years. I've got a sweetheart back home that I should've married before I left. If God allows it I'm going home and I'm gonna marry her just as soon as I can. I'm honored that you'd ask me, but I gotta go home."

Wallace nodded his head slowly.

"I thought that's what you'd say, but I had to ask."

He poked a stick into the fire, then looked at Joseph.

"We'll be going to Birmingham in the next few days. When we get there we'll see if we can get you a train to Atlanta. I don't know how you can go back to North Carolina from there, but I figure a man that broke out of a Yankee prison camp and got all the way down the Mississippi this far, he'll figure out a way."

Wallace smiled and walked away.

Birmingham was a sizable town with an active population. Joseph waited while Wallace talked to the stationmaster.

"You're in luck, Youngblood," Wallace told him. "There's a full load of horses going outta here tomorrow morning headed for Atlanta. I've got you a ride on that train. You'll have to stand up though. The only room is on the cattle cars with the horses."

"That's fine with me," Joseph said smiling. "I've put up with a lot worse than that just getting this far."

Wallace walked over to him and extended his hand.

"Well, this is it for us. We'll be moving on. We gotta meet up with General Forrest in a few days."

The two men shook hands, and Joseph thanked him. The cavalrymen mounted their horses and rode away taking the extra horse, leaving Joseph at the station.

The cattle car was crowded, dirty, and shaky. Joseph looked through the cracks as the train chugged down the track heading east. He was at the front of the car with two other men who'd also hitched a ride on the train. He listened to them complain about the discomfort of having to stand up for the entire ride. They also griped about the heavy odor of horse manure that permeated the car. The black smoke and soot blowing into the compartment from the engine smokestack also gener-

CHAPTER SEVENTEEN

ated considerable discontent with Joseph's fellow passengers. Joseph said nothing in response. He thought of the freezing nights at Camp Morton, riding Morton's Mule, and the hundreds of deaths he had seen. He thought about the ride down the Ohio and the Mississippi in his cramped tobacco cubicle. Joseph examined his bayonet wounds, which were now mostly healed. Then he smiled to himself as he surveyed his surroundings.

"Quite nice, quite nice," he whispered.

Joseph did learn something important from the two men. They informed him that the train was only passing through Atlanta. The horses were on their way to Confederate general Joseph E. Johnston's Army of Tennessee. These men were on their way back to their units. According to them, Johnston's whole army was now camped at Dalton, Georgia, somewhere north of Atlanta.

"All you have to do is stay on the train," the men advised him. "You'll get a ride that much closer to home."

Joseph decided to ride all the way to Dalton if he could. He was pretty sure from what he'd learned from the men at Camp Morton that the 60th North Carolina was with Johnston. That would mean that his two brothers, J. N. and Hiram, would be there. He only hoped that they were safe. Joseph knew that the army had seen some hard fighting, and he feared that they might have been wounded or killed. No matter what he would discover regarding his brothers, he knew he could walk into western North Carolina from that part of Georgia. He could find out in Dalton where the worst of the fighting was and select a route which would avoid trouble. It all seemed reasonable at the time.

Chapter 18

──APRIL 1864──

Hoopers Creek, North Carolina It was a beautiful day, with dogwoods in bloom and leaves popping out on the hardwoods. The tranquil setting did much to disguise the difficulties encountered by those who resided in the mountains. So many young men were gone off to war; far too many had gone never to return. The small coves, valleys, and towns were now sprinkled with maimed men who had returned from the battlefield, often injured both in body and spirit. Those that recovered physically might never recover emotionally. Most every family housed a limbless, blind, or otherwise disabled young man. Deserters roamed everywhere avoiding the war and conscription agents. Cold Union prisons in the far north held many of their loved ones captive. Some families simply didn't know where their loved ones were or what fate had befallen them. Some realized that they'd probably never know.

Starvation and depravation had converted many loyal Rebels into doubters or opponents. The strong-arm discriminatory regulation of the new Confederate government had forced many otherwise respectable families to engage in criminal activity. It was only through the devotion and tenacity of the dedicated men who remained in the trenches that the infant nation continued to exist. They persevered in spite of the death and destruction on the battlefield and the extreme hardships forced on their families at home.

CHAPTER EIGHTEEN

Delia Russell looked out over the sprouting green grass that dominated the property around the farm. It looks so peaceful, she thought. Yet nothing was peaceful. Every belly was growling with hunger. Every citizen was wary of the other. The main concern for most people was basic survival.

Delia worried about Joseph constantly. Indeed, she feared his death. Yet thoughts of his return were her only grip on sanity. Visions of him and dreams of the two of them together made her happy at times. "He must be alive," she thought to herself. "Without him I can't go on."

Today was a happy day with something to look forward to. Joseph's little brother was coming to take her for a ride. Pinkney Youngblood was only a boy of thirteen, and like so many others he'd been forced to grow up fast. He was home taking care of the farm with Bill, who'd been spared further exposure to the war by way of the paid substitute. With the oldest and the youngest still at home, the Youngblood farm fared better than most. Still, it was not a happy home. The elder Youngblood was sick and weak, partly from illness and partly from worry over his sons. The Youngblood patriarch was now among the most ardent of the disgruntled.

Delia was delighted when the youngster rode into the yard. He said he wanted to show her something, something he seemed to be quite proud of. So they had talked at church the previous Sunday and made their plans. Delia didn't really care what Pinkney was going to show her. She just looked forward to the day's entertainment and some time away from her father. Robert Russell's physical and emotional decline had continued. When he wasn't complaining he was drinking. Delia seemed to be the one that he leaned on and the one that everyone else counted on to keep the senior Russell somewhat stable.

Delia had dressed in her work dress. She would be riding in the buggy with Pinkney on a rough road. It seemed that Delia had taken on such a powerful role at home that her mother often relinquished her normal parental controls.

Pinkney climbed off his horse and met Delia on the steps.

"Mornin', Miss Delia," he said, taking off his hat and doing his best to act grownup.

"Good morning to you, Pinkney," she replied politely.

"Are you ready? We're going up on Bearwallow Mountain. But don't you worry about a thing. I'll protect you," he said confidently while exposing a small pistol in his belt. The sight of the small revolver was a bit disconcerting, but Delia said nothing.

"Where on Bearwallow are we going?" she asked.

"You'll see," he said as he tied his horse and went to the buggy.

The ride up Hoopers Creek was uneventful. Pinkney did all the talking while Delia took in the scenery and enjoyed the beautiful day. He described the trees in great detail and shared the things he had learned to do on the farm. He was especially proud of his work with the livestock.

When they were almost at the top, Pinkney broke off the main road and started down a winding trail that twisted to and fro between the laurel and rhododendron. He guided the buggy along the steep, sometimes rocky path. To Delia the trail seemed to be getting dangerous, but to Pinkney it appeared to be entertaining. Pinkney parked the buggy and tied off the horse. The youngsters continued from there on foot.

The pair emerged from the trail and entered a little clearing that was completely surrounded by heavy growth. At the edge of the clearing was a small corral that housed two beautiful brown and white Appaloosa mares and their two young colts. Delia stared at them in awe and disbelief as she watched the young horses dance around the corral.

"Oh, Pinkney, they're beautiful. Just beautiful."

"I've been raising them myself. I took care of 'em without any help at all," he said with obvious pride.

Delia eagerly rushed over to the corral. One of the colts approached her and accepted her hand almost freely as she petted the young animal. The two mothers munched on mountain grass, paying little attention to the visitors. Delia was captivated. Her father had sold off most of their horses, and they hadn't had little ones since she was a child. Her heart melted as she beamed at the two little colts.

CHAPTER EIGHTEEN

"I keep them hidden up here 'cause Bill says some bushwhacker or somebody might try to steal them. He says that things is so bad that some folks might even try to eat 'em."

The two of them fed the horses and played with them for over an hour. The day had warmed and was quite pleasant. They sat under a nearby walnut tree where they could watch the horses and enjoy the mountain scenery.

"Miss Delia, do you think Joseph is alive?" Pinkney asked with a nervous tone.

"Oh yes, of course he is," Delia answered frantically.

"I don't know. Sometimes I just fear the worst. Lots of men die in those prisons, ya know."

"He is alive and he will come home. You just wait and see."

Tears came to her eyes as she was forced to face the worst possibilities. Pinkney recognized that he had upset her.

"Oh no, Miss Delia, I don't mean to say that I don't think he's coming home. I just worry about it, that's all." He changed the subject back to the horses and suggested that they get a drink from the spring nearby.

"Sometimes I feel guilty about not fighting. All my brothers have gone off to war, but Pa and Bill won't let me go."

"You're only thirteen and your family already sent four sons to the war. Don't you think that's enough?" Delia asked, trying to make him feel better.

"I don't know. I just feel like I oughta go. I said so at the supper table and my pa didn't like it. But Bill, he really didn't like it. He got mad and said that he would chain me up before he'd let me join," Pinkney said, indicating he was surprised at their response.

"I reckon my folks don't feel the same way about the war anymore. They say all they want is out of it. They just want Joseph, J. N., and Hiram to come home and for folks to leave us alone," he said with an air of disappointment.

"Can I tell you a secret, Miss Delia?" he asked her with some reservation.

"Of course you can. I mean, you can if you want to. I sure won't tell anybody," she said reassuring him.

She was expecting something about a sweetheart or girlfriend, but Pinkney blurted out, "Hiram is at home. He snuck off from the army and came home. That's the third time he's done it in the last year."

Delia was puzzled.

"Doesn't he have a furlough?" she asked.

"No, he just sneaks off, but he always goes back," he said, trying to justify the circumstances.

"Won't he get in trouble?" Delia asked.

"He says he won't, but Bill worries about it something awful. He says Hiram's asking for trouble. Bill won't let him go out of the house when he's home. He's afraid he'll get arrested or something. Hiram says lots of 'em do it and he ain't the only one. He says there won't be trouble as long as he goes back."

"I don't know," Delia said worriedly.

"I don't think that's good."

"You won't tell now, will ya? Please don't tell nobody."

She touched his hand, "Oh, no, I won't tell a living soul."

The ride down the mountain was both fun and relaxing, with Pinkney playing the role of grownup and Delia playing right along. She enjoyed his attention and felt comfortable with him because he was Joseph's brother. What a delightful day it had been!

Pinkney and Delia said their good-byes, and she thanked him for the wonderful day. Delia went into the house and was greeted by her mother, who was out of bed for a change.

"Where's Papa?" Delia inquired.

"I believe he's in the study," her mother answered.

Delia walked down the hall and into the study to find her father sitting at his desk. He had the moneybox out and on the table. He was counting what was left, as he so often did. Delia looked closer and noticed that he had her velvet pouch laid out on the table and that he

CHAPTER EIGHTEEN

was holding Joseph's coin in his right hand. The beautiful German coin gleamed brightly in the lamplight.

Delia was disturbed.

"What are you doing with that?" she said, pointing at the coin.

"Just looking at it," he answered calmly. "You know the day might come when we have to use this," he said.

Delia was enraged.

"Give that back to me, it doesn't belong to us. It's Joseph's," she said defiantly. She reached and took the coin from his hand.

"Besides, you still have money left," she said, trying to get his mind off the coin.

"You might as well forget him. He's dead anyway. Nobody survives those Yankee prison camps that long," he blurted out in a cruel tone.

Delia looked beside him and saw the bottle. Obviously he'd been drinking again and it angered her.

"If you'd stop spending your money on that whiskey," she responded bitterly.

"How dare you talk to me that way! I'm your father."

He had risen to his feet and raised his hand as if to strike her but stopped himself. He half-sat and half-stumbled back into his chair. He took another drink and looked away from her.

"Here, take your damn coin. Don't matter anyway," he said half-grumbling.

Delia took the coin and dropped it back into the velvet pouch. She put the pouch and the rest of the contents back into the box. Russell ignored her while she put the box back into its hiding place and covered the hole with the paneling.

"Please, Papa. Don't drink so much," she said pleading.

He ignored her again. Delia waited for a moment, then went to bed.

Chapter 19

— APRIL 1864 —

Dalton, Georgia Joseph jumped off the train and walked into town with a lively step. There were men, horses, and wagons everywhere. Pre-war Dalton was a small, sleepy village with a few farmers and a lonely street of merchants. But with Joe Johnston's army stationed in the area, the village had turned into quite a boomtown. Joseph decided to look for the post office, thinking he might get information on the location of the 60th North Carolina there. Before he was able to locate the post office he was approached and stopped by a Confederate captain. The officer seemed to stare at Joseph with suspicion.

"Where do you think you're goin' soldier?" the captain asked in an accusatory tone.

In an effort to avoid confrontation, Joseph answered deferentially.

"I'm trying to find the 60th North Carolina, sir," he answered.

Three other Confederate soldiers now joined the captain.

"Is that your unit?" the officer asked.

"No, sir, but my brothers are there, I think."

The officer studied Joseph carefully, then asked. "You wouldn't be a deserter now, would ya? Do you have any papers?"

"No, sir, I don't have any papers," Joseph said. "I've been in a Yankee prison camp for over a year. I escaped back in November and have finally made it here from Indiana."

CHAPTER NINETEEN

The officer looked at him doubtfully while Joseph told him the highlights of how he had gotten from Indiana to Georgia.

"That sounds like a mighty tall tale to me," the officer responded.

One of the other men interrupted. "Sir, I believe the 60th North Carolina is camped up at Crow Valley. If this feller's telling the truth he oughta know some of 'em."

"I reckon that's so. You come with us, boy," the captain said belligerently.

One of the men retrieved a horse for the officer while the other three walked with Joseph. Joseph thought about the army that he had volunteered to fight with. At Sharpsburg he'd had about all the Confederate army he could stand. Joseph had been through so much, and they'd treated him unfairly. After escaping from prison he'd been so glad to see those gray uniforms again. But this man had rapidly reminded him of his earlier discontent. He made up his mind about his future as he walked. The escaped prisoner of war hoped to have a reunion with his brothers but just as soon as he could he was going home.

The long walk also provided Joseph with time to worry about what the captain might do if there were no familiar faces in the 60th, or if they didn't find the 60th.

The captain led the way toward a clearing with a large cluster of tents bunched in the middle. Another officer was walking toward them, paying little or no attention to the small party.

It wasn't until he was right beside them that Joseph recognized him.

"J. L., is that you?" Joseph blurted out.

The man stopped, and Joseph's escort stopped at the same time.

The officer looked puzzled as he stared at the group, trying to figure out who'd spoken his name.

"That's you, ain't it, J. L? You're J. L. Ward from Hoopers Creek."

Ward looked confused as the escort party watched with interest.

"Do I know you?" he said, not recognizing the person calling his name.

"I reckon you do. I'm Joseph Youngblood. I've known you since you pushed me into Cane Creek when I was just a little tot." Joseph smiled widely, displaying his decayed teeth.

At first the words still didn't register; Joseph had changed so much. Ward stepped closer, and then his face lit up. He took one more step, as if to verify what he was seeing.

Ward took Joseph's hand and grabbed his shoulder, shaking him vigorously.

"Well, I'll be damned! Good lawd in heaven, it is you, ain't it? Folks said you was dead. I'll be damned. Where in the hell have ya been?"

Joseph started his explanation as they continued to pat each other and shake hands.

"I've been in a Yankee prison camp. Camp Morton up in Indiana. Me and another feller escaped, and I found my way back here, head'n home."

"Well come with me. Let's get you rested and something to eat."

Joseph's escort party now conceded to his story and said their terse good-byes.

"I've got news for you. Your brothers are in my command, J. N. and Hiram both," he said smiling.

"Then they're all right?" Joseph said happily.

"Oh sure, they're fine. Hiram ain't here though. He snuck off again. I 'spect him back any day. I wish he'd quit doin' that. He's gonna get me and him both in a heap of trouble."

The two friends walked the short distance back into camp and approached a circle of men gathered around a campfire.

"Look what the skunks done drug in!" Ward announced loudly. The men around the fire looked up curiously. Joseph looked right at J. N. and smiled widely. J. N. looked at him without expression. It was clear that he did not recognize the heavily bearded stranger, his own brother.

Joseph looked at Ward and laughed.

"It's a real sad day when your own brother won't speak to ya, ain't it?"

J. N. instantly recognized the voice of his brother. He jumped to his feet, nearly falling over another man sitting between them. The two brothers embraced, something they would have never done before. J. N. began excitedly slapping Joseph on the back and then stepped away and looked into his face.

"Damn, Joseph, we thought you were dead," he said, momentarily choking on his words.

CHAPTER NINETEEN

"Hell, I thought I was dead too," he said laughing through tears of joy. "A Yankee prison ain't no place to be anytime, and it's the worst place to be in winter time."

There were lots of friends from home in the regiment, and his arrival turned into a celebration. The men gathered around the fire and listened to the details of his escape. Many of them teased him for not bringing the Yankee tobacco with him when he got off the boat—at least a little of it, they said.

As the evening wore on more men returned from picket duty. Joseph always checked the faces of each man to see if he knew them. One face stood out above all the others. It was black.

Joseph was surprised at the sight of George Mills. Mills, the well-known former slave from Henderson County, was very close to the Bryson family, and they had given him his freedom before emancipation. Joseph remembered George from the battle at Sharpsburg and the tragic death of his master and friend Watt Bryson.

George walked into camp dressed in a Confederate uniform. Joseph had heard talk at the prison about the manpower shortage and how the government was allowing black men to join up. Obviously the talk was true.

Joseph got up from the fire and walked over to Mills and extended his hand.

"Do you remember me, George? I'm Joseph Youngblood," he said warmly.

At first Mills didn't know him, but then a broad, toothy smile spread over his face.

"Yez, sir, I sho do. I 'member ya real good."

"Yo's one a dem dat hep me fin' Massa Watt at Antietam. I 'members ya real good."

He shook Joseph's hand and walked with him to the fire.

"How'd you end up in the army?" Joseph asked in disbelief.

"Well, sir, I brung Mr. Watt home. It took me a spell, but I gits him home. Then Mr. Bryson done went 'n gives me my freedom. I sez, since I be free I can do what I wants, so I wanna do what Watt done. I went to de army."

"Well, I'll be damned," Joseph said shaking his head. "I'm so glad to see you, and I'm real proud you made it home with Watt."

"Oh yez, sir, dat money you 'n dem other men give me, well I takes it and buys Mr. Watt a grave box. Then I gits on a train for part way. Then I be on a wagon part way 'n dis and dat. Lotta folks hep me on de way. They knowed Mr. Watt be a captain 'n all. When I gits to Greenville, Tennessee, folks done come all de way from Hendersonville to meet me and hep me de rest of de way."

As the men settled in for the night, Joseph got his first chance to talk to his brother alone.

"Tell me the truth about things, J. N. How is it? What am I gonna find at home? How is everybody in the family? Do you know if Delia is still waiting for me?"

J. N. looked around as if to be sure no one could hear.

"Joseph, things ain't good. Folks back home are starving to death. Delia's still waiting, and I reckon she will be until one of ya is dead. You don't have to worry about her, but everything else has gotten ugly."

He got quiet for a moment, then continued slowly.

"With no supplies coming in folks don't have no way to cure nothin'. There's hardly any meat. Everybody's livin' on scraps. All the men are gone, so ain't much crop-farmin' gettin' done. Worst of all is that some folks have done gone plain bad. There's lots of 'em just hiding out and running wild. Nobody's property is safe. These men are just taking what they want. The Home Guard does what they can, but they're nothin' but a bunch of young boys and very old men. They're usually outnumbered and outgunned; they can't do much.

"Then there's plenty of 'em that take advantage of everything and everybody. They come down out of the mountains, robbing and killing people."

He looked again as if he were checking for observers.

"That still ain't the worst of it. Folks don't talk about it, but most of the victims are women. It's the kinda thing nobody wants to talks about, but word gets around and it's frightening, Joseph. I worry about Delia. Joseph, I don't guess you realize, bein' on the run and all, but we're losing this war. None of us have shoes; we don't have food half the time.

CHAPTER NINETEEN

I don't know, it just don't look good."

J. N. shook his head in despair and continued his unleashing.

"That damn Hiram is still too young to have any sense. He's gone back home three times. He got caught once and was in a real pickle. General Johnston took command from General Bragg and pardoned everybody or he'd a been in a real bad way."

"What about my old regiment? Do you know where they are?" Joseph asked.

"After you got caught at Sharpsburg they came back to North Carolina for a good part of last year. It's a good thing too. They weren't at Gettysburg or they mighta been wiped out. Last I heard they're back in Virginia."

J. N. looked at his brother with a painful expression on his face.

"Joseph, if you go home they'll send you back to your regiment. You know they will. They made Will Garren go back, and he can't hardly use his left arm."

"Yea, I know that. But if they'll let me stay long enough to marry Delia and have a little honeymoon, I'll go back. I reckon if what you say is true this war can't last too much longer."

"No, it can't," J. N. said angrily. "But these damn fools may not quit until we're all layin' under grave rocks."

Joseph pondered what he'd said. If he'd made it this far he'd keep on, he decided.

The men prepared to bed down for the night, and Joseph sought tent space to avoid sleeping in the open through the cold night. Tents were in short supply and in poor condition. Some of the little tents had three men in them.

Joseph scouted the camp asking for help.

"You'll have to crowd in with J. N. and his bunkmate," one man told him.

"What about the tent down there?" Joseph said, pointing to a tent off by itself.

"Well, you can't stay there. That's George's tent," the man said in a tone that demonstrated that he wouldn't be willing to sleep with a black man.

This war had changed nothing for some, Joseph thought. Here was a black man willing to join up and fight for the South and no one was willing to share a damn tent with him.

"By God, I'd be proud to be in a tent with that man," Joseph said angrily. "I've slept with a hell of a lot worse in my day."

Joseph stormed off, marching down the hill.

"George, would you be willing to let me share your tent?"

George Mills grinned from ear to ear.

"Yez, sir, Mr. Joseph. Be mighty glad to."

Joseph slept through the night and woke up to the smell of frying bacon.

"Cookie was saving this bacon for Sunday, but since you're here we're gonna eat it now. Kind of a welcome Joseph breakfast," Ward said lightheartedly.

The men talked as they gobbled the bacon. There were no eggs or bread to go with it, but they didn't care. It was mighty good eating to these hungry men. Throughout the camp breakfast, Joseph took a good deal more teasing about the tobacco and his failure to bring any of it with him.

"Hell, ya might as well drowned, you ain't no good to us without any of that tobacco," one man said as they all laughed.

In the middle of their joyous meal a voice coming from the edge of camp penetrated the cluster of men.

"I smell bacon," the voice shouted.

"I'm mighty hungry."

On the sound of his second phrase, Joseph heard it clearly. It was Hiram. He walked into camp greeting all the others without realizing his brother was there.

J. N. looked at him and pointed at Joseph. Then J. N. stole the line used by Captain Ward.

"Look what the skunks drug in," he said, smiling and pointing at Joseph.

Hiram looked at Joseph and studied his face. He ran toward him

CHAPTER NINETEEN

and started to talk but only got the word "Joseph" out before breaking into tears.

"Damn, I never thought I'd see you again in this world," he said, trying to regain his composure. The others laughed, and the happy reunion overcame the uncomfortable embarrassment of the tearful moments.

The pleasant reminiscing continued throughout the early morning as Captain Ward left the Youngblood brothers alone. Many of the men came back and forth from duty exchanging greetings and news from home. The men demanded a song from Hiram, and they all got quiet as he sang "Lorena" while the men dreamed of home. When he'd finished, the men cheered and settled into normal conversation.

"How long you gonna stay here, Joseph?" Hiram asked him.

"I want to go home something awful. I'm gonna stay here tonight, then I'm leaving in the morning. I'm going home, and I'm gonna marry Delia just as soon as she says she'll do it," he said smiling.

"I wouldn't worry about what she says. It's that papa of hers you gotta get past," J. N. said, indicating that he thought that Bob Russell might be a problem.

"I don't give a damn what he says as long as she'll marry me. If she'll marry me I'll just up and take her away," Joseph said defiantly.

Their conversation continued as the brothers enjoyed their happy reunion. Joseph was telling one of his prison stories when he noticed J. N. looking past him. Joseph watched his brother's eyes and saw something he'd seen before. He'd seen that expression on the battlefield; it was the face of a terrified man. Joseph's mind raced as he turned his head to look behind him, searching for the source of fright.

Joseph was confused. He watched as a small cluster of men moved toward them. It was Captain Ward with a Confederate major and a group of armed guards. When they got closer, Joseph could tell they were coming right toward him and his brothers. They came to a halt just a few feet away. Joseph looked into the eyes of Captain Ward and saw a sickened expression. He became aware of his own fear as his hands began to tremble.

"Hiram Youngblood? Which one is Hiram Youngblood?" the major shouted.

Hiram meekly raised his hand.

"I reckon I'm him," he said shaking.

The major looked at him and shouted, "You are under arrest for desertion."

"I didn't desert. I came back," Hiram almost squealed.

"Guards, take him," the major ordered.

Joseph looked at Captain Ward.

"Can't you do something, J. L.?"

Ward looked back at him with fear in his eyes.

"I can't do nothin', Joseph."

The major looked at Ward as the guards surrounded Hiram.

"Be sure the other private Youngblood understands his orders," the major said gruffly.

"What's he talking about, J. L?" Joseph asked.

"You've been ordered to stay with this regiment. Joseph, I'm sorry."

Joseph's mind whirled. How could this be? His emotions twisted between shock, fear, and anger. What could he do? How was he going to get out of this?

"They're crazy!" Joseph yelled at Ward. "I ain't staying. I've got a regiment already!"

He watched Hiram being marched away. Hiram looked over his shoulder at his two brothers, and Joseph could see the terror on his face.

"He's just a boy!" Joseph screamed at Ward. "He's just a damn boy!"

Things settled down for a moment, and Joseph approached Captain Ward and told him calmly.

"I'm leaving, J. L. You can shoot me if you want, but I'm leaving."

"Don't do it, Joseph. I won't try to stop you. If ya go, ya go. But it will make it that much harder on Hiram when he faces court-martial."

The thought of putting his brother at risk stopped him in his tracks.

"But what about my regiment?" Joseph appealed.

"That doesn't matter, and you know it. They'll just send a message to

CHAPTER NINETEEN

Virginia. You're now in the 60th North Carolina," Ward said bluntly.

"How bad is it for Hiram?" Joseph asked.

"I don't know. Johnston warned everybody not to go AWOL anymore. Some folks say he's gonna make an example out of these men. He had fourteen of them arrested, most of 'em from North Carolina."

—— MAY 4, 1864 ——

It was a gray and dreary morning as the men assembled on a gradually sloping hill. Joseph thought it curious that many other regiments were already in formation on the hills above them. The 60th had been called into formation but had been directed to leave their muskets behind. Soon the whole army was gathered there. It was an awesome scene, nearly forty thousand men spread across the rolling hills of north Georgia's Crow Valley.

They were marched into position, and there they waited. Joseph looked below and saw the dreadful sight that provided the answer to the days of anguish over his brother's fate. He'd stayed with the army in an attempt to help his brother.

"Oh God, no," Joseph whispered aloud as he took in the sights in front of him.

At a low point in the valley where all the army could see stood fourteen vertical stakes in the ground. Beside each stake was a crude wooden casket and a hole obviously shaped for a grave.

Joseph looked at J. N. and saw the tears in his brother's eyes through those of his own. He turned back to the horrible scene unfolding on the ground below. From off to the left a group of guards marched the fourteen condemned men toward the stakes. The men were all dressed in shabby clothes and were barefoot. One by one the men were tied to the stakes. Joseph could clearly see Hiram being tied to the fourth stake from the left. His head hung to one side as his body assumed an ignominious posture.

Joseph and J. N. now sobbed openly. He thought of rushing to save him but knew he'd be shot. He held out hope for a last-minute reprieve from General Johnston, but none came.

Once all the men were tied the officer ordered the guards into position.

Joseph turned his head away and saw the tears of other men in the regiment. He gritted his teeth in painful anguish and looked back to the ghastly scene just as the order to fire was given. The results of the first volley were painfully inconclusive. Many of the guards had missed intentionally, unable to bring themselves to shoot their comrades.

Joseph could see that Hiram was hit in the arm but was still alive.

"Please God, do something," he prayed. There was a pause and then some confusion among the death squad. Joseph started to run forward but was grabbed and held by his neighbors. J. N. just slumped to his knees and cried aloud. For a moment, Joseph held out hope that his brother would be spared yet.

Then the officer ordered one man forward with a musket. He ordered him to place the gun barrel to the breast of one of the condemned men. The guard looked at the officer with revulsion as he anticipated the order.

"Fire," he ordered.

The shot rang out.

Then the officer ordered more guards forward. He went down the line, pulling the guards' musket barrels forward and pressing them into the chests of the condemned.

One by one he went down the row until all fourteen of the poor souls were dead.

Joseph was in shock, numb and unable to move. A mixture of rage and sadness overwhelmed him. The world had gone mad, he thought. Nothing he'd been through had prepared him for this. He looked into the eyes of his surviving brother and could see the hate and anger etched in his face. The two battle-hardened veterans sobbed openly.

"No more," he said to himself.

"This Confederacy can go to hell."

When they returned to camp, Ward sought them out.

CHAPTER NINETEEN

"I'm so sorry, I couldn't do nothin'," he said, shaking his head.

"The general has ordered extra guards to be placed around the camp. Don't you two try nothin' stupid. They're ready for it. You'll get yourself shot."

It was three o'clock in the morning when Joseph and J. N. made their exit from camp. They'd talked it over and decided that they'd rather be shot than stay another day in this madness. Both men were so enraged and overcome with sadness that they were not thinking clearly. Hate consumed them, clouding their judgment. They knew that there was a good chance they'd be caught. Still, they were desperate enough to try.

As Ward had warned, it was not a good night to attempt such an escape. There was too much moonlight and only a slight wind to cover the noise made by their footsteps. The two brothers walked among the tents as if loitering. They made it to the edge of camp when they heard a shout and an order to halt. The two men dashed into the woods and ran as fast as they could.

As they came over a little rise J. N. tripped. Joseph stopped to help him just as a figure in gray approached through the woods. They dove into a hole made by the roots of a fallen tree. They covered themselves as much as possible with leaves and limbs. Joseph heard footsteps rustling nearby. Both men lay silent and anxious. Joseph's heart pounded from the mixture of fear and adrenaline. Joseph knew that if they were caught they would be shot. He thought that maybe the guard hadn't seen them. Soon all hope was dashed by the sight of a gun barrel gleaming in the night as it pointed directly at the two men hiding in the hole.

Joseph looked up into the eyes of a Confederate soldier with a black face. It was George Mills. The men stayed frozen in their positions, staring upward as Mills held them at bay. Slowly he pulled the gun away and turned his head toward camp. Then he shouted into the night.

"Don't see nothin' over here, sir. Must'a been a possum or somethin'."

He turned his back on the two brothers and walked toward camp.

Joseph and J. N. waited until it was quiet. Then they climbed out of their hole and sprinted into the darkness. The Youngbloods were now erstwhile Confederates.

CONFEDERATE STATES OF AMERICA
ARMY OF TENNESSEE

EXECUTION LIST
Dalton, Georgia
May 4, 1864

Jacob A. Austin	Private
Alfred T. Ball	Sergeant
William R. Byers	Private
Reuben A. Dellinger	Private
Asa Dover	Private
Joseph A. Gibbs	Private
Jesse Hase	Private
Wright Hutchings	Private
Christopher Ledford	Private
George W. McFalls	Private
James M. Randall	Private
Michael Ward	Private
Hiram Youngblood	Private
E. F. Younts	Private

Chapter 20

―― SEPTEMBER 10, 1864 ――

Knoxville, Tennessee The late summer sun baked the earth as Matthias Dees and his two sons walked the dusty road to the outskirts of Knoxville. When they approached the bridge that crossed the French Broad River, they found it heavily guarded.

"Halt," one of the guards shouted well before the trio reached the east end of the bridge.

Dees raised his right hand high into the air and shouted back loudly as if addressing the flock. "I'm Reverend Matthias Dees, I am. Me 'n my boys wanna join the Lord's army 'n fight for the Union."

"Advance slowly and put your hands in the air," the guard instructed them.

Dees and his boys did as they were told, while two guards advanced quickly and searched the men. Since they were carrying only knives they were allowed forward.

"So, you want to join the Union army?" the sergeant asked him.

"Yes sir, brother, we does. We're willin' to offer our lives to save the Union. We does in lovin' memory to my dear missus."

In reality the mother of these Dees offspring was a poor mountain woman who also happened to be Matthias Dee's half-sister. Dees had never bothered to marry her. She had died mysteriously more than a decade before the start of the war, but Dees saw an opportunity to revive her and embellish her memory.

"Yez, sir brother, we been loyal Union men all along. We's men of God. I had a little church up in 'em hills of North Carolina 'n 'em Rebs done burnt it down and kilt my lovely wife. God rest her soul. Then they went'n kilt my two little girls. Me and my boys want to join the Union to set things right."

The sergeant looked at him skeptically. Then he and the other soldiers looked at each other and laughed.

"Well, where was you when they was doin' all this? Why didn't ya fight then?" the sergeant asked sarcastically.

Initially stumbling at the inquiry, Dees quickly found his voice.

"Oh, ah, well me'n the boys was off doin' missionary'n. We was ministerin' to some po folks. Ah, yea, black folks it was too. Poor souls."

The sergeant shook his head in disbelief and laughed.

"Well, ain't that somethin', preacher. Sho was mighty fine of ya, now. But you can't join the army here; you'll have to go into Knoxville. We're changing guard here in about an hour. You can go in with us."

"Thank ya, brother, thank ya, the Lord bless ya," Dees said nodding vigorously. "We'll keep ya in our prayers. Won't we boys?" he said taking off his hat.

His two sons quickly followed suit and took theirs off. The sergeant rolled his eyes and walked back to his post, ignoring the effusive religious gesture.

"Hey, Sarge, ya reckon them boys is really gonna be praying for ya?" one of the guards asked. The other men laughed while the sergeant scratched his beard.

"Shit, the only thing them boys is praying for is a bigger bounty."

The Dees boys and their small escort marched into the middle of town and stopped in front of a large stone structure. It appeared to be an official building of some kind. Many Union soldiers were going in and out of the building, and Dees watched them with interest. It seemed that a significant number of them were officers.

The sergeant recognized a major and called for his attention.

"Sir, these men approached the bridge we was guardin', and they say

CHAPTER TWENTY

they wanna join up." It was apparent from the sergeant's tone and demeanor that he did not completely welcome the shabby-looking crew. The major looked at them carefully, studying their ragged clothes and bare feet.

"So, you fellers think you wanna be in the Union army, huh?" The major looked at the sergeant and winked.

"Ya, sir! We sure doz, we wanna fight for the Lord's side."

Dees took off his hat and again motioned for the boys to do the same.

"So you're a man of God, are ya?" the major asked.

"Oh, yes sir. Praise be to God," Dees shouted theatrically.

"I guess you bein' a man of God and all, you probably don't want to take no bounty, you just wanna fight for the Lord?" the major said smiling.

Dees stuttered, and his face turned ashen. He was lost for only a second or two when he recovered.

"Well a, ya see, sir, me'n my boys wouldn't take nothin' for ourselves, but we needs that bounty to build our little church back," Dees said, bowing his head and holding his hat over his heart.

He paused for a moment, then pointed east toward the mountains as he continued the sermon.

"Ya see, sir, we had a little church over in North Carolina, we was doin' the Lord's work, yea we was. Me 'n the missus 'n my boys. Me 'n the boys went off doin' ministerin' fer po' black folks. Trying to hep 'em, ya know. While we was gone the Rebs come ridin' in, and they kilt my wife 'n my two little girls. Sad, sad thing, it was, may God rest their souls. Then they went 'n burnt down our little church."

Dees was now almost wailing as he whipped himself into a frenzy.

"So me'n the boys done decided that we was gonna come fight for the Union, yes sir. We wanna be fightin' for the Lord's army. What little bit we git for layin' down our lives for the Lord we gonna give to the church. We goin' back to them hills and do the Lord's work, rebuild our little church. Yes sir, brother."

The major looked at him and scoffed. "If you're a preacher, then I'm Abe Lincoln."

The sergeant and the guards all laughed with him.

Suddenly a loud voice startled them.

"Why are you laughing at this poor man?"

The major and the guards looked up to see General Alvan Gillem standing on the steps. He was a dominating presence, in full uniform, dark blue with dual rows of brass buttons down the breast. Gillem had on a large cavalry hat with gold tassels on the brim and his collar was decorated with gold stars, indicating the rank of major general. He had a heavy beard that hung halfway down his chest. His large brown eyes were deep set and topped by heavy dark eyebrows. Gillem was a man who liked to flaunt his rank as long as he was not near a battle.

Gillem climbed down to the last step.

"I heard your story, Reverend, and I'm real sorry to hear about your church. These Rebels need to feel the wrath of God, don't you think?" he said, asking the disheveled character for his opinion.

Dees lit up instantly.

"Oh yes, sir, the wrath of God, an eye for an eye, just like it says in the good book!"

Gillem turned to the startled major and the guards.

"Just because a man's poor doesn't mean he won't be a good soldier. Get these men over to the adjutant's office and sign them up."

He started to walk away, then looked back.

"Get them some shoes too."

Sensing his opportunity, Dees intruded, "Ah, Mr. General, sir, me and my boys can ride. Do ya reckon we could sign up to be in the cavalry?"

"By all means, Reverend. Didn't you say you were from North Carolina?"

"Yes, sir, we did that," Dees replied.

"Well good. We have a unit with some men from western North Carolina in it. I think you'll do well there."

"Major, these men are to be assigned to the 13th Tennessee Cavalry."

"Yes, sir," the major responded promptly.

"Tell me, Reverend, do you know your way around the North

CHAPTER TWENTY

Carolina mountains?" Gillem asked with a serious tone.

"Oh my, yes sir! Me 'n the boys knows 'em mountains likes the back of our hands. Yes sir."

"Good," General Gillem replied. "I think that will come in handy someday."

―― JANUARY 1865 ――

Nashville, Tennessee: Headquarters, U.S. Army of the Cumberland General George Thomas called his adjutant-general into his office. Thomas was tired and uncomfortable as a result of the stresses brought on by years of war. He sat in his favorite cushioned wooden chair and puffed on a large cigar. He twisted around in the chair and put his feet on the desk. His blue uniform was clean but crumpled from several days of wear.

"I have a copy of that report from General Sherman."

"Yes, go ahead, Major."

Thomas leaned back as he waited to hear the old message that he'd heard about previously.

The adjutant read in a monotone voice until he came to the controversial part.

> Until we can repopulate Georgia, it is useless to occupy it, but the utter destruction of its roads, houses, and people will cripple their military resources. By attempting to hold the roads we will lose 1,000 men monthly and will gain no result. I can make the march to Savannah and make Georgia howl. We can push into Georgia and break up all the railroads and depots, capture its horses and Negroes, make desolation everywhere.
> General William T. Sherman

Thomas looked out the window and puffed the cigar again. "So this is what it's come to," he said as if talking to no one in particular.

"Were you talking to me, sir?" the major asked.

"No, not really, Major. I guess I was talking to myself."

"I'm concerned about where this war is going to lead us. What will our nation become? Things are really getting out of hand," the general said as he stared out the window and into the distance.

"They made Georgia howl all right, but I'm afraid it will haunt us for years to come. I just hope the papers don't get wind of General Davis's decision to cut the pontoons out from all those freedmen at Ebenezer Creek. It won't make the Union army look too good, freeing slaves, then drowning them," Thomas said sadly.

"Over four hundred men, women, and children were drowned by the very army that was supposed to protect them."

"I don't think we really know yet the full extent of what went on down there. If we're going to reunite this country we'd better conduct ourselves as soldiers and not bandits or worse."

Thomas got up and walked around the room engrossed in deep thought. He seemed to emerge from his thoughtful state.

"This division of cavalry we're putting together for General Stoneman needs some work. We've got one brigade made up of three regiments from the Department of Kentucky. They served under Stoneman up there. What were those regiments?" Thomas asked the adjutant.

The major shuffled his papers again and read them off.

"That would be the 11th and 12th Kentucky and the 11th Michigan, sir," he responded quickly.

"Then we have the brigade made up of General Gillem's men, the 8th, 9th, and 13th Tennessee Cavalry," Thomas said thoughtfully as he studied the large map on the table.

The general laughed disgustedly, then mumbled out loud, "Gillem's men are mostly drunks or bounty hunters or both."

"We'll need one more brigade to make up a full division for General Stoneman."

Then Thomas turned to his adjutant and asked, "Do you know much about General Gillem and these Tennessee regiments?"

CHAPTER TWENTY

"No, not much, sir, just that General Gillem was credited with trapping and killing Confederate General John Morgan in Greenville, Tennessee," the major stated calmly.

General Thomas laughed lightly as he continued to study the map.

"What a farce. Gillem didn't even know he was there. Some of Gillem's men stumbled on Morgan by accident. Morgan went to sleep at some friend's house without his guard. Gillem wasn't within miles of the action. He never is, if he can help it. He didn't even know about Morgan until it was all over. General Gillem would still be a lieutenant if he didn't have big connections in Washington."

Thomas laughed some more. "Hell, if he'd known Morgan was anywhere around he probably would've hightailed it in the other direction."

"About the only real credit Gillem deserves is for joining with the Union at the beginning of the war when most Tennesseans went the other way," Thomas said.

"Stoneman wants him because Gillem is from Tennessee, and he has big political connections in Washington. Many of his men are from Tennessee, and he's got one hundred or more who are from North Carolina. Stoneman thinks they'll make good scouts," Thomas added.

"Well, that seems to make good sense to me, sir. They ought to know the ground," the major said.

"Yes, you'd think so, Major, but a lot of those men are deserters from the Confederate army. They wouldn't fight for them, so I'm not so sure they'll fight for us."

Thomas got up from the table and walked across the room.

"President Lincoln is a wise man, but for the life of me I can't figure out why he thinks a man can be trusted when he joins up simply to get a bounty," he continued his thoughtful evaluation out loud to his trusted adjutant.

"It's because of Gillem and his drinking companion, Vice President Johnson, that Lincoln left several states out of the Emancipation

Proclamation. The vice president, Gillem, and many other Tennesseans on the Union side are pro-slavery. Most of Gillem's men are part-time criminals at best. Have you seen some of those men, Major?" he asked.

"No, sir, I'm not familiar with the Tennesseans," he replied.

"Well, enough discussion," Thomas said, indicating that he'd reached a decision.

"We are going to need some strength in Stoneman's division. Convey my order to Colonel William Palmer. He is to report to Knoxville as soon as possible with the 15th Pennsylvania. We'll add the 12th Ohio and the 10th Michigan to make up a brigade for him. With Palmer along as a brigade commander, it will be harder for some of Gillem's command to run amuck. Inform Stoneman that he can have Gillem as divisional commander," Thomas stated flatly. "Get my orders off to Palmer immediately."

—— MARCH 20, 1865 ——

Knoxville, Tennessee Colonel William Palmer and the 15th Pennsylvania Cavalry rode into Knoxville with some local citizens gathered to cheer them on. The early days of Confederate dominance in Tennessee were long gone. Unctuous converts now joined the truly loyal Unionists of the state. The end of the war was within sight, and almost everyone knew it.

The festive reception embarrassed Palmer, but there was no need to concern himself with it. He had military matters to consider. The 15th Pennsylvania was to report to the quartermaster for supplies. Palmer would be leading his men on a long campaign, and General Thomas was equipping them with the latest in military technology. Stoneman's cavalry was being outfitted with Spencer carbines, the new seven-shot repeating rifles.

Palmer had served as secretary to the president of the Penn Central Railroad before the war and was considered an able administrator. He was raised a Hicksite Quaker and valued honesty and integrity above all

CHAPTER TWENTY

material things. Palmer was recognized as an accomplished and respected military officer. Early in his career he had helped form the 15th Pennsylvania Volunteer Cavalry. The young officer was only twenty-four years of age at the time. Additionally, he required personal references from home before he accepted men into his command.

Palmer's military career was most remarkable. He'd been granted a captain's commission at the beginning of the war. Later he was captured at the battle of Antietam after volunteering for a dangerous assignment. Palmer was caught behind enemy lines in civilian clothes and nearly executed as a spy. After spending months at Castle Thunder prison in Richmond, Virginia, he was exchanged and returned to duty.

Palmer led a charge at Red Hill, Alabama, in January 1865 for which he received the Congressional Medal of Honor. Palmer never commented publicly about the medal.

Palmer had charged a Confederate position with about one hundred men; the Confederates had more than two hundred. Palmer and his men captured their guns and two hundred prisoners without losing a single man.

"It should be obvious," Palmer said humbly. "The Confederates didn't fight or I wouldn't be here. No man deserves a medal for taking men that don't fight."

General Thomas, who had recommended Palmer for the medal, knew the real circumstances at Red Hill but that did not concern him. Palmer's overall performance, repeatedly tested over years of hard fighting, proved him worthy of the honor.

Palmer's men gathered their supplies and made camp. He reported to General Stoneman and prepared to take his position with the division.

"You'll command the 1st Brigade, Colonel Palmer; General Brown will command the 2nd, and Colonel Miller the 3rd. General Gillem will carry out my orders as divisional commander. Our mission is to advance into enemy territory, destroy all railroads, depots, and military buildings. We will free any slaves we find and destroy all property belonging to citizens contributing to the war effort," Stoneman said.

"Sir, how are we to determine who is contributing to the war effort?" Palmer asked.

Stoneman was puzzled at first, then responded, "We'll have to determine that as we go, Colonel."

"General Grant has approved the mission, and he suspects that we'll not meet any sizable force that a thousand men can't repulse. We'll travel as a full division when possible. I'll divide the command as necessary. If we have larger areas to attack we'll divide to the company level or even into smaller units," Stoneman continued as he spread a map onto the field table in his headquarters tent.

"First we'll head into southwestern Virginia and destroy the salt works in Saltville and the railroad. Then we'll turn south into North Carolina and head east. Our most important goal, as far as I'm concerned, will be to free the Union prisoners at Salisbury, North Carolina. Then we'll turn back west, destroying all railroads and bridges we can find," Stoneman said, completing the highlights of his briefing.

"Sir, what about the conduct of the men? Should we not caution them considering the fact that we will be in a great deal of contact with civilians?" Palmer asked, indicating that he was concerned about this issue.

General Gillem steamed at Palmer's question.

"Colonel Palmer, these 'civilians,' as you called them, are just as much the enemy as the troops are. They have been feeding and supplying the Confederate army. Remember what General Sherman said: 'We are not fighting a hostile army. We're fighting a hostile people.'"

"Yes, General Gillem, I am well aware of what General Sherman said. By now the whole world knows it. The world is also aware of what went on in Georgia, and the conduct of some men will forever stain the honorable record of the U.S. Army. I don't hold General Sherman responsible for the actions of those men, but I want to see to it that it does not happen again," Palmer said.

"These Rebels have caused death and destruction, and they are traitors! They need to feel the firm hand of God," Gillem responded with apparent anger.

CHAPTER TWENTY

"That's enough, gentlemen," Stoneman said. "Your point is well taken, Colonel Palmer; we'll have no lawlessness on this mission. We will leave tomorrow morning."

Palmer returned to his regiment where he found the officers of the 15th Pennsylvania waiting for him.

"Sir, have you seen those Tennessee and North Carolina men? They look like animals," Captain Weand almost shouted to Palmer. "Surely we're not riding with those men. We'll be more likely to be shot in the back than by the Confederates."

"Restrain yourself, Captain. You can't judge men by their looks."

"Sir, we talked with some of them. Most of 'em are bounty men. Several of them smelled like whiskey stills. Some of them seem to be loyal Union men, but there's a bunch of them that ain't nothing but bounty men or convicts. They won't be worth a damn in a stand-up fight!" Weand was insistent, and the other officers joined in expressing concern.

"Those men know the land, captain. General Gillem has selected them just for that reason," Palmer told his men calmly.

"But sir, they're openly talking about settling old grudges and worse. I think someone should say something to General Thomas."

"Enough!" Palmer shouted at his staff while raising his hand. "We'll not judge anyone on such frivolous information. I will hear no more of it. We will ride with them and do our duty honorably. Do you understand?"

Captain Weand and the other officers looked at each other in silence.

"Yes sir," Weand said, and the others followed.

Palmer turned and went into his tent. He wondered, "What will history say of our deeds and how will God judge us?" He began to pray for the safety of his men and for the Union. He also prayed that this war would end soon before it got worse.

Chapter 21

―― SEPTEMBER 1864 ――

Ducktown, Tennessee Joseph and J. N. had been on the run for months now. They were afraid to go home and afraid not to. Life as deserters had proven more difficult than they'd imagined. The worst part was finding food. The mountains had provided fall berries and nuts of a wide variety. The berries alternated with insects had been their main meal for weeks. Both men were suffering from dysentery, and they desperately needed more food.

"We've got to get some meat, Joseph, or we're going to die," J. N. said nonchalantly. Joseph didn't respond.

The two men rested by a creek near the cave that had been their home since late May. Both men were gaunt, emaciated figures having all the appearance of savages. Long, shaggy beards covered their faces, and their hair hung in tangled strings around their ears and down to their shoulders. They often bathed in the creeks, but the cold water and the absence of soap failed to clean the accumulated filth from their tired bodies. Both men had terrible teeth, and J. N. suffered from a serious gum abscess.

"Maybe we can kill a deer," J. N. said without much confidence.

Joseph sat in silence, not paying much attention to his younger brother. His fantasy of Delia dressed in her wedding gown kept his mind occupied. He imagined a happy time with all his family and friends there.

CHAPTER TWENTY-ONE

At other times he continued to relive the horrors of war. He often lay awake at night thinking of Hiram and how insane Confederate officers had murdered him. Joseph would never get over the rage that those horrific memories ignited.

"I sure wish we'd gotten out of there with our muskets," Joseph said as his mind returned to the reality of their life on the run.

"Me too," J. N. responded.

"We might be able to trap something. Maybe we could spear a deer."

"I'm up for tryin' anything. I'm so hungry. I just don't want to eat no more grubs or bugs."

"Don't say bad things about those bugs. Without them we'd already be dead. Bugs kept me alive the last time I was on the run," Joseph said as he remembered his harrowing escape from Camp Morton.

"Let's go see what we can find. We may have to come down out of the mountains a little to find something," J. N. said as he rose to his feet.

The two men began their hike toward the little hamlet of Ducktown. They'd scouted the area before and knew of several homes in the area. The pair hadn't approached them for fear of discovery. It didn't matter which side the families were on as they could be arrested or shot by either side now.

The brothers watched the small log cabin from a distant hill for most of the day. Smoke came from the chimney, and they observed at least one woman and two children.

"Look at that field, J. N. It's a cornfield that's been harvested. There's got to be a corncrib around somewhere," Joseph said, pointing at two small outbuildings. J. N. peered over the land, then nodded in agreement.

"Joseph, I'll bet there's corn in one of those shacks."

"Yea, I bet so. We'll wait 'til dark and then go down there."

"I hope I don't starve before then." J. N. pulled his ragged, floppy hat down over his eyes and lay back on the ground as if he were taking a nap.

Joseph sat upright and continued to watch the house from their distant perch.

When it was sufficiently dark Joseph rousted his dozing younger brother.

"I hope you've got supper," J. N. said, not losing his Youngblood sense of humor even in their sad state of existence.

"I hope I've got dinner too. We'll see."

It was after eleven when the two deserters approached the shacks. The lanterns were out, but smoke came lively from one chimney. The two desperate men snuck quietly to the first shack and slipped inside without incident. This time, Joseph and J. N. were in luck. They found the corncrib on their first try. Some of the corn was not totally dry yet, but that didn't matter to the starving Youngbloods. The condition of their teeth made munching on the hard corn kernels a challenge. They chewed with difficulty but managed to eat their fill. The two former Confederates sat down in beds of corn shucks and straw. The brothers wiggled down into the straw and made themselves a comfortable mattress. It was the most comfortable bed either man had experienced in months. Both fell into a deep sleep.

It was mid-morning when Joseph awoke with a start. Fear coursed through his veins as he assessed their vulnerability. He listened carefully, for a good ear was essential for men constantly on the run. As he absorbed the indicators within his environment he began to relax. Joseph heard nothing but birds and the babbling spring nearby. Rising from his makeshift bed he peered through a crack in the shack wall. No one was about. No threatening sight or sound could be detected.

Joseph returned to his sleeping brother and shook him gently. J. N. lurched in fear as his instinct automatically alerted him.

"Shh, there ain't nobody around," Joseph told him in a whisper.

Joseph went back to the crack in the wall and peered out once again. Still there was no sign of activity in the house or yard. Joseph continued to watch for several minutes. J. N. went back to eating corn.

"I think they may be gone off somewhere," Joseph said as if he couldn't believe their luck.

The two fugitives had lost track of the calendar. They had no way of knowing it was Sunday morning and the family had left their little farm and gone to church.

CHAPTER TWENTY-ONE

Joseph slipped out into the yard and crept toward the cabin. He pressed himself against the wall and slid his body toward the window. He slowly leaned over and looked into the cabin. He was sure of it now. No one was home.

He dashed back to the corncrib and alerted his brother. J. N. had already loaded a sack full of corn to take with them.

"They're gone, J. N. We've got the place to ourselves."

"Let's look around and see if we can find some meat."

The two deserters cautiously slipped around the other side of the cabin where they came across a pigpen. Inside the pen was a large hog with a number of smaller piglets milling about. The two men looked at each other and smiled widely, displaying their decaying teeth.

"Let's get one," J. N. said as he started for the pen.

"Wait a minute, you damn fool. When you go after one of them pigs that mama is going to raise hell."

"What are we gonna do, just stand here and look at 'em?"

"No, we're gonna get one, but we'd better have a plan. Are there any more of those big sacks in the corncrib?"

"Yea, there's several of 'em."

"Go get one and bring it here."

J. N. fetched a sack and returned while Joseph continued to watch the pigs.

"When we get in that pen you take a stick and chase the mama and keep her busy. I'll take the sack and catch one of the pigs."

The plan seemed simple enough, but the two men found the actual hunt a little more difficult than making a plan. Once the men were inside the pen all the pigs went to scrambling and squealing. The noise created by the human invasion was deafening to the ears of the two deserters. Instead of the mama pig being chased by J. N. the tables were turned. As soon as J. N. advanced on her she charged him, chasing him around the pen and attempting to bite him as she squealed and snorted.

Joseph fared little better. As he dove for the first piglet she dodged him. He splashed headfirst into a pool of mud and animal manure. He was immediately on his feet chasing another. Meanwhile J. N. screamed in horror as the sow pinned him in a corner. He desperately climbed the wall as the huge animal nipped at his feet.

As Joseph chased one pig, then another, he noticed a smaller one with a limp. He focused on this one and chased him into an opposite corner. He dove forward, trapping the animal in the mud between his body and the ground. Joseph grasped one of his hind legs and held on for dear life. The little pig squirmed violently and squealed at a tremendous volume. Joseph had the sack in his other hand. He wrestled the pig as he positioned the sack and slipped it over the terrified animal's head. The pig escaped his grasp and dashed forward. Fortunately for the fumbling hunters, the panic-stricken animal dashed straight into the sack. The misdirected pig allowed Joseph to complete the capture.

"Help!" J. N. screamed as he struggled desperately to get away from the angry mother. Joseph looked at his brother and burst out laughing. Now covered with mud and pig manure, both men were an unsightly mess.

"Let's go, boy!" Joseph yelled as he started for the gate struggling with the heavy sack.

J. N. struggled to the side and climbed over the high fence, flopping clumsily to the ground on the other side. The sow went back and forth on the inside of the pen seeking to attack the strange invaders.

The confined pig struggled inside the sack as the two men looked at each other and laughed.

J. N. eyed the house with interest.

"Let's go see what we can get inside the house."

Joseph looked at the little cabin and thought of the woman and little children he'd seen the evening before.

"We've got enough to last us a while. Let's don't go in their house. You get that sack of corn and we'll head for the mountains."

It was a day's hike back to their cave. The travel was slow because of the heavy burden of the sacked pig. They took turns carrying the heavy load as they trudged into the mountains. Their hideout was located near the physical point where Tennessee, North Carolina, and Georgia meet.

CHAPTER TWENTY-ONE

When they arrived at their little camp Joseph found a pine knot that was solid and heavy with a good stick still attached to it. He decided to use it to slaughter the pig.

Another plan was necessary to ensure that the pig did not get away when they took it out for the kill.

"You hold his hind legs real good, while he's still in the sack. No matter what don't turn loose," Joseph instructed his younger brother.

"Are you crazy? I ain't about to turn loose of this meal," J. N. shouted back at him.

"When you get a hold of his legs I'll roll the sack back so I can hit him in the head."

The two hungry men got into position and began the process.

"Have ya got 'em?"

"Yea, I got 'em. Just get it done."

Soon the pig's upper body was exposed. He squealed and struggled, but J. N.'s determined grip held the animal in place. Joseph raised his makeshift club and swung it downward, missing the head and striking the snout. The pig squealed louder and Joseph swung again. This time the club hit him in the side of the head. The blow was not fatal, but it sufficiently stunned the animal so that Joseph could strike again. He hit him several times until the pig lay motionless and bleeding. They pulled the animal from the sack and shoved a knife blade at an angle up and under his ribs. The now-dead animal was prepared for cooking.

The two men feasted on roast pork throughout the night. Both men were so full they could hardly move without a groan.

"What a feast," J. N. commented as the two men fell off to sleep.

It was early morning when Joseph got up to relieve himself. He walked through the woods a short distance until he found a comfortable spot. His mind drifted as he strolled over to the little mountain stream that had been their primary source of water for months.

He enjoyed a drink of fresh, cool water before heading back to feast again on fresh pork. When he topped the ridge to head back to the cave he heard the dogs. At first he wasn't sure what he had heard, but soon the noise was louder and closer. He ran a little farther up the ridge and

THE SECRET OF WAR

looked west. Through the foliage he could see two men following a pack of dogs.

Joseph ran back to the cave as fast as he could to wake up J. N.

"Get up! Get up! They're coming after us."

It took J. N. a few seconds to absorb the frantic calls from his brother, but life on the run had taught them to be constantly alert.

J. N. leaped to his feet, rubbing his eyes at the same time.

"Grab the food sack," Joseph yelled as he wrestled a big piece of pork into the other sack. The two men ran out of the cave and headed up the ridge line toward the higher mountains. The sound of the dogs was much louder now, and Joseph knew they were in real danger. In their condition it would be hard to outrun the dogs.

They broke through a patch of laurel into a semi-clear area created by a chestnut canopy. Joseph saw the flame and puff of smoke before he heard the sound. Buckshot whizzed over their heads, narrowly missing the two fugitives. Both men dove and rolled just in time to avoid a second shot fired by another man.

"They've flanked us!" J. N. shouted in panic.

"This way," Joseph shouted as he stumbled and rolled down a hill.

Two more shots came from behind them, this time from muskets. J. N. fell and rolled again, dropping his sack of corn.

The two fleeing men knew the lay of the land, having explored the area for months. Joseph yelled as loud as he could.

"Head for Carolina!" He continued to shout as they ran. It was difficult, but Joseph still held onto the sack of pork.

The two men pulled close together, and Joseph called out instructions as they continued in flight. Two more musket balls popped through the tree limbs, causing them to duck instinctively.

"We've got to split up! Head for the high country. Get into that laurel and rhododendron."

"I'll see ya at dinner," J. N. called out as he faded to the right and parted ways with his brother.

Joseph was thankful for the full stomach and the rest. He calculated that their chances were much better because of that. He knew if they

CHAPTER TWENTY-ONE

could get far enough into the foreboding mountain forest the pursuers would likely give up the chase for fear of their own safety. Joseph gasped and panted as he continued to run diagonally up a long ridge line. He made it to a long chine and began to follow it. An hour had gone by when he heard shots in the distance behind him. Fear gripped him, not only for himself but also for his younger brother. He heard another shot, but he had no choice but to continue moving. Joseph prayed for J. N. and begged God to spare him.

Joseph ran on for another two hours until he finally stopped, totally exhausted and unable to continue. He struggled to hear but had difficulty because of the pounding of his own heart and the noise created by his strained lungs gasping for breath. It was some time before he was rested enough to hear well. There were no sounds save those of the forest.

Joseph rested as long as he could, then continued his trek. His mind was overpowered by images of what might have happened to J. N. He thought of the gunshots and wondered why the pursuers were so intent on killing them for stealing a little corn and a pig. The tenacity and scope of their effort puzzled him.

When night fell he made it to the reconnoiter point. He began to bird whistle, seeking a response, but heard nothing. He whistled again as he fretted over the fate of his brother. This time the familiar whistle came back to him from the other side of the laurel thicket. He ran toward the sound and met J. N. in the middle. The two men grabbed each other and chuckled.

"Damn, what took you so long? I've been here all day," J. N. said, still breathing hard. "You never could keep up with your little brother."

Joseph just smiled and patted his brother on the back as the two men sat down for a rest.

"They damn near killed us. This war sure has made people mean," J. N. said with the same puzzlement that had occupied Joseph's mind.

"Yea, you'd think we killed somebody or something."

"They must have had ten or twelve men after us," Joseph said as he pondered the question.

The next day the two men hiked until dark, well back into the North

THE SECRET OF WAR

Carolina mountain wilderness. Their objective now was to find a new hideout.

In the early evening they came upon a little stream where they started to drink. Joseph heard a stick pop behind him. He rose up to scan in the direction of the sound. He found himself staring into the muzzle of an antiquated musket. At first he thought their pursuers had followed them all the way back into North Carolina, but then he realized that the man holding the musket was another deserter. His condition was that of a ragged, dirty outlier. Joseph could see remnants of an old Confederate uniform. Just then three more men appeared from behind the first man.

"Howdy, friend," Joseph said meekly as he raised his hands into the air.

"We're just one of you. Hidin' from this stupid war."

The other men approached with muskets pointed. The two Youngbloods were truly frightened. These were dangerous men, and they knew it.

"I've got some fresh pork here," Joseph said as he pointed to the sack lying beside him. "You're welcome to eat a bite."

The strange men looked at each other and seemed to relax their guard slightly.

One man, who seemed to be the leader, motioned for one of the other men to come forward. The man approached still pointing his musket at Joseph. He squatted down and picked up the sack, then backed away.

One of the other men smiled slightly, then happily spoke to the others.

"I can smell it from here. Whew wee!"

The man who was the leader calmly asked the two fugitives. "Where's ya boys hidin' ya guns?"

"We ain't got no guns," Joseph said with his hands still in the air.

"Search 'em," the man said.

The other two men stepped forward and searched both of them. Finding nothing, they searched the ground around them.

"Nothin' here, Cal," one of the men called back to the leader.

"All right, I reckon you boys ain't lawmen."

CHAPTER TWENTY-ONE

The quartet of Confederate deserters lowered their muskets and dove for the sack of pork. Joseph and J. N. lowered their hands and watched as the hungry men devoured their treasure.

"Hope ya don't mind," the leader said with a gap-toothed grin.

"No, you go right ahead. We've had plenty," Joseph responded, still fearful of what these men might do.

As the men continued to eat, full stomachs began to relax the tension. Soon all six men sat together on the ground talking. As the strangers took their fill the leader tore off two small pieces and gave them to Joseph and J. N.

"You boys on the run, are ya?" he asked.

"Yeah, we been hidin' out for months."

"Why don't ya tie in with us? We ain't got much, but we gets by."

"Why, much obliged. We might just do that," Joseph answered with a wide grin.

"We've been running hard for two days. Men and dogs chased us like madmen."

"Yeah, all we did was steal a pig and some corn. You'd think we killed somebody or something the way they came after us," J. N. added.

The four outliers looked at each other, then back at Joseph.

"Which way'd y'all come from?"

"We were down on the Tennessee side, near a little village called Ducktown."

The four men looked at each other again and chuckled. It was clear to Joseph and J. N. that the men knew something they didn't.

The leader looked at them and smiled through his gapped teeth.

"I reckon there ain't no harm in tellin' ya. They was fixen to git ya for what we done." The other three laughed aloud.

"We was down that way ourselves, a few days back, a Sunday evenin' it was. We had a bad hankerin' for a gal. Bein' there ain't nary a one up here in the mountains, we come upon a little home place down yonder. It was just a gal and some children." The leader went back to chewing his pork while the other men laughed again.

Joseph disguised his disgust and faked his own laugh.

"I reckon that was a heap of fun," Joseph said laughingly while he attempted to extract more information.

One of the other dirty men spoke up, "Yea, a heap o' fun. Them boys went fer the mama, but I had me a time with the little un. She sure was a sweet thang." All four men snickered as Joseph looked at his brother.

"She squealed and squalled louder'n a pig at the slaughter," the leader said as he chewed on his pork. The strangers laughed even louder.

Joseph and J. N. feigned a laugh as they glanced at each other in horror. Both knew that the men with dogs would have killed them, believing that they had committed this crime.

"What happened to 'em after y'all were done?" Joseph asked, still feigning amusement.

"Oh, well ya see, ya can't leave nobody to put an eye on ya later. We'll teach ya boys 'bout that if ya wanna run with me'n my men. We had us a day with 'em; then we cut their throats and left." All four men laughed aloud again, but Joseph and J. N. were unable to fake it any longer as they listened in disgust.

The cluster of men sat by the creek and chatted for over an hour. They told stories of home and war. The strangers did most of the talking while the Youngbloods listened. The two continued to pretend that they would join up with the marauders.

The group hiked on into the mountains and made camp in a little cove in southern Macon County in the southwestern corner of North Carolina. As they settled down for the evening Joseph discussed with Cal all the things they might do together. The Youngbloods continued to gain Cal's confidence until the group loosened their watch on the brothers. Just after nightfall Joseph signaled to his younger brother. J. N. said he was going for a drink. When he was out of sight, Joseph followed. As soon as they were out of camp they were on the run again. Fleeing from the other deserters, Joseph and J. N. struggled through the darkness for several hours before they felt safe enough to rest.

As it began to rain the pair found shelter under a small rock outcrop. The fugitives huddled together to warm each other in the cold, damp

CHAPTER TWENTY-ONE

air. They had nothing to eat, no weapons, and no matches. Even their knife had been lost in the frantic escape from Tennessee.

—— JANUARY 1865 ——

Joseph and J. N. had talked about it for weeks. They knew of men hiding out who had gone into Chattanooga and surrendered to the enemy. One of them said to them when he left that he was going to "swallow the yellow dog," a term Confederates used to describe taking the oath of allegiance to the United States. J. N. was for it from the beginning, but Joseph couldn't bring himself to do it. He had not forgotten Malvern Hill and Sharpsburg where so many of his friends and neighbors had been killed. Most of all he remembered Camp Morton and the torture and starvation he'd experienced there.

"I ain't a Yankee either, Joseph, but if we don't do something we're gonna starve to death or freeze to death," J. N. pleaded with his brother. "We can't go home, we'll end up like Hiram. We're both very weak. If we get sick we'll die," he continued.

"What do you think the Yankees will do if we go over and surrender to them?" Joseph asked.

"I ain't sure, but at least they'll feed us, won't they?"

"Maybe, maybe not. They didn't feed me much up in Indiana," Joseph said bitterly.

"I know they'll feed us if we join up," J. N. said.

Joseph looked at his brother angrily.

"Don't you ever say that to me again. I'll die before I join them. I hate the Confederacy, but I'll hate the Yankees for the rest of my life for what they did to me. Besides, they'll make us kill our own. I ain't ever gonna do that. No matter what it ain't right to fire on your own people."

"Sure, Joseph, sure. But the rest of your life ain't gonna be very long if we stay up here in the mountains all winter," J. N. said solemnly.

"All right, I'll swallow the damn dog, but I ain't joining up with 'em," Joseph conceded.

The walk into Chattanooga was a long one. Starting before daylight, they arrived in Cleveland at midday on the fourth day of their hike. They encountered Union pickets. There were Union soldiers everywhere, and the two former Confederate soldiers were soon marching toward Chattanooga with other deserters who were now surrendering to the enemy in significant numbers.

Upon arrival in Chattanooga they were put in a large horse corral with about sixty other prisoners. It was nothing more than a dirt rectangle, but it was heavily guarded. The Union guards gave them beans, bread, and coffee, which the Youngbloods gobbled up rapidly. They were greatly surprised when the guards in charge gave them more food when they told them that they were still hungry.

"They never did nothin' like that when I was at Camp Morton," Joseph told J. N. in a manner that indicated he was pleasantly surprised.

The next morning an officer came into the corral and instructed the prisoners to come forward.

"You men can join the Union army and get your freedom. You'll be given clothes, food, and shoes. You'll have to take the oath. Any of you who want to join step over to the table," he said in a businesslike tone.

Joseph and J. N. approached the officer and got his attention.

"Excuse me, sir, we don't want to shoot at our own people, but we're willing to take the oath," Joseph told him with great humility. He didn't want to anger his keeper.

The officer looked at Joseph's bare feet and emaciated condition and shook his head incredulously.

"That's fine with me, Reb. I don't give a damn. You'll be shipped to Louisville, then on to Camp Morton. We just gotta make sure you won't take up arms against the United States again."

Joseph's heart sank at the mention of Camp Morton, but he was too sick and too weak to object.

The two brothers got in line and took the oath.

Chapter 22

―― JANUARY 1865 ――

Hoopers Creek, North Carolina Delia could hardly wait for Pinkney to arrive. She was now seventeen years old, and life had so little to offer during these desolate days of war. Her brief outings with him not only represented recreation, but also provided her with an all-important link to Joseph. Pinkney Youngblood and Delia Russell had come to share many common interests. They talked about everything during their rides. The escape from reality seemed to lift their spirits.

Pinkney arrived right on time. He also enjoyed these outings with Delia, as the atmosphere at the Youngblood home was now very sad. News of Hiram's execution and the desertion of Joseph and J. N. had left the family devastated. It wasn't so much that two of the boys were now Confederate deserters but that their fate and whereabouts were unknown. No one knew if they had been captured or killed. The only thing that was known for certain was that Hiram was dead.

Joseph had written Delia only once from Dalton, Georgia, after the execution. Delia had been so excited. She was ready to start planning for her wedding, when hope seemed to be so cruelly dashed. She couldn't accept the fact that they'd shot Hiram Youngblood. He was only nineteen years old, and after all, he'd gone back to his regiment. She couldn't understand it and would never accept it.

THE SECRET OF WAR

When the pair reached the top of Bearwallow Mountain it was cold but tolerable considering it was January. Pinkney was on the mountain often, tending to the four horses he had hidden there. The two colts were getting quite large, but they were still very playful and active. He'd built a tiny shelter at the back of the cove to help protect them from the winter winds, and he worked diligently to keep them safe.

"Pinkney, do you have to bring that gun with you all the time?" Delia asked with a troubled tone, as she looked at the small revolver he always carried in his belt. She knew of this necessity, but still she hated the ubiquitous instruments of death.

"Yes, Delia. Bill told me to. There's deserters and bushwhackers everywhere in these mountains now."

"But you couldn't stop men with muskets, could you?"

Pinkney gave the question serious thought. "No, really I guess not, but the pistol might help me get away without being killed. Besides, Delia, I might need it to protect you."

Delia felt a chill run through her body as she contemplated what he'd said. Why had God allowed things to get so bad? She knew Pinkney was right. Bushwhackers would kill them both. Killing seemed to be so common that no one cared anymore.

Eventually their time expired, and they headed for home.

Delia guided the buggy back into the yard where Zeke met her and helped her put Ole Star in the barn.

"Did y'all have a good ride, missy?" Zeke asked her.

"Oh yes, Zeke. It's so pretty up there," she responded happily. "Is Papa home?"

"Yessum, he be in de house, I 'spect," Zeke said, turning his head away.

Delia knew that wasn't a good sign.

"Is he drinking again, Zeke?"

"I reckon so, missy," Zeke said with sadness and concern in his voice.

Delia went into the house to find her father in the study with the jug sitting on the table beside him.

CHAPTER TWENTY-TWO

"Well, well, look at ya, look what you've come to. Running around up in the mountains," Russell said to his daughter with a cruel sting in his voice.

"Papa, I've been riding in the buggy. What's wrong with that?"

"Mixing with them damn Youngbloods, I reckon."

"The Youngbloods are good people, Papa. Please don't say bad things about them."

"There a bunch of damn traitors. They should've shot the rest of 'em while they were at it," Russell said as he took another drink of corn whiskey.

"Don't you ever say that! Joseph fought for his country. He was nearly killed at Malvern Hill and nearly died in that Yankee prison. They shot Hiram for no good reason. It's so awful. I hate the Confederates," she screamed at him as she'd never done before. "All you do anymore is drink and complain. You don't do anything to help." Delia burst into tears and ran from the room.

"And you ain't marrying that damn Kraut neither. I won't allow it," he shouted after her.

Nanny Mills caught up with her in the hallway.

Delia wrapped herself in old Nanny's arms and cried. Nanny held her close and talked to her softly.

"Things gonna git better, child. Things gotta git better."

Delia looked up into her warm, black face.

"When, Nanny? It just goes on and on, and gets worse and worse."

Nanny didn't answer; she just patted her on the back.

"Come wit' me, child. We bes' be fixin' supper."

They went into the kitchen, and Delia did her best to get her mind off of the confrontation she'd had with her father.

"What's for supper, Nanny?" Delia asked.

"Black eyed peas 'n cornbread, yum," Nanny said.

"Nanny, that's all we've had to eat for over a week."

"Them peas is mighty good, yea they is," Nanny responded.

"There isn't anything else, is there, Nanny?" Delia asked her.

"No, reckon not. But spring be comin'; Zeke be growing greens soon," she said, trying her best to be positive.

Delia studied the situation while cleaning the table.

"Well, there is one sure thing in all of this," she said sarcastically.

"What ya talkin' 'bout, child?" Nanny asked, not sure she really wanted to know the answer.

"Papa's money doesn't matter anymore. You can't buy anything with it anyway. Nobody has anything to sell."

Chapter 23

―― MARCH 28, 1865 ――

Watauga County, North Carolina Sergeant Pete LaFerre of the 11th Michigan Cavalry was originally a French citizen. He'd come from France to Canada just three years before the war started. Only a year later he had fled across the border to avoid Canadian authorities. "For something he was not guilty of," he told his fellow soldiers. Joining the U.S. Army and going to war was something he considered an opportunity.

LaFerre was a rough man of stocky build who weighed more than two hundred pounds. His heavy beard had grown to a thick mass that rested on his barrel chest like juniper growing over a fallen log. His huge eyebrows and convoluted facial hair left little visible of his face. He had a deep, booming voice and was especially fond of corn whiskey, having been introduced to the potent brew by his new comrades from North Carolina and Tennessee.

LaFerre became a natural ally to the regiment's scouts. These men thought like he did. They were always helpful in pointing out opportunity. In addition, the scouts knew the land, and they shared his enthusiasm for corn whiskey. They also seemed to know how to find it. Each regiment was assigned scouts with local knowledge. Most of the scouts came from the 13th Tennessee Cavalry.

LaFerre was not one to volunteer for anything dangerous, but whenever the regimental scouts, Reverend Matthias Dees and his sons, went scouting, LaFerre was often with them. They preferred to ride ahead of the regiment, spying and scouting possible approaches for the cavalry. Other members of the 11th sometimes accompanied them depending on the opposition anticipated.

On the morning of March 28th, the 12th Kentucky and the 11th Michigan attacked the town of Boone, North Carolina. The resistance they encountered was a disappointment to some. LaFerre and about twenty of his men encountered an old farmer in a field working with his plow horse.

"I ain't got nothin to do wit dis confounded war. Can't you let me keep my horse?" Jacob Council pleaded with the soldiers.

LaFerre laughed gruffly and looked at the other soldiers.

"I think de man be resisting authority of de U.S. Army, no?"

The others looked at him, catching on to the joke.

"Oh yea, he's puttin up a heap o' fuss," one of the men said, his voice oozing with sarcasm.

LaFerre calmly pulled his Colt .44 revolver and shot the old man in the stomach. Council lay in agony only briefly before dying. The Michigan cavalrymen nonchalantly rode away looking for yet another source of entertainment.

Several members of the 13th Tennessee Cavalry were well acquainted with the area, having been born and raised nearby. This particular group was not out for entertainment but rather to settle old scores. They rode up on the home of Warren Green with no warning. Having no reason to believe that Union solders would harm him if he didn't resist, he stepped out onto porch unarmed and unsuspecting. By the time he recognized the men he was confronting, it was too late. He was shot through the throat by a round fired from a Spencer carbine. The bullet had been fired by a neighbor from nearby Avery County. Green's wife and five children watched in horror as he bled to death on the front porch.

Meanwhile the advance troops of Stoneman's cavalry ran wild through the town of Boone. As the community was being pillaged, General Gillem arrived to the cheers of his men. Stimulated by the

CHAPTER TWENTY-THREE

events of the day Gillem ordered the county buildings burned.

It was well into the evening when the rest of the division caught up with the regiments involved in the attack. Colonel Palmer and the 15th Pennsylvania arrived in the late afternoon. Palmer and his officers began to interact with the citizens, and Palmer was disturbed by what was reported.

Acting on information supplied to him by a middle-aged woman, Palmer stopped and searched four men belonging to the 13th Tennessee Cavalry. Upon finding a woman's ring and other jewelry, Palmer arrested them.

Palmer approached General Stoneman upon his arrival at Boone.

"Sir, I have arrested four of General Gillem's men for robbery. They accosted two elderly women in their home and took their private property at gunpoint."

Stoneman was disturbed by the report.

"Are you sure, Colonel Palmer?" he asked, hoping that there was some other explanation.

"Yes, sir, I'm sure. I found the property on their person myself," he said.

General Gillem burst upon the scene during the conversation.

"How dare you arrest my men!" he screamed.

"They acted in violation of civilian and military law. I had no choice," Palmer said calmly.

"Liars! They're all a bunch of liars!" Gillem screamed again.

"I found the women's property on these men myself," Palmer stated.

Gillem turned to Stoneman.

"My men bought those rings from those thieving Rebel harlots," Gillem said fuming.

"They paid them, fair and square."

Gillem turned back to Palmer.

"Don't you dare arrest one of my men again."

Shifting his gaze once more to Stoneman, he said, "I demand that my men be released immediately."

"Very well, General Gillem. Colonel Palmer, release those men,"

Stoneman said with an indecisive demeanor.

"Yes, sir, but I request that we do everything possible to maintain military discipline," Palmer stated with agitation.

Gillem again flew into a rage.

"You mind your own damn business, Palmer. I'm divisional commander and don't you forget it."

"I'm fully aware of your position, sir." Palmer saluted and left the room.

——— MARCH 29, 1865 ———

Boone, North Carolina General Stoneman called the brigade commanders to his headquarters tent for a brief meeting. Military assignments were being given along with travel routes. General Gillem, General Brown, Colonel Miller, and Colonel Palmer were all present.

"Gentlemen, we will move all captured prisoners to Tennessee. From there they will be taken to Camp Chase, Ohio. General Tillson has ordered Colonel Kirk to bring up the 2nd and 3rd North Carolina Mounted Infantry Regiments to take up guard position here in Boone. Colonel Kirk's mounted infantrymen are natives of the region. They will secure our rear position here. General Tillson will follow in a few days with the 1st Colored U.S. Heavy Artillery to fortify the mountain passes," Stoneman said, laying out his plans while pointing at a map.

"We will move out tomorrow morning. It will be necessary to divide our forces. There is not enough forage to keep four thousand men and horses fed on a single route. General Gillem, you will take the 3rd Brigade to Wilkesboro. I will take the 1st and 2nd Brigades with me across Deep Gap, and we'll reconnoiter with General Gillem in Wilkesboro."

The ride across Deep Gap was uneventful for the 1st Brigade. They crossed the crest of the Blue Ridge at an elevation of more than three thousand feet and endured an exhausting climb up the winding trails.

Stoneman rode in his carriage at the rear of the column. Unsure of what to expect in the way of opposition upon their approach into Wilkesboro, Palmer began to divide his unit into company-size

CHAPTER TWENTY-THREE

elements in order to probe the enemy.

As the main body of the 15th Pennsylvania neared the town, couriers came galloping back to the regiment.

"Sir, Captain Weand urges you to come forward at once."

"Very well, Corporal," Palmer responded.

"Major, you're in charge until I return," he shouted as he turned his horse toward Wilkesboro.

"Lead the way, Corporal," Palmer shouted.

The cavalrymen rode several miles and made two turns down side roads before coming into a clearing. The smoke was visible well before they got to the scene. When they rounded a bend in the road the troopers came upon Captain Weand and his party. They were transfixed as they watched a large farmhouse go up in flames. The fire was fully engaged, and even though they were more than three hundred feet away, the heat and smoke were stifling.

Weand was off his horse, kneeling on the ground and talking to a young boy of about ten. The youngster was sobbing uncontrollably.

"What's going on here, Captain? Why did you burn a civilian home?" Palmer asked angrily.

"Sir, we didn't burn it. It was on fire when we got here. It seems that General Gillem's men got here first," Weand said with an accusatory tone.

Palmer was relieved to learn that his men hadn't started the fire, but he was still puzzled as to what had transpired.

"Why did they burn the place?" Palmer asked with growing concern.

"We don't know, sir, but you may want to hear what the boy has to say," Weand said with an expression that showed his disgust.

Palmer went to the boy and tried to calm him, but he continued to sob. Finally he began to talk in broken spurts.

"The Yankees came. . . They broke into our house."

The boy lost his composure again and was forced to pause.

"I climbed in the kitchen cabinet and hid out. . . I was so scerred! Nobody was home . . . 'cept me, Mama, and my big sister. They wanted money . . . gold 'n silver and such. I heard my mama say she'd give 'em everything she had."

259

The child started to speak but burst into tears again, this time wailing loudly.

"I heard noises . . . then . . . then."

He cried some more and appeared unable to speak. He seemed to force himself to continue.

"I heard my mama screaming. I heard my sister screaming! They screamed something terrible!"

The boy stopped and cried some more.

"I was so scerred. . . I didn't know what to do. I wanted ta hep 'em, I swear I did!"

He broke down once more, then continued.

"I was so scerred. . . I got out of the cabinet. . . I went and ran for the woods behind the house. I hid there. . . I was so scerred I couldn't move. I heard them Yankees, laughin' and howlin' like dogs."

The terrified youngster looked up at Palmer, then back at Weand. Before he could speak he broke down again. "Then I heard gunshots. . . I heard them men laughing again."

He looked back at the men with tears in his eyes. "I wanted to go back in there . . . to kill them men . . . honest to God I wanted to go back in there, but I froze plum up. I couldn't move none!"

Palmer looked at Weand, and each man saw the sickness in the other's face. Palmer turned his attention back to the boy.

"Did you see the men?"

"No sir, I was hid in the cabinet."

"Did you hear any of them call a name?"

"No . . . I don't think so. But one of 'em talked funny. I ain't never heard nobody talk like that."

"Can you tell us anything else about these men?" Palmer asked, frustrated by the sparse information.

"No sir. I only seen 'em from a ways off when they come ridin' up. I ran and hid."

Captain Weand interrupted.

"Sir, when we got here the fire was goin' pretty good. We could still go in the house, but we couldn't get upstairs 'cause of the smoke. I had to order my men out," he said sadly.

CHAPTER TWENTY-THREE

"I understand, Captain. You did the right thing. I don't think you could have saved anyone," Palmer said, now growing angry.

Palmer turned his attention back to the boy.

'Son, do you have any other family around here?"

"Yes, sir, my granny lives in town."

"Captain, see that this young man gets to his grandmother's house safely."

"Yes, sir," Weand responded.

Palmer stood erect and started to leave when the boy spoke up again.

"Mr. General, sir," the boy said, fighting back his tears again.

"Yes, son, what is it?"

"I did hear one of them men call out to another one of 'em."

"Did you hear a name, son?" Palmer asked anxiously.

"No sir, not just exactly; he called another feller Reverend."

Palmer looked back at the house and the roaring flames shooting high into the air. There would be no trace of evidence, and he doubted that the bodies could be identified. Palmer climbed back onto his horse.

"Take good care of that boy, Captain," he said firmly, then rode away.

Chapter 24

——APRIL 12, 1865——

Salisbury, North Carolina It was just after daylight when Stoneman called his officers together.

"Gentlemen, I was held as a prisoner during part of 1864, and I can tell you that there is no greater horror for a soldier than that of being captured and imprisoned," Stoneman said while obviously becoming emotional.

"It is our duty to liberate our fellow soldiers who are being held in the Salisbury prison. We have reports that there may be as many as ten thousand of our brothers being held there. This is the most important part of our mission," he said, looking directly into the eyes of his officers.

Stoneman rolled out the map and gave each commander his instructions.

"We will divide into four parties. The 11th Kentucky will cross at Grant's Creek. The 13th Tennessee will cross below them. The 8th Tennessee will capture the bridge and then General Brown will follow, crossing the bridge. Colonel Miller, you will go east and destroy the railroad," Stoneman said as he outlined basic assignments. "Colonel Palmer, you will take the prison. Major Barnes, you will collect enemy prisoners and make a tally of stores and supplies located in Salisbury."

"Men, this is the biggest challenge we've faced on this raid. They have artillery and possibly a substantial garrison there," Stoneman said.

Stoneman knew something that most of the others did not. He

CHAPTER TWENTY-FOUR

shared it only with the divisional commander, General Gillem. Very soon he would be leaving the command. His main reason for seeking this command had been to try to restore his tarnished reputation and to free the prisoners at Salisbury. He knew that the war was ending and this was to be his last campaign. His intentions were to leave after he'd accomplished those goals. It was very important to him that this final mission be a successful one.

Moments before he separated from his officers Stoneman looked directly at each of them and sternly gave one last command.

"I want no more crimes of any kind committed. All of you are to be sure that your men conduct themselves properly. If anyone is caught stealing or committing any other crime, they will be punished. Is that understood?" The officers nodded, indicating their understanding, and Stoneman dismissed them.

General Gillem assembled his officers and scouts to give them their orders.

"Now listen to me, men. I don't want to see any trouble out of anyone on this mission. Stoneman will be leaving after we free those prisoners and I'll be in full command. I don't want any trouble. Is that clear?"

Within the hour the full division was in position. The attack began in the center with Brown's men riding across the bridge over Grant's Creek. The Confederates defending the bridge on the other side broke and ran. Palmer's men followed and met little opposition. Miller's men attacked the garrison at the west side of Salisbury and were greeted by a cheer from the enemy. The defense of that part of the line had been assigned to the recently freed Irish "Galvanized Yankees." Instead of putting up a strong resistance for the Confederates, they welcomed the Union soldiers and promptly joined them.

Palmer reached the prison easily but to great disappointment. When Stoneman arrived he was devastated. The prisoners were gone, having been moved only days before, dispersed to various other camps in North Carolina. Stoneman's primary personal objective was not obtained.

Stoneman sat on a masonry wall and held his face in his hands.

Palmer went to console him.

"Sir, we got here as quick as we could," Palmer lamented.

"It's not your fault," Palmer told Stoneman in an empathetic tone. He'd come to appreciate Stoneman. Palmer knew he wasn't the greatest of leaders and didn't always seem focused, but he'd performed admirably for the most part. Palmer knew that Gillem and his men were a little more than Stoneman could handle, but he also recognized that Stoneman had tried his best to control them.

"All this way, all this effort, and they're gone. I so wanted to see the look upon those men's faces," he said sadly.

"You know, Colonel Palmer, I wanted to see their faces so I could see what I looked like that day. You know, what it was like for me the day I walked back to freedom."

"Yes, sir, I know. I will never forget that day either," Palmer said.

Stoneman looked up at him. "Yes, that's right. You were once a prisoner too, weren't you?"

"Yes, sir, I was at Castle Thunder. I really thought I was going to die."

Both men were contemplating their next moves when Major Barnes approached.

"General Stoneman, sir!" Barnes shouted.

"Yes, what is it, Major?" Stoneman replied impatiently.

"Sir, it seems that Governor Vance had turned Salisbury into a major supply point because of the railroad. The town is loaded with a king's ransom in supplies!" Barnes said excitedly.

Palmer interrupted him briefly.

"It looks like your mission may have been more successful than you thought, general."

Stoneman brightened up quickly.

"Go on, Major. What have you found?"

Barnes pulled papers from his frock coat and read from a list.

"We found 10,000 stand of arms, 1,000,000 pounds of ammunition, 10,000 pounds of artillery ammunition, 6,000 pounds of powder, 3 magazines, 6 depots, 10,000 bushels of corn, 75,000 suits of uniform clothing, and 250,000 blankets." Barnes looked up with his smile growing broader.

CHAPTER TWENTY-FOUR

"They were English blankets too, General."

Stoneman and Palmer could restrain themselves no longer. Both men let out a howl and Stoneman jumped to his feet.

"That ain't all, sir. There's more," Barnes said beaming.

"Go on, Major! Go on!" Stoneman shouted at him.

"We also took 20,000 pounds of leather, 6,000 pounds of bacon, 100,000 pounds of salt, 20,000 pounds of sugar, 27,000 pounds of rice, 10,000 pounds of saltpeter, 50,000 bushels of wheat, 80 barrels of turpentine, $15,000,000 in Confederate money, and a lot of medical stores which our surgeon says is worth $100,000 in gold."

Stoneman and Palmer erupted in a cheer. Both men began slapping Barnes on the back and asking for more detail.

"The loss of those stores will do far more damage to the enemy than freeing the prisoners, sir," Palmer said to Stoneman, smiling broadly.

"Did you say 100,000 pounds of salt?" Stoneman asked, knowing how valuable the commodity was.

"Yes sir," Barnes stated confidently.

Palmer asked if he had any information on casualties.

"Almost none reported so far, sir, just a few injuries. Most of the Rebs cut and ran. There wasn't much of a fight to it," he said.

Sensing the need to support his commander, Palmer reached out his hand.

"Congratulations, General, you have achieved a great success. Your victory is a major step toward ending the war," Palmer said formally. He shook the general's hand again.

Stoneman beamed openly.

"Yes, yes. They will say this was a great victory! I've won a great victory!"

"Sir, may I add that this victory will result in those prisoners being free soon. All prisoners, I might add," Palmer continued congratulating Stoneman.

"Yes, you're right, Colonel! Without these supplies the enemy will be unable to carry on this war. In the end we'll free all the Union prisoners, and soon I think."

"Major, get my adjutant. I want to send a message to General

Thomas right away!" Stoneman shouted the command while shaking Colonel Palmer's hand for the third time.

"Colonel Palmer, fetch the other officers. I want to invite them to a bonfire. It's going to be the biggest bonfire in North Carolina history!"

―― EASTER SUNDAY, 1865 ――

Saint James Episcopal Church, Lenoir, North Carolina General Stoneman looked out over the churchyard. There were throngs of Confederate prisoners and hundreds of freed slaves gathered in two large clusters near the church. He was proud of himself. He'd redeemed his reputation. His command disasters early in the war and his embarrassing capture by home guards in Georgia were distant memories. The men seemed to respect him, and he felt very good about his triumph in Salisbury. He felt certain that the capture of those enemy supplies would be recognized in Washington as a great accomplishment toward winning the war.

The war is almost over, he thought. This is no time to take chances. Quit while you're ahead.

He was troubled to some degree about what would go on after he left, but he'd have to leave that to others. He'd made his decision. He was going home.

Stoneman sent for his brigade commanders. Soon they were all gathered in the church rectory, which was now serving as headquarters.

"Gentlemen," he said calmly. "We have a large number of prisoners and many freed slaves in our charge. I have made the decision to leave the command. I will take the prisoners and the freedmen and return to Tennessee by way of Watauga County."

He looked out the window again and pointed at the slaves.

"I want to make sure they get to freedom safely," he said earnestly.

"I will leave tomorrow morning. I will take an escort guard with me as far as Boone, where General Tillson and our support troops are waiting. General Gillem will take command.

CHAPTER TWENTY-FOUR

"The war is all but over, but there is one more objective that should be accomplished before you return to Tennessee. There is only one strong garrison left," he said, looking directly at Gillem. "It's Asheville. You must take Asheville. I trust you will do so without delay."

The meeting disbanded, and Stoneman left. All the officers crowded around General Gillem except one. They were all congratulating Gillem on taking command and attempting to seek his favor. Colonel Palmer walked out into the churchyard and looked to the west. Those poor people, he said to himself. He wondered what fate lay ahead for them.

Palmer slipped into a melancholy state. He reverted back to his religious upbringing. Hicksite Quakers believe that God speaks to individuals through their consciences. Palmer had done his best to follow the spirit of God by following his conscience. He didn't know a soul in western North Carolina, yet he felt the weight of God's will upon him as he contemplated the future of this mission under the command of General Gillem.

Seeking relief from his despair, Palmer walked into the empty sanctuary of Saint James Church. He slowly walked forward and knelt in front of the church altar. He bowed his head and prayed:

> Almighty God in heaven,
> Grant me thy wisdom, that I may know your truth.
> Grant me thy protection as I may be cast among the evil.
> Grant me thy strength so that I may defend the meek in thy name.
> Grant me the courage to stand against the powerful in defending the righteous.
> In thy name I pray.
> Amen.

Chapter 25

—— APRIL 13, 1865 ——

Lenoir, North Carolina Colonel Palmer bounded down the steps of the little house where he'd quartered for the night. He felt rested and strong, and he'd made peace with himself and God the night before.

"I will follow my conscience and do what is right. I will do so at whatever perils my military career may face. I will follow God's direction," he promised himself just before he fell asleep.

Stoneman was seated on his carriage, and the escort guard was already in place. Palmer shook his hand for the last time and saluted. The two men said their farewells. Stoneman gave the order to move out, and Palmer watched as the strange procession of soldiers, former slaves, and prisoners snaked its way through the town of Lenoir.

General Gillem immediately called the officers to a meeting. Palmer was the last to arrive. When he entered the room there was suddenly a strange silence. The uncomfortable moment lasted only briefly when Gillem spoke up. There was an unrestrained boastfulness in his tone.

"Gentlemen, I am now in full command," he bellowed.

Palmer looked at his aide without saying a word, then turned his attention back to Gillem. Palmer was thinking, "I wonder if he thinks we don't know that?"

"My first orders are for Colonel Palmer."

"Colonel Palmer, I will be separating the command. You will take the 1st Brigade down to Charlotte and destroy any bridges you find over the Catawba River."

CHAPTER TWENTY-FIVE

Palmer was stunned. "But sir, there's no tactical reason for that. It will take me days to catch up with the rest of the division," he said, appealing his case.

Gillem fumed. "How dare you tell me what is tactical. I'm a West Point graduate. I'll tell you what is tactical and you will carry out my orders. Is that clear, Colonel?"

Palmer lost his speech. He knew what this meant. With Stoneman gone and his brigade out of the way, the pillaging and plundering would go completely unchecked. He tried to find the words to argue, but there were none. He had to accept it. There was only one thing he could say.

"Yes sir, it's clear," he replied weakly.

"Good, Colonel. That's very good, because the first man in this division who fails to follow my orders will be arrested. We are still in a combat situation in enemy territory, and I will not tolerate any insubordination," Gillem said, obviously relishing his new power.

"Does anyone else wish to debate tactics with me?" Gillem asked in a challenging tone. Some of the other officers chuckled slightly at the question, but the room remained silent.

"Good. Then this meeting is over."

"Oh, by the way, Colonel Palmer. I want you on your way to Charlotte within the hour. Is that understood?"

"Yes, sir, I will muster my men at once," Palmer said.

All the worry and anguish of the night before had been pointless. He was helpless, and he knew it. There was so little resistance left to slow Gillem down that by the time Palmer got to Charlotte and back, the division would be in Tennessee.

"God help the poor people in his path," Palmer prayed silently, then left the room.

Gillem watched Palmer's exit, then turned back to his officers, displaying a wide grin.

"Remember, gentlemen, we are to make these Rebels pay with all the blood we can extract and all the pain we can deliver. We can do whatever we want as long as we claim we are out saving some poor nigger slave.

You've riden hard and witnessed the deaths of many comrades. We are entitled to the spoils of war."

The officers laughed and cheered simultaneously.

"Prepare your men to begin the march."

—— APRIL 20, 1865 ——

Swannanoa Gap, North Carolina Matthias Dees rode alongside Corporal LaFerre just a few lengths behind General Gillem. Dees looked behind them, and he could still see smoke in the distance. The buildings they had burned in Rutherfordton the day before still smoldered.

"Ya know, Pete, gettin' word on ole Abe being shot is 'bout the bes' thang goin'. General Gillem is madder than a hornet. I believe he's gonna let us do what we wanna without much fuss," he said laughing.

"Ya, de village of Morgintoon make goot fire, no?" he said smiling.

"Yep, I reckon that's so, burnt down the whole highfalutin town. Damn, that were fun!" Dees said.

Dees patted the two sacks hanging on either side of his horse.

"I reckon I'll need me another bag when I git up thar where all 'em rich folks on the mountain lives. Hell, and I got the good stuff on me," he said feeling of his waist.

The formation came to a stop and General Gillem convened his officers.

"Colonel Miller, when we get to the gap, you take two companies of your men forward. Have them ride all the way to the top of the gap. Tell them to check both flanks. There could be a few home guards there, so be ready for a little trouble."

Asheville, North Carolina Delia and her father skipped breakfast. They wanted to be ready to meet friends in the lobby of the Eagle Hotel. When they reached the lobby they found it crowded and very busy.

"What's going on?" Russell asked the desk clerk.

"Ain't you heard?" the man shouted back excitedly. "The Yanks is on the way!"

Delia's heart fluttered, and she immediately felt weak.

CHAPTER TWENTY-FIVE

"Oh my God, save us! Papa, what will we do?" she asked him, her voice burdened with fear.

"Let's don't panic. Maybe they won't make it this far," Russell said as if he doubted his own words.

"We'll go to General Martin and see what's really going on," Russell told Delia as if he had a plan.

Confederate General James Green Martin was the Western District commander for North Carolina. His headquarters were nearby, and Russell had gotten to know him since he took command of the Confederate garrison in Asheville.

When they stepped out into the street, people were running everywhere. Men, women, and children were going through town by every means of transportation. Horses, carts, and wagons were loaded with all that could be carried.

As the Russells crossed the town square they could see Confederate soldiers forming in the middle of the square. More were arriving constantly, and it was obvious that the soldiers were preparing for a fight.

Suddenly two formations pulled into the square. Horses pulled two cannons as the men guided them. Russell recognized the men as Jeter's Battery, normally stationed north of the town. Porter's Battery had already moved their two guns toward Swannanoa Gap.

Just as Delia and her father arrived at Martin's headquarters the general was giving orders to another man.

"General Martin, sir, could I have a word with you?" Russell asked, his voice laden with apprehension.

"No, not now," Martin replied quickly and dashed back into the building.

Another young officer stood at the door and seemed to be directing others. Russell approached him at about the same time two other men did.

"Sir, tell us what is happening!" one man said urgently.

"Yes, please, man, tell us," Russell shouted.

Delia stood in the background as the young officer let several soldiers pass and then turned his attention to the civilians. She moved closer in hopes of hearing what he would say.

The young man looked at the small cluster of men now gathered at the steps and began to address them.

"Scouts have come in from McDowell County. The Yankee cavalry is headed this way. They burned down Morganton and Rutherfordton. General Martin is assembling all available men. We're going to station ourselves at Swannanoa Gap before they get there with as many men as we can get," he said rather calmly.

"We got word to Colonel Love in Waynesville last night, and he and a good portion of the 69th are on the way. No need to panic yet. We may be able to hold them off if we get to the gap first," he said reassuringly.

"If Colonel Love gets here we can do it," he said, emphasizing the importance of the colonel's arrival.

The town square became even more crowded with people. More soldiers were arriving every minute. Suddenly a rider appeared galloping frantically to the front of Martin's headquarters. He was so excited he couldn't wait to see the general without announcing his news to the people gathered outside.

At the top of the steps he wheeled around and pointed to the west. "Colonel Love's coming! He's just down the road, and he's got four hundred men!" A huge cheer erupted from the civilian bystanders gathered around Martin's headquarters.

Before he could get in the door Martin rushed out to meet him.

He grabbed the man's lapel and shouted at him, "Are you sure?"

"Yes, sir! Yes, sir! I saw them there just down the road and moving fast!" the man shouted as he pointed westward. Suddenly more noise could be heard from behind the buildings on the west side of the square. People could be seen looking in that direction, pointing and waving.

Within minutes Colonel Love appeared on horseback. He swung his horse to the side, and his men came running into the square. There were rows of them, six wide and continuous. They wore ragged Confederate uniforms and carried muskets. Some of the soldiers were Cherokee Indians.

The civilians clapped and cheered as the men continued to file into town. Martin now had parts of the 62nd, the 64th, and Walker's Battalion

CHAPTER TWENTY-FIVE

of Thomas's legion, which made up part of the 69th North Carolina Infantry. A total of nearly seven hundred Confederate soldiers were gathered on the town square.

Delia was stunned at the sight of so many armed soldiers. The scene was quite frightening.

"What are we going to do, Papa?" she asked him anxiously.

Robert Russell only stared. He was transfixed by the scene unfolding before them and only shook his head.

"Papa, shouldn't we go to the hideout now?" Delia asked him, hoping to get his attention.

Colonel Love dismounted and ran to Martin's headquarters. Before he could get inside Martin met him on the steps. The two men could be seen conferring, but the others could not hear what was being said. Soon Love saluted the general and dashed over to where all the men were assembled. Delia could see a cluster of a half dozen men gather around Love in the middle of the square. Within seconds the circle dispersed. Colonel Love mounted his horse and called out the order for the men to march. The Confederates started down South Main Street at a steady run.

The crowd cheered, roared, and clapped. Men on the veranda waved their hats as the last formation started down the hill past the Eagle Hotel.

"Papa, Papa, shouldn't we go to the hideout?" Delia asked him as she tugged at his sleeve.

Obviously annoyed, he turned back to her.

"No, we'll stay here."

"But what about Mama, Mary, Sarah, and John? What about Zeke and Nanny?" she said, now frantic.

"Hush, child!" he snapped at her. "Can't you understand that the Yankees are coming toward Asheville? If they were to make it through Swannanoa Gap they'd be coming this way. If we hear of it then we'll head out to Fletcher and go to the hideout. Everyone out there will be better off if we stay here and find out what's happening."

What he told her did seem to make sense. Besides, she was so frightened and unnerved by what she had witnessed that she couldn't think clearly. They walked back to the hotel, and she prayed as they walked. "Oh God, please save us, protect us, help our men. Please, oh God."

Many people were gathered at the hotel, and the lobby and parlor were abuzz with conversation and commentary on what might occur. The large number of men Martin was able to assemble gave comfort to those gathered at the hotel and the townspeople in general. There was nothing they could do but wait.

General Gillem felt no reason to be seriously concerned, so the division took its time. Even with the 1st Brigade gone Gillem still had 2,800 men with him. The fact that his men were armed with repeating rifles added to his confidence. He felt sure that with the new rifles he could bring more firepower to the field than twice his number with muskets. General Gillem felt that if he got into a serious fight all he needed to do was bring all his force to battle. He assumed that he would encounter nothing more than a home guard detachment. That was what they were used to.

"Find the enemy and brush them aside, Colonel Miller," Gillem told him officiously.

Miller's scouts went forward without incident. While scouting the lower end of the gorge they captured a man who'd been cutting trees in an apparent attempt to block the road. He was dressed in civilian clothes and appeared to be a civilian. The man was taken back to Colonel Miller.

"What's your name?" the Union colonel demanded.

"Charles Wesley White," the man answered him with his head held high.

"What were you doing up there?" Miller inquired further.

White looked defiantly at the soldiers who'd captured him.

"Well, I was doin' a little loggin' when these here Yankees interrupted me," he said smiling. "This dang war done fouled up everthin'. A feller can't get no work done."

"There's no point wasting time with this ignorant fool. Move the first two companies into the gorge and start up to the gap," Miller said.

CHAPTER TWENTY-FIVE

"Sir, it's mighty narrow in there. There are two steep ridges on both sides. It's real steep at the far end where the trail winds up to the top," he said with concern.

"So, what does that matter?"

"Well, sir, we can't bring our full force to the field in there. It's a bad place to be caught in an ambush. We'd be shooting straight up and they'd be shooting straight down on us."

"Look, soldier, it's several days' ride around to another pass, and we'll find the same thing when we go there. So the general says we're crossing here. Move those two companies into the gorge."

"Yes, sir," the man said, shaking his head as he rode back to the front of the column.

Confederate Colonel Robert Love watched from the center of his line at the top of Swannanoa Gap. He was elevated well above the valley floor and had a clear view of the trail as the line of blue began winding its way toward the barricades. Two scouts were out front several lengths ahead of the first company of the 12th Kentucky Union Cavalry. The Union soldiers were crowding into each other as the traffic slowed. They were slowly maneuvering their way around the felled trees when Love gave the order to fire.

The lead scout at the front of the Union column was looking up at the ridges trying to see if there was anything suspicious on the tops. He saw the flames about a half second before he heard the sound. There were hundreds of musket balls raining down on the men at the front of Gillem's procession. The first musket volley was followed by simultaneous blasts from Porter's two guns. That was followed quickly by two more blasts from Jeter's two Napoleon cannons.

Many of the men in blue were hit, some falling dead immediately. Scores of horses were hit, and those men still alive and able were scrambling for cover. Many dashed on foot into the woods on their hands and knees. Spencer rifles and other accoutrements were left behind, scattered randomly. Those at the rear of the column took flight on horseback as fast as they could go. Many men were running into each other, some falling off their horses. Several Union soldiers fired blindly up at the ridge tops with little or no effect. Still others tried to crawl into thickets or under brush.

General Gillem was positioned at the rear surrounded by a heavy guard. He was chatting and laughing with his fellow officers when he heard the roar. He turned to face Major Barnes with a sick expression on his face. Barnes could see the fear in the general's eyes.

"What in the hell was that?" Barnes asked as his horse fidgeted unsteadily at the noise.

"I don't know, but if that was muskets, it was hundreds of them!" another officer shouted.

Gillem was dumbfounded. His face turned ashen. What could this be? he wondered.

Soon two riders approached.

"Sir, Colonel Miller reports that there is a full division of Confederate infantry in front of us. They are at the gap and in force. Colonel Miller awaits your orders, sir!"

Gillem turned crimson with anger. He didn't know what to do.

"Goddamn it, don't those Rebel fools know the war is over? What the hell are they doing up there?" he shouted as he whacked his hat onto his leg.

"Goddamn it, why does this have to happen to me?" he said in a low, disgusted tone.

Gillem turned back to the messenger.

"Get Colonel Miller up here."

As Gillem waited for Miller he began to tremble. "Maybe we can go up the sides and flank 'em," he said to himself. Then he worried, "What if I am captured or even injured?" Indecision gripped him.

As he continued his attempt to control his own panic, several bleeding and wounded men were carried by. Gillem looked at them with growing trepidation. Just behind the wounded was Colonel Miller. Miller was bareheaded, having lost his hat in the frenzy.

"Sir, they have at least two thousand men at the gap! It appears to be

CHAPTER TWENTY-FIVE

veteran troops. They must have been reinforced or something," he said while gasping for breath.

"They've got artillery, sir!"

"Sir, the situation is impossible. The walls of the gorge are very steep. We'll be cut to pieces if we don't get out of here."

Gillem sat on his horse in silence trying to think of a way out of this. He continued to stare in silence, unable to regain his composure. Miller and the other officers watched as Gillem moved his mouth but nothing came out.

More musketry rattled in the distance as Gillem floundered.

Gillem continued his mental evaluation as his men scrambled around him in chaos. He thought to himself, "If there were two thousand men on that ridge, then there might be more. There could be cavalry coming in behind them as they waited."

Suddenly Gillem was overwhelmed with fear. We could be wiped out or captured, he thought. He was used to encounters with old men and boys, not the whole damn Rebel army.

He was now consumed by panic. His mind clamored for a face-saving explanation.

"All right, all right, we have to care for these men. Order the retreat, Colonel," Gillem said meekly.

The wait back in Asheville had been excruciating for everyone. Delia looked around the hotel parlor at the people, and she could see the fear in their faces. Everyone in town carried the same worry and anxieties. What would happen if their men couldn't hold the gap?

It was almost dark when a rider came into town. Delia heard someone in the crowd shout.

"There's a rider in the square."

Everyone in the hotel poured out into the cool evening air to hear the news. There was a lot of commotion, and Delia was at the back of the group that had emptied out of the hotel. There were many other ladies with her. Soon there was cheering, then more cheering and people running through the streets.

"What happened? Please, what happened?" screamed one of the women standing with Delia.

A young man who seemed to be hysterical screamed back at her.

"We whooped 'em! We whooped 'em good! Our boys whooped the Yankees!"

Delia screamed with joy and the woman beside her almost collapsed. Delia had to help hold her on her feet.

Robert Russell grabbed her arms and shouted, "I told you so!"

Chapter 26

——APRIL 23, 1865——

Columbus, North Carolina General Gillem paced impatiently as he waited for his scouts to return. It was midday, and he was finishing his activity reports.

"Don't you want to include the list of casualties from Swannanoa Gap?" Major Barnes asked him.

"Hell no, we ain't saying nothin' about that battle," Gillem stormed back at him.

"Well, ah, yes sir, if you say so." Barnes was taken aback by Gillem's defensive reaction.

"Just don't say a damn thing. You leave that out of the report. This war will be over soon, and nobody will remember it. Besides, I may get another chance at them damn Rebels up there in the mountains," Gillem said, his words laden with hollow confidence.

"I'm going to make those ignorant bastards pay, and pay dearly," Gillem said grimacing.

At that point Captain Scott interrupted them.

"Sir, Corporal LaFerre and his scouts are back."

"Good, good. Send them in right away," Gillem said anxiously.

LaFerre walked in with the Dees boys behind him.

"Sir, we scout de enemy at Howard Gop," LaFerre said in his heavy French accent.

Gillem walked from behind his field desk and looked straight at Dees. "What did you boys see up there?" he asked anxiously.

Dees smiled broadly, sensing that the stage was his.

"Well sir, me'n the boys went up through 'em woods on a little deer path," he said, trying to build suspense and promote himself.

"It was real dangerous, but me 'n the boys, we knowed the ground real good. We been all over this here country," he continued while pointing up at the mountain ridges.

"Well sir, we snuck up real close to 'em. We was on that little mountaintop just yonder," again pointing at something no one could see.

Dees's grin widened.

"Sir, there ain't but 'bout fifteen or sixteen men thar. Most of 'em looked like old men 'n little boys. I tell ya, sir, we could take that gap real easy."

Dees nodded, and his boys followed his example. Soon all of them, including LaFerre, were smiling and nodding at the general. Gillem stepped away and pondered what he'd heard. He looked up in the direction of the mountains. Secretly fearing that he'd face another force like the one at Swannanoa Gap, Gillem hesitated. Then he turned back to Dees.

"Are you absolutely sure?" he asked while he tried to hide his trembling hands.

"Yes, sir, I is. I swear to the Almighty himself." With that Dees removed his hat and bowed his head.

"Major, get General Brown at once. We'll seize Howard Gap this afternoon and hold it through the night. We'll move in force to Hendersonville tomorrow morning. That's our last obstacle before we attack Asheville."

Gillem paced some more as he contemplated his advantage.

"LaFerre, you and your scouts stay close by. I may need you tomorrow. I need men who know the land."

Robert Russell sat at the table with his family gathered around him. He ate

CHAPTER TWENTY-SIX

slowly and in silence. The word had come yesterday, and it was obviously true. The legendary Confederate general Robert E. Lee had surrendered the Army of Northern Virginia to the Yankees.

Robert Russell's anxiety was taking a toll on everyone around him. Where would it go from here? What would become of him? Where was Joe Johnston and the rest of the Confederate army? Could he be arrested, maybe tried and hanged? Russell had returned home elated that Confederate troops had stopped the Union advance from coming to Asheville. The news seemed to be so much better, only to be followed by the dreadful news of Lee's surrender of the Confederacy's main army.

Delia broke the silence.

"Papa, what are we going to do?" she asked fearfully. Everyone at the table looked at him, but he sat in silence. It seemed that he hadn't heard the question.

Mary and Sarah sobbed openly as the anxiety continued to build on the family.

Nanny Mills went around the table serving grits and greens to all. She followed with cornbread while Delia poured water from a pitcher. She did her duties without expression or change in demeanor, conducting herself as if everything was normal.

"Papa, corn meal and a little bit of greens is all we have left to eat. Should we go somewhere?" Delia asked persistently. Still there was no answer. Robert Russell sat deep in thought. But Delia would not be deterred.

"Papa, what are we going to do?" she inquired again.

Russell flew into a rage. He swiped his hand across the table, knocking his plate and glass to the floor and breaking them both. He stood up, wobbling on his bad leg.

"I'm about to be taken to prison or maybe hanged!" he said screaming. "All you can do is whine about supper! Nobody has done a damn thing around here except me. All any of ya do is complain."

He stepped from the table, reaching for his cane to leave. Before he could clear the room, they heard shouting outside, apparently coming from the direction of Jackson Road. Delia got up and ran to the door where she could see someone galloping toward them yelling excitedly.

It was Samuel Justus, a fourteen-year-old boy who lived nearby. He was yelling and shouting so frantically that Delia could not make out his words. He came riding into the yard and toward the house. By this time the whole family had left the table and come to the door while Zeke was running up from his shack to see what the commotion was about. Justus pulled up the horse in front of their porch.

"The Yankees are here! The Yankees are here! Thousands of 'em!" he shouted, fighting for breath.

"They're everywhere; they're in Hendersonville!"

Delia and her sisters gasped.

Delia's heart sank, and she felt sick to her stomach. She caught her breath, then uttered quietly, "Oh my God, save us!"

Mary Russell swooned and fainted. Nanny and Delia caught her just in time. Sarah cried aloud.

"They're shootin' up everything, robbin' people, and arresting anybody that's a Confederate," the boy continued excitedly. He looked at Robert Russell and shouted, "and they're arrestin' all slaveowners!"

Russell's face was ashen. Stunned, he looked around in absolute panic.

"Ya better git outta here. They'll be here any minute. I saw 'em in Fletcher!" the boy howled.

Russell came out of his momentary trance.

"Zeke, hitch up the wagon! Hurry, hurry!" he shouted frantically.

Zeke was running to the barn before he finished his words.

"Boy, you go by Hutch's place, and be sure they know about this. You hear?"

"Yes, sir." Then Justus turned his horse and rode away at a gallop.

Russell looked at his family and knew that he couldn't take everyone in the wagon. His major concern was that he escape immediately.

"Girls, you help your mother get your things and git to the wagon now!" he shouted impatiently.

CHAPTER TWENTY-SIX

"Nanny, you help the girls. Delia, you stay with me."

As soon as they were alone, Russell turned to Delia.

"Listen, now, you listen good! There ain't enough room for all of us to go now. We're going to the hideout, and as soon as we can unload I'll send Zeke right back. It's only a couple of miles. You stay here and gather up all the silver and china, get all the valuables you can carry. Grab all the food you can get too. I can't stay; they'll be after me. I'll leave Nanny here to help you," he said in a most serious tone.

Delia's heart pounded, and her mind raced. She knew that there would be little time, but she understood what she must do.

"Now one more thing, Delia. Don't let Nanny see you, but you must get the moneybox down. Take it to the cellar and bury it a foot deep. Put something over it so it don't look like nothin' is buried there. Do you understand me, child?" he asked, shaking her by the shoulders as he talked to her. "You gotta bury it. Our lives depend on it."

"Yes, yes, Papa. I understand," she said shaking with fear.

"It's all I have left. We must protect it!"

Zeke pulled up in front of the house, and the girls were already coming down the stairs. Nanny helped Mrs. Russell as they executed the hasty assemblage in the yard. Zeke helped them onto the wagon, and they were gone in an instant. Ole Star strained at the heavy load as she pulled them into the road and off toward the hideout.

Delia tried to compose herself, but she couldn't stop shaking. She ran back into the house and shouted at Nanny.

"Get some boxes, Nanny. Hurry!"

The two of them worked frantically but carefully. The china was quite old, and Delia feared breaking it. Nanny talked to her as they worked.

"Now don't ya fret none, Miss Delia. Zeke'll be back," she said as her own voice cracked with fear.

They carried boxes onto the porch and placed them in position. Delia worked in the kitchen, and Nanny went to the smokehouse and collected what she could. They lost time dropping things, and Nanny had to retrace her steps to retrieve the smokehouse key she'd forgotten.

Time flew by as Delia's panic grew. Nanny came running into the house. She screamed loudly, "He's a comin'! Ole Zeke, he's a comin'! I sees him comin' down de road!" She laughed her deep, bellowing laugh that Delia had heard all her life. "I tol' ya so. Zeke be comin'!"

Just as she started down the steps Delia heard gunshots in the distance. She screamed and tripped on the steps, crashing forward onto the ground. Nanny picked her up while Zeke was already loading the boxes. It took them only seconds, and they were in flight. They could hear more gunshots as they pulled away.

Ole Star frothed at the mouth and sweat ran over her body as she fought to meet the demands of her driver. The wagon carried them toward the hideout and safety. The sun was setting as they made the left turn up Souther Road, and soon they were out of harm's way.

Delia fell into Nanny's arms and burst into tears.

"Oh God, what's going to happen to us?" she mumbled as she hugged the old woman tightly.

After a slow pull up Souther Road they were at the hideout. Great relief was apparent on the faces of all who made it to safety. Wash Hutchison was so glad to see them that he ran out on his knees. His affection for Delia was now obvious to everyone. Wash's emotions were spilling out verbally as he ran to her. "I'm so glad you're all right," he said as he looked up at her in admiration.

"I'm so happy you're here safe. Thank God!"

He took her small hand in his and continued to talk to her.

"I was so worried about you," he stuttered, almost choking on his words. Delia reached down and patted him on the shoulder.

"Thank you, Wash. I'm so thankful to you. You built this hideout. I don't know what we would've done without it. Thank you." He beamed with pride at having pleased her.

Hutch Hutchison was already there with the rest of his family. He was busy adjusting things and arranging all of the recently arrived contents. Then Hutch helped Bob Russell up to the blind they had built to see if they could spot any activity down in the valley.

CHAPTER TWENTY-SIX

"Got to hand it to your boy. We'd be in a heap of trouble if we didn't have this hideout," Russell said, expressing genuine appreciation to Hutch.

"Yea, I know. It was well worth it."

Everyone began to settle in for the night and got as comfortable as possible. It was quite late when a visitor arrived. It was Pinkney Youngblood. He scared them at first, but they were all glad to see him. He'd been scouting on his own, carried by a good horse. He'd come to check on Delia.

Everyone gathered 'round as he told what he knew. His folks were already hidden out up on Bearwallow, and he was headed that way.

"The Yankees are in Fletcher already," he said, resigned to it.

"I saw at least one to two hundred on horseback. They're arresting people and shootin' at anybody that don't surrender," he added calmly. "Anybody that's got anything to do with the government is being arrested. They're arresting slaveowners too." He looked up at Russell. "But that ain't the worst of it. They're burning down public buildings and all homes that they take a notion to. They got guides with 'em, traitors I reckon, telling 'em where to go and who to git."

The Russells all gasped at the same time.

"Papa, they'll burn our house," Mary screamed.

Russell's heart sank. What could he do? He had no manpower. He couldn't fight them. He could only hope.

"Maybe they won't. Asheville is their real target. Maybe they'll move on," he said, his voice cracking.

Pinkney Youngblood got up to leave.

"I hope you're right, Mr. Russell, but I don't think so. Come daylight they'll be coming up Hoopers Creek," he stated as he reached for the horse's reins. He climbed on and bade farewell to the small group of refugees. He looked at Delia affectionately and spoke to her. "You take care now, Miss Delia."

Hendersonville, North Carolina Corporal LaFerre approached Major Barnes. "De scouts wish to speak to ze generelle. No?"

Barnes spoke to Gillem, and the men were invited in.

"Yes, what is it?" Gillem asked.

"Well sir, me and my boys here, we knows this country mighty good," Dees expounded.

"Go on," Gillem said as his interest grew.

"Well, I was kinda thinkin' we outta be keepin' a watchful eye out for them Rebs we run into back at Swannanoa Gap," Dees said, indicating by his tone that he could somehow foresee a threat.

"Ya see, General, there's a road, not many folks knows 'bout it, but for sure 'em Rebs knows about it, and course me'n the boys knows 'zackly," he boasted.

Gillem squirmed in his seat as he heard this.

"Go on, tell me more."

"Well ya see, sir, 'em Rebs could move five thousand men over that road comin' crossways. They could hit our flank, sir," Dees said, emphasizing his apparent belief that he had learned enough military parlance to discuss plans with a general.

"I see," the general said worriedly. "What do you suggest?" he asked in all seriousness. Dees was enjoying his new role and continued to present himself as an expert.

"Well sir, just give the corporal here a few men, and me and the boys'll ride up thar tonight and make sure there's nothin' comin' at ye flank in the morning."

"Very good," Gillem said. He turned to Major Barnes smiling. "This man knows what he's doing. You did an excellent job scouting Howard Gap; you do the same over there. Don't let any sizable force surprise us. Corporal, if you run into any Rebels up there, burn 'em out!" Gillem said with a vicious tone. "Don't wait to see who's in there, just torch 'em. If anybody asks you, you're freeing slaves."

Dees smiled broadly and attempted a clumsy salute. Then he and his party left.

As soon as the men gathered up supplies Corporal LaFerre led twenty hand-picked troopers into the street. They left Hendersonville and rode toward Fletcher. As the party moved along the dirt road one of

CHAPTER TWENTY-SIX

the men asked Dees a question. "Is there really a road through there?"

Dees looked at him as if he were the town fool. "Sonny boy, there's a road up thar all right. If'n ya had to, you could march a herd of goats over it, but that'd be 'bout all." He and LaFerre laughed loudly.

Dees whispered to LaFerre. "Now I know where them rich folks resides. I knowed 'em before the war. I gots me a debt to settle with one 'em. Old man Russell paid me with bad money, that Confederate shit. I aim to git my money back, one way or t'other."

"Now Pete, I tell you there be some pretty peaches ready for picking up yonder on Hoopers Creek. That old bastard got some pretty lookin' phillies, three of 'em I reckon. They ought to be 'bout ripe for the pickin', I'd say."

LaFerre looked back at him and smiled. "Ooo la la!" he said kissing his fingertips.

Fletcher was a ghost town when they arrived except for Union soldiers and a few brave citizens that had decided to stay. They rode up Howard Gap Road and crossed Cane Creek, then made the left up Jackson Road, following the exact same route James Russell had followed four years earlier when he'd frantically announced the start of the war.

"First we got a stop to make," Dees said, revealing that he was up to something. He led the men to the home of Isaac Justus. Justus was a locally famous distiller of the finest corn whiskey. Justus and his family were gone, but it took Dees and the cavalrymen only minutes to break into his cellar and find twenty-six jugs of whiskey. The Union soldiers stopped long enough to have a good drink. They tied the jugs onto their horses and continued up Jackson Road.

As the squad of Union cavalry rode into the Russell yard, they soon discovered the house vacant.

"Damn, damn it all," Dees said angrily.

"I had me a hankerin'. Damn it! We ain't had nothin' since that darky in Morganton."

"Maybe zey be near, no?" LaFerre asked.

"Maybe so, Pete, maybe so," Dees said, rubbing his stringy beard. "We'll go up on that little hill thar and wait a spell. Maybe they'll come back later if they go to figurin' it's safe," Dees said thoughtfully.

"Besides, we got some whiskey to drink."

Delia felt such relief. She sat in her little family cubicle and said a prayer of thanksgiving for their sanctuary and safe delivery to it. Just as she had finished her father called her outside and guided her away a short distance from the hideout structure.

He looked to see if anyone was listening.

"You did bury the money, didn't you?"

Delia's heart sank. She gulped trying to catch her breath. She tried to speak but was dumbfounded. Her eyes opened wide as she stared blankly back at him.

"Oh God, Papa," she finally uttered.

"I, I was in such a hurry. We heard gunfire!"

"You mean you didn't bury it?" he was now screaming at her.

He grabbed her shoulders and started shaking her.

"I told you to bury it!" he screamed. The commotion had now attracted the attention of the others. Wash Hutchison scooted outside on his knees.

"Be quiet. There could be Yankees down there," he told them urgently.

Russell got quiet out of fear, but his rage grew stronger.

He gritted his teeth and shook Delia wildly.

"I told you to bury it, Goddamn it! I told you! They'll burn down the house. We'll lose everything! Don't you understand?"

He was almost yelling again.

Finally his emotions overcame him and he reeled around and slapped her. Years of stress and fear tormented him as he fretted over the last of his financial holdings. Russell kept shouting, mumbling, and crying. "I told you, I told you," and he continued to strike her.

Nanny Mills came out of the hideout and ran toward them. Russell was now completely out of control. Delia was crying and begging him to forgive her. He was initially slapping her with his open hand when he

CHAPTER TWENTY-SIX

stopped to catch his breath. He reached for his thick hickory cane, picking it up with his right hand. Delia was now down on the ground with her knees in the dirt as he raised the hickory shaft high above her. Before he could bring it down Nanny grabbed his arm and twisted the cane from his hand. In a instant she wielded it around and lashed him across the side of the head, knocking him to the ground.

Stunned and disoriented, Russell climbed to his knees. Delia burst into louder sobs and crawled to her father.

"Papa, I'm so sorry. I'm so sorry. I'll go back. I promise I'll go get it," she said babbling through her tears. "Please forgive me!"

She tried to grasp his arm, but he pushed her away.

"I'll have you hanged, nigger," he shouted as he pointed at Nanny Mills.

"You hush, you ain't ownin' me no mo. I doin' what I wants. You bes' not be hittin' Miss Delia no mo or I be takin' a stick to ya agin," Nanny shouted at him, as she lost control of her own emotions.

"I be callin' the sheriff on ya fo beatin' a woman," Nanny said defiantly as her eyes flared.

Robert Russell stood on his knees and broke down into tears. No one had ever seen him cry, and the experience was a complete surprise for Delia and her family. The whole group of refugees was now outside watching the bizarre incident unfold.

Delia looked at Zeke.

"Zeke, you'll go with me, won't you? Please, please go with me," she begged him.

"I don't know now, Miss Delia; it ain't safe down yonder. I don't know," he said not wanting to disappoint her.

Delia rushed to Nanny.

"Please, Nanny, Zeke's got to go with me. I need him," she said crying and begging.

"No child, it jus' ain't safe. Ya gots ta stay here. Dat money ain't worth it," she said shaking her head.

She turned back to her father and wiped the tears from her face.

"It's all right, Papa. I'll go by myself," she said with a steely resolve.

"Child, don't ya go doin' nothin' like dat. Please," Nanny pleaded with her as she took her hand. Delia tore away from her.

"I'm going and that's that."

"Zeke, where is Ole Star?" she asked in a demanding tone.

"Now Miss Delia don be doin' dat," Zeke said trying to reason with her.

"Where is she?" Delia screamed at him.

"All right, all right, missy. I go wit ya," Zeke said, resigning himself to her demands.

"I reckon 'em Yankees won't do nothin' to a ol' black man no way," Zeke said softly.

Before they left, Hutch gave Zeke a small revolver. He motioned toward Delia and whispered to him. "You must protect her."

Zeke nodded affirmatively while tucking the revolver into his pocket. Zeke had difficulty but was able to negotiate the wagon through the darkness and onto the main road. As they headed toward the Russell home there was an eerie silence dominating the night. The only noise was the plopping of Ole Star's feet and the creaking of the wagon. Delia began thinking of Joseph and the gold coin he'd given her. She was glad they were going back, just as much for Joseph's coin as for her father's money. Delia knew that if the house was burned down, the money and the gold would be lost. She would be heartbroken if the coin was gone too.

As Delia and Zeke approached the house they slowed the wagon and Delia walked ahead on foot. It was soon evident that no one was around. Delia ran back to the wagon, and they rode on into the yard. They crept up to the house while scanning constantly for intruders. As they slipped down the dark hallway, Delia picked up a lantern. She raised the glass and then whispered to Zeke, "Give me a match."

The two of them fumbled in the darkness, and Zeke whispered back to her.

"Miss Delia, don't be lightin' nothin'. A body might see."

"I can't see, Zeke. I can do it much faster if I have a light."

"Please, missy, don't go lightin' nothin'. Please!" he said worriedly.

CHAPTER TWENTY-SIX

"It won't take but a minute, and we'll be gone."

On the little hilltop just a short distance from the house twenty Union cavalrymen sat with their horses tied while they told bawdy stories and drank corn whiskey. By now the majority of them were seriously intoxicated.

"Hey, Pete! Look, there's a light down there," a trooper shouted to LaFerre.

Dees and LaFerre jumped to their feet. They stared toward the house and saw the light.

"Holy damn!" Dees shouted, looking back at LaFerre. "I sure hope one of them fillies is runnin' loose!"

"Saddle up, men!" Dees blurted out as he ran for his horse. Troopers began scrambling, bumping into each other and falling as they went. Soon they were all mounted, and Dees said to LaFerre in a loud whisper, "Pete, you take some men round back, me'n the boys'll go in up front," he said with slurred speech, giggling as he finished.

"Now don't ya let nothin' get out the back."

The drunk and disorganized cavalrymen galloped into the night. One man was knocked off his horse by a tree limb, causing the others to burst out in laughter as they helped him remount. They were off again, galloping through the yard and up to the house. LaFerre and a dozen troopers were soon in the backyard. The men quickly dismounted and pulled their weapons.

As they approached the house the light went out. They tried the door, and it was unlocked. They crept through the house and down the hallway checking rooms, pointing their weapons as they approached.

"Hey, Reverend!" one of the troopers shouted.

"I got somethin' here!"

Dees ran in the direction of the sound and looked around the room. He found the trooper immediately, but at first he didn't see anything. When he saw movement in the shadows, he smiled. Dees pulled out a match and struck it. Hovered in the corner was a tall, elderly black man with a pistol in his hand, and he appeared to be hiding something behind him. The match went out, but he quickly lit another.

"Git me a lantern, boys," Dees said calmly as his eyes cut sharply toward them.

When the lantern was lit and the room was fully illuminated two small feet and the figure of a woman in a dress could be seen standing behind the black man. Dees studied the scene. There were now a half dozen troopers in the room with their guns pointed at the terrified pair cornered in the back. There was a large hole in the wall beside the fireplace, and pieces of paneling lay in front of it.

"Drop the gun, nigger!" one of the troopers shouted.

"I ain't droppin' nothin'," Zeke replied. "Ya jus be lettin' us go, an ya kin have dis place."

Pete LaFerre walked into the room wielding his .44-caliber Colt revolver.

Even though he was intoxicated, he quickly assessed the situation.

"No trouble, please, please," he said smiling and raising his left hand.

Delia hid behind Zeke trembling in fear. She clutched the moneybox in both arms. All she could think of was that she should never have lit that lantern.

"Oh God, why did I light that lantern? Why, why didn't I listen to Zeke?" She wanted to cry, but she was too afraid.

The big one, who talked funny, calmly walked closer. He was smiling, waving his hand back and forth in a gesture that indicated he meant no harm. Suddenly an incredible roar stunned Delia's ears. Flame belched from the end of his revolver and smoke flooded the room, blinding her for a flash of a second. She stood frozen in horror as the scene unfolded in front of her. The smell of burning cordite scorched her nostrils.

The bullet hit Zeke at an angle. It tore through the lower part of his lung, tearing at his liver before bursting his spine. The bullet passed through him and into the wall behind. Zeke dropped instantly, flopping to the floor like a wet rag. He lay motionless, staring helplessly at the mass of feet and legs in front of him. The old slave felt no pain as his

CHAPTER TWENTY-SIX

blood poured onto the floor and pooled under him. He tried to move, but his body did not respond. He felt cold and faint as the darkness passed over him. His eyes were still open, but he could see no more.

The little cluster of soldiers broke into a roar of laughter at the sight.

"Well, well!" one of them howled in a drunken stupor.

"Look what the nigger was hidin'."

"Whew, ain't she a pretty thing," another shouted as the others all laughed.

Dees approached her, cocking his head and eyeing the box clutched in her arms. He reached for the box, and she pulled away from him. The others roared with laughter.

"What's the matter, Reverend? Can't ya git a little box from a little girl?"

They all laughed some more as Dees shoved her into the corner and tore the box from her arms.

Delia cowered in fear as her face twisted in anguish. She was trapped and she knew it. Delia made up her mind, and she branded into her brain one message. She would fight. She would fight to the death.

The soldiers brought in jugs of whiskey howling and cheering as their sadistic game of cat and mouse continued. LaFerre stepped in front of the others. He turned, took off his hat, and bowed. The men gave a loud roar. He turned to Delia.

"Madame, I request ze waltz," he said sarcastically. The soldiers roared and laughed as they drank.

LaFerre pinned her in the corner and tried to kiss her. Delia fought frantically, lashing out at him and screaming wildly. She tried to run and fell over Zeke's body. LaFerre was on her quickly. Delia found strength she was unaware of before. She managed to pull herself away, crying and sobbing as she fought. He came after her again, but she twisted free and dashed back into the corner. There was another loud roar from the rowdy audience.

Delia tried to dash by him again, but this time he grabbed her arm and threw her back into the corner. He had her pinned there, smashing his lips against her cheek. His rough beard scratched her, and his foul alcoholic breath repulsed her. She used her fingernails and lashed at his face. He howled as the others in the room cheered.

Matthias Dees slipped away from the others, but he could still hear the roaring and cheering as he worked in the kitchen. The box proved much more difficult to open than he'd originally thought. He struggled anxiously because he didn't want to miss out on the entertainment yet he had to be the first one in the moneybox. Dees was well aware that the girl had distracted his competitors.

Eventually with a great deal of effort and all the strength he could muster the box popped open. Dees examined the contents carefully. Inside there were many large stacks of Confederate currency.

"Worthless shit," he screamed as he threw them aside. He continued his hunt and found five leather pouches, three of them containing twelve silver dollars. He opened the other two and gasped. There were twelve two-and-one-half-dollar gold pieces in each one.

"Whewee!" Dees sighed to himself.

The last item was a purple velvet bag. Dees had never seen anything like it. He lifted it out of the box and pulled the drawstring. Inside was a single gold coin. It was huge; he figured it was at least one full ounce. He held the coin up to the lantern light and smiled. Dees pulled the coin to his lips and kissed it. Replacing it in the velvet pouch he took all the gold coins and most of the silver. Dees left one bag of silver and all the Confederate money. Hearing the roaring festivities in the other room he was ready to make his move. He stepped into the hallway to see if anyone was looking, then slipped out the back door. Dees went over to his horse and hid the treasure in his saddlebags.

Dees dashed back into the house and into the room full of soldiers. He watched for a few minutes while he took several sips of corn whiskey. By now all the men were fully intoxicated.

Dees stepped in front of the men and shouted. "Hey Pete, can't ya break that little colt?" The men roared and toasted with their jugs.

CHAPTER TWENTY-SIX

"Show him how to do it!" one man yelled to the screaming delight of the others.

LaFerre looked over at him and laughed hysterically.

"Oui, oui, miseur, s'il vou plait," LaFerre said with a sweeping bow toward the terrified young woman in the corner.

Delia did not recognize Dees at first in his blue cavalry uniform. But as he approached her with that same demonic grin she'd seen years before, she identified him immediately.

"Oh God!" she gasped.

"Get some rope!" one of the men yelled.

"He'll have to lasso this one!" Again all the men hooted and laughed.

"I'll get the rope," another shouted.

Dees turned around and spoke to them calmly.

"Ya city boys ain't got no good sense for nothin'. That ain't how ya do it. Me'n the boys will show how to tame this here wild one," Dees said, indicating that he had something else in mind.

"Rupert, y'all go out thar and git that harness off her horse," he said slyly. "They ain't gonna be ride'n that wagon no how."

There was mumbling, discussion, and speculation about the harness among the men. Rupert soon brought the harness inside and handed it to Dees. Dees stood before them as if he were giving a training lesson.

"Ya see, boys, if you tie a filly like this here one to the bedposts you can't roll 'er over. If you put the harness on her, that'll take some of the fight out of her and you kin roll'er every-which-a-way." The men let out a loud cheer as Dees tossed the harness to one of them and he started at Delia.

She watched all of this, trapped in the corner with nowhere to go. Once again, she resolved to fight to the death. No matter what it took she would fight. She recoiled in the corner and braced herself to lash at his eyes. He came at her quickly, and she was surprised by his speed. She tried to move to her left, but he cut her off.

She only caught a glimpse out of the corner of her eye, but it was too late. Dees wheeled around from the side and slammed her in the jaw with a cavalry revolver. The weight of the heavy metal pistol crashed into her face with such force that it popped her upper left molars completely out of their sockets. The slightly downward motion of his blow broke off her lower molars at the gum line and fractured her left mandible, dislocating her jaw.

Her head spun and her eyes rolled. She slammed into the wall and slid to the floor. Blood spilled from her mouth as she unconsciously spit out her teeth. Her ears were ringing such that she could no longer hear.

Dees calmly holstered his pistol and turned to the men watching.

"Grab her, boys, and take her over by the bed," he ordered as if he were an officer in command. Four men quickly ran over and grabbed each of her limbs. Delia lay limp as they carried her. Her mind whirled as she looked into the faces of the men who carried her. She didn't even hear the command when Dees yelled out loud. "Strip her boys! Strip her plum necked!"

The men were in a frenzy as they tore at her clothes. One man pulled a large knife and cut off the more difficult attachments. When she was totally naked they stood her up in the middle of the room.

"Bring me that harness!" Dees yelled. Two men held her up while Dees took Ole Star's harness and slipped it down over Delia's head, then over her arms. He had to stretch and pull as the leather device tightened around her. In an instant her arms were trapped against her sides and her small breasts protruded through the leather straps.

"Throw the bitch on the bed!" Dees yelled as he began to jerk off his boots. Then he stripped off his pants. The men howled and cheered as he climbed onto the bed. Men were on either side holding her so that she could not move. Her mind whirled and then she seemed to float without feeling. Endless thoughts crossed her mind as the horror continued. Images of her family and her childhood flashed before her. She thought briefly of Joseph and their plan of marriage. Now, she thought, that can never be.

"I am dead," she said to herself. "I am dead." The words continued to cycle through her mind over and over again. There was nothing she could do, so she said it again. "I am dead." Eventually, the events of the

CHAPTER TWENTY-SIX

physical world no longer mattered; Delia was dying.

She seemed to reach calmness within herself. Her plight was desperate. In her mind, death was the only option.

"I am dead." The words continued their endless rotation. The events going on around her seemed unreal.

She looked down at Dees. Then she stared at the ceiling, rolled her eyes back, and closed them. In her mind she died. She felt no more.

Throughout the night the men took their turns. They drank their whiskey and cheered each other on as the degradation continued. She felt none of it, and her mind drifted as if she were floating on air.

As the sun rose most of the men were still intoxicated. LaFerre paraded around the house nude except for his cavalry hat and gun belt. He and Dees were laughing and dividing up the one small bag of silver dollars when they heard a rider approach. It was another scout. Dees ran out on the porch to greet him.

The rider shouted at Dees.

"You men come on into Asheville. General Gillem says Sherman and Johnston signed a truce down east of here somewhere. Now we got one. General Gillem and that Confederate general signed a truce this morning. We've been given free passage through Asheville."

Dees tucked his shirt into his trousers and shouted back.

"We'll be headin' in soon as we can saddle up. Tell the major we're comin'."

Colonel William J. Palmer had driven his men hard. They had followed their orders and completed their mission. The ride had taken them out of the way for days, but they were now close to catching up with the main body. Palmer had brought his men through Hickory Nut Gap in the Blue Ridge. It was steep and rugged but breathtakingly beautiful. At the top of the gap they approached Sherrill's Inn. Palmer had arrived late the night before and was now being served breakfast by local women who were less than friendly to the men in blue uniforms. Unbeknownst to Palmer and the other Union officers the women had taken off their stockings and shook them over their eggs. It was meant to look like pepper, but to the southern women who'd done it, the act provided them with a satisfying feeling of resistance.

One local man was somewhat friendly. He was also knowledgeable. Palmer approached the man and asked for his help.

"I'm trying to catch up with General Gillem. I understand that he's in Henderson County somewhere. Is there a road from here over to Hendersonville without going into Asheville first?" he inquired.

"Yep, I reckon there is, but it ain't much," the man responded.

"Could you lead me over that road?" Palmer asked.

"I ain't fer helpin' you Yankees shoot nobody," the man said calmly.

"We don't want to shoot anyone. I just want to see if I can find a shorter route," Palmer said earnestly, trying to reassure the man.

"I reckon I could oblige ya' on that," the man said scratching his head.

Palmer turned to Captain Weand. "Captain, prepare my horse and bring a dozen good men. We're going scouting."

The ride from Hickory Nut Gap over the backside of Bearwallow Mountain was rugged and steep. It wasn't far into the scouting trip that Palmer realized that bringing a full brigade of cavalry over this route was not practical. From a tactical standpoint the scouting trip was a waste.

Palmer continued on, not because of a military mission, but because he was entranced with the incredible beauty of the place. He was somehow drawn further. He felt an uneasy tranquility in the air and wondered if God was communicating with him. At each turn in the trail they went higher and higher. Palmer thought of his faith and silently prayed for guidance.

Dogwoods and other native flora were in full bloom. Palmer thought he should go back, but something called him onward. They came to a highland meadow with a small babbling stream running through it. The top of the mountain was bald, beckoning them to the top.

Palmer rode forward and gasped as he looked out over the landscape. He could see for miles. Captain Weand and the others joined him on top.

"This is the most beautiful sight I've ever seen," Weand said wistfully.

"Magnificent," Palmer added.

CHAPTER TWENTY-SIX

"Shouldn't we go back now, Colonel?" Weand asked him.

Palmer started to say yes, but something unseen and intangible stopped him.

"This day is lost anyway, Captain. We may as well enjoy the ride."

They continued on, down the headwaters of Hoopers Creek, stopping to take a drink and to rest the horses.

The tension at the hideout was at a peak. Nanny Mills paced back and forth praying out loud. Her words could only be deciphered by God as her speech was rambling and broken.

Hutch approached Bob Russell while Wash remained frozen at his position at the lookout point.

"Good God, Bob. They've been gone all night. We've got to do something!"

"What can we do?" Russell snapped back at him. "Maybe they had to leave the wagon and hide in the woods or something," he said unconvincingly.

The pair had been gone more than twelve hours. Everyone at the hideout shared the same gloomy fear. Something must have gone terribly wrong.

Wash Hutchison was beside himself. He scanned the valley searching for any sign of Delia and Zeke. Suddenly his eyes caught some movement out beyond the trees below. He scurried forward on his knees trying for a better look. It took several minutes, but he figured it out. Wash turned and dashed along the ground, scurrying on his knees back to the hideout structure.

Wash was so excited that he could hardly talk when he pointed behind him and yelled at the two older men.

"There's a horse down there," he said almost screaming. "It's Ole Star!"

Tears came to his eyes as he shouted again.

"She ain't got nobody with her. No harness, no halter . . . she's bare!" he said as he burst out crying.

The two older men ran to the lookout point. Hutch got there first with Bob Russell hobbling along behind. Wash joined them and pointed out the horse grazing below.

"Let's go down there. We gotta help!" Wash cried out.

"We can't do nothin'," Russell said, cowering in the direction of the hideout.

"We gotta!" Wash shouted.

Hutch looked down at his footless son perched on his knees.

"Wash, we can't do nothin'. If we go down there, what happened to them will happen to us."

Wash was livid. He screamed at the two older men frantically.

"You damn cowards!" he shouted through his tears. "Somebody's gotta help Delia!"

"I'll go without you, by God," he shouted with determination.

Wash immediately scurried forward and straight down the hillside toward the valley where Ole Star grazed. He fell and tumbled as he went, scratching his hands and face repeatedly. He sobbed and cried as he struggled to make his footless body perform as he demanded. It was a great distance to travel on his knees, but he was determined and continued struggling. Along the way he began to talk to her through his tears.

"Hold on, Miss Delia, I'm comin', please hold on," he repeatedly murmured as he half-crawled and half-stumbled toward the house.

It was a strange feeling that drew Palmer to this place. The beauty and the scenery entranced him, but he was bothered by something inexplicable.

"Let me see your field glass, captain," Palmer said calmly as they looked out at the beautiful view of the valley beyond.

Palmer raised the glass and scanned the pristine setting below. Suddenly he caught sight of movement. His military instinct immediately drew him to it. At first he couldn't make out what he saw. Was it an animal? Palmer wondered. Upon closer inspection he determined it was a man. But his movement was strange. He must be wounded, Palmer concluded.

"Captain Weand, take the glass and look over there," Palmer urged the junior officer.

CHAPTER TWENTY-SIX

"What is it, sir?" Weand asked curiously.

"I'm not sure. It looks like a wounded man," Palmer said in a tone of disbelief.

"Mount up men, we're going down there," Palmer said sternly.

When they first came upon Wash they thought him mad. He was very dirty and didn't appear to be able to stand. He babbled and cried incoherently. The footless man had scratches and cuts over his face and hands.

His speech was indecipherable.

"Calm down, man. We're not going to hurt you."

"She's just a girl, a beautiful young girl," Wash blurted through his tears.

"What are you talking about?" Palmer asked again.

"They got her; I know they got her!" he managed to say before bursting into tears again.

Now it all added up for Palmer. He'd seen this before, remembering the poor young boy who'd lost his mother and sister. Obviously there were others. As his calculations brought him to his conclusions, Palmer looked up into the eyes of Captain Weand. The two men faced each other, and no words were necessary.

"Mount up men; give me a hand with this fellow," Palmer said as they threw Wash Hutchison onto the back of Weand's horse.

The troopers were gone, and only the scouts remained. LaFerre was now dressed, and he and Dees were making their final plans.

"Boys, get the lanterns and set this place on fire. I'll get the horses ready."

LaFerre went back upstairs to have one last look for valuables as the Dees boys lit the lanterns and prepared to burn Delia alive. When Dees was making a final search of the house, he saw the riders coming. He studied the men in the saddles and recognized that one of them was Palmer.

Palmer and the troopers from the 15th Pennsylvania rode into the yard in a rush, drawing their weapons as they dismounted. The fire had already been started in two places when the Dees sons spotted Palmer. LaFerre drew his revolver and tried to make it out of the front door. He had dashed through the opening when he saw Palmer. Although LaFerre was a big man, he was surprisingly agile. As he moved he pointed his pistol and fired. The bullet was on line toward Palmer, but there was a support post between the two and the bullet struck the post instead of the intended target.

LaFerre prepared to fire again, but he was too late. Palmer fired from a crouched position, striking him in the chest and killing him instantly.

Rupert Dees and his brother came out of the back of the house with pistols spouting flame and smoke. Captain Weand and the other troopers cut them down with multiple shots from their Spencers.

Palmer ran around the house just as it happened. He took one look at the growing fire. It was apparent that the house would soon be fully engulfed. Just then a horse galloped from behind the smokehouse and dashed toward the pasture.

"After him, men!" Weand yelled.

"No, stop! Let him go," Palmer shouted.

"We've got to put out the fire. There may be people in there."

"Move, get water!" Palmer screamed. "Come with me, Captain! Search the ground floor. I'll go up!"

Palmer dashed up the stairs and overtook the sad little man who was already climbing the steps on his knees. Palmer reached down, took him by the hand, and hoisted him up the last four stairs. He dashed into a bedroom as the footless man scurried behind him. They found nothing, so they quickly entered the next room.

Shock and rage flew over Palmer as he reacted to what he saw. A young girl lay coiled in the fetal position in the middle of a bed. He ran to her and could see that her nude body was restrained in a horse harness. She was covered in dried blood, bruises, and other evidence of her horrible ordeal. Palmer ripped off his double-breasted officer's frock and wrapped it around her. Sweeping her into his arms, he turned toward the door.

The crippled man looked up at him with pain and anguish on his tearful face. "She's just a little girl," Wash sobbed loudly.

CHAPTER TWENTY-SIX

Smoke filled the room, and Palmer recognized the seriousness of the situation.

"Come, help me, we've got to get out!" he said to the little man as he ran down the stairs. Wash followed him, half-climbing and half-falling.

Captain Weand and the others were now in the house. They had quickly assembled a bucket brigade and eventually put out the two fires.

Palmer laid Delia outside on the grass. She lay limp and speechless. She stared blankly into the distance, completely ignoring the presence of her rescuers.

They gently unwrapped her, exposing her body only long enough to cut the leather harness from her body. Wash sobbed uncontrollably through it all. Palmer felt sick as he looked at the dazed young girl and the pathetic little man who obviously loved her.

"Please, Delia, talk to me," Wash pleaded through his tears.

She stared unseeing and unresponsive. The soldiers found a large full-length coat for her. As they dressed her, she lay limp, never speaking or acknowledging their efforts.

Palmer looked at Wash.

"Do you know where this girl's family is?"

"Yes," Wash said while not taking his eyes off her.

"They're hiding up in the hills."

"Captain Weand, take this man up there. Help him bring her family back down here. We'll stay with the girl," Palmer said sadly.

"You may assure them that no harm will come to them."

Wash and Palmer moved Delia back into the house.

When Palmer's men returned with the family most of the Russells rushed into the house and to the upstairs bedroom where Delia lay motionless. Robert Russell rushed into the study desperately searching for the moneybox. He saw the open void in the wall. Searching all over the first floor, he finally found it. It was broken open and empty. Russell dropped to his knees and wheezed, trying to catch his breath. He threw the box to the floor and buried his face in his hands.

Colonel Palmer left the family alone with Delia and led Nanny Mills to the back porch where Zeke's body lay under a quilt that covered his lifeless body. She sat beside him and talked softly to him as she cried quietly.

Upstairs Delia's sisters tried desperately to elicit some kind of response from her. Their efforts were in vain. Delia lay limp, eyes fixed at the ceiling, never making direct eye contact with anyone.

Palmer sought out Robert Russell and spoke softly to him.

"Sir, on behalf of the U.S. government, I would like to express my deep regret for what has happened."

Russell looked up at him, his eyes flaming with hate.

"We have nothing; we're going to starve to death," was all he could think of to say.

Sensing that he could be of no further assistance, Palmer prepared to leave.

"Sir, one of them got away. I'll do everything possible to bring him to justice," Palmer said firmly. Russell did not respond.

"I am leaving six men to guard your home. I'll leave them here until it's safe. I have to get back to my brigade. If you need me I'm staying at Sherrill's Inn just over the mountain," Palmer said pointing toward Bearwallow.

Palmer mounted his horse and looked at Captain Weand.

"I want that man apprehended. Find him if you can."

"Yes sir," Weand responded, and the two men led their party up Jackson Road.

Chapter 27

―― APRIL 28, 1865 ――

Hickory Nut Gap, North Carolina Union colonel Palmer sat on the front porch at Sherrill's Inn waiting for Captain Weand. He was up at daybreak because he had not slept well the night before. His sleep was constantly interrupted by haunting visions of the poor young girl they'd rescued. Her blank, lifeless stare troubled him greatly.

"Good morning, sir," Captain Weand said, interrupting Palmer's thoughts.

"Good morning, Captain," Palmer replied.

"I want you to take a group of your men and see if you can catch up with General Gillem in Asheville. I feel certain they are in the vicinity," Palmer said thoughtfully.

"I don't know, sir. Since General Gillem signed that truce with the Confederates they may have just gone on back to Tennessee," Weand said.

"Maybe so, Captain, but we still need to know where they are and what's going on. It's not that far to Asheville, so if you get started now you should be back by this afternoon," Palmer said.

Late that day Palmer watched them coming up the hill toward him, and he wondered why they were riding so hard. Sherrill's Inn rested on a high ridge overlooking the verdant pastures below. This mountain perch had a long porch which provided a great view of the galloping men riding toward the inn. It was obvious to him that the formation was Captain Weand and his party returning from Asheville. Then Palmer noticed that Weand had a couple of extra men with him. He assumed that they must be men from the 2nd or 3rd Brigade.

The men dismounted, and the horses were tied. Weand hastily marched onto the porch and asked to see Colonel Palmer. The two strangers stood behind him, each wearing the uniform of Union soldiers.

"What's the urgency, Captain Weand? It looked like you were riding those horses mighty hard," Palmer said seeking an explanation.

The two strange soldiers stood in silence while Weand made his report.

"Sir, I'm afraid I have terrible news," Weand said bowing his head.

Palmer cringed, fearing another horror similar to the one they'd come upon on Hoopers Creek.

"Well, come out with it, Captain, I may as well hear it," he said, resigning himself to be exposed to another tragedy.

"Sir, this is truly unfortunate," he said raising his hands in disbelief. "General Gillem signed a truce with the Confederates. Both sides agreed to give each other forty-eight hours notice if hostilities were to be resumed. I have seen it and I copied down the words for you to see for yourself." Weand pulled out a piece of paper and began to read.

"The Confederates supplied rations and forage for our men to pass through town to Tennessee. Confederate General Martin opened his home and had all the Union officers as guests for dinner. Our entire division was given free passage through town and they rode through without incident. The Confederates disbanded and went back to their farms," Weand began shaking his head from side to side as he talked.

"Go on, Captain, get to the point," Palmer said.

"Well, sir, on the night of April 26, the same day they'd been granted passage, Gillem's men rode back into Asheville with their guns belching fire and smoke. No warning. No nothing. They shot up the place and went on a wild rampage. The town was given up to plunder. Union

CHAPTER TWENTY-SEVEN

soldiers broke into every home in Asheville as far as I can tell. They robbed everybody, taking anything they wanted," Weand said disgustedly.

Palmer jumped to his feet.

"Where was General Gillem while all this was going on?" Palmer demanded.

"That's just it, sir. Gillem wasn't there. Once they got to the other side of Asheville, General Gillem took off to Tennessee and apparently sent his men back into town!" Weand said, making a direct accusation.

Weand added one more comment, "It was reported that General Gillem left his command to take a seat in the new Tennessee legislature."

Palmer's face flushed. "Who was in command then?" Palmer demanded.

"It was General Brown, sir," Weand responded. "Sir, that's not all. They arrested all the Confederate officers and some civilians and put them in animal transport cage wagons, and Brown is taking about thirty of them back to Tennessee. He also placed the county judge in jail, a man named Bailey," Weand continued as his disgust escalated. "Sir, they rode their horses into buildings and homes. They broke out all the glass in town and burned the public buildings. I interviewed several women who were beaten and robbed in the street, and some of them were even forcibly stripped of their jewelry," Weand said, obviously repulsed by the entire incident.

Palmer shouted to his adjutant, "Order the men to assemble at once." He was now furious at what he had learned.

"Corporal, get my horse ready! We're going to Asheville," Palmer said, not really sure of what he would do when he got there.

Palmer looked at the two strangers and pointed at them.

"Did you arrest these men, captain?" Palmer asked angrily.

"No, sir, they're dispatchers. We just offered to show them where you were. They came into Asheville looking for you about the same time we got there."

"Do you have dispatches for me?" Palmer asked.

"Yes, sir, we do," one of the men said, stepping forward with a leather saddlebag.

"I am Sergeant Clapton. I have a dispatch from General Thomas," the man said curtly while opening the bag and handing the dispatch to Palmer.

The others stood silently while Palmer read.

Palmer looked up at Captain Weand and smiled. "It's about time they got around to this," he said happily.

"What is it, sir?" Weand asked anxiously.

"Captain Weand, these are orders from General Thomas. I have been promoted to brevet brigadier general," Palmer said in apparent disbelief. He had been waiting on the promotion since November, and it never seemed to come through. It had been so long that Palmer had given up on it.

"Well, hallelujah!" Weand shouted. The rest of Palmer's staff cheered and congratulated him.

"There's more captain," Palmer said.

"What, sir, what is it?" Weand asked.

Palmer looked up and, unable to restrain himself, he smiled again. "I've been given command of the entire division," he said excitedly. There was a general cheer of approval from those gathered at the inn. Palmer raised his hand impatiently.

"Enough of that. We've got work to do."

Palmer turned back to Weand.

"Those Confederate prisoners that were being taken to Tennessee, how far along are they?" he asked.

"They were just leaving Asheville this morning, General. They couldn't be too far,"

Palmer turned back to the dispatchers.

"You men wait here, I'm sending orders for you to take back with you."

Palmer directed his adjutant to take down the order.

"All prisoners are to be freed at once. I will be in Asheville as soon as I can assemble the brigade." Palmer barked at his adjutant, "Have all officers report to me immediately."

When he'd finished he directed the two dispatchers to ride with urgency until they caught up with the prison wagons.

CHAPTER TWENTY-SEVEN

"Captain Weand, come with me. I want to talk to you in private."

Palmer led Weand to the inn's small, private library and closed the door.

"Tell me, Weand. How wicked did it get in Asheville?" Palmer asked.

"I don't know for sure, sir, but I think it was pretty bad."

"Tell me, Captain, did any women report similar violence like we saw on Hoopers Creek?" Palmer asked.

Weand looked at Palmer in disbelief. He started to speak but then held himself. The captain shook his head disgustedly. "May I speak openly, sir? Man to man?" Weand said, his voice tightening with aggravation.

Palmer looked at him, somewhat taken aback.

"Yes, Captain. I would like for you to speak openly."

"Well, sir, it's like this. You're now a general and you're supposed to be smarter than I am. But sir, you asked a stupid question," Weand said, verbally questioning his superior officer. Palmer wanted to interpret Weand's obvious scolding, but he didn't. "Very well, Captain. I invited you to speak openly. Continue."

"I've ridden with you through this war for thousands of miles. We've been all over the south, and we've come to know southern people. I'm surprised, sir, that you would not understand them by now," Weand said further chastising Palmer.

"What do you expect these defenseless women to do when they get raped by Union soldiers? Come walking into town waving at Union officers and shouting out loud: Hey, a bunch of your men just raped me," Weand continued with sarcasm oozing from his voice. "Do you really expect that they think Union officers are going to do anything about it? Do you think they'd be comfortable telling the details of what happened with a stranger in a blue uniform? Would she even bother to tell her own family? Indeed, sir. She would not.

"No, sir, not one woman reported to me that she was raped. I'll also guarantee you that the poor young girl we pulled nude and bleeding from that burning house yesterday will never tell any Yankee soldier what happened to her either." Weand continued his tirade.

"I expect there were plenty of rapes in Asheville on that night. I also expect that there were probably several thousand down in Georgia when Sherman's men went into the business of making Georgia howl. I'll bet you none of those women went chasing after General Sherman anxiously telling what was done to them.

"I'll also bet that in almost every case when a woman died in this war it was because some men were as foolish as you. They thought she might tell, so it was just as easy to kill her. That boy we found when we first came into North Carolina. We both know what happened to his mother and his sister.

"For the life of me I can't figure it out. The ones who are the meanest, who conduct themselves the worst and commit the most crimes, are the locals. These are home Yankees. Men from North Carolina and Tennessee—they're the ones doing the worst of this to their own people.

"Most of 'em are nothing but bounty men and drunks. I said it back when we first got orders to go on this mission. Their only real loyalty is to plunder."

Palmer looked back at him with a firm stare. Weand caught himself and twisted uncomfortably as he awaited Palmer's reaction, thinking maybe he'd gone too far.

"Thank you for your honesty, Captain Weand," Palmer said looking away. "I'm afraid everything you've said is true."

"You can go now, Captain."

"May I tell you one more thing, sir?" Weand asked him.

"Yes, you may," Palmer replied.

Weand stood erect.

"Sir, all the sympathy I once felt for the Tennesseans has now turned to contempt. All that sympathy has been transferred to their enemy," Weand said defiantly.

Palmer shook his head in agreement. "Yes, that's understandable, Captain. We have work to do. Let's get into town and see what we can do to set things right."

"Yes, sir," Weand said as he started to exit.

CHAPTER TWENTY-SEVEN

"One more thing, Captain," Palmer said stopping him at the door. "Thank you again for your honesty."

Palmer rode into Asheville and went straight to the town jail. Colonel Miller was waiting for him as word had already reached him that Palmer was now in command.

"You are to release all prisoners at once. You can't expect to hold them after a truce," Palmer barked to Miller. "And find General Brown. I want the entire 2nd and 3rd Brigades assembled in the town square as soon as possible." Palmer watched as Judge Bailey was released from his cell.

Union officers immediately began to worry about what Palmer might do. They knew of his strict moral code and how he would feel about the events of April 26. Many of these officers quickly went about finding duties that would excuse them from the called assembly.

On the north side of town General Brown sat writing his report, taking great pains to distance himself from what had happened and denying knowledge of the majority of the questionable activities.

"General Brown, one of the scouts is here to see you," his adjutant called to him.

"Very well. Send him in," Brown said impatiently.

Matthias Dees came in, removing his hat as he entered.

"General, sir, I heard tell that General Gillem's done gone back to Tennessee?" Dees asked nervously.

"Yes, so what of it?" Brown replied.

"Well, sir, ya see, General Gillem was sendin' me to go scout for Colonel Kirk. Ya know, the 3rd North Carolina Mounted Infantry," Dees said anxiously.

"Kirk's got a whole mess of local men. What does he need you for?" Brown asked.

"Well, ya see, sir, I'm from up yonder in East Tennessee right next to Mitchell County. Kirk's got some problems up thar that I kin help him with. That's what General Gillem said, sir."

Brown thought for a minute. He knew the war was over and couldn't care less. He calculated that Dees probably had some reason for wanting to get out of town. Brown didn't believe the story, but he calculated that it didn't matter much.

"Well, the war's over anyway. I'll approve it. You go on up to Colonel Kirk."

Dees quickly mounted up and rode into Madison County. He was not present for Palmer's assembly in Asheville.

Palmer dismounted and walked into the home of Judge and Mrs. Bailey. He had asked that all of the town officials and Confederate officers gather there. Palmer walked straight to General Martin and saluted him respectfully.

"Sir, it is with deep regret that I learned that our troops violated the truce. Their action has disgraced the honor of the U.S. Army. On behalf of the government I offer my sincere apology," Palmer said in his most formal tone. The reception was cool, and there was a pervasive air of skepticism in the room. The Confederates reacted slowly, and General Martin finally spoke.

"Thank you, General Palmer. Certainly, we were shocked and dismayed at the conduct of your predecessor, General Gillem," Martin said curtly.

"I give you my word, General Martin. I will do everything in my power to apprehend any Union soldier guilty of criminal activity," Palmer added.

Martin looked at him incredulously. "That would be about your whole army."

Palmer spoke quickly. "Not the whole army, sir. May I remind you that the 1st Brigade was not here," Palmer said defensively.

Martin nodded affirmatively, conceding the point.

"One of my officers tells me that the worst of the crime was committed by local men who joined the Union army," Palmer said.

Martin looked back at the others assembled there and bowed his head.

CHAPTER TWENTY-SEVEN

"They're not our people anymore. Besides, many of them are from East Tennessee," he said begrudgingly.

Palmer made his exit and rode back to the square where the whole division stood in formation. It was an assembly of more than three thousand men. He divided up his officers and then shouted his order as loud as he could.

"A terrible crime was committed out on Hoopers Creek. One of the men who did it got away. I am offering a reward, twenty-five dollars in gold, to any man who can identify who committed that crime," Palmer said, watching for a reaction. No one came forward.

"All of you are to empty your pockets and hold the contents in your hands. My officers will come by and collect all civilian property. Any man who fails to do this or attempts to conceal stolen property will be arrested."

There was a low rumble among the men, and slowly they began to move in mass. The officers moved down the lines with baskets, collecting the ill-begotten gains. There were many watches, rings, and various types of women's jewelry. Pairs of officers worked the lines until each company had been checked.

When the unpleasant exercise was completed Palmer returned to Judge Bailey's house. Soon the officers followed with the baskets.

"Sir, I will leave it to you to sort out this property and return it to the rightful owners," Palmer said formally.

General Martin, Judge Bailey, and the others looked at him in disbelief. More baskets were arriving as Palmer continued to speak.

"I only regret that I can't do more. Gentlemen, there are some things I can't fix."

"Thank you. Your attention to this has been greatly appreciated. You are an honorable man," Judge Bailey said as he watched the officers stack the baskets.

"I must go now," General Palmer said. "I've been ordered to take the division south in pursuit of Jefferson Davis. General Tillson will be here in a few days to take over Union command in Asheville."

Palmer saluted, turned, and walked out the door. He gave the order to march. Stoneman's cavalry division rode down South Main Street in near perfect formation, past the Eagle Hotel, on the same path that had guided thousands of local boys off to war.

Chapter 28

―JUNE 1, 1865―

Hoopers Creek, North Carolina Nanny Mills stayed with Delia constantly. She bathed her and fed her. The days turned into weeks, and still there was no improvement in Delia's emotional condition. She stared blankly in no particular direction. She made no eye contact nor did she respond to any stimulus. Caring for her was difficult. Her broken jaw was slow to heal, and she had to be fed liquids by the use of a hollow piece of cane. Nanny used the cane to give her soup, broth, and other nourishment. Eventually Delia progressed to the point of eating small spoonfuls of grits or oatmeal.

Despite Nanny's best efforts, Delia had lost weight. The youthful glow of her skin and the pinkness of her complexion had left her. She exercised only when Nanny forced her to get up and walk around the house. Her eyes were sunken, and a severe depression was visible on her left cheek where her molars were missing.

Nanny waited anxiously for her anticipated visitor to arrive. Delia's brother had survived the war and had returned home. He'd arranged for Dr. Fletcher to call on Delia. Nanny held out great hope that maybe he could do something for the poor girl.

Dr. Fletcher was a prominent local physician, having been a surgeon in the Confederate army. He was the late Captain Solomon Cunningham's brother-in-law and could be trusted as a friend of the family. He knew of Delia's secret.

"Good mornin' to ya, massa doctor," Nanny said subserviently as James brought Dr. Fletcher up to Delia's room. He approached Delia and examined her, carefully looking into her eyes and taking her pulse. He listened to her heart with a horn designed to aid in the effort. He looked into her mouth and examined the injury to her jaw and teeth.

During the entire examination Delia stared straight ahead. She offered neither cooperation nor resistance.

"Are you the woman who cares for her?" Dr. Fletcher said, looking at Nanny Mills.

"Yez, sir, I is," Nanny replied.

"Is she always like this?" the doctor asked, pointing at Delia.

"Yez, sir, she don't say nothin', she don't do nothin'. She don't eat nothin', 'lessen I feeds her," Nanny replied sadly.

"Does she do anything at all?" he asked in disbelief.

"No, sir, she jus' be hidin' in her own world," Nanny said shaking her head from side to side. "She don't sleep none at night. She be afraid of de light."

"What do you mean, she's afraid of the light?"

"Well, sir, if ya lights de lantern she go to screamin' and a carryin' on somethin' awful. Yea, she sho does."

"How long does she do that?" the doctor asked curiously.

"It don't be for long 'cause we puts the lantern out," Nanny said shaking her head.

"You mean she stays in the dark all night?"

"Yez, sir, she don't sleep none neither. 'Bout daylight, she falls off to sleep some. Most nights she jus sit in de dark and stare at de wall," Nanny said, concern in her voice.

Dr. Fletcher examined her further and asked Nanny more questions. He looked at Delia's tormented face, scratching his head. He packed his bag and walked into the hallway with James and Nanny following close behind.

"What's wrong with her, Doc?" James asked earnestly.

"I hate to be the one to tell you this, but I'd say her brain is damaged, probably from a blow to the head," he said with a grim expression.

CHAPTER TWENTY-EIGHT

Nanny gasped and put her hand over her mouth.

"What do dat mean?" Nanny asked tearfully.

The doctor paused briefly and turned to James.

"She doesn't know anything. Her mind is gone. She doesn't know who you are, she doesn't know who she is." He looked at Nanny Mills and added, "nor who you are."

"What about her getting upset over the lantern being lit? Don't that show that she's aware of something?" James said desperately.

"No," the doctor replied confidently. "Her eyes are probably injured from the fire, and the light probably hurts her eyes. That's all.

"I'm sorry to tell you this, but she'll most likely be this way the rest of her life. I saw men like this on the battlefield. They never recover," Dr. Fletcher said sadly.

He shook James's hand and left the house.

Nanny Mills ran back to Delia. She sat beside her and put her arms around her. "I don't kere what dat doctor be sayin'. You gonna git well, yea ya is. I gonna nurse ya 'til ya gits well. Ya hear me child. I gonna nurse ya 'til ya gits well."

Nanny burst into tears and held Delia closely.

Delia's arms lay limp at her side. She made no motion or sound other than normal breathing. She continued to stare straight ahead in silence.

James Russell went back upstairs late in the day to find Nanny sitting at Delia's bedside. He wondered what they would do without this wonderful black woman who was now free to go wherever she wished.

James walked over to her and took her hand.

"God bless you, Nanny."

She looked up at him and managed a slight smile.

"Dat doctor, he be wrong. Miss Delia gonna git better."

"Sure, Nanny, she'll get better some day," he said in a weak effort to support her.

James pulled a small amount of change from his pocket and put it on the night table beside the bed.

"Nanny, you take this to Fletcher tomorrow and get some flour and bacon for you and Delia. Maybe you can get her to eat a little more. If not, you can eat it."

"Thank ya, Massa James. That be mighty nice of ya," she said as she looked up at him.

James left them alone as the sun began to set over the mountains west of Hoopers Creek. He walked down the hall and looked out the window.

"How did it all happen?" he whispered as he thought of what the war had done to them all.

Nanny Mills sat with Delia into the night as she always did. When she fell asleep Delia was sitting in her nightgown staring at the wall. Nanny often slept in the same chair beside Delia's bed.

When Nanny first woke up she found nothing unusual. It was dark and quiet. She reached over to adjust the covers for Delia when she noticed something was wrong.

"Oh Gawd! Oh Gawd, Lawdy!" Nanny screamed to the top of her lungs.

She jumped up and ran down the hall.

"Oh Gawd! Help! Help!" she continued her screaming and shouting.

James Russell was already out of bed and running down the hall. The rest of the family was now up, and the entire house was in a state of sleepy confusion.

James grabbed Nanny by the shoulders and shook her.

"What's wrong? What's happening?" he yelled at her, trying to make sense of her screams.

"Miss Delia, it's Miss Delia!" she screamed.

"What Nanny, what?" James questioned her as his mind conjured up the worst.

"She be gone! She's gone! Miss Delia, she's gone!"

James rushed down the hall and into her room. There was only a little light, but he could see that the bed was empty. He lit the lantern and searched around the room. Delia was nowhere to be found.

Robert Russell and the rest of the family were gathered outside the

CHAPTER TWENTY-EIGHT

door. James turned to them and shouted.

"Search the house!"

The family began running room to room. They searched all the closets and under the beds. Still they could not find her.

"Someone best get the sheriff," Robert Russell said nervously.

Eventually the family regrouped in the downstairs hallway.

"We've searched the whole house; she's not here," Sarah said in a voice laced with panic.

"All right, let's get lanterns, and we'll search the yard and the barn. Hurry, let's get looking," James shouted urgently.

Lanterns were collected, and the family dispersed. James started around the house toward the smokehouse when he noticed that one of the double storm doors to the cellar was open. He approached and looked into the dirt cavern that made up the basement for the house. It was pitch dark, but when he held the lantern to the door he heard a muffled, rustling sound.

James Russell crept down the steps. He heard more sounds as he reached the floor and the light from his lantern flooded the dirt cellar. He scanned the dark, cavernous basement as best he could with the limited light from the lantern. Off in one corner he saw her.

"Oh my God, Delia! What are you doing?"

Delia sat on her knees in the corner of the basement wearing nothing but her nightgown. Her hair was a stringy mess, and she was covered with dirt. Tears ran down her face mixing with the dirt, creating muddy smears all over her face. James ran over to her, but she screamed and hid her face from the light.

"What is it, Delia? For God's sake, what are you doing?" he begged for an answer.

Delia only sobbed and covered her eyes with her soiled hands. As he got closer he could see that she had gouged out a hole in the dirt with her bare hands. At the bottom of the hole was a small fruit jar containing the small amount of change that he'd left on the night table in her room.

She was in the process of burying it.

James took his sister in his arms and rocked her gently. Tears came to his eyes as he spoke aloud to her.

"Poor Delia, what are we going to do?"

Chapter 29

——JULY 12, 1865——

Indianapolis, Indiana J. N. Youngblood walked over to the hospital with the camp guards. They weren't guarding him anymore. They were just trying to help. The war was over, and almost all the prisoners had gone home. J. N. had stayed behind. Most of the men he'd bunked with left two weeks earlier. It was pretty simple really; all they had to do was take the oath and they could go. Many had already taken it once but were required to do so again. They were completely on their own and had to walk, but at least they were free.

J. N. had delayed as long as he could but couldn't wait any longer. As he entered the hospital he thought to himself, "What a horrible day this is." The only thing close to this experience was Hiram's execution.

He went to Joseph's bedside and held his hand. Joseph's breathing was labored and raspy. He took only short, choppy little breaths, and he could hardly move. The doctors had expected him to die already and had said he wouldn't last much longer.

"Hey, Joseph. Can you hear me?" J. N. said, looking into the gaunt, ashen face of his gravely ill brother. Joseph cut his eyes in J. N.'s direction but was too weak to speak or move.

J. N. nodded saying matter-of-factly, "It's all right, Joseph, I know you're sick."

"I came to see you before I have to go, Joseph," he uttered with his voice cracking.

"The war's over, and I've got to go home. I can't stay with ya no more." He broke down crying as he spoke the words.

"As soon as I can get home I'm going to get Bill, and we'll come up here in a wagon and bring you home. You hang on now."

J. N. felt a slight squeeze of his hand, and he looked into his brother's eyes. Joseph nodded slightly and winked. J. N. knew that he was giving his blessing, telling him it was all right. Joseph coughed some more as J. N. cried quietly. J. N. sat for a while without a word being spoken.

Finally, J. N. got up to leave, and Joseph closed his eyes. J. N. walked out into the corridor of the building and spoke to the doctor.

"Does he have any chance, Doctor?" J. N. asked desperately.

"No, I don't think so," the doctor said bluntly.

"He's barely breathing now. Most only last a few days or a week after they get to this point. I'm sorry."

J. N. looked up and down the corridor of the prison hospital. Most of the beds were empty now. The only ones left were a few men who were too sick to leave, waiting to die.

His tears overcame him again as he walked out of the door and into the prison yard. He stepped out of the gates and looked back one last time.

"Good-bye, Joseph," he said sadly as he began the long journey back to the mountains of North Carolina.

Weeks had gone by when the last of the prisoners were moved and Camp Morton closed for good. A local charity organization made up of area churches volunteered to take the last of the sick prisoners from Camp Morton. There were only eight left, and they were all gravely ill. Two had severe head injuries and were totally unaware of their surroundings. The other six clung to life. The doctors didn't expect any of them to survive.

When the prisoners were moved the scene was understandably chaotic. Upon their arrival at Gabriel House they were greeted and placed with a group of compassionate women. The care received at the hands of the ladies was a good deal better than that of the hospital. The cleanest

CHAPTER TWENTY-NINE

bandages and the best sanitary practices were used, and the women provided highly nutritious food.

When the prison staff carried these dying men to Gabriel House, they were brought in on stretchers. When they were placed in their beds the sergeant in charge walked into each room, which had two beds. He walked over to Horace Whitley's bunk and put a chalkboard nameplate on it. The plate read "Joseph Youngblood." At the foot of the bed where Joseph lay near death, the plate read "Horace Whitley."

Nanny Mills had struggled with her secret for as long as she could. She kept hoping she was wrong, but she couldn't pretend any longer. The frightened Nanny paced the floor constantly and chewed at her nails until they bled.

Nanny went downstairs at a time when she knew that James would be alone. She couldn't talk to Bob Russell anymore. No one could. Russell hardly spoke to anyone. He was filled with hate and remained in an almost constant state of agitated despair. Had it not been for James, the Russell farm would not be functioning at all. Nanny thanked God for sparing him.

When she approached James she was shaking. She started to talk but stood silent.

"Good mornin', Nanny," he said calmly.

When there was no response he looked at her curiously, detecting that something was wrong.

"What is it, Nanny?" he said.

She tried to talk the way she had planned, but planning it and doing it were very different things. She started to stammer and tears came to her eyes.

Now James was really concerned. He had great confidence in the strength of this black woman, and her strange behavior was alarming.

"Tell me, Nanny, what is it? What is eatin' at you?"

She began to choke out words, a few at a time. At first it made no sense, but as she went on her message became clearer.

"Well, ya see, Massa James. I takes care of Miss Delia all de time," she stammered in choppy phrases. "I feeds her, I walks her, and I bathes her."

She paused briefly as if trying to catch her breath.

"I know that. Go on, Nanny. Finish what you were saying," James prodded.

"I don know, Massa James, I don know!" she said, now crying openly.

James grabbed her shoulders and talked to her in a serious fatherly tone.

"Look, Nanny, I think you better tell me what's on your mind."

She looked up into his eyes, and her lower lip rolled. She burst into tears and blurted out the words.

"Miss Delia, she don't have no bleedin'. I think she be with child."

James Russell looked at her as his eyes widened. He stepped back to catch his breath. He grew pale and felt faint.

"Oh my God. Papa was afraid of this," he said in a sickening tone. "Dear God, what are we going to do?"

He fell back into a chair, and Nanny watched as tears dribbled down his cheeks. James Russell had maintained a brave and steadfast composure for four years of gruesome battle. He could be strong no longer. His family had fallen apart, and he had no idea how they could cope with more adversity.

He looked up toward the second floor and shook his head.

"Poor Delia, how will she cope with this?" he mumbled as he buried his face in his hands.

Chapter 30

―― SEPTEMBER 12, 1865 ――

Asheville, North Carolina Pinkney Youngblood was sad, but he was also proud. He had raised these two colts during the war and had managed to keep them hidden and safe. Pinkney hated to sell them, but he knew it had to be done. The family needed the money, and they could find no other way.

Pinkney knew horses well. He may have looked like an easy mark for the men at the stockyards, but he wasn't. The same could be said of Pinkney that was said of all Youngbloods, that "he can squeeze the ink out of a greenback."

Saturday at the stockyards in Asheville was the best time and place to trade. Pinkney led the two horses attached by a single rope on the trek toward Asheville. He followed the Asheville Road until he crossed the Swannanoa River at Gum Springs. Pinkney rested for a few minutes, then continued, following the river to its confluence with the French Broad. From there the stockyards were in sight. The youthful Youngblood paid his stall fee and prepared for the sale.

A good part of the day had passed, and still he hadn't sold the two horses. At the far end of the shed he saw a group of men dressed in fancy clothes. One tall, slender man stood out among the others; he seemed to be leading the group. As they walked in his direction he saw that they were drinking, passing a jug from man to man. They were loud and vociferous.

THE SECRET OF WAR

The man beside Pinkney looked in their direction and cursed under his breath.

"Bunch a damn Yankee carpetbaggers," he said in a low voice.

As the group approached, Pinkney turned his back and began brushing one of the horses, and he pretended not to notice the little entourage.

"Hey, kid, that thar is some mighty pretty colts ya got," one of them said.

Pinkney continued to brush the horse and mumbled a quiet, "Thank you."

"This here's Mr. Matthias Dees; he's a county commissioner," one of the men said, pointing to a man in a dark green velvet frock coat.

Pinkney didn't turn around. He just kept brushing.

"Them horses for sale, boy?" Dees asked.

"Naw, they was, but nobody's payin' nothin' today. I'm just gettin' ready to take 'em home," Pinkney said calmly.

Dees looked around at the men with him.

"Well, boys, maybe this kid ain't seen a body with the means," he said, obviously bragging about his own wealth.

Pinkney sized him up quickly. He could see that the man was intoxicated and might represent an opportunity.

"Yea, I reckon that's right. They ain't nobody here today with the means, as you say." He emphasized the word "means" and then resumed brushing the horse.

Dees tucked his thumbs under his suspenders and puffed out his chest.

"Well, boy, I reckon I can buy anythin' ya got," Dees said slurring his speech. The men in his party all nodded and mumbled their approval at the comment.

Pinkney turned and looked at him incredulously.

"Naw, not these horses. They're fine animals," he said, baiting the man's ego as he continued to brush.

Dees looked at the rest of his group. He raised the jug and took another sip of corn whiskey. He wiped his mouth on his sleeve and looked back at the horses.

CHAPTER THIRTY

"What doz ya say to sellin' 'em horses for gold?" he asked confidently.

"Well, I might sell for gold if a man had any," he said dubiously.

Dees staggered a little as he dug in his pockets. He pulled out some greenback and asked him, "How 'bout this?"

"I thought you said you had gold," Pinkney answered.

"I do, somewhere," Dees said as he continued to stagger around while rummaging through his pockets.

He looked at his friends laughing and said sloppily. "I got gold, ain't I boys?"

The men all laughed, nodding in affirmation while Dees continued to search himself. Knowing that he had everyone's attention Dees grabbed himself at the crotch as if he were still searching himself. He twisted from side to side, then thrust his hips in a vulgar motion. His little traveling cadre burst into laughter at the sight.

Dees returned to rummaging through his own pockets when he froze in place and altered his expression to a twisted grin.

"Aha! I found it," he said laughing again.

He pulled a pouch from his coat pocket and opened it up.

Pinkney continued to brush the horse and act busy.

"I give ya this here solid gold piece fer 'em horses," he said as he stumbled backward.

"Maybe," Pinkney said, still keeping his bargaining position open. "Let me see."

At first he doubted that it was real or that it contained enough gold to pay for two quality horses. He took the coin and examined it.

Pinkney's faced flushed, but none of the intoxicated men noticed. His pulse quickened, and he broke into a cold sweat. His heart beat so loud that he could feel it. Pinkney recognized the coin immediately but said nothing. He made the trade with Dees and watched with some regret as they led the horses away.

Pinkney looked for familiar faces, hoping for more information. He spotted Joseph Hamilton at one of the stalls.

Some of the Union men were so out of genuine conviction. Many of them were honorable citizens who sincerely believed in preserving the Union. They hadn't joined at the end just for the bounty or for personal advantage; they had been Union men from the beginning. One of those men was Joseph Hamilton. He'd been a captain in the 2nd North Carolina Mounted Infantry and was well known to many, including the Youngbloods.

"Excuse me, Mr. Hamilton, I'm Pinkney Youngblood. I believe you know my father," he said respectfully.

Hamilton looked over at him, at first unsure as to who he was. Then he smiled and shook his hand. "Yes, sure. Pleased to see ya."

"I wanted to ask you a question if I could," Pinkney said shyly.

"Why sure, what is it?" Hamilton asked pleasantly.

"That man going there with the green frock coat. Do you know him?"

Hamilton looked up and his eyes focused on the man in question. His smile faded and his expression changed.

"Yea, I know him, boy. You best stay away from him. He ain't no good. I know him from the war," Hamilton said with an ominous tone.

"I wanna be sure I get his name right. What's his name and where does he live?" Pinkney persisted.

"His name is Dees, Matthias Dees. He's a county commissioner, if you can believe that. He lives up in Mitchell County. He comes down here right regular on Saturdays," Hamilton answered as he stared at the boy curiously. His weathered eyes narrowed as he evaluated the youngster.

"What do ya wanna know about him for?"

"Oh, nothin'. I sold him two horses. I was just curious," Pinkney responded nonchalantly.

Pinkney said good-bye to Hamilton, then started on the long walk home with the gold coin in his pocket.

Chapter 31

—— OCTOBER 1865 ——

Hoopers Creek, North Carolina Robert Russell waited anxiously. He was curious as to why this visit was taking place. He didn't see much of anyone these days and hadn't seen any Youngbloods for quite a while. Bill, the oldest of the five Youngblood boys, had approached him at church. He'd asked for permission to come by for a visit. Russell could tell that Bill had something serious to discuss.

When the wagon pulled into the yard he could see that three of the boys were on the wagon. Hiram had died in the war, and no one knew where Joseph was. Russell didn't care much one way or another. He knew no one would ever marry Delia now, not even one of those Krauts.

Russell met them at the door while Nanny Mills swooned over them. Russell was annoyed by her intrusion. Bob Russell invited them in, and Nanny offered to bring refreshments. The group went into the parlor and took their seats. They were still engaged in small talk when James Russell came downstairs and joined them.

"It's a real pleasure having you boys by for a visit. What is it ya got on your mind?" James asked pleasantly.

"Yea, I've been real curious about that myself," Bob Russell added.

Bill, J. N., and Pinkney Youngblood all looked at each other as if to decide who would speak. The younger two gestured to their older brother as if to defer. Bill slowly began to speak.

"Sometimes it's best just to show somebody something rather than trying to tell it," Bill said calmly. He looked back at J. N., and Pinkney reached in his pocket. He pulled out a fancy-looking envelope and handed it to Mr. Russell. Robert Russell fished into the envelope and looked back at the Youngbloods with a confused stare. He couldn't possibly imagine what was in the envelope.

He put on his spectacles and began to read. The others in the room just watched. Nanny Mills came back into the room carrying a tray loaded with refreshments. She smiled at the Youngbloods and then left again. Russell finished reading the short note inside. He took off his glasses and handed the letter to James.

"I'm very sorry. The war has taken so much from all of us. I'm very sorry," he said.

James opened the folded sheet of paper and noted the nice heading at the top of the page: Gabriel House, Indianapolis, Indiana.

> Dear Mr. Youngblood,
> It is with deep regret that we inform you of the death of your son Joseph. He was entrusted to our care after the closing of the prison at Camp Morton. He was well cared for during his last difficult hour. We pray that the Lord is with you in your time of grief. May you be comforted in knowing that a minister accompanied him at the time of his passing and that he now rests with the Lord.
>
> With Sympathy,
> Sisters of the Lord,
> Gabriel House

James Russell got up and walked out of the room, hiding his tears. He was not really that close to Joseph, or any of the Youngbloods, but he'd fought the war from the beginning at Camp Patton all the way to Appomattox. Young Russell served with these men. He couldn't take any more of it, and the news of Joseph's death brought back the inescapable sadness. Up until this moment he had also held out hope

CHAPTER THIRTY-ONE

that Joseph would come home someday and possibly do something to help his sister.

Robert Russell watched his son, and his expression hardened. "Those goddamn Yankees, may they all burn in hell," he said.

The Youngblood boys looked at each other, seemingly unsure as to how to react. Bill spoke up first.

"Seems to us that there's plenty of blame to go around on both sides," he said with his own anger rising as he thought of Hiram's execution at the hands of a Confederate firing squad.

James came back into the room.

"I'm so sorry; it's so tragic. Please God, quit taking our boys," he said as if in prayer.

"We have something else that we'd like to ask you about," Bill said calmly. Then he turned back to his brothers.

"Go ahead, J. N., show 'em," Bill said.

J. N. pulled out a pouch and opened the drawstring. He pulled out a large gold coin and placed it on the table in front of the Russells. James looked at it and then looked up at the Youngbloods in obvious confusion. Robert Russell leaned over, putting on his spectacles. He studied the coin and then picked it up and turned it over.

"Well, I'll be damned!" he exclaimed.

"I'll be damned!" he shouted again in excitement. He looked up at the Youngbloods and then back at James. Apparently unable to speak, he got up and hobbled over to the fireplace. He ripped the paneling out of the wall and pointed to the hole that was exposed.

"That coin was right in here the night the Yankees came!" he said almost screaming. "Where did you get that coin?"

James stood and tried to calm his father.

"Now wait a minute, Papa. There could be other coins like this one. It might not be the same one," he said.

"That's it! Damn it. I've never seen a coin like that anywhere else," he shouted in an adamant voice.

"Calm down, Papa, let them finish."

Bill spoke calmly and thoughtfully to both men.

"Yes, there are other coins like this, but only four others. We have the other four. Each was individually marked and given to us by our father. His grandfather brought them from Germany. We know this coin was Joseph's. We just wanted to know for sure that it was taken from here. We knew Joseph left it with Delia. He told us so." Bill finished his talk without saying how they'd gotten it back. Pinkney put the coin back in his pocket.

"Goddamn it, what are you going to do about it?" Bob Russell screamed.

Bill Youngblood's demeanor changed to calm, almost distant. Then he looked back at Robert Russell and evaluated his emotional state.

"Nothing, there's nothing we can do about it. Pinkney found it in the pasture. We don't have any idea who took it," Bill said calmly.

"Damn!" Robert Russell fumed.

"I'd give anything to catch them bastards that took my money! But at least I'm gonna get my money back. You are giving me the coin, aren't ya?" The Youngbloods ignored the question.

Pinkney spoke up as part of the well-rehearsed plan the Youngbloods had devised.

"By the way, Mr. Russell, me and Delia used to go riding together. We were good friends," he explained. "Could I see her?"

Russell scowled at them, obviously annoyed. "No, she don't see nobody. She can't talk no how."

Pinkney looked at James and obviously intended to appeal to him.

"I know she can't talk, but she knew me pretty good. It might do her good to see me," he pleaded.

"Papa, I don't see how it would hurt none. Let him go up and see her."

Robert Russell didn't answer, and James took his silence to mean he'd accepted the idea.

"You can go up and see her, but you've got to understand. She does not recognize anyone. She can't speak. The doctor says she has severe brain damage," James said in a capitulating tone.

"We've heard. I won't do anything to disturb her. I just want to visit with her a little."

CHAPTER THIRTY-ONE

As the Youngbloods continued to execute their plan Pinkney went upstairs to Delia's room with James. Pinkney stood at the door, indicating that he expected to be left alone with her. James went back downstairs where he found the men talking over farm matters. He was soon fully engaged in the conversation.

Pinkney slowly walked around in front of Delia's bed. She was sitting upright looking out the window. He maneuvered to a position where he could see her face and was shocked at what he saw. Her skin was ashen and her eyes sunk deep in their sockets. Her skin was stretched over her facial bones, giving the impression of an age much greater than her years.

Her expression was lifeless and her weight loss so extreme that her appearance was skeletal. Pinkney gasped, covering his mouth with his hand. Determined to regain his composure, he took the small wooden chair at the foot of her bed.

He sat down and looked at her, waited a minute, and then spoke softly. "Hello, Delia, remember me?" he said with a slight smile. "I remember what great times you and I had up on Bearwallow, looking after those horses. Do you remember that, Delia?" he said, looking for some reaction.

Delia didn't move. Her expression was unchanged, and she stared straight ahead with the same blank look.

Pinkney got up from his seat and moved around into her line of sight. He peered into her eyes, and she turned her head and stared out the window. He looked toward the door to see if they were still alone. Turning back to face her, he walked around in between the bed and the window. She continued to stare.

He sat on the bed beside her and began talking.

"You've got to help me, Delia, you've got to. No one else can," he said searching her eyes for some sign or movement.

"Delia, I think I know who attacked you," he said staring at her. Pinkney thought he saw a twitch in her eyes, but still she did not respond. He reached in his pocket and pulled out the gold coin and held it so that she'd have to see it. Her eyes widened, he was sure of it. He held it in front of her face again, and she turned her head.

"Help me, Delia," he said forcefully. Once again she turned her head.

He moved around to the other side of the bed and sat beside her again. Pinkney saw a tear slide down her cheek. He smiled and took her hand. It lay limply in his as he grasped her shoulder and pressed very close.

"Do you know the man who came here that night?" he asked. Tears now filled her eyes and her face tightened. But she continued to divert her stare away from Pinkney. "Answer me, Delia! Was it a man named Matthias Dees?" He almost shouted at her.

Delia turned away again and began to sob openly, and then she began to register eerie, fearful howls as the memories came flooding back. She twisted and lurched, as if to try to remove her body from the pain. Pinkney tried to calm her, but she tumbled off the side of the bed and curled into a ball after she hit the floor. Pinkney ran around to find her beside the bed with her eyes covered.

"Answer me, Delia!" he pleaded.

She uncovered her face, displaying a tortured expression. She stared up into his face, looked directly into his eyes, and nodded her head frantically up and down. Then all the pain that she had held inside emerged. Collapsing from the emotional weight she had carried for so long, Delia broke down completely into a sobbing, incoherent state of despair. She curled into a tight fetal position and cried uncontrollably.

The door to the bedroom burst open. James Russell and Nanny came running into the room.

"What did you do to her?" James screamed. Nanny ran around the bed and helped her up.

At first, he said nothing. He just stared at her. Then he looked at Nanny Mills, then at James.

"Nothing," he said. "I didn't do anything. Something must have scared her." Then he excused himself, turned, and walked out of the door.

Chapter 32

—— NOVEMBER 1865 ——

Indianapolis, Indiana Joseph shook as he took his broth, looking up at the elderly lady who fed him. He could see the kindness in her eyes. He looked around at the clean and tidy surroundings and wondered where he had landed this time.

Joseph's recovery had been tenuous and slow, but recently he had seemed to gain just the tiniest bit of strength each day. Most important, his delirium was gone. He'd had long and horrible nightmares, and the heat of his fever drove him to near madness. So he was very grateful to be coherent.

He raised his head to the lady feeding him and managed to speak for the first time in months.

"Where am I?" he asked weakly.

She smiled down at him and replied sweetly. "My, we are getting better, aren't we?"

He wasn't sure she heard him so he asked again.

"Where am I?" he asked, not remembering that he'd been told when he awakened earlier.

"You're at Gabriel House, a house of the Lord," she said beaming. "God has surely blessed you. We thought you had passed on many times.

"I believe your fever is nearly gone."

"How long have I been here?" he asked trying to raise his head.

"A long time, a very long time," she said while holding his head to feed him.

Joseph drifted off again and fell into a deep sleep. When he woke again he felt a little stronger than before. The meal had done him good.

Alone and still confused, he tried to lift himself out of the bed, but he was too weak. He watched and waited for some time when another lady came into his room.

"Well, you are awake again," she said happily. "Bertha said you were coming around. It's a miracle. Surely God is with you."

Joseph vaguely remembered the conversation with the other woman. "Where am I?"

"You're at Gabriel House of the Lord. You were a Confederate prisoner at Camp Morton, and when the war ended they brought you here. We've been caring for you for many months now. You were not expected to live, but I think God has decided otherwise."

Joseph listened to her words and tried to remember how he got there. He suddenly felt hungry. "Can I eat something?" he asked meekly.

"Getting your appetite back, are you?" she said smiling. "That's a good sign."

Joseph ate quickly, consuming the oatmeal offered him, and then he dozed off again. When he awoke it was the middle of the night and there was no one around. He began to form many questions and resolved to get them answered as soon as the nice ladies returned in the morning.

The same lady that was there the first time he awoke was sitting there when he awoke again.

"Good morning," she said cheerfully.

Joseph looked up at her and decided that her serene and pleasant demeanor reminded him of his own mother.

"What month is it?" he asked.

"It's November 1865," she said while leaning over him and touching his forehead.

It took a moment for the date to register in Joseph's mind.

CHAPTER THIRTY-TWO

"My God, I've been here for months then!" he said. "Where is my brother?"

Bertha looked confused.

"I don't know. We weren't aware that you had a brother. Was he here with you?" she asked sincerely.

"Yes," Joseph said, still partially confused.

"Does my family know I'm here?" he asked.

"Oh yes," the lady said smiling.

"They write occasionally to see how you're doing. We have letters for you that they sent in case you ever woke up. Looks like it's time for you to have them," she said with the same sweet smile.

Bertha left the room and returned with some envelopes bound in a cluster by a string. "They are going to be so happy to hear that you're better. It's a miracle." She continued talking while she untied the string. Then she took one of the letters and handed it to Joseph.

His hands shook from weakness as he took the letter from her. He stared at it briefly trying to get his eyes to focus. Finally he was able to read the intended recipient's name. It was plainly printed in bold letters on the front of the envelope: "Horace Whitley."

Joseph looked up at Bertha.

"Thank you, ma'am, but this ain't mine," he said as he calmly handed it back to her with an unsteady hand.

Bertha looked puzzled and upset.

"Of course it's yours. There's no one else left but you."

Joseph frowned as he looked back at her.

"Ma'am, I know I'm mighty sick, but I know who I am. I'm Joseph Youngblood from Henderson County, North Carolina."

Bertha's face wrenched into a stunned expression. She got up and walked out of the room and came back with another lady. The other woman looked at Joseph and looked back at some papers she carried in her hand.

"You're not Horace Whitley who was with the 8th Louisiana Infantry?" the woman asked with a sick look on her face.

"No, ma'am, I'm Joseph Youngblood. I'm right sure of that."

The two women turned simultaneously and looked at each other with ghastly expressions.

"Oh my God!" one of them said as they looked back at him. "There's been a terrible mistake."

Chapter 33

——NOVEMBER 1865——

Hoopers Creek, North Carolina The days were long and tortuous for the Russells. The family struggled with questions about Delia's future, the baby, and the family. Would Delia be physically able to take the trauma of childbirth? Most important, what was the best way to handle this delicate situation? Maybe someone would take in this illegitimate child. Delia certainly couldn't be counted on to raise the child. Her sisters couldn't, for they saw the child as the "devil's child."

Robert Russell continued to spiral out of control emotionally. He sat in silence most of the time and continued to drink. James was forced to take over as head of the household, playing peacemaker between his father and everyone in his path and trying to keep everyone's spirits from collapsing.

Nanny Mills's workload had tripled. She was paid now but very little. In addition to her regular duties, Delia required constant care, and Nanny made an extra effort to spend time walking her and talking to her. Nanny still carried on as if she was still an active member of the family. Her determination to coax Delia back to health was fervent and unwavering.

In the evenings she often sung field songs to her that she'd learned as a child. She seemed to see a light in Delia's eyes that no one else could see.

It was late afternoon when Delia began to show signs of labor. Nanny was not a midwife, but she had been involved in the delivery of many babies. She often assisted the slave's midwife when she lived on the Livingston farm. Initially she concluded that this must be false labor, as Delia's baby was not expected until January. But suddenly the pains became more persistent in the evening hours. By late evening, Nanny realized that Delia was in full labor.

James sent for the area midwife, Mrs. Addie Whitaker, from up on Mud Creek. Upon her arrival there was little conversation. James had met with her earlier and explained the circumstances. Her discretion could be counted on.

Addie entered the room cheerful and confident, quickly outlining Nanny's duties for the evening. The two women began the vigil that lasted throughout the night. Delia remained in the same catatonic state that had imprisoned her mind since the attack. She did not acknowledge anyone around her, and while her face revealed her pain, her voice did not.

Just before daylight the baby arrived. Despite Delia's diminished physical condition and her less-than-cooperative participation, Delia gave birth to a small but seemingly healthy male child. The majority of the family was relieved and thankful that the delivery had gone so well. Secretly some of them had expected tragedy of some kind.

Delia did not react to the newborn in any way. Addie coaxingly talked to Delia as she placed the baby at her breast. But Delia coiled back at the attempt, and Addie instructed Nanny to seek out the services of a wet nurse, while she made do with milk from one of the bottles sometimes used for baby calves.

As the sun rose Addie placed the baby in the bassinet. She looked at Delia, who was now drifting off to sleep. Nanny had returned and Addie spoke softly to her.

"You should probably let Delia be around the baby for a few days, just to see if she'll take to it. But I don't know if she'll ever be able to care for that baby. The Russells probably need to make plans. I'll speak to James."

"I don know how Massa Russell's gonna take to dis little un," Nanny said in a worried tone.

"Miz Russell done say it be de devil's child."

CHAPTER THIRTY-THREE

Addie didn't respond.

"I'll be going now, but I'll come back this afternoon to check on her," Addie said. She looked back at Nanny and smiled. "Delia's lucky to have you, Nanny."

Nanny got up and walked over to the bedside.

"What's we gonna do, Miss Delia? What's we gonna do?"

She walked back across the room and looked down into the bassinet at the sleeping baby.

"Don ya fret none, missy. Nanny gonna be right here wit' ya." Nanny plopped her exhausted body down into the chair by the bed. In a few minutes she was fast asleep.

Robert Russell had been awake all night, well aware of what was happening upstairs. He had not gone up to check but had stayed in his study sipping whiskey and wallowing in self-pity. This was one challenge that he could not face.

Robert Russell couldn't help but remember how happy he had been when they had first bought this farm. The former slavemaster remembered when the future held the promise of prosperity. Now he had lost nearly everything, selling off half of his land to keep from losing the house and the whole farm. He couldn't help but be furious at the small amount he had received from the sale.

"I was robbed, same as if a man had held a gun on me," he lamented as he took another long drink.

Now he was burdened by shame. It was a deep and ugly shame that would curse him and his family forever. No one in the community spoke of it in public. It was never mentioned, but everyone knew.

Robert Russell felt completely helpless. If he knew who had broken into his home, took his money, and raped his daughter, he would surely kill them. If he knew how to find them, he'd go looking. If he knew how to make this all go away, he would.

Slowly as the whiskey bottle drained and the sun rose, Robert Russell's self-pity turned to fury. While the rest of the family was still sleeping, he clumsily rose to his feet and grabbed his cane. He paced around the room, seething with frustration and rage. His mind raced uncontrollably, and his thoughts became confused. He needed an answer. He felt an overwhelming need for control.

Robert Russell walked down the hallway of the quiet house and looked up toward the second floor. His mind whirled in an intoxicated state of vengeful rage. His frenzied need to restore his former life led him to climb the stairs.

"I do not want to see this baby," he thought. "I do not want to see it." But his legs seemed to be making decisions for him. An indescribable force led him, and even though he tried to go back down the stairs, he couldn't. He paused between steps, not knowing if the next step would take him up or down. Finally he reached the landing and shuffled down the hall, still pausing intermittently, indecisively.

"Why am I going in here? I do not want to see this thing, this devil's child."

As the sun began to rise a little higher he stepped quietly into Delia's room. Delia finally slept fitfully and Nanny lay slumped and snoring. In the corner he saw the bassinet and walked over to peer inside.

He stood and stared into the bassinet as if transfixed.

"My life is destroyed, and now I'm to be burdened with the likes of you," he whispered almost silently.

His mind settled enough to calculate the risk. "Nobody will question it; nobody could blame me," he told himself. "Everybody knows that you're the devil's child; nobody will do a thing."

Anguished and tormented, he twisted his face and squinted his eyes. He leaned on his cane and reached down into the bassinet. Suddenly he found someone to punish, someone to answer for his pain. It was a chance to retaliate for the years of misery and suffering.

Robert Russell placed his hand around the infant's tiny neck. The baby's eyes opened briefly as he glared up at his grandfather. The grip of Robert's hand was quick and strong; there was no sound. There was no cry, no scream.

The little face turned purple, and the bantam body quivered. It was

CHAPTER THIRTY-THREE

over quickly, in just a minute or so.

Robert Russell looked around to find both women still sleeping. He turned on his heels and carefully snuck out of the room and down the hall to his bedroom.

Chapter 34

―― DECEMBER 1865 ――

Hoopers Creek, North Carolina It had been years since there'd been such a festive occasion at the Youngblood farm. The festivities had been organized to celebrate a miracle. Joseph was alive and coming home. The family had received the letter in the mail days before his arrival, and his brothers had traveled to Knoxville to pick him up at the train station and bring him home.

The wagon pulled into the yard, and the crowd erupted in a loud cheer. Friends, relatives, and neighbors from all around had come to welcome Joseph back. It was early December, and the weather was still quite pleasant. Joseph sat on the front seat of the wagon as they bumped along the rough road and into the yard. He waved weakly and fought back tears as they pulled up to the house. People followed along beside the wagon and reached for his hand as they went by.

Joseph climbed down and greeted the throng of well-wishers. His mother and father rushed to him and hugged him at the same time. He was wrapped in their arms for several minutes before he turned them loose. Tears were visible in most everyone's eyes as the reunion with his parents touched all those who witnessed it. His brothers beamed with happiness as they watched.

Elizabeth Youngblood looked at her son and gasped.

"You look terrible!" she screeched, wiping a tear from her eye.

CHAPTER THIRTY-FOUR

Joseph was still quite pale and emaciated, and he'd aged to twice his years. He looked over at his brothers and smiled warmly.

"Well, all y'all look mighty pretty to me!" he said loud enough for all to hear. Everyone cheered again.

"Yep, even my brothers look damn pretty right now."

The family went into the house while people continued to gather on the porch, in the kitchen, and anywhere there was room. Soon the grounds were covered.

Joseph had told the story of waking up at the Gabriel House to his brothers on the way home. All the guests wanted to hear the story too. He repeated it many times, and he always got a laugh when he recounted how he told the ladies he knew who he was, even if they didn't.

Joseph walked out on the porch and looked up and down the creek valley. He took a deep breath and thanked God for finally bringing him home alive. He also thanked God for ending the horrible war that had taken so much from so many. He watched the ladies bring more food, and he remembered how hungry he'd once been.

Bill joined him on the porch.

"Little brother, we thought we'd never see you again," he said patting him on the back.

"I never thought I'd make it back," Joseph responded.

Bill looked at his brother and secretly fretted about his condition. His teeth were bad and his weight loss was frightening.

"Damn, you're skinny, boy," Bill teased him.

"That ain't gonna last long," Joseph said with a wink. "Besides, you need some help. I can see you been eatin' my part and yours while I was away."

Both men just smiled and enjoyed the moment.

"I ain't gonna do nothin' but eat for the next month."

"Good, we'll see to it," Bill said.

Joseph looked out toward the road and saw them coming. At first he didn't recognize them; they looked so much older. David Garren now walked with a conspicuous limp. Will Garren's left arm hung limply at his side. Seeing his old comrades brought his heightened emotions to the surface once more. Tears came to his eyes as he watched them walk into the yard.

Joseph hobbled down the steps and hurried out to meet them. The three men hugged and cried. Display of such emotion would have been unthinkable four years earlier.

Bill, Jasper Newton, and young Pinkney came out and joined them as well. They all hugged while shaking hands with each other.

"I wish I'd gone to war with y'all," Pinkney quipped as he listened to their stories.

All the older men turned and glared at him in astonishment.

"Don't you ever say that again," Bill said solemnly.

Pinkney was taken aback, but he understood their sensitivities. It just bothered him that the rest of them shared something that he wasn't a part of.

Will Garren looked at him and smiled.

"We all wanted to go once. But look at us now," he said sadly as he gazed around at the other veterans.

"I can't use my arm, David can't walk right, and Joseph's lucky to be alive. Hiram and Elisha have gone on to the Lord. No, boy, we're all damn glad you didn't have to go."

The Garrens went to the house and joined in the eating and drinking as the celebration carried into the night. Joseph was the happiest he'd been in four years. Still there was a void that he'd have to fill. He longed for his beloved Delia. He had to see her. His brothers had told him on the trip home the horrible truth about what happened to Delia. He'd already made up his mind that he'd marry her anyway.

The truth about what happened to Delia nearly killed him. Joseph fell into an ignominious state of despair for hours. It was an attitude that could often be found in the hearts and minds of surviving men all over the South.

CHAPTER THIRTY-FOUR

Joseph didn't understand why his brothers had insisted that he not see Delia yet. There was something they had to tell him first.

Joseph had been home a few days. He'd gained weight and walked farther each day. The good food and rest were having a most positive effect.

"I haven't felt this good in years," he told J. N. as they sat on the porch.

"You're sure looking a sight better too, but you still ain't pretty," J. N. said while eyeing his brother up and down.

"You seem stronger. You know I wouldn't have left you in that hospital up in Indiana if I hadn't believed you were a goner."

"It's all right, J. N. I reckon I was a goner. There wasn't nothin' you could do anyway."

Joseph sat quietly looking into the distance. He began to ask questions about Delia.

"Look, J. N. I know it's bad, but I've got to go see her," he said with determination.

"I'm going over there today with or without your help."

"I know, Joseph. Bill and I talked about it this morning. We've got something to tell you before you see her," J. N. said in a foreboding tone.

Joseph was now very curious as he realized that his brothers were up to something serious.

The four remaining Youngblood boys gathered in the kitchen late that night after their parents had retired. Joseph sat at the table and waited as his brothers gathered around. J. N. looked out the door as if to see if anyone was near. Pinkney lit a lantern, and they all sat down at the table.

Bill began the discussion.

"Joseph, there's something we know that no one else knows."

Joseph looked around the table and detected that this conversation was very serious.

"We haven't told anyone except Will and David," J. N. added.

Joseph was getting impatient. "Well, if you told them, don't ya think it's time you told me?"

"That's why we're here," Bill replied, slightly annoyed. "You see, Joseph, the night Delia's house was robbed there were a number of men involved. A Union general named Palmer came and saved Delia's life.

"Palmer's a good man, Joseph. He tried to do right," Pinkney added.

"Go on, tell me the rest," Joseph said quietly.

"Palmer and his men rode up to the Russell place while the Yankees that did it were runnin' away. They had set the house on fire with Delia in it. They were going to burn her to death. Palmer killed one of 'em, and his men killed two others," Bill continued. "They had robbed the place too, took all the money in the house.

"I talked to Palmer later. He said one of 'em got away. He said they would've gotten him too, but the house was about to burn down, so they had to let him go to put out the fire."

Joseph scooted back in his chair and put his hands to his face and rubbed his eyes.

"I'd give anything to get that man," Joseph said sadly.

He looked up to find his brothers looking at each other. Bill looked at J. N. and told him quietly.

"Go ahead, J. N."

J. N. reached in his pocket and pulled out one of the rare German coins and laid it on the table. Joseph looked at him in confusion, knowing that all his brothers had one. Bill then reached in his pocket and laid his beside it. Pinkney produced his and laid it in a line with the others. J. N. then pulled out a fourth coin.

"This one was Hiram's," J. N. said, as he placed it beside the others.

There was still one space left. Joseph knew that the missing coin was his. He had left it with Delia, and he knew it had been taken during the attack on her house. Pinkney reached in his pocket and pulled out the fifth coin and laid it in line with the others.

Joseph's eyes bulged. He looked at his brothers in astonishment and then returned his gaze to the coins. He picked up the last one and held it to the light. He rolled it over and over in his hands. It had the same dates and marks that he was familiar with. He looked around at his brothers wide-eyed.

"Good God almighty! That's my coin!" he shouted, trying to gain control of himself.

CHAPTER THIRTY-FOUR

"Yes, Joseph, you think we don't know that?" Bill said condescendingly to his little brother once more.

"My God, where did you get it? Delia had this coin," Joseph said excitedly.

Bill grinned a sly grin and said, "Yes, we know that too, Joseph."

"How did you get it?"

Bill looked over at Pinkney and smiled.

"The kid here, he's pretty sly. He's a pretty good horse trader too," Bill said pointing at Pinkney. Pinkney was proud of the recognition he was receiving.

"The kid raised some horses during the war, and he managed to keep them hidden. He went down to the stockyards in Asheville to sell them, and a drunk man paid him with this coin."

Joseph's lip curled and his face reddened.

"Is he the man that attacked Delia?" he asked angrily.

Bill paused briefly, then nodded affirmatively.

"Yes, he is."

Joseph asked, "Are you sure?"

"Absolutely certain," Bill replied, looking at Pinkney.

"We did some snooping and found out that he was a scout with the 13th Tennessee Cavalry. He was with Stoneman's men when they came through. A lot of 'em were men from these parts. He is from Mitchell County."

"That don't mean he did it," Joseph said.

"No, it doesn't," Bill replied.

"Tell him, Pinkney," J. N. said to the youngster.

"Joseph, me and Delia got to be friends during the war. She didn't talk about nothing except you coming home and marrying her. We used to ride up on Bearwallow where I had those colts hidden. She loved it up there."

"Go on, boy, tell him the rest," Bill interrupted him.

"Well, you see, everybody says she ain't got a brain anymore, but it ain't so. I know it. I went over there, and I asked her about this man.

349

Delia wouldn't talk to nobody, but she told me. She shook her head up 'n down real clear like. It was Dees. She cried and screamed and carried on something awful."

Joseph climbed to his feet and paced about the room.

"My God! It was a local man!" Joseph said between clinched teeth. "What did you say his name was?"

"A man named Matthias Dees," Pinkney answered.

"Do you know where we can find him?" Joseph questionied.

"Yes, we found out. We've been working on this for a while, and we know where he lives and when he comes and goes," Bill answered. "Nobody outside this room knows about it except David and Will Garren."

Joseph stared through the window into the darkness beyond. He thought about Malvern Hill and Antietam. He had so wanted to come home and live in peace. But there could be no peace for Joseph as long as this man walked free.

"What about the law? Will they do anything?" Joseph asked.

"The Union army runs things now, and they won't do nothin' to him cause he's a so-called Union man," J. N. responded with bitterness.

The war had taken its toll on Joseph physically and mentally. But there was really no choice in the matter. There were certain codes among proud mountain men. These rules of conduct were often unspoken and unwritten, but they dominated life in the mountains. These codes exceeded the value of all earthly things. Certain values were more important than life itself. He'd have to pick up a gun one more time. He knew that there would be serious risk and that it could cost him his life.

"I will not live in disgrace. I know what I've got to do," he said bluntly. "I don't see that I have much choice. How would a man live with himself?"

"No, Joseph, it's what we've got to do," Bill said stoically.

Joseph turned back to the table and saw his brothers looking at him

CHAPTER THIRTY-FOUR

with rigid determination in their expressions. Bill got up from the table and walked to Joseph and took his hand. His other brothers got up and joined them. Joseph looked into their eyes, and he knew that he was home.

The men pretended to organize a hunting trip and met at their old camping spot. It was the same place that had been the scene of happy times before the war.

Joseph was surprised at how calm he felt. He was stronger now but still not the man he once was. But he was resolved about what he must do.

When the Garrens arrived they were jovial as ever. They'd brought the wagon and Pinkney brought the horses. Will invited Joseph over to the wagon for a look. He unrolled a large blanket in the back and displayed two British-made Enfield rifles. Joseph picked one of them up and held it to his shoulder. He knew the weapon well, and it felt all too familiar in his hands. He embraced the rifle like an old friend.

"How did you manage this?" Joseph said, pointing at the two military weapons.

"Easy," Will laughed. "When everyone went over at Appomattox to surrender me and a bunch of men from the 25th, well, we just took off walking south. We had to hide from some Yankees every now and then, but we made it home just as good as the next feller. Only we kept our guns."

"Hell, we didn't need any help from the Yankees. We just up and quit."

The men went over their plans carefully. Joseph couldn't get over how relaxed everyone was. It reminded him of the early days of the war, when spirits were high but experience was limited. All these men, except one, were now hardened veterans of one of the most ghastly wars in history.

"Pinkney, you know you'll be staying here at the camp. You understand that, don't you?" Bill said staring at him sternly.

"Yes, I know," Pinkney replied, dejected.

"What we're doing here depends on every man doing his job," Will said, patting him on the shoulder with his good hand.

"I still wish I could go," Pinkney complained.

Joseph walked over to his youngest brother and talked to him emphatically.

"I know you want to go. But look at us; we're a bunch of old men. We've been shot up and suffered like no man oughta have to. We've seen horrors so bad that we'll never go to sleep at night again for the rest of our lives without thinkin' about it. We don't want you to be like us if you don't have to. We need you to stay here and keep this camp. You leave the rest of what has to be done to us. We've been through it before." Joseph looked at his brother and smiled warmly.

"Now remember, if anything goes wrong, you didn't know nothin' about it. You understand?" Joseph said as he held his shoulder.

Pinkney looked up and nodded. "You boys be careful now."

The men split into two groups. Joseph and David Garren rode horses with Bill. Will Garren and J. N. sat in the wagon for the long ride. They traveled all the way across Buncombe County and camped for the night above the French Broad River. Then they waited.

The next morning they moved to a place on the road that gave them a commanding view in both directions. Will Garren had studied Dees at the stockyard, and it was his job to identify him. It was Saturday, and there was a good chance he'd be coming this way.

J. N. gave the signal when they saw him approaching. The others took their positions. Joseph turned to David. "Remember, don't fire unless I miss," Joseph said in an attempt to leave his friend out of the unpleasant duty. David gave him a steely look but didn't reply.

J. N. was already moving back to his position with the horses. Will Garren stayed out on the road beside his wagon looking at the wheel. Joseph checked his musket and laid it over a log. His pulse quickened a little, and he felt the old pounding of his heart. He thought of the men he'd killed in the war and the men he'd seen die.

"Never seen one that deserves it like this man," he said to David as they waited in ambush.

CHAPTER THIRTY-FOUR

Will Garren was his usual self. When the rider approached Will called out to him.

"Hey, mister, don't I know you?" he said jovially.

"I've got trouble with my wagon."

Joseph took his sight and laid the bead on the center of the man's chest. He could hear them talking as he waited for the signal. He saw Will look casually in both directions and then heard him say something.

Will Garren asked him, "Ain't you Matthias Dees?"

Dees seemed somewhat suspicious, but he responded, thinking his name might favorably influence the man.

Garren smiled looking up at him.

"Land sake, Matthias Dees," Garren said, taking off his hat and placing it over his chest. To the men in wait the removal of his hat was the confirmation signal.

With military precision both muskets fired, one only a fraction of a second behind the other. Two musket balls struck Dees in the chest only inches apart. The force of the shots violently knocked him off his horse and to the ground. Dees looked up at Will Garren as he walked over and looked down at him.

"I don't reckon you'll be botherin' nobody else," Garren said calmly. Dees took several painfully labored breaths. He moved his mouth and made slight gurgling sounds as he fought for air. His mouth moved as if to speak, then he slumped and died.

Joseph and David came out of their hiding place. J. N. and Bill came riding in with the horses. Bill took Dees's horse and rode off on a trail with it. J. N. and Joseph pulled Dees well into the trees up over a ridgeline and into an area of exposed rock. They pushed the body into a natural cavity and covered it with rocks. Then they placed several larger rocks on top of the pile. The muskets were wrapped in blankets and hidden in the slot built under the wagon frame. David got on the wagon with his brother, and they headed toward home on the main road. The Youngblood boys met up with J. N. well up the trail going off in a different direction. They rode on for miles, leaving Dees's horse miles from where the rider lay.

It was well into the night when they all made it back to camp. No one was nervous except Pinkney.

"Damn, I'm glad to see y'all," Pinkney said.

The older men were so calm that Pinkney thought maybe Dees hadn't come by and they'd have to try again. Maybe Dees hadn't gone to town this Saturday.

"What happened? Tell me what happened," he urged.

David Garren walked over to him and put his hand on his shoulder.

"It's over. We got him."

"Thank God. All I've been able to think about is what that man did to her. Thank God you got him."

Joseph looked at David and asked him why he'd fired.

"You said not to fire unless you missed. I didn't like where you was aiming. It looked to me like you were off a little. I considered that a miss," he said calmly. "Really, Joseph, I figured that if you missed I might not get off a good shot. I figured we couldn't afford to take a chance on missing."

Joseph stared into the fire that Pinkney had built.

"I killed a lot of men in the war. I never felt good about it, never," Joseph said quietly. "But I felt real good about this. I can live my life now. If I have to die for it, then I'll die proud."

He looked into the faces of his brothers and friends around the fire and smiled. "Now I just got one more thing to do, and I'm gonna do that soon as we get home."

Joseph climbed down from the wagon and swiftly headed into the house. He had a lively step and a determined look. He knocked on the Russells' front door and waited until Nanny Mills came to the door.

"Lawdy me! It sho is good to see ya, Mister Joseph," Nanny said affectionately. "I be so happy when they said ya was alive."

Her black face was beaming, but then she paused and began to frown.

CHAPTER THIRTY-FOUR

"Ya know, Miss Delia, she ain't right," Nanny said with a warning in her tone. "She ain't herself no mo. She don even look like herself."

"Ya bes' git yo'self ready cause she ain't a pretty sight. They sez she don't know nobody." The old black lady whispered to him. "But I don believes it."

She looked up the stairs and then turned back to him.

"No sa, I don believes it."

Joseph took one look toward the stairs. He thanked Nanny, then moved past her. He climbed the stairs with his boots pounding, and marched down the hall with the same confidence he had displayed in Virginia four years earlier.

He made the turn into the room but slowed when he saw her.

Delia lay in bed with the same blank stare in her eyes she'd had for months. She lay still and silent facing the window.

Joseph stopped in the center of the room and watched her. There was no reaction from her. He stepped closer and spoke her name.

"Delia," he said softly, as he crept closer to her bed. She did not respond.

He approached her slowly, fearing he would startle her.

Joseph sat down on the edge of the bed and talked softly.

"Delia! Oh Delia. It's going to be all right. I'm home now and I'm here to stay," he said as he slid closer to her. "I know all about what happened. A lot of terrible things happened in that war and there's nothing we can do to change that." His voice cracked with emotion.

Still Delia stared into the distance as he talked. But he continued with his appeal.

"What's important is that we take our lives back. That couldn't be done with a man like Matthias Dees still roaming the mountains." He paused, hoping for a reaction, but there was none.

"I want you to know, Delia, that Dees is dead!" he said bluntly.

Joseph was convinced he saw a movement in her eyes when he said the words, but now she was stone still.

"You'll never have to worry again now that I'm home."

Joseph walked around the room and stood between her and the

window. Her eyes found the wall, and she stared at it as he pleaded with her.

Joseph reached in his pocket and exposed the gold coin in his right hand. He placed it in front of her eyes, using only two fingertips to hold it.

"Pinkney got it back, Delia. It's going to be all right. We killed Matthias Dees."

He saw it. Her lower lip quivered. He was sure of it!

He took her hand and knelt down at her bedside, staring up at her.

"Delia, do you remember that night at Calvary Church behind the bell tower? Do you remember the oath I made the night before I left? Well, I still mean it, Delia."

Joseph saw her eyes water and a painful expression form on her face. He clutched her hand and stared straight at her. "I have returned to fulfill the promises of my oath." He paused briefly to compose his emotions, then he began speak slowly.

> It is to thee that I commit my heart.
> It is to thee that I commit my life, my spirit, and my soul.
> It is to thee that I will return to take as my wife.

Joseph saw her break as his own emotions overcame him. Delia was sobbing freely, and she burst out with an enormous cry of painful relief. He rose to his feet and sat beside her on the bed, taking his hand and placing it his around hers.

"Will you marry me, Delia?" Joseph muttered, fighting his turbulent emotions.

She paused briefly, unable to move. She mustered her courage and turned to face him. She looked into his eyes, and it was over. Delia's long nightmare of unimaginable darkness and total solitude was over. She allowed her mind to begin the difficult journey back into the world she had known.

She only nodded at first, unable to speak; then she cried out.

"Oh God, Joseph! Yes! I will," she managed to say before she

CHAPTER THIRTY-FOUR

completely broke down in his arms. He held her, quietly rocking her back and forth. She fought for a smile through her tears as she looked up at him.

"It's going to be all right, Delia," he whispered to her.

Outside the room at the edge of the steps the old nanny collapsed, sliding down the wall with her face buried in her hands. She cried her own tears as she mumbled into her hands hoping to muffle the sound.

"Thank ya, Lord, thank ya."

Chapter 35

—— JUNE 1, 1866 ——

Fletcher, North Carolina The crowd that gathered at Patty's Chapel that warm June afternoon was larger than it might have been just a few years earlier, but the hardships of war had heightened people's interest in life's normal pleasures. Most of the families from Cane Creek and Hoopers Creek were well represented there. Delia's parents, surrounded by the rest of the Russells, looked on with relief.

It was a simple ceremony, and thankfully so because the heat in the little church was rapidly rising beyond endurance. The church choir sang an old hymn as Joseph and Delia gazed at each other as husband and wife. Delia had gained back some of her weight, and the youthful glow was back in her smile. There was still fear hidden deep in her eyes, and she was still very quiet. The noticeable depression in her jaw would be with her for life. But now at least she would have a life. Her beloved Joseph had returned, and for him she would smile.

Everyone spilled into the churchyard, and the celebration began. There was fried chicken, fresh corn, and tomatoes spread on a collection of white tablecloths. There was also lots of tea and cold water. Out behind the church young men were sneaking sips from several brown jugs. A genuinely festive mood was in place, but there was also a lingering void in the back of people's minds because of the memory of those who hadn't come back. This melancholy spirit would always linger in

CHAPTER THIRTY-FIVE

the mist of the mountains. The images of war would visit them in their dreams for the rest of their lives. It was the haunting memory of the many who were gone, never to return, that troubled them most.

Joseph Youngblood looked into the eyes of his new bride and resolved to put it all behind them, to leave the memories in the past. He would heal the wounds that had very nearly destroyed them all. Joseph looked around the churchyard. Just within the scope of his limited view there was a man with one leg; two others were missing arms. There was a blind man sitting under a tree. Many others limped or hobbled in pain. Perhaps worst of all were the mental scars that they carried. Four years of war had exposed them to horrors that wouldn't have seemed possible just a few years earlier.

In the corner of the churchyard a small assembly had formed. The Garrens, Joseph's brothers, and various other former soldiers were chatting happily. Joseph looked at the small group and realized that among these men were the people who would help rebuild the devastated community. They were good men, and he was thankful that they had survived.

As people gathered around the newlyweds and congratulated them Joseph's mind focused on the little group gathered in the corner of the yard and the old black woman serving refreshments. He excused himself from Delia and walked across the churchyard.

He and Delia had planned a short honeymoon, but Joseph had loose ends to tie up before he left. As he strolled across the yard he watched the old Nanny as she worked happily. No one had been more pleased to see Delia marry than Nanny Mills. But there was a silent sadness about her; Joseph saw it and understood it. The Russell children, Delia in particular, had been her life. Zeke was gone, and Delia's marriage meant that she would be leaving. She was unsure of her future and unsure of herself. She was free now, but freedom wasn't that easy. It was a difficult time for everyone, but even more difficult for former slaves. Joseph understood that Nanny needed them, but he also knew that they needed her. Delia was better, but her life would be difficult as the memories were sure to haunt her. Nanny could help in the difficult times, and Joseph knew it.

"Hey there, Esther Elizabeth Mills, we did it!" Joseph said, calling her by her real name.

The old black face lit up in a smile, and she said back to him, "Ya sho did!" As she answered him she followed with a low, grumbling laugh. "Ya sho did."

Joseph pulled away from her and looked into her eyes. She wasn't saying anything, but he knew what she was thinking.

"Well, Nanny, I guess you know Delia is gonna be coming up to the farm with me when we get back," he stated in an ordinary way. The smile on her black face faded slightly, but then she caught herself.

"Yez, sir, I reckon dat be so." Her eyes drooped to the ground as she answered him.

"Well, I guess I'd better be talkin' to these men," Joseph said as he motioned toward the group in the corner of the churchyard.

"Yez, sir, I reckon so," Nanny said as she secretly worried about her own future.

Joseph started to turn away, then shifted back toward Nanny and took both her hands in his.

"By the way, we'll only be gone a few days, so you don't have much time to get packed," he said as his weathered face beamed with a fresh smile.

Nanny looked up at him with a confused look.

"What's ya' mean, git packed?" she said, trying to sort out the meaning of his words.

"Well, unless you've got a better offer somewhere, we want you to come with us. The pay ain't much, but we can give you a dollar a week and room and board. I mean, get packed because you're coming to live with us; that is, if you want to. You don't have to, you know. You're free now," Joseph said as he watched her large eyes open wide in obvious astonishment.

Nanny let out a scream that startled everyone in the churchyard.

CHAPTER THIRTY-FIVE

"Does ya mean it? Does ya really mean it, Mr. Joseph?"

Joseph looked across the churchyard, and his eyes caught Delia's. She heard the little squeal, and her heart filled with joy for she knew what the commotion was about.

Joseph looked back into the shining black face and told her firmly.

"As I vow to the Lord, I mean it. We don't want to go without ya," he said happily.

Nanny screamed again and lunged into him, wrapping her big arms around him and lifting him off the ground. She hugged him tightly and laughed. Joseph laughed with her. She finally turned him loose, and he excused himself.

"Yez, sir, yez, I be packed. Don ya worry none 'bout me. I be packed when ya gits back home. Dat's easy, I ain't got nothin' to pack."

He could hear Nanny talking to herself as he walked away.

Joseph slowly moved toward the cluster of men gathered in the corner of the churchyard.

"Hey, here comes the happy groom," Will Garren blurted out as he approached.

"You'll be gettin' fat soon," his youngest brother Pinkney told him.

He stepped up to the group and extended his hand to each man.

"Congratulations, Joseph, you deserve every happiness," David Garren told him in a sincere voice.

When the little cluster of men settled down and the joking stopped, Joseph looked around at his old friends with a serious expression.

"You men know Delia's a lot better. She's eating, working, and smiling once again. But she's still got a long way to go. She's gonna need a lot of help," Joseph said with his voice cracking.

The men's heads began to droop as they all thought of what she'd been through. It was something they all knew, but no one ever spoke of it. Secretly they all felt some sense of guilt. They had gone to war to protect their families, and they had failed.

"I ask you, I pray you, men. I don't want what happened to her to ever be mentioned again. I don't want to ever speak of it, to ever hear of it again. I want Delia's secret kept so those of us who know carry it to our graves," Joseph said as tears formed in his eyes.

There were general murmurs of agreement and understanding. The men began swearing to the secret spontaneously. Will Garren represented them all as he spoke to Joseph.

"I vow to never speak of it again."

"I will carry it to my grave. I vow it on my life," David Garren said firmly.

The other men nodded and affirmed their promise. Joseph thanked them and returned to Delia's side. He escorted her to the wagon while everyone cheered them on. He looked into her eyes and made her one last promise.

"I swear on my life, I'll never leave you again."

——— JANUARY 17, 1928 ———

Pinkney Youngblood was now an old man. Like all the others he'd carried the secret a long time. If it would ever be told he was the last one living who could tell it. The family members sat around the little house on Hoopers Creek and listened intently as he revealed what had been buried in the minds of those who lived it. Many of them shed tears of their own.

"Ya know, he never did leave her again. Joseph died in 1907, but he was with her every day until the last. Even after he died she could never be left alone. Somebody has stayed with her constantly every minute of the day since that night on her eighteenth birthday, April 24, 1865. She was so torn up by what happened that she never did get over it. Oh, she lived what some people called a normal life, but it wasn't ever peaceful.

"I want you to know why I decided to tell the story of what happened. I thought I never would, you know. I was there that day we all decided never to tell of Delia's secret. It's not a pretty thing, not an easy thing.

"I'd lie awake at night thinking about it. Sometimes I'd cry. We all felt

CHAPTER THIRTY-FIVE

guilty, you know. None of us protected her. None of us was able to stop it.

"As the years went by and I learned more about it, one thing became clear to me, something I wish Delia had known.

"What happened to Delia is something that happened all over the South wherever that war reached, wherever it touched: Sherman's Bummers in Georgia, Wilson's Cavalry in Alabama, and anywhere else the armies went.

"It happened in the north too, in cases where the war reared its ugly head up there. It's certainly happened in many places since. I often thought about the women of Europe during the Great War. I don't know of any particular incident, but I'm sure it happened. It happened over and over, I'm confident.

"I know it was a stain on the Christian Crusades of the Middle Ages. Those fools told themselves it was acceptable because they saw the women as infidels. We know it happened to women in the colonies during the Revolution.

"It's a crime that is as old as time. In every case where war rears its vile head women are attacked. They have been the innocent victims of wars for time immemorial. Many of them died; some like Delia survived. But for those women forced to live in that dark shadow of shame, it has been a death of its own. It's some kind of living death where a woman is never at peace but always livin' in fear.

"The reason I decided to tell of Delia's secret is because after years of study and contemplation I've reached the conclusion that it's not just Delia's secret at all. It's not just a secret for the women of the South. It's not just our secret. It's the secret of war."

"If you bring these leaders to trial, it will condemn the north, for by the Constitution, secession is not rebellion."

SALMON P. CHASE
Chief Justice of the United States Supreme Court, 1868

Historical Perspective

The account of the capture and attack on Delia Russell Youngblood by Union soldiers in April 1865 was first recounted to me by my aunt, Burdette Youngblood Horton. She told me this piece of family oral history as she lay dying of congestive heart failure at Memorial Mission Hospital in Asheville, North Carolina, in 1989. She was born in 1906 and was the only remaining sibling in a family of three Youngblood children. My mother, her younger sister, had died just a few weeks earlier.

When Aunt Burdette first told me the story I was unsure what to make of it. She died shortly thereafter, but the memory of what she reported captivated me. I'd sometimes lie awake at night thinking of my great-grandmother and what she must have experienced. The troubling thoughts continued so that eventually I determined that I would try to investigate and sort out at least some of it in documented history.

My study has lasted for almost fifteen years and led me to countless hours of research and investigation. Within a short time I found two more living granddaughters who knew the story, Madge Cunningham Stedman and Bessie Wolfe Ward. Both women told the same story that Aunt Burdette had recounted. There were some minor differences in detail, but the basic story was the same.

While both women were helpful, it was Bessie Ward who added the most new information. She told me, "They made me stay with Maw, but I didn't want to." Bessie stated that she was a "sickly child," and as a result she was designated to stay with Delia Russell Youngblood. "She could never stay alone, you see," Bessie added.

The behavior she described was consistently reported from all those who knew Delia. In her day there was no name for posttraumatic stress disorder (PTSD) or obsessive-compulsive disorder (OCD). They just said that Delia was "peculiar."

THE SECRET OF WAR

While researching the Civil War history of western North Carolina I spent a great deal of time trying to identify which Union solders were here and when. I was investigating war crime, so one can imagine my surprise when I encountered the impeccable Palmer. On the surface, he seemed like any other Union officer I was tracking. I continued to investigate the record, and it began to reveal a very exceptional man. The official record indicates that he not only disapproved of the conduct of some Union soldiers but also actively tried to stop it.

Palmer's story does not end with western North Carolina. After the war, he moved to Colorado and helped build the nation's rail system. He founded the city of Colorado Springs, Colorado, and founded Colorado College. He became a regional hero in that area. A monument to Palmer stands in a prominent position in the center of Colorado Springs. Visitors to Durango, Colorado, ride the old narrow gage railroad from Durango to Silverton that Palmer built. Visitors stay at the General Palmer Hotel, which he constructed before the turn of the century.

After the war he was often referred to as "General Palmer." He was actually a brevet brigadier general. Brevet is of course a temporary rank, and he held that rank for only a short period. The original promotion order was dated November 1864, but when I examined the original document in the archives at the Colorado Pioneer History Museum I discovered that the document was not signed and activated until March 22, 1865. Since Palmer had already left East Tennessee with Stoneman's Cavalry, he was not aware of the promotion until some time later. Study of the record indicates that he was probably notified of the promotion at Hickory Nut Gap, North Carolina, late in the evening of April 27, 1865. This is also when he was notified that he had been placed in command of Stoneman's division.

Palmer's outstanding character and conduct did not end with the war. He was a model citizen after the war. Unlike many of the railroad moguls who developed the rail system in the American West, Palmer never accumulated great wealth. When he sold his railroad late in life, he distributed the proceeds among his employees.

American history, military or otherwise, has not produced a more outstanding citizen. He has gone largely unnoticed by most of history outside of Colorado. There are many reasons for this, some of which will perhaps never be identified. Certainly he had enemies and others who may have simply been envious of him. He angered many in the Union hierarchy who wanted harsh treatment inflicted on the defeated South. Many of these men harbored a level of hatred and vindictiveness that Palmer most certainly did not share. His opposition to criminal conduct certainly angered many who harbored vindictive attitudes molded by hate. Most notable among these men was Brevet Major General Alvan Cullen Gillem. The fact that Gillem was a West Point man, a common bond shared with President Ulysses S. Grant, makes it even more revealing that Grant fired Gillem his first day in the White House.

HISTORICAL PERSPECTIVE

Although Palmer was not a West Point man, he should be a primary example to that institution. His conduct in the execution of military tactics was exemplary, and his ethical conduct tested in the midst of a sea of pollution stands at a level with Washington, Lee, and Eisenhower, or any other soldier in American history.

My original intent was to expose war crimes that occurred in the American War Between the States when I started the project that became *The Secret of War*. In the end I think my most important discovery is that perhaps one of the most outstanding military officers in the history of the United States had been lost to obscurity.

DELIA RUSSELL YOUNGBLOOD
Mrs. Youngblood, shown in this 1898 photograph, is a great-grandmother of the author. Note: an apparent depression of the left jaw.

HISTORICAL PERSPECTIVE

JOSEPH YOUNGBLCOD
Private Joseph Youngblood of the Twenty-fifth North Carolina
Infantry Regiment, Confederate States of America. Youngblood is a
great-grandfather of the author. The photograph was taken in 1898.

THE FAMILY OF JOSEPH AND DELIA YOUNGBLOOD
Thomas Revis Youngblood (top row, far right), is a grandfather of the author.
The photograph was taken in 1898.

HISTORICAL PERSPECTIVE

CAPTAIN SOLOMON CUNNINGHAM
Confederate Solomon Cunningham was elected captain by the men of Company H, "Cane Creek Rifles," Twenty-fifth North Carolina Infantry Regiment, on April 30, 1862. He was wounded at the Battle of Malvern Hill, Virginia, July 1, 1862. He was later killed at the battle of Fredericksburg, December 13, 1862.

THE SECRET OF WAR

THIS HOUSE near Fletcher is the oldest wooden house in Henderson County still inhabited. Built in 1845 by Branch Merrimon for whom Merrimon Ave. in Asheville was named, the house was bought in 1856 by Robert Russell. Robert's son John inherited the house and lived in it until he died in 1927. Two of John Russell's daughters now occupy the house. They are Miss Monnie Russell and Mrs. Sue Anderson. The house has been in constant use by the Russell family for the past 104 years.

ASHEVILLE CITIZEN-TIMES, ASHEVILLE, N. C.
Serving WNC Since 1870   Sunday, July 17, 1960

THE MERRIMON/RUSSELL HOUSE
This is the house where Delia Russell Youngblood was captured and attacked by Union soldiers on the night of April 24, 1865. It was her eighteenth birthday.
(PHOTOGRAPH COURTESY ASHEVILLE *CITIZEN-TIMES*)

HISTORICAL PERSPECTIVE

THE MEADOWS

The Meadows was the home of Daniel and Mimi Blake. The Blake family held more slaves than any other family in Henderson County (59 slaves, 1860 U.S. Census). The house was built in the 1850s of native stone with ornate hardwood paneling and eight individually designed fireplaces. The structure still stands approximately seven tenths of a mile east of Calvary Episcopal Church in Fletcher, North Carolina.

(PHOTOGRAPH COURTESY OF MICHAEL AND JUDITH McKNIGHT)

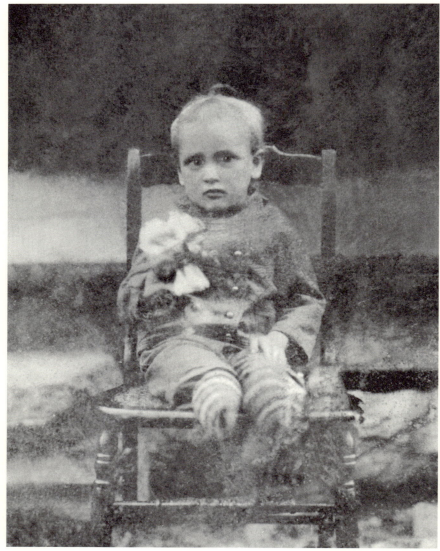

THE FOOTLESS MAN
DANIEL WASHINGTON "WASH" HUTCHISON
This tintype photograph was taken when Wash Hutchison was three or four years old (approximately 1850). It is believed that the photographer selected the footless Hutchison because he was considered a "curiosity" at the time. Wash Hutchison is a great-grandfather of the author.

HISTORICAL PERSPECTIVE

JAMES R. PAYNE AND MELINDA REEVES PAYNE WITH OLDEST CHILD
James M. Payne, of the Third North Carolina Mounted Infantry Regiment (Union), is a great-great-great-grandfather of the author's daughter. The letter featured on the cover is regarding his death in 1865.

COLONEL WILLIAM J. PALMER WITH OFFICERS
Palmer, second from right, was awarded the Congressional Medal of Honor for meritorious service at Red Hill, Alabama, in 1865.
(PHOTOGRAPH COURTESY THE U.S. ARMY MILITARY HISTORY INSTITUTE)

HISTORICAL PERSPECTIVE

MAJOR GENERAL GEORGE STONEMAN
George Stoneman was a Union cavalry commander who did not ride a horse.
He traveled by carriage due to severe hemorrhoids. After the war he served
as governor of California from 1883 to 1887.

(PHOTOGRAPH COURTESY THE U.S. ARMY MILITARY HISTORY INSTITUTE)

MAJOR GENERAL ALVAN CULLEN GILLEM
Gillem served as divisional commander of Stoneman's Cavalry throughout most of the raid. He was in full command from April 15, 1865, through April 26, 1865.
(PHOTOGRAPH COURTESY THE U.S. ARMY MILITARY HISTORY INSTITUTE)

Index

1st Brigade 235, 258, 268, 274, 312
1st Colored U.S. Heavy Artillery 258
2nd Brigade 235, 258, 306, 311,
2nd N.C. Mounted Infantry 258, 328
3rd Brigade 235, 258, 306, 311
3rd N.C. Mounted Infantry 193, 258, 311, 374
10th Michigan 234
11th Kentucky 232, 262
11th Michigan 232, 256
11th Michigan Cavalry 255
12th Kentucky 232
12th Kentucky Union Cavalry 275
12th Ohio 234
13th Tennessee 262
13th Tennessee Cavalry 230, 232, 255-257, 349
15th Pennsylvania 234, 237, 257, 259, 302
15th Pennsylvania Cavalry 140, 141
15th Pennsylvania Volunteer Cavalry 235
24th North Carolina 102, 106
25th North Carolina 102, 104, 106, 110, 133, 134, 137, 203, 351
25th North Carolina Infantry 76, 81, 85, 114, 125, 135, 369, 371
26th North Carolina 102, 104, 106, 109
35th North Carolina 102, 135
48th North Carolina 102
49th North Carolina 102
56th North Carolina 106
60th North Carolina 156, 171, 173, 207, 214, 215, 223
62nd North Carolina 272
64th North Carolina Infantry 121, 125, 148, 272
69th North Carolina Infantry 272, 273
8th Louisiana Infantry 337
8th Mississippi Cavalry 204
8th Tennessee 262
8th Tennessee Cavalry 232
9th Tennessee Cavalry 232
Alabama 204, 363
Aldridge, James E. 116
Allen, Colonel 148
Allen, David 119
Allen, David J. 115
Allen, Joseph J. 117
Allen, Lawrence 121, 148, 158
Allen, Mrs. 119
Allen, Reverend 103
Allen, William 117
Allison, Isaac 115
Almon, Henry G. 114
America 74
Anders, David H. 114
Anders, George W. 115
Anderson, Jasper N. 116
Anderson, Josiah M. 116
Anderson, Martha 87, 88, 91, 148, 159, 162
Antietam 217, 235, 350
Antietam Creek 133, 137

Appalachia 29
Appomattox 330, 351
Arial, Harvy O. 114
Arkansas 57
Army of Northern Virginia 114, 281
Army of Tennessee 207, 226
Asheville 75, 79, 83, 85-87, 95, 121, 147, 151, 153, 157, 267, 270, 271, 273, 277, 280, 281, 285, 297, 298, 305-312, 314, 325, 349, 365
Asheville Road 85, 120, 325
Atkins, Alfred A. 117
Atlanta 206, 207
Austin, Jacob A. 226
Avery County 256
Bailey, 307
Bailey, Judge 311-313
Baldwin, R. L. 86
Baldwin store 86
Ball, Alfred T. 226
Baltimore, Maryland 38
Bane, George W. 117
Banks, Henry H. 114
Barksdale, General 133
Barnes, Major 262, 264, 265, 276, 279, 285, 286
Barnett, Columbus V. 114
Barnwell, 8, 71, 119, 153
Barnwell, Dave 153
Barnwell, John A. 115
Barnwell, Saphronia 153, 154
Bearwallow Mountain 67, 68, 95, 210, 252, 285, 298, 304, 333, 349
Beaucatcher Mountain 78
Bertha, 336, 337
Bill of Rights 59
Biltmore 7
Birmingham 206
Bishop, 71
Black Mountains 80
Blackman, Jacob 117
Blake, 62, 86
Blake, Daniel 40, 53-55, 64-67, 69, 72, 120-122

Blake, Fredrick 69, 71, 75-77, 79, 81, 89, 121, 123
Blake, Mimi 54, 63, 120
Blake, Mrs. 55, 67
Blue Ridge Mountains 184, 258, 297
Boone North Carolina 256-258, 266
Boyd, Daniel A. 114
Bragg, General 219
Brookhaven Mississippi 204
Brooks, David W. 114
Brown, 172, 173, 177
Brown, General 235, 258, 262, 263, 280, 307, 311, 312
Bryant, Columbus D. 114
Bryson, Samuel H. 117
Bryson, 71, 137, 217
Bryson, Watt 135-137, 217, 218
Buchanan, Julius L. 116
Buchanan's brigade 107
Bull Run 103
Buncombe County 22, 77, 113, 114, 352
Burke County 80
Burnside, 88
Byers, William R. 226
Byrd, Robert 117
Cagle, Leonard C. 118
Cal, 246, 248
California 376
Calvary Church 356
Calvary Episcopal Church 54, 67, 92, 120
Camp Chase Ohio 258
Camp Morton 164, 170, 174, 178, 197, 207, 216, 239, 249, 250, 322, 330, 336
Camp Patton 75, 79, 330
Canada 255
Cane Creek 51, 65, 68, 81, 215, 287, 358
Cane Creek Rifles 75, 81, 102, 371
Cannon, Watson R. 114
Carland, 71
Carson, Newton F. 114
Cartner, Daniel W. 114
Case, Elisha G. 118
Castle Thunder 235, 264
Casualty List 114

INDEX

Cataloochee Creek 192
Catawba River 268
Chambers, George W. 116
Charleston 52
Charlotte 268, 269
Chattanooga 249, 250
Cherokee County 77, 116
Cherokee Indians 272
Cherokee trails 79
Clapton, Sergeant 308
Clarke, William 106
Clay County 77, 116
Clements, Joseph R. 114
Cleveland 250
Clingman, Thomas 55-59, 62, 65-67, 76-78
Cogdill, Joseph W. 117
Collins, Joseph A. 117
Colorado 366
Colorado College 366
Colorado Pioneer History Museum 366
Colorado Springs 366
Columbia South Carolina 52
Columbus North Carolina 279
Company B 121, 122
Company H 76, 102, 106, 107, 111, 113, 371
Company I 112
Congressional Medal of Honor 235
Continental Congress 58
Cooper, 196
Cooper, Bill 192
Cooper, John 192-194
Council, Jacob 256
Courtney, John H. 114
Cowan, David L. 117
Cowan, James W. 117
Crawford, Andrew J. 117
Crew House 107
Crow Valley 215
Cunningham, Preston 1
Cunningham, Saphrona 146
Cunningham, Solomon 67, 71, 72, 75, 82, 89, 101, 102, 106, 107, 115, 123, 130-133, 138, 146, 315, 371

Cunningham, Tekoa "Cora" Youngblood 1, 2, 6, 7, 11
Dalton Georgia 207, 214, 226, 251
Davis, General 232
Davis, Jefferson 150, 313
Dearing, Saint Clare 77
Declaration of Independence 57, 58, 60, 61
Deep Gap 258
Dees, 38, 93-95, 279, 280, 286-288, 291-293, 296, 297, 301, 302, 312
Dees, Carl 37
Dees, Matthias 36-39, 50, 84, 89, 90, 122, 124, 125, 151, 152, 191-196, 227-230, 255, 270, 287, 291, 294, 295, 301, 311, 326-328, 334, 350, 353, 355, 356
Dees, Rupert 37, 90, 124, 125, 151, 191, 192, 194, 196, 295, 302
Dellinger, Reuben A. 226
Dotson, Josiah H. 114
Dover, Asa 226
Drake, Elias A. 114
Drake, Nathan 153-155
Ducktown Tennessee 238, 239, 247
Dunker Church 133, 137
Durango, Colorado 366
Eagle Hotel 79, 87, 147, 270, 273, 314
Early, 133
Ebenezer Creek 232
Edmonds, Samuel R. F. 114
Edney, Balous 75
Eisenhower, 367
Ellis, Governor 57
Emancipation Proclamation 233, 234
England, David H. 118
Enloe, Thomas J. 115
Europe 363
Execution List 226
Faison, Paul 106
Featherston, Calvin R. 115
Fie, John C. 116
Fletcher, 71
Fletcher, Dr. 46, 315-317
Fletcher, Sam 153-155

Fletcher N.C. 6, 7, 36, 37, 51-53, 67, 68, 84, 86, 92, 119, 147, 155, 173, 273, 282, 286, 287, 317, 358
Forrest, General 205, 206
Forrest's Cavalry 204
Fort Donelson 88
Fort Henry 88
Fort Sumter 52, 53, 55, 57, 68, 141
Fowler, 71
Fowler, William H. 118
France 74, 255
Frederick the Great 74
Fredericksburg 127, 146, 148, 371
Freeman, 71
French Broad River 125, 227, 325, 352
Frizzle, James H. 117
Fry, Neely D. 116
Gabriel House 322, 323, 330, 335, 336, 345
Garland, George W. 114
Garren, 8, 42, 67, 68, 71, 76, 107, 359
Garren, Absalom 43
Garren, David 39, 40, 44, 68, 78, 108, 111-113, 115, 130, 345-347, 350, 352-354, 361, 362
Garren, Elisha 39, 40, 68, 69, 72, 76, 78, 82, 101, 107, 108, 113, 115, 130, 346
Garren, Henry 135, 136
Garren, Lieutenant 135-137
Garren, Will 39-41, 69, 76, 81, 82, 104, 108, 110-113, 130, 219, 345-347, 350-353, 361, 362
Garren, Williamson 115
General Palmer Hotel 366
Georgia 207, 215, 231, 232, 236, 242, 266, 310, 363
Georgia's Crow Valley 223
Germany 74
Gettysburg 172, 219
Gibbs, Joseph A. 226
Gillem, Alvan Cullen 230-237, 256-259, 263, 266-270, 274-277, 279, 280, 286, 297, 298, 305-307, 311, 312, 366, 377
Gillespie, James L. 114
Glendale Virginia 102

Grant, General 236
Grant, President Ulysses S. 366
Grant's Creek 262, 263
Granville 88
Green, Jeremiah 116
Green, Warren 256
Greenville Tennessee 195, 218, 233
Griffin's brigade 107
Griffith, William D. 116
Gudger, Jessie Giles 114
Gum Springs 325
Hamilton, Joseph 60-62, 327, 328
Hammond, 71
Hase, Jesse 226
Haywood County 77, 116, 191
Head, Anderson C. 115
Hemphill, Robert S. 117
Henderson, 71
Henderson County 22, 65, 69, 75, 77, 80, 91, 115, 119, 121, 122, 136, 159, 172, 217, 298, 337
Hendersonville 1, 6, 85, 218, 280, 282, 286, 298
Hendersonville News 6
Heth, General 148
Hickory Nut Gap 297, 305, 366
Hicksite Quakers 234, 267
Hill, General 103
Hilton Head 88
Hogsed, Walter L. 118
Holbert, Joseph 152-155
Holder, Hamilton 114
Holder, Lyttleton I. 115
Home Guard 218
Hood, 133
Hooper, Daniel H. 117
Hoopers Creek 1, 2, 4, 6, 8, 9, 15, 19, 22, 24, 25, 41, 45, 48, 65, 67, 68, 75, 76, 81, 83, 100, 144, 151, 172, 208, 210, 215, 251, 285, 287, 299, 306, 309, 313, 315, 318, 329, 339, 344, 358, 362
Hoopers Creek Road 49
Hoopers Creek Valley 13, 95, 127, 160
Horton, Burdette Youngblood 365
Howard Gap 279, 280, 286

INDEX

Howard Gap Road 51, 287
Huger, General 103, 105, 106
Hutchings, Wright 226
Hutchison, Daniel Washington 125-128, 160-162, 169, 284, 288, 299-303, 304, 373
Hutchison, John 125
Hutchison, W. W. "Hutch" 125-129, 282, 284, 285, 290, 299, 300
Hyatt, Samuel P. 114
Icard Station in Morganton 80, 85
Illinois 60
Indiana 178, 199, 200, 202, 214-216, 249, 321, 335, 347
Indianapolis 164, 168, 177, 180, 181, 321, 330, 335
Ingle, Albert L. 114
Ingram, Joel 115
Ingram, Robert 115
Inman, William P. 116
Irish "Galvanized Yankees" 263
Jackson, 121
Jackson, Stonewall 103, 104
Jackson County 77, 117
Jackson Ms. 172
Jackson Road 37, 41, 48, 51, 52, 153, 282, 287, 304
Jacob, 139, 140, 142, 143, 164-166, 168, 170
James River 103
Jeter, 275
Jeter's Battery 271
Johnson, Benjamin C. 116
Johnson, Creed F. 115
Johnson, Vice President 233
Johnston, 297
Johnston, General 219, 224
Johnston, Joe 214, 281
Johnston, Joseph E. 207
Johnston's store 84
Jones, 61
Jordan, James H. 116
Joyce, William M. 114
Justice, A. I. 6, 7

Justice, Reverend 9
Justice, William W. 114
Justus, Isaac 287
Justus, Samuel 282
Keever, David M. 117
Kelly, George W. 117
Kentucky 57, 171, 172, 176, 177, 184, 185, 199, 232, 256
Kentucky Cavalrymen 165
Kirk, Colonel 192-196, 258, 311, 312
Knight, Thames M. 115
Knoxville 148, 227, 228, 234, 344
Kuykendall, John Allen 115
LaFerre, Pete 255, 256, 270, 279, 280, 285-287, 291-295, 297, 301, 302
Lanning, 8, 51, 71
Lanning, John 51
Laughter, Hampton 115
Ledford, Christopher 226
Lee, Robert E. 103, 104, 131, 281, 367
Leesburg Virginia 130
Lenoir North Carolina 266, 268
Lewise, 71
Lilley, Thomas 118
Lincoln, President 42, 55-57, 59, 65, 149, 233
Lister, Thomas R. 115
Little Sorrell (Horse) 104
Livingston, 17, 18, 84, 340
Livingston, John 16, 18
Livingston, Susannah 19
Lockaby, William C. 118
Long, Henry C. 118
Long, Peter G. 117
Longstreet, 131
Louisville 177, 181, 186, 199, 250
Love, Mathew Norris 115
Love, Robert 272, 273, 275
Macon County 77, 117, 248
Madison County 121, 125, 147, 148, 159, 312
Magaha, Thomas J. 118
Magruder, General 104, 105
Mahone, General 106

Malvern Hill 105, 111, 114, 119-121, 123, 132, 133, 138, 139, 197, 249, 253, 350, 371
Manassas, Virginia 78
Marion, Joyce 112
Marshall 125, 147
Martin, James Green 271-274, 306, 312, 313
Martin, William J. 116
Maryland 57, 131-133, 135, 170
Massachusetts 58
McCracken, Joseph M. L. 116
McDowell County 272
McDowell, J. C. 154, 155
McFalls, George W. 226
McKillop, Jacob 115
Memorial Mission Hospital
Memphis Tennessee 197
Merrill, Henry C. 115
Merrimon, 15, 18, 36
Merrimon, A. S. 55, 56, 58-62, 147, 148, 157-159
Merrimon, Branch 15
Miller, Colonel 235, 258, 262, 263, 270, 274-277, 311
Miller, James 112
Mills, Esther Elizabeth 360
Mills, George 9, 135-137, 217, 220, 225
Mills, Nanny 16, 18-22, 24, 29-34, 41, 45-47, 49, 53, 70, 71, 83, 95, 96, 98, 99, 122, 144, 149, 150, 162, 163, 253, 254, 273, 281-284, 288, 289, 290, 299, 303, 315-318, 323-324, 329, 330, 334, 339-342, 354, 355, 357, 359, 361
Mills, Zeke 16, 18-21, 24, 28, 29, 31, 33, 39, 50, 84, 92-100, 122, 128, 129, 136, 137, 144, 149, 162, 252, 254, 273, 282-284, 289-293, 299, 304, 359
Mills River 38, 85
Mississippi 172, 202, 203
Mississippi River 206, 207
Mitchell County 36, 122, 192, 311, 312, 328, 349

Moody, Joseph H. 117
Morgan, General 184
Morgan, John 165, 233
Morgan, Perminter P. 115
Morganton 78, 80, 85, 270, 272, 287
Morris, B. T. 122
Morton, Oliver P. 164
Morton's Mule 167, 207
Moss, John J. 117
Mount Sterling 191, 195
Mountain Planting 29
Mud Creek 340
Nashville Tennessee 231
Netherland, George M. 118
New Albany Indiana 177, 183
New Bern 88
New Orleans 186
New York 58, 60, 76
Nix, Francis 116
North Carolina 7, 15, 17, 37, 40-42, 56-58, 75, 78, 81, 127, 157, 158, 191, 193, 194, 206, 207, 219, 223, 228-230, 233, 236, 237, 242, 246, 248, 251, 255, 262, 263, 266, 267, 270, 271, 286, 310, 315, 322, 329, 337, 339, 344, 365, 366
North Carolina Infantry 76, 81, 85
North Carolina Mounted Infantry 193
North Carolina Regiment 102, 104, 121
Norton, William V. 117
Ohio 184
Ohio River 165, 177, 181, 184, 207
Old Fort 80
Ole Star (Horse) 17, 18, 20, 21, 23-25, 30-32, 34, 46, 48, 51, 52, 84-87, 91, 92, 147, 155, 156, 160, 252, 283, 284, 290, 296, 300
Otis, 8, 9
Owen, Richard 165
Owenby, Francis M. 116
Pace, 8
Palmer, William J. 140-142, 234-237, 257-261, 262-269, 297-314, 347, 348, 366, 375
Parker, Henry H. 117

INDEX

Parker, Samuel J. 117
Parker, William J. 116
Parris, Alfred W. 117
Patty, Reverend 41, 42, 62, 119
Patty's Chapel Methodist Church 6, 7, 9, 40-42, 358
Payne, Cary J. 116
Payne, James M. 374
Payne, Melinda Reeves 374
Pearson, William I. 115
Peeler, Jacob F. 118
Penland, Alexander M. 115
Pennsylvania 142, 172
Pinner, Solomon B. 115
Pitillo, Fred 52
Pitillo, James 52
Polk County 121, 122
Porter, 275
Porter's Battery 271
Queen, John B. 117
Raines, Christopher C. 118
Raleigh 78, 81, 85
Ramsey, Anderson W. 115
Randall, James M. 226
Ransom, Robert 102-106, 135
Ransom's brigade 110, 133, 203
Ray, William C. 118
Red Hill Alabama 235, 375
Reese, Isaac 117
Richmond 103, 235
Riddle, Marvil M. 115
Roach, Mrs. Lonie 7
Rose, David 165
Rough and Ready Guard 79
Russell, 8, 71, 90, 136, 354
Russell, Delia 16, 17, 19-35, 41-50, 53-55, 63, 64, 68-75, 80, 83-88, 91-94, 99-101, 119, 120, 122, 123, 125-130, 137, 144-150, 152, 153, 155-163, 166, 173, 184, 187, 198, 202, 209-213, 218, 219, 221, 238, 251-254, 270, 271, 273, 277, 278, 281-285, 288-297, 299, 300-304, 315-320, 324, 329, 332-334, 339-342, 346-350, 355-363

Russell, James 16, 17, 19, 20, 22, 23, 36, 39, 47, 48, 51, 52, 85, 92, 120, 124, 147, 287, 316-320, 323, 324, 329-334, 339, 340
Russell, Joe Lee 16-18, 22, 24-26, 28, 29, 31-38
Russell, John 16, 22, 35, 92, 144, 150, 273
Russell, Mary 16, 19, 22, 25, 27, 30, 44, 100, 273, 281, 282, 285
Russell, Minerva 22
Russell, Robert "Bob" 15-25, 28, 35, 36, 38-43, 50, 52-55, 59, 64, 70, 83-91, 93-100, 120-122, 126-129, 144, 145, 150, 152-155, 157-162, 209, 213, 221, 253, 270, 271, 273, 278, 280-285, 285, 287-289, 299, 300, 303, 304, 318, 323, 329-332, 339, 341-343
Russell, Sarah 16, 19, 20, 22, 25, 27, 30, 43, 96, 273, 281, 282, 319
Russell, Susannah (Mrs.) 16, 18, 22, 30, 41, 45-48, 83, 92, 93, 96, 97, 150, 283
Russia 74
Ruth, Braxton R. 116
Rutherfordton 270, 272
Rutledge, Henry Middleton 77, 101, 102, 105, 106, 116, 123, 130, 131, 138
Saint James Episcopal Church 266, 267
Salisbury 236, 262-264, 266
Salisbury prison 262
Saltville 236
Sarah, 175
Savannah 231
Scersey, David W. 118
Scott, Captain 279
Scruggs, Richard M. 118
Sedgwick, John 133, 134
Sellers, Felix H. 118
Seven Years War 74
Sharp, William W. 116
Sharpsburg 133, 138, 170, 215, 217, 219, 249
Shelton Laurel 158
Shenandoah Valley 103
Sherman, William T. 231, 236, 297, 310, 363

Sherrill's Inn 297, 304, 305
Shufordsville 86
Silverton 366
Smathers, William Burton 117
Smith, C. W. 104
Smith, George W. 116
South Carolina 53, 88
South Carolina militia 52
Souther Road 126, 160, 284
Southern Appalachia 38
St. Louis 184, 185
Stanton, Edwin 165
Stedman, Madge Cunningham 1, 365
Stewart, Joe 192
Stoneman's Cavalry 366, 377
Stoneman's Division 366
Stoneman, George 232, 234-237, 256-258, 262-269, 314, 349, 376
Summey, 71
Swannanoa Gap 79, 85, 270-273, 275, 279, 280, 286
Swannanoa River 79, 91, 325
Taylor, Dan 172-174, 177
Taylor, Jesse W. 116
Taylor, Wilbourne 116
Tennessee 57, 155, 172, 185, 192, 193, 195, 196, 202, 227, 233, 234, 237, 242, 247, 249, 255, 258, 266, 267, 269, 305-308, 310, 311, 313, 366
Terry's Gap 151, 153
The Meadows 53, 55, 63, 120
Thomas, George 231-235, 237, 266, 308
Thomas's legion 273
Thompson, James W. 118
Tillson, General 258, 266, 313
Transylvania County 77, 118
Turner, Alice 183, 185-187, 202
Turner, Howard 165-172, 172, 174, 176-186, 188-190, 202, 203
Turner, Juliana 182
Turner, Toad 181-190, 197-202
Tuscaloosa Alabama 205
U. S. Army of the Cumberland 231
U. S. Constitution 58-60
United States 59

Vance, Zebulon Baird 55-62, 79, 102, 104, 106, 109, 110, 145, 147, 148, 157-159, 264
Vermillian, James M. 116
Vicksburg 186, 187, 189, 201-203
Virginia 57, 78, 102, 114, 119, 121, 129, 137, 140, 155, 158, 219, 223, 235, 236, 355, 371
Walker, 131
Walker's Battalion 272
Wallace, Lieutenant 204-206
Ward, 8, 71, 156
Ward, Bessie Wolfe 365
Ward, Claude 84, 85
Ward, J. L. 121, 215, 216, 220-225
Ward, Michael 226
Warm Springs 87
Washington, (D.C.) 56, 78, 177, 233, 266
Washington, (George) 367
Watauga County 255, 266
Watson, Benson N. 117
Waynesville 272
Weand, Captain 237, 259-261, 298, 299-311
West Point 106
Wheeler, 71
Wheeler, Sam 71
Wheeling, Samuel 116
Whitaker, 8, 71
Whitaker, George W. 115
Whitaker, Mrs. Addie 340, 341
White, Charles Wesley 274
Whitley, Horace 323, 337
Whittemore, James B. 115
Wilkesboro 258, 259
Williams, 113
Williams, Lewis D. 115
Williams, Sidney 113
Willis Church Road 103
Wilson, John C. 118
Wilson, Robert 118
Wilson's Cavalry 363
Wolfe, Mrs. H. H. 7
Yancey County 192

INDEX

York, Jeffery S. 116
Youngblood, 24, 42, 49, 65, 68
Youngblood, Bob 12, 13
Youngblood, Delia Russell (Mrs.) 1-4, 6, 7, 9-14, 365, 368, 372
Youngblood, Dovie 7
Youngblood, Elizabeth 344
Youngblood, Hiram 39, 66, 146, 173, 207, 211, 212, 216, 219-224, 226, 239, 251, 253, 321, 329, 331, 346, 348
Youngblood, J. N. 39, 40, 44, 66, 146, 173, 207, 211, 216, 218-221, 223-226, 238-245, 247-251, 321, 322, 329-331, 347-350, 352-354
Youngblood, James 119
Youngblood, Jasper Newton 346
Youngblood, Joseph 4, 6, 9, 10, 25-29, 31-35, 39-41, 43-49, 63, 64, 66-75, 77, 78, 80-82, 85, 87-89, 92, 102-104, 106-113, 120, 123, 124, 130-143, 145, 146, 148, 155, 156, 162-190, 197-207, 209, 211-226, 238-251, 253, 290, 296, 321-323, 329-332, 335-338, 344-362, 369, 370
Youngblood, Pinkney 7-13, 39, 66, 128, 146, 209-212, 251, 252, 285, 325-330, 332-334, 346-352, 354, 356, 361, 362
Youngblood, Reuben 24, 25, 39, 65, 67
Youngblood, Revis 7
Youngblood, Russell 7, 9, 10, 13
Youngblood, Thomas Revis 370
Youngblood, William "Bill" 39, 41, 43, 66-69, 76, 78, 81, 82, 102, 104, 111, 112, 124, 130, 146, 173, 209, 211, 212, 252, 331, 322, 329-332, 345-353
Younts, E. F. 226